Still Holding Out for You

Real American Country
Book 4

Jennifer Carr

Edited by
Ashley Andrews

Published by JCarr Writes, LLC (jcarrwrites.com)

Edited by Ashley Andrews

Cover by JCarr Writes, LLC

ISBN-13: 979-8-9870638-5-9 (paperback)

ASIN: B0F6RF51VN (digital)

Still Holding Out
for You - Playlist

If you like to listen to music while you read, there's a Spotify playlist curated specifically with a song for each chapter of *Still Holding Out for You.*

Scan the QR Code below to coordinate your reading and the song.

A Note to the
Reader/Content Warning

Dear Reader,

Thank you for picking up *Still Holding Out for You*. Before you dive in, I want to offer a gentle word about the story ahead.

This book explores several difficult and emotional themes, including chronic illness, cancer, death, grief, and the vulnerability that comes with love and loss. While this is ultimately a story about hope, healing, and the courage it takes to keep choosing love in the face of life's hardest moments, there are scenes that may feel heavy — especially if you've experienced something similar in your own life.

Please know that your well-being matters more than anything. If you find yourself needing to pause, take a breath, or step away — that's okay. Stories can be powerful mirrors, but they can also stir up pain we thought we had tucked away. Take care of yourself in whatever way feels right for you.

You are not alone. And if you choose to walk through this story with me, I hope you find both tenderness and truth on the pages — and maybe even a reminder that love, in all its forms, is always worth holding out for.

With love and gratitude,

Jennifer

Present Day

Austin

The mirror didn't lie. I adjusted my tie for what felt like the hundredth time, staring at the man looking back at me. A man with a name printed on not one, but three nominations at the Country Music Academy Awards—Song of the Year, Album of the Year, and Entertainer of the Year. A man I hardly recognized.

Never in my wildest dreams did I think I'd be here. Not after everything.

The muffled sound of giggles drifted from the next room, and I turned toward the door. My mom had Allora, my seven-year-old whirlwind, in stitches. "Mom, you sure you're good?" I called out, stepping closer.

"We're fine, Austin." Mom's voice was warm and steady, her pride unmistakable. She appeared in the doorway, Allora perched on her hip. My daughter's grin lit up the room. "Go on, enjoy this night. You've earned it. The three of you deserve this."

Allora squirmed free, landing on the bed with a bounce before throwing her arms around me. "Win, Daddy!"

"I'll try, Cupcake." I kissed her forehead, holding her a beat longer than usual. "Be good for Nana, okay?"

"I will!" she promised, her green eyes sparkling with excitement. My daughter's grin lit up the room. She had her mother's smile—bright, mischievous, a little untamed.

"I love you, baby girl."

"Love you too!"

I turned to Mom, who rested a hand on my shoulder. "We'll be cheering for you," she said softly.

I nodded, swallowing past the tightness in my throat, and slipped out the door before I could second-guess myself.

The waiting car whisked me toward the venue, but my thoughts were scattered. The bright Nashville skyline blurred through the window as I stared at my reflection, trying to steady the storm brewing inside. It felt like just yesterday I'd been a man who'd sworn off music for good. And now this.

I reached for my phone, a habit I still hadn't broken.

Before I could stop myself, my fingers hovered over the screen, half-typing a message I already knew I wouldn't send.

Almost there. Nervous. Say something to calm me down.

The response was already in my head, as familiar as breathing.

You've got this, cowboy.

I let out a breath and set the phone aside, my hand tightening into a fist against my leg. I knew what she'd say. I didn't need the words to hear them.

The red carpet was a whirlwind of flashes and questions. Smiling. Posing. Answering. But inside, I was still back in the car, caught between the past and the present.

Inside, the theater buzzed with energy, the anticipation electric. I took my seat beside Christopher Jordan, my producer, my friend, and one of the few people who'd seen me at my worst.

The first category—Song of the Year. My stomach tightened as the nominees' names echoed through the speakers. "And the winner is... Austin Blake for 'Holding Out for You.'"

The room erupted in applause.

I stood frozen for a moment, a rush of emotions tightening my chest. Christopher nudged me, a wide grin on his face. Slowly, I made my way to the stage, the crowd's energy carrying me.

The presenter handed me the award, her smile warm as she stepped aside. I stood at the microphone, searching for the words.

I took a deep breath and began, "This is for you and because of you, Willow. I wouldn't be standing here if not for you. Every step, every song—you were there, leading me forward. You carried me this far."

A pause. A breath. A quiet promise.

"I've got us from here."

The audience was silent, absorbing the weight of my words. I smiled, a bit shakily, and looked into the camera. "Allora, sweetheart, I hope you're in bed asleep. Daddy loves you."

A ripple of laughter from the audience, easing some of the tension in my chest.

"I want to thank my parents for pushing me and always being there for me. Mom, Dad, I love you." I paused, gathering my thoughts. "And Chris, thank you for believing in me, for encouraging me, and for giving me the opportunity to make music again."

I wrapped up my speech and made my way back to my seat, where I watched the performances between awards, my heart still racing. The night continued, with more awards and more anticipation. Each time my name was called—Album of the Year and finally, Entertainer of the Year—the emotions built up, until I was barely holding it together.

As I stood on stage for the third time, clutching the biggest award of the night, tears blurred my vision. "I never thought I'd make music again," I admitted, my voice cracking. "But here I am, because of all of you. Thank you."

The applause was deafening as I made my way back to my seat, my heart full. I had made it. We had made it.

Chapter 1

Austin

Nine Years Earlier

I wiped the sweat from my brow, straightening up to admire the work I'd done in the barn. The Montana sun was blazing outside, but I didn't mind the heat or the labor. There was something satisfying about a hard day's work on the ranch. The scent of hay and wood filled the air as I looked around at the neatly stacked bales and freshly cleaned stalls. My parents had owned this place for as long as I could remember, and it was in my blood just as much as the music that pulsed through my veins.

"Austin!" My older brother Connor called from the other end of the barn. He was elbow-deep in the engine of one of our tractors, his face smeared with grease. Connor was a veteran Marine and the best mechanic in town. He saw the world differently than most, but he was the best brother I could ask for.

"Yeah?" I shouted back, walking over to him.

"Hand me that wrench?" he asked, not looking up from his work.

I grabbed the tool and passed it to him. "Here you go."

"Thanks." He took it and continued working, completely focused. I watched him for a moment, admiring his dedication and precision.

Nearby, Connor's three-legged military K9, a German Shepherd named Charlie, padded over. I squatted down, giving him a hearty pat on the head. "Hey there, Chuck," I greeted him with a grin.

Connor glanced over, his expression exasperated but silent. I knew he didn't appreciate the nickname, but he never said anything about it.

"How's my favorite three-legged friend doing, huh?" I asked in a playful tone, ruffling Charlie's fur. "You know, I call you Chuck just to mess with Connor, right? Your real name's Charlie, but I think you know that already." Charlie's tail wagged enthusiastically, and I chuckled. "Good boy."

Connor shook his head slightly, but a small smile played at the corner of his lips. "He listens to you more than me sometimes," he said, his voice a mix of fondness and mild annoyance.

I stood up, brushing off some stray dog hair. "Nah. He just thinks that voice means I brought him a treat. Hey, I was thinking about heading to The Hole in the Wall in a little while. You wanna join me?" I asked, trying to keep my tone casual.

Connor paused for a moment, his hands stilling on the engine. "No," he finally said, his gaze returning to his work. "Thanks, though."

I nodded, not surprised but still hopeful. "Alright, well, if you change your mind, let me know. Maybe Chuck here can convince you to come along," I added with a wink at the dog.

Charlie barked softly, almost as if he understood the invitation. I gave him one last pat before heading out, leaving Connor to his work and hoping one day he'd take me up on the offer.

After finishing up my chores, I headed to the house to clean up. Tonight was one of those nights I looked forward to—singing at the Hole in the Wall, our local bar. It was a small place, but it had a loyal crowd, and I loved the energy of performing live.

I threw on my favorite pair of Wranglers and a clean shirt, running my fingers through my hair to make sure it wasn't too unruly. The mirror reflected a young man with a bright smile and an eagerness that had yet to be dulled by life's challenges. I grabbed my guitar and headed out.

Driving through Bitterroot, I thought about how much this place meant to me. I'd grown up here, and most of the faces I saw around town were the same ones I'd seen my entire life. There were the occasional mountain resort guests that wandered into the place, but for the most part, The Hole in the Wall was a locals' hangout.

The name itself came from the owner having bought the old building, picturing it as a place for locals like a little hole in the wall place to get away for a few hours. When his daughter quipped something about the place literally having plenty of holes in the wall so his dreams were definitely coming true, he'd laughed so hard he knew right then what he was naming the place.

As I walked into the bar, the familiar sounds and smells greeted me. The chatter of patrons, the clinking of glasses, and the warm, wooden interior made me feel right at home. I set my guitar case down near the small stage and made my way to the bar.

"Hey, Austin!" called out Shelly, the bartender. She was a petite woman with a sharp wit and a heart of gold.

"Hey, Shelly. How's it going?" I asked, sliding onto a stool.

"Busy as usual. What can I get you?"

"Just a beer to start with," I replied, giving her a wink.

As Shelly poured my drink, I scanned the room, recognizing most of the faces. Old man Jenkins was at his usual spot, nursing a whiskey. The Larkin brothers were engaged in their weekly pool game, and a group of young locals were gathered around a table, laughing and chatting.

A couple of new faces caught my eye—probably tourists from the resort. I smiled to myself, wondering what they thought of our little hole in the wall.

Shelly handed me my beer, and I took a long sip, savoring the cold, crisp taste. "Thanks, Shelly," I said, giving her a nod before heading over to a group of familiar faces.

"Hey, Austin!" Maggie, a long-time friend from high school, greeted me with a hug. "You ready to sing for us tonight?"

"Always," I replied with a grin. "Wouldn't miss it for the world."

As I made my rounds, I stopped to chat with the Larkin brothers, teasing them about their game. "You boys still can't beat each other, huh?"

One of them, Ben, laughed. "Nah, we're too evenly matched. You should give it a try, Austin. Maybe you can break the tie."

"I'll stick to the guitar, thanks," I said, giving him a playful shove.

A little while later, I found myself at the table with the tourists. "Hey there, folks. First time here?" I asked, flashing my most welcoming smile.

A woman in her early thirties nodded. "Yeah, we're staying at the resort and heard this place has great live music."

"You heard right," I said, leaning in a bit. "Hope you enjoy the show. Name's Austin, by the way."

"I'm Jackie, and this is my husband, Tom," she introduced. "We're looking forward to hearing you play."

"Well, you're in for a treat," I replied with a wink, making Jackie blush slightly.

The night wore on, and as showtime approached, I took to the small stage. The familiar buzz of anticipation filled the air as I tuned my guitar. I looked out at the crowd—my friends, a couple of cousins, and the occasional new faces—and felt a rush of gratitude. This was my home, and these were my people.

"Good evening, everyone," I said into the microphone, my voice steady and confident. "Let's make this a night to remember."

I launched into my set, a mix of old favorites and some of my original songs. The audience responded with enthusiasm, and I fed off their energy. This was my escape, my way of connecting with people and sharing a piece of my soul.

As the night wound down, I finished my final song to a round of warm applause. The energy in the room left me buzzing, like it always did. Shelly handed me a fresh beer as I stepped off the stage, the adrenaline from performing still coursing through my veins.

"Great set tonight, Austin," she said, sliding the drink across the counter. "You had 'em hooked from the first note."

"Thanks, Shelly," I replied, taking a sip. "Nothing like playing for your own people, huh?"

A voice broke through my thoughts. "Hey, Austin."

I turned to see Jackie and Tom approaching, their excitement unmistakable. Jackie's eyes were alight as she said, "That was incredible. You've got an amazing voice!"

"Thank you," I said, grinning. Compliments like that never got old, but they always caught me a little off guard.

Tom stepped forward, shaking my hand. "Listen, I don't want to take up your time, but we need to talk. I'm a producer for a show called *Real American Country*. It's a competition for country artists based in Nashville, and we're looking for people with raw talent—people exactly like you."

Jackie nudged him, grinning. "I told him he had to talk to you. He just thought we were on vacation. But when I saw there was live music, I wasn't about to let him miss this. Now, I bet he's glad I insisted," she said, as she nudged him with her elbow.

Tom chuckled. "She's persistent, and she's not wrong. You've got something special, Austin. The kind of presence that can't be taught."

I hesitated, the weight of his words settling on my shoulders. The idea of performing on a bigger stage was thrilling—and terrifying. "I don't know what to say," I admitted, glancing around the bar. "I've never really thought about something like that."

"Take your time," Tom said, handing me a card. "But I hope you'll give it a shot. You never know where it might lead."

I stared at the card, his words circling in my mind. The chatter of the bar seemed to fade as I looked around at the familiar faces—the same faces I'd been singing to for years. This was home.

But Tom and Jackie had planted a seed.

This place was my home, but an opportunity like this felt too big to ignore. I knew I had a lot to consider, but one thing I knew for certain—if I said 'yes', my life would get a lot more interesting.

Chapter 2

Austin

I kicked off the tangled sheets, my feet meeting the cool wooden floor as I fought to shake off the remnants of a restless sleep. I stared at Tom's business card on the nightstand, picking it up, then setting it back down. Over and over.

Every time I closed my eyes, I saw the bright lights of a Nashville stage, the hum of an expectant crowd. But then, like a gut-punch, the image shifted. The distant rumble of the tractor. The creak of the barn door swinging open. Dad's worn hands gripping a hay bale. Connor's constant presence under the hood of an engine. The thought of stepping away felt like cutting a thread in the only life I'd ever known.

I finally pulled myself together and headed out to the kitchen of the small cabin I shared with Connor on our family's property. We'd built the place a few years back, giving us some space while still being close enough to help out on the ranch. I poured myself a cup of coffee, the smell and warmth helping to steady my nerves.

After a quick breakfast, I headed out to the barn. Dad was already there, tending to the horses. His graying hair and weathered face were familiar comforts, but the thought of leaving him to handle the ranch without me tugged at my heart.

"Mornin', Dad," I said, walking over to join him.

"Morning, son," he replied, looking up with a smile. "How'd last night go?"

"It was great. Had a good crowd," I said, trying to sound casual. "Met some folks from Nashville. They're here on vacation."

Dad raised an eyebrow. "Nashville, huh? That's quite a ways from here."

"Yeah, they were really nice. One of them is a TV producer," I said, thinking about the business card in my pocket.

Dad nodded, returning to his work. I grabbed a pitchfork and started mucking out the stalls, my thoughts still swirling. The physical labor helped clear my head, but the weight of the decision loomed over me. Leaving the ranch would mean leaving my family short-handed, especially Dad. And Connor—change wasn't easy for him. He had found a routine that worked, and I didn't want to disrupt that.

After a while, I decided to take a break. I walked over to where Connor was working on the same tractor from yesterday. He often came over to help with the heavy repairs, even though he owned the mechanic shop in town with our granddad. Charlie lay nearby, keeping a watchful eye on his surroundings.

"Morning, Connor," I called out.

"Morning," he replied without looking up.

I watched him work for a moment before speaking. "Hey, can we talk for a minute?"

Connor glanced up, wiping grease from his hands. "What's wrong?"

"Nothing's wrong." I hesitated, then pushed ahead. "I met a couple last night—Tom and Jackie. Tom's a TV producer working on a country music reality show called *Real American Country*. He thinks I'd be good for it."

Connor set down the wrench, turning to face me fully. He studied me for a moment, his gaze steady. "You want to go?"

"I don't know," I admitted. "I'm worried about leaving Dad short-handed and how that might impact you. And I know change isn't exactly your favorite thing."

Connor was quiet, his expression hard to read. Finally, he said, "We'd figure it out."

"You really think so?"

"You've got the talent."

The words were simple, but coming from Connor, they landed heavier than I expected. He wasn't the type to hand out compliments just to make someone feel good. That meant something. It meant he believed it.

"You'd be okay with it?" I asked, knowing that change was not one of Connor's favorite parts of life. Though he'd come a long way in dealing with it since we were kids.

"We'd manage," he said simply, picking up the wrench again. After a pause, he added, "You should try."

I blinked, caught off guard by the certainty in his voice. Connor wasn't one for big speeches, but in those three words, I felt more belief than I'd ever dared to feel for myself.

Charlie padded over, and I bent down to scratch behind his ears, glancing up at Connor. "What do you think, Chuck? Should I go for it?"

Connor huffed. "He says yes. So do I," he deadpanned.

I stood up, feeling confident about my next move. "Alright, then. I'll call Tom and see what the next steps are."

As I walked back toward the house, the card in my pocket felt heavier than before—like a promise, or maybe a challenge. And this time, the fear didn't outweigh the excitement.

Chapter 3

Willow

The gentle sway of Spanish moss in the breeze caught my eye as I eased the car to a stop outside the office building. The cobblestone street shimmered faintly, polished smooth by years of use.

I parked outside the office, my fingers tightening around the steering wheel as I glanced at the clock. Twenty minutes early. Not bad, considering I'd already spilled coffee on my blouse, misplaced my car keys, and spent the drive here wondering if today was the day I finally quit.

My guitar case sat on the back seat, a reminder of the life I was chasing outside of this job. Last night, I'd spent hours rehearsing for The Driftwood gig, strumming until my fingers ached. Now, as I headed into the market research firm, the contrast between my dreams and my reality felt sharper than ever.

The office hummed with fluorescent sterility—the buzz of computers, the rhythmic clacking of keyboards, the lifeless hum of an air conditioner working too hard. It smelled like paper, burnt coffee, and boredom. The place was far less inspiring than the music I loved.

I settled into my desk, pulling up the client report I'd been working on. My boss, Jackson Trent, would likely be breathing down my neck before long.

Jackson wasn't just a micromanager—he was the kind of man who let his presence linger too long, his words sticky and gross like humidity after a summer storm. He appeared at my desk without warning, his cologne cloying, the kind that smelled expensive but felt like suffocation.

"Gracin," he said smoothly. "Those figures ready yet?"

"Almost," I replied, keeping my tone even.

He leaned in, bracing one hand on the desk beside mine. Too close. Always too close. "Make sure it's flawless. You know how much is riding on this client."

"Of course," I said, forcing a smile that didn't quite reach my eyes.

He hovered—not saying anything, just watching. Waiting. For what, I never knew. Then, finally he turned and walked away, leaving the scent of arrogance and overconfidence in his wake.

By lunchtime, the tension in my shoulders had eased slightly. I stepped outside, letting the warm Savannah air wrap around me as I walked to my car. The guitar case in the back seat caught my eye, and I found myself itching to reach for it almost instinctively.

I drove to Forsyth Park, the familiar green space offering a much-needed escape. Sitting on a bench near the fountain, the weight of my guitar was as familiar as my own heartbeat. I slid my fingers over the frets, plucking out a melody that had been haunting the edges of my mind for weeks. It wasn't polished, not yet, but it had potential. A little like me, I supposed.

The first few notes drifted into the air, mingling with the distant laughter of children and the rhythmic splash of the fountain behind me. A few passersby slowed their steps, casting curious glances in my direction. That was the thing about music—no matter where you were, it made people stop and listen.

My voice came next, soft at first, then steady:

Lost between the lines of who they want me to be,
Chasing dreams they said were never meant for me...

The words weren't finished, but they were real. They were mine.

Growing up in Savannah meant living in a world of expectations. My father, a prominent lawyer, had charted a path for me long before I could choose one for myself. Law school, the family firm, a future as structured as the Spanish-style architecture that lined the streets of my childhood.

But music had always been my refuge. I'd spent hours as a kid playing the upright piano in the living room or sneaking my guitar outside to strum under the stars. My mother had been my quiet supporter, slipping me encouragement when my father wasn't looking.

When I turned down law school to pursue music, the disappointment in his voice was a weight I carried long after I left home. "You're throwing away a future, Willow," he'd said. My brother Caleb, ever the dutiful son, hadn't understood my choice either. But music wasn't a choice—it was who I was.

Later that evening, back at the duplex I shared with Gemma, the strains of my new song still echoed in my mind.

"You're late," Gemma teased as I walked through the door, kicking off my shoes. She was already at the kitchen counter, chopping vegetables.

"Work ran long," I said, setting my bag down. "Jackson was in rare form today."

Gemma made a face. "Slimeball Trent strikes again. Please tell me you told him off."

"Not this time," I replied with a tired laugh. "But at least I'm done for the day. Now I can focus on The Driftwood."

Her face lit up. "Finally! You've been waiting for this gig forever."

I nodded, feeling a mix of excitement and nerves. "I'm ready, I think. I just need to change clothes."

Gemma leaned against the counter, her expression softening. "You're going to blow them away, Willow. I can feel it."

Her confidence buoyed me, and as I browsed my closet, the tension of the day began to melt away.

The Driftwood was more than just a gig. It was a chance to prove —to myself, to my family, to the world—that I could do this.

Chapter 4

Willow

The Driftwood buzzed with low chatter, laughter bouncing off the walls and glasses clinking here and there. My fingers gripped the smooth and familiar neck of my guitar, my heart pounding ninety to nothing in my chest. I flexed my hands, trying to shake off the nerves creeping in.

I belonged here. At least, I had to believe that.

The place smelled like old wood and citrusy drinks giving me something to focus on as I tried to steady myself in the chaos as the crowd waited, buzzing with anticipation.

"Deep breaths," I whispered to myself, rolling my shoulders to shake off the nerves.

Gemma's voice drifted over from her seat at the bar. "You've got this, Willow!" she called out with a grin, her confidence radiating across the room.

The spotlight snapped on, casting a warm glow over the small stage. My boots clicked softly against the worn wooden planks as I stepped into its center. The light was softer than I'd expected, like an embrace rather than a glare, but it didn't stop the prickle of nerves running down my spine.

"Good evening, everyone," I said into the microphone, my voice steady despite the flutter in my chest. "Thank you for being here tonight. My name is Willow Gracin, and I'm so excited to share some music with you."

The first chords wavered—just for a second—but then muscle memory kicked in. My fingers danced over the strings, finding their rhythm, steady and sure. The opening notes floated into the room, and conversation softened as heads turned toward the stage.

With each verse, I felt my nerves unravel, replaced by something else—something electric.

By the time I reached my third song, my confidence had built. The applause between sets was soothing, easing my doubts. I introduced my new song hesitantly, the vulnerability of sharing something so personal making my voice feel thick in my throat.

I swallowed against the knot and adjusted the guitar's strap over my shoulder. I could still hear my father's voice in my head, crisp and disappointed. I could still feel the sting of Caleb's disapproval, the weight of expectations I never asked for.

"This next one's new," I said, forcing my voice to stay steady. "It's about finding your place in the world, even if it's not where people expect you to be."

I exhaled slowly. And then, I let the music speak for me.

The first notes hung in the air, tender and tentative. As I sang, memories flashed through my mind—my father's disappointed frown, Caleb's careful words of caution, my mother's quiet encouragement. The emotions poured out, raw and unfiltered, as if I were singing directly to them.

When the final chord echoed through the room, there was a moment of silence, the kind that felt almost sacred. Then the applause came, louder and more enthusiastic than I'd dared to hope for.

After the set, I mingled with the crowd, exchanging smiles and thank-yous as patrons stopped me to share their thoughts. Gemma joined me, practically glowing with pride.

"You were amazing," she said, pulling me into a quick hug.

"Thanks, G," I replied, my heart still pounding from the adrenaline of performing.

That's when I noticed him—a man standing near the back of the room, his sharp gray suit standing out against the casual crowd. He was in his early forties, with salt-and-pepper hair and an easy confidence that seemed to command attention without demanding it.

He approached with a warm smile and extended his hand. "Willow Gracin?"

"That's me," I said, shaking his hand.

"Mitch Haynes," he introduced himself. "I'm a music producer based in Nashville. I was in town visiting family, and I try to catch live music wherever I go. I'm glad I stopped in tonight."

His voice was smooth and unhurried, with the slightest Southern drawl.

"Thank you," I said, my mind racing. A Nashville producer? Here, tonight?

"I have to say, your set was incredible," Mitch continued, his tone genuine. "You've got something rare, Willow. There's an authenticity to your voice and lyrics you don't hear much these days."

I blinked, trying to process his words. I'd spent years chasing this feeling, this moment, but now that it was happening, my brain refused to catch up.

"Wow," I managed, feeling a blush rise to my cheeks. "That means a lot. Thank you."

Mitch nodded, his expression thoughtful. "I'd love to sit down with you and talk about a project I'm working on. It's a country music reality show called *Real American Country*. We're looking for talent, and I think you'd be a great fit."

The words hit me like a thunderclap. A reality show? It was an opportunity beyond anything I'd imagined, but the idea of stepping into that kind of spotlight felt overwhelming.

I wanted to believe him. But was I really ready for something this big?

"That's incredible," I said, trying to keep my voice steady. "I don't know what to say."

"Say you'll think about it," Mitch replied with a kind smile. "No pressure tonight. Here's my card. Let's meet tomorrow and talk more."

I took the card, studying it before meeting his gaze. "Thank you, Mr. Haynes. I'll be there."

"Call me Mitch," he said. "Looking forward to it."

Gemma nearly tackled me as soon as Mitch walked away. "Willow, oh my gosh!"

"Did that just happen?" I asked, staring at the card as if it might disappear.

"Yes! And you're meeting him tomorrow? This is huge!" Gemma's excitement was infectious, but beneath my smile, I felt a swirl of doubt.

"It's a lot," I admitted, running my fingers over the edges of Mitch's business card. The cardstock was thick, the embossed letters pressing into my fingertips—a physical reminder that the chance meeting had been real.

This was what I wanted. Wasn't it?

Gemma looped an arm around my shoulders. "You're ready for this, Willow. I've always known it. Now the world's going to know it too."

Her confidence steadied me, but as we stepped into the cool Savannah night, the weight of the opportunity settled on my shoulders. Mitch had seen something in me, something real—but was I ready to believe in myself the way he did?

For now, I let the applause, the music, and Gemma's unwavering faith carry me home.

Chapter 5

Willow

The Blue Door Café buzzed with morning chatter, but the noise barely registered over the pounding in my chest. Sunlight streamed through the windows, reflecting off the ceramic mugs, the warm scent of coffee curling around me. I wrapped my hands around my own cup, letting the heat anchor me.

This was real. A real meeting with a Nashville producer.

My fingers tapped against the table, restless. What if I wasn't ready? What if he changed his mind overnight?

He arrived precisely on time, his sharp gray suit and relaxed demeanor standing out among the casual crowd. As he approached, I stood, extending a hand.

"Good morning, Willow," he said, his smile warm and genuine. "Thanks for meeting me."

"Thanks for inviting me," I replied, as I took my seat.

Once we'd settled, Mitch wasted no time. "I meant what I said last night—your performance was incredible. You've got talent, but more than that, you've got heart. That's rare, and it's what people connect with."

His words left me both flattered and cautious. "Thank you. I've always wanted to share my music with people, but this feels big."

"*Real American Country* isn't just a singing competition, Willow," Mitch said, leaning forward, his voice steady and sure. "It's a launchpad. You don't just get fans—you get a chance as a career. You get a chance to live the life you've been dreaming about."

The weight of his words pressed into me. A real career. The kind that didn't involve side gigs at bars or cramming music into the spare moments between shifts at a job I didn't love. A chance to prove—to myself, to my father, to the world—that this wasn't just a dream.

"But it's also a risk," I said, voicing the fear that had kept me up the night before. "What if I'm not ready? Or what if I try and fail?"

Mitch leaned forward, his gaze steady. "Every artist feels that way, Willow. But the ones who succeed are the ones who try, even when they're scared. You've got the voice, the story, and the drive. The rest? That's just hard work and heart."

I swallowed hard, his words settling into the pit of my stomach. "What would it look like? If I said yes?"

He outlined the basics—auditions, contracts, the grueling schedule of filming and performing. It was overwhelming, but for every daunting detail, there was a spark of possibility.

As we wrapped up, Mitch handed me a folder. "Take this. It's a draft of the contract and some information about the show. Read it over, talk to your family, and let me know."

"Thank you," I said, meaning it. "I'll think about it."

Mitch smiled. "Good. Just remember—you're ready for this, Willow. Don't let fear hold you back."

The Gracin family dinner table was a place of tradition and familiarity—plates of Mom's lasagna, the soft clink of silverware, and conversations that often carried the weight of expectation. Tonight, though, the air was heavy with something else.

I cleared my throat as the conversation lulled. "I have something to tell y'all."

Three sets of eyes turned toward me: Dad, his expression expectant; Caleb, with his lawyer's gaze already analyzing; and Mom, a flicker of concern softening her features.

"I've been offered a spot on a reality music competition called *Real American Country*," I began, my voice steady despite the knot tightening in my chest. "It's an opportunity to share my music on a national stage."

The silence was deafening.

Dad set down his fork carefully, like he needed to physically brace himself before speaking. "Willow. We've talked about stability. You have a good job—a future. Why throw that away for something so uncertain?"

The word "uncertain" carried more than doubt—it carried disappointment.

"Because music is what I love," I replied, trying to keep the frustration out of my voice. "I've been working toward this my whole life."

Caleb exhaled sharply, setting his glass down with a quiet clink. "Who's behind this? What's the angle?" His lawyer's gaze locked onto mine, searching for weaknesses.

"There's no catch," I said, pulling Mitch's card from my pocket and sliding it across the table. "His name's Mitch Haynes. He's a producer from Nashville, and he believes in me."

Dad sighed, rubbing his temples. "Believing in you is easy, Willow. But believing this industry won't chew you up and spit you out? That's harder."

Silence stretched between us, thick and unyielding.

Mom reached for the card, her expression thoughtful as she studied it. "It's a big opportunity," she said softly, glancing at Dad.

"It's a gamble," Dad countered. "And gambles rarely pay off. What happens if this doesn't work out, Willow? Have you thought about that?"

"I have," I said firmly. "And I'd rather take the risk than spend my life wondering 'what if.'"

Caleb sighed, his pragmatic side warring with something gentler. "I'll look into this Mitch Haynes and review the contract. If it's legit, and if you're serious about this, I'll support you."

Relief flooded through me. "Thank you, Caleb."

Dad's frown deepened, but Mom placed a hand on his arm. "She needs to try, Frank. And we need to let her."

Later, I found Dad in his study, the soft glow of his desk lamp casting long shadows across the bookshelves. He was hunched over a stack of papers, his reading glasses perched on the bridge of his nose.

"Hey, Dad," I said softly, stepping inside.

He looked up, and for a long moment, he just looked at me. And in his eyes, I saw everything—his worry, his pride, his struggle to hold onto both at once. "Willow."

I hesitated, then crossed the room to sit in the chair across from him. For a moment, neither of us spoke. The air felt heavy, filled with things unsaid. Finally, he sighed, leaning back in his chair and removing his glasses.

"You're my youngest," he began, his voice low. "My baby girl. It's hard not to want to protect you."

"I know," I said gently, folding my hands in my lap. "And I appreciate it. But this is something I need to do."

He nodded slowly, his eyes searching mine. "I just don't want to see you get hurt. I've seen dreams turn to dust, and it's not an easy thing to come back from."

I swallowed hard, his words hitting a place deep inside me. "I've thought about that. But I have to believe in myself, even if it's scary. And I'll have Caleb, and Mitch, and people who believe in me, too."

"And me, too," he said quietly. The words came softly but carried so much weight, his gaze unwavering. "You'll have me, too."

My chest tightened, and I nodded, blinking back the sudden sting of tears.

"But promise me you'll be careful," he added after a moment, his voice thick with emotion.

"I promise," I said, my voice steady despite the lump in my throat. The words felt like a pact, carrying more weight than I'd expected.

He gave a small nod, his expression tinged with both pride and reluctance. "I trust you to know what's right, Willow. Just be careful. And remember, whatever happens, you're not alone."

"Thanks, Dad," I said softly, rising from the chair. "I promise."

As I turned to leave, I paused at the doorway, glancing back at him. He was already reaching for his glasses, but the look on his face stayed with me—a mix of love, worry, and something that felt like quiet hope.

The next day, my phone buzzed with Caleb's name.

"Hey, Willis," he said, using the nickname he'd given me when we were kids, his tone lighter than I'd expected.

"Hey," I replied, my heart pounding. "Did you talk to Mitch?"

"I did," Caleb said. "And I can see why you trust him. He's legit."

Relief flooded through me. "Thank you for checking, Caleb."

He hesitated, then added, "I'm proud of you, Willow. For going after this."

Tears welled in my eyes. "That means everything to me."

Back at the duplex, Gemma and I sat cross-legged on the floor, takeout containers spread between us.

"To big dreams and scary risks," she said, raising her spring roll in a toast.

"To having the best friend a girl could ask for," I replied, clinking my fork against hers.

As we laughed and ate, I felt the weight of the past few days ease.

Later, as I sat with my guitar, the fear crept back in. But for the first time, it didn't feel bigger than the excitement.

Chapter 6

Austin

My boots hit the Nashville tarmac with an eager thud, the heel-toe rhythm of my stride a steady beat to focus on so the nerves inside me stayed in check. With a tug at my old cap, I looked around the bustling airport, feeling both excited and nervous. A face that looked oddly familiar bobbed in and out of view, but as far as I knew, I didn't know anyone else here.

My hand found the folded edge of paper in my back pocket—the document I'd pored over countless times on the flight. Pulling it out, I scanned the faces once more, committing them to memory. Amidst the headshots, Levi Brooks's stood out: the guy had a jawline like it was chiseled from Tennessee limestone itself, and eyes that seemed to hold a steady confidence.

"Levi Brooks," I said under my breath. And as if on cue, there he was, standing by baggage claim, a guitar case slung over his shoulder and a duffle bag at his feet.

"Levi?" I ventured, stepping forward with an extended hand. "I'm Austin Blake."

"Thought that was you," Levi replied, his handshake firm and sure. "Ready for this rodeo?"

"Born ready," I quipped, though a flutter of doubt rippled through me. Was I though? I guess we were going to find out.

We made small talk on the ride to the house, the city blurring past the car windows. The green Tennessee countryside gave way to a sprawling estate. The farmhouse, if you could call it that, looked like it had been pulled out of a magazine—white columns, wraparound porches, and enough windows to let in the kind of light every artist dreamed of.

"Sweet mercy," I breathed.

"Twelve thousand square feet of opportunity," Levi said, his voice tinged with awe.

"Or six acres of atomic pressure," I muttered, but my grin gave me away.

We stepped out onto the property, and for a moment, all I could do was drink in the view. Hills rolled away to the horizon, the lushness of the landscape a vivid backdrop to the journey ahead.

"Best get used to it," Levi said, clapping me on the shoulder. "This place is home for the next little while."

I stepped through the grand foyer, my boots echoing against polished hardwood floors. The house felt alive, buzzing with possibility. Cameras were everywhere, tucked into corners like they were waiting to catch the first spark of drama or magic.

"Feels like walking onto a movie set," I murmured, my voice lost in the cavernous space of the formal living room where a fireplace big enough to roast an ox dominated one wall.

"Or into the lion's den," Levi added, but there was a twinkle in his eye that told me he was more excited than afraid.

We found our way to the great room, where huge windows offered a panoramic view of the backyard. Another massive fireplace whispered promises of cozy winter nights, though the heat outside argued we wouldn't need its warmth anytime soon. The furniture was arranged to invite conversation or late-night gatherings.

"Alright, gentlemen," a producer approached us, clipboard in hand and a headset firmly in place. "We'd like you two to hang out here. As the others arrive, we want to capture those first impressions."

"Got it," I said, nodding. My heart thrummed with anticipation, the performer in me waking up. This was just another stage, albeit one with higher stakes than I'd ever known.

We both sat on either end of one of the couches, Levi's posture relaxed but his eyes sharp. I, on the other hand, felt a surge of energy propel me to my feet. I couldn't sit still; not now, not when the air was thick with promise and potential.

As each contestant walked through the door, I was there to greet them, my hand extended, my smile easy. Some were shy, clinging to the walls like ivy, while others entered with all the fanfare of a head-lining act. But they all got the same Austin Blake charm—a joke, a compliment, a shared look of can-you-believe-we're-here?

"Welcome wagon much?" Levi teased during a lull in arrivals.

"Someone's gotta do it," I replied with a shrug, though I knew he was right. My nerves were singing, and this—this camaraderie, this show of spirit—was how I kept them at bay. It was in my nature to make connections, to build the bridges I'd someday need to cross. And in this house, under these lights, every handshake was the foundation of something more.

"Next up, Real American Friendships," I joked, earning a chuckle from Levi. But really, wasn't that part of it? We may have been here as individual competitors but we were also here as part of a group. And when twelve different personalities converged under pressure, anything could happen. So harmony was the name of my game.

Then she stepped inside like she already belonged here—shoulders back, chin high, her eyes scanning the room with a quiet kind of wonder. It wasn't arrogance—it was something different, something that made me want to watch her longer than I should have.

Confidence radiated from her like a melody from a well-tuned guitar. I felt my breath hitch, words lost somewhere between my brain and my lips.

She caught my gaze for a split second—just long enough for my breath to hitch, long enough to wonder if she'd felt it too.

"Earth to Austin," Levi murmured, his elbow nudging me gently in the ribs. I blinked, the spell momentarily broken.

"Right, yeah." My voice sounded strange to my own ears, but I shook off the sudden fog and stepped forward. "Hey there! I'm Austin."

"Willow," she replied, her smile lighting up the room like the stage lights above us. "This place is incredible, isn't it?"

Even her name sounded like a song, a smooth melody you wanted to play over and over.

"Sure is," I managed, hoping my grin didn't look as goofy as it felt plastered on my face. As she drifted further into the house, her presence seemed to linger in the air, a note held just a bit too long at the end of a song.

"Smooth," Levi commented dryly, but I barely heard him over the thrumming of my own heartbeat.

Before I could think too deeply about the effect Willow had on me, another arrival drew our attention. Christopher Jordan stepped through the threshold, his demeanor the polar opposite of Willow's exuberance. He was friendly enough, offering a nod and a modest, "Hey, y'all," before giving the space a quiet once-over.

"Chris, right?" I said, stepping up with an outstretched hand which he shook firmly yet briefly.

"Christopher, but yeah." His tone was amicable, if reserved, a slow drawl that suggested deep roots and deeper thoughts.

"Place is something else, huh?" I tried, aiming for conversation.

"Never seen anything like it," he agreed, his words few but genuine. His gaze wandered around the great room, lingering on the fireplace before he found a spot by the window, content to observe rather than plunge into the thick of introductions.

I glanced back toward where Willow had mingled with a couple of other contestants, her laughter ringing clear across the room, then to Christopher's solitary figure by the window. Two different tunes, both part of the same unfolding concert that was this experience. And I couldn't wait to see how they'd blend with my own.

The last of the arrivals filtered through the door just as twilight began to paint the horizon with hues of orange and lavender. We were a motley crew of dreamers, each with a guitar case or instrument in tow, our footsteps echoing against the pristine floors of the grand farmhouse that would be our home for the coming weeks.

"Alright folks, listen up!" A production assistant clapped her hands, gathering us in the great room. Her clipboard was gripped in hand as though it was her weapon, a clear sign of her serious demeanor. "Dinner's at seven sharp in the dining room—trust me, you don't want to miss it. Tomorrow's call time is eight AM; we start filming your backstories then." Heads nodded, and murmurs of acknowledgment filled the space. "For now, feel free to relax. Get to know each other. For better or for worse, you're going to be like family soon enough."

A communal sense of relief seemed to ripple through the group, the kind that comes when the last piece of an unfinished puzzle clicks into place.

The dining room was a sight to behold. A long, polished table stretched out beneath a chandelier that sparkled like a constellation, its light casting a warm glow over the assembled group. The scent of grilled meats and fresh vegetables wafted through the air, mingling with the chatter and laughter that began to fill the room. Seated among newfound friends and soon to be rivals, we dug into the feast, a perfect accompaniment to the stories and dreams being shared.

After dinner, we all wandered out onto the sprawling patio, the vast Tennessee sky stretching above us, stars just beginning to pop out one by one. The patio was lit by string lights that cast a soft, golden glow, creating an atmosphere of casual intimacy. Comfortable seating arrangements invited us to gather in small groups while still all being able to fill the space.

From my place by the railing, I caught sight of Willow again. She was standing with Harper Lane, another contestant whose voice, I remembered from her profile, was said to rival the soulful croon of Emmylou Harris. They chatted with the ease of old friends, their laughter floating on the evening air.

Willow's presence was magnetic, her smile bright enough to be seen even in the waning light. It wasn't just her confidence that captivated me—it was the way she threw her head back when she laughed, genuine and unguarded, or how her eyes sparkled with an innate joy that suggested she didn't just live life, she embraced it wholeheartedly. I found myself studying the curve of her lips, the way her hand brushed her hair away from her face, and the graceful gestures that punctuated her conversation.

"Quite the view, isn't it?" Levi's voice pulled me back from my silent admiration.

"Uh, yeah," I stammered, a little too quickly. "The landscape's unreal."

"Wasn't talking about the landscape," he chuckled, nudging me with his elbow before wandering off to join a group nearby.

I shook my head, trying to clear the fog of infatuation that had wrapped itself around my thoughts. Focus, Austin. This was a competition, after all. But even as I reminded myself of the stakes, my gaze drifted back to Willow wishing I could bask in her energy. There was something about her—more than just a pretty face or a potential rival for the title. She had an aura, a light, and I couldn't help but feel drawn to it like a moth to a flame. And I didn't care how cliché that sounded. It was the God's-honest truth.

The laughter and chatter on the patio melded into the symphony of crickets as twilight deepened. I excused myself with a grin and a plan. Trying to hurry, I slipped back into the great room where my guitar leaned against the plush couch, waiting like an old friend.

"Missed me, didn't you?" I murmured to the instrument before striding back outside, the door swinging shut with a gentle thud.

As I stepped onto the patio, the conversations quieted, expectant eyes turning my way. My pulse quickened—not from nerves, but from the sheer thrill I got just from thinking about performing.

Strumming a chord to signal the start of my impromptu entertainment, I caught Willow's gaze across the flickering lights, her silhouette outlined by the warm glow of the setting sun.

"I think it's time for some music," I announced, voice confident as my fingers danced along the strings.

Her smile reached me before her laughter, warm and inviting, and it was all the encouragement I needed. It was as though we were already in sync because when I launched into Alabama's "Dixieland Delight," she was right there with me. Her voice harmonized effortlessly with mine, smooth, warm, a perfect fit alongside my own. It was effortless—like we'd sung together a hundred times before.

My pulse quickened, but it wasn't just from the music.

Across the flickering firelight of the fire pit, her eyes met mine, and something unspoken passed between us. A spark.

"Rollin' down a backwoods, Tennessee byway, one arm on the wheel..." The words flowed from us, our voices mingling with the dusk. Others joined in, clapping their hands and tapping their feet, but through it all, my focus never wavered from Willow and my smile never faded.

Song after song filled the air, each one tapering off as the night drew on and the group dwindled, contestants retreating into the comfort of the house or the promise of rest before the competition began in earnest.

I lingered, hoping for a moment alone with her, but Willow was encircled by a few holdouts, their laughter pealing into the night. I watched her animatedly recounting a story, her hands painting pictures in the air, and felt a tug in my chest. She was talented, no doubt about that. There was definitely a sense of admiration but also there was something else, something deeper.

Realizing I might not get the chance to speak to her, I started toward the house, guitar in hand, forcing myself to think about chords and lyrics instead of the conversation that never happened. But just as I approached the doorway, a voice stopped me in my tracks.

"Hey, Austin, wait up!" Willow called out, her approach light and unhurried. She had extricated herself from the group.

"Oh, hey," I replied, turning to face her with a smile I hoped looked casual and not as overeager as I felt.

"Wouldn't miss a chance to thank you for the music," she said, her tone genuine.

"Thanks," I chuckled, leaning against the doorframe. "You're not so bad yourself. Where'd you learn to harmonize like that?"

"Shower. Car. Anywhere I can belt out a tune without someone telling me to pipe down," she quipped, and we shared a laugh that felt as comfortable as a broken in pair of boots.

"Good places, all solid acoustics," I nodded sagely, playing along. "We might have to make this a regular thing if we don't wear out our welcome first."

"Or get voted off," she added with a playful wink.

"Then let's make sure we leave 'em with something memorable," I said, the words tinged with a challenge, hopeful for more evenings like this one.

"Deal." She extended her hand, and I shook it, her grip firm and promising.

"Goodnight, Austin Blake."

"Goodnight, Willow Gracin."

She turned away, but I stood there a second longer, like a fool, watching until she disappeared inside.

I ran a hand through my hair, exhaling sharply. I came here to win a competition. Not to get distracted by a girl with a voice like honey and a smile that could make a man forget his own name.

Stepping back into the great room, the guitar now resting in its case by the couch, I could still feel the warmth of Willow's handshake lingering on my skin. Now inside it was just me and the faint hum of the camera equipment.

I sank down onto one of the plush armchairs, the leather cool against my back. My heart hadn't quite settled yet, still keeping time with the rhythm of the evening. Willow apparently had that effect—an energy that seemed to buzz through me, electric and infectious.

I tried to shake off the sensation, but it clung to me, that feeling of excitement for what lay ahead. Not just the competition; that was a given. But the possibility of more moments with Willow, more music, more shared glances across the firelight.

"Get a grip, Austin," I muttered to myself, standing up. I strode across the room, flicking off lights as I went. There was an early call tomorrow, rehearsals or interviews or some such thing, and I needed to be on top of my game.

But as I climbed the stairs to the bedroom assigned to me that I shared with Levi, I couldn't help but replay the night. Her smile when she said my name, the easy banter, the way her eyes had locked with mine as we sang—it was all too easy to imagine doing it again.

Chapter 7

Willow

The steady hum of the airplane engine tried to distract me, but it couldn't drown out the thoughts colliding in my head. Excitement. Doubt. What if this was the best thing I'd ever done? What if it was the biggest mistake?

I traced the edge of the boarding pass still tucked into my notebook that I'd been holding onto like a lifeline, my fingers restless. My entire life was in transition, suspended between two places—Savannah and Nashville, security and the unknown.

Excitement warred with nerves, twisting my stomach into a tight knot. I gripped the armrest and closed my eyes, replaying the last few weeks—the goodbye dinner, the nervous energy buzzing through my apartment, and my dad's hesitant but heartfelt encouragement.

"Willow, you'll knock 'em dead," Gemma had said, raising a glass in toast. Her blue eyes sparkled with unshed tears, mirroring my own.

"Here's to chasing dreams, and to always keeping home in your heart," my father added, his voice steady despite the emotion I knew was brimming beneath the surface.

We'd sat around the table talking about what I was heading for and what I'd be up against. The details were sparse but I knew enough that I could explain how twelve of us would be competing for a million dollars and a recording contract with one of the big labels. Every week we'd perform according to the theme of the week and every week viewers would vote for their favorite. The contestant with the lowest number of votes would go home and it would all start again the next week.

Mitch had explained that chances were pretty high that any of us that actually wanted a contract in the end would probably not be hurting for offers but he couldn't promise it. Apparently, none of us would be less than really good at what we'd be bringing to the table. This had made my dad a little defensive because he was a lawyer and guarantees meant dotted lines with every 'i' dotted and 't' crossed. I assured him Mitch was not making any kind of promise or guarantee. He just thought I was talented enough to pick up a contract on my own even if I didn't reach the finish line. Being on the show would put me in a better position either way.

After dinner we'd sat around the living room talking longer about Caleb's latest case and a project Gemma was working on. My dad stood and began handing something to everyone in the room but me. I stared at my Dad waiting for an explanation. The expression he wore was of sheepish pride as he held up a handful of what looked like metal buttons.

"Vote for Willow" they read, surrounding a picture of me holding my guitar. The campaign-style pins were both corny and incredibly sweet, the kind of thing only a father could get away with. Tears pricked at the corners of my eyes as I took one from his hand.

"Dad, I—"

"Should've done this sooner," he cut in, his voice rough like he was clearing it from emotion. "I want you to know, I'm really proud of you, Willow. No matter what happens in Nashville."

My chest ached as I threw my arms around him, holding on tighter than I had in years.

"Thanks, Dad. That means everything to me," I said, the tears

spilling over as I hugged him tight. There was a tremble in his arms that told me he felt the gravity of this moment just as much as I did.

"Your old man's learning that supporting your dreams is like backing the right horse in a race. Can't help but feel like I've won already, just seeing you chase after them."

"Even if I don't make it?" I asked, pulling back to look at him.

"Especially if you don't make it. Because you tried, Willow. And trying takes guts." His eyes locked onto mine.

"Besides," he added with a wink, "with these buttons, how could America resist?"

I laughed through my tears, clutching the button like a talisman.

It didn't take long to make it through baggage claim and out to the car waiting for me. The moment the sedan pulled up to the curve of the sweeping driveway, my heart did a little two-step in my chest. The mansion that sprawled before me was something straight out of a movie —all wrap-around porches and windows winking in the afternoon sun like the eyes of a man who knows he's got a good hand at poker.

"Here goes nothing," I murmured to myself, clutching the handle of my guitar case like it was the only thing keeping me tethered to the ground. My boots crunched on the gravel as I took in the sprawling colonial farmhouse that would be home for the next few weeks.

The sheer size of it, the white columns standing guard like sentries had me enamored. The massive front doors opened and my jaw hit the floor. I was so taken by the opulence that I nearly missed him. Nearly.

"Hey there! I'm Austin." His voice, warm as molasses, drew my gaze like a magnet. There he stood with a smile that could've outshone the high beams of an eighteen-wheeler. Austin, as I'd soon learn, was the epitome of a country boy dream, from the brim of his worn ball cap down to those Wrangler jeans that clung to him in a way that made a girl wonder if denim had finally met its destiny.

"Willow," I managed, feeling the flush creep up my cheeks as I approached. Was it the Tennessee heat or just him?

His grin was infectious, the kind that sparked a light inside that you didn't know had been flickering.

"This place is incredible, isn't it?"

"Sure is," he said, and I could tell by the twang in his voice that he was country charm and mischief personified. He had an ease about him, like he'd been born on a front porch swing.

Stepping past him into the grand foyer, I couldn't help but feel like I was walking into the first day of the rest of my life. As his laughter followed me, mingling with the echoes of my footsteps, I thought about how music had always been my guiding star, leading me to this very spot.

"Earth to Austin," someone called out, and I turned to see another contestant nudging him playfully. Austin blinked, breaking whatever reverie had held him captive, and laughed it off. But as I walked further into the house, I had the strangest feeling that there was more to the place than just music.

The room was bright and warm, light from outside radiated through windows, casting a spell of hope and renewal. As I wandered through the space, my hand brushed against the luxurious velvet of a sofa, a silent observer of my awe. The massive room was alive with murmurs of conversation and the steady clicks and blinking lights of cameras from every angle. My heart raced in anticipation - every smile, every note sung, would be captured by those unflinching lenses.

"Remember why you're here," I whispered to myself.

About that time, in walked Lanie Tisdale, with all the subtlety of a tornado ripping through the Georgia plains. She was dressed to impress, like she was about to take over Music Row, throwing exaggerated waves at cameras that weren't even filming yet.

"Hey, y'all!" Her saccharine voice grated on my nerves as my body instinctively tried to escape her presence.

She waltzed in like she owned the place, tossing her hair over one shoulder as she scanned the room like she was picking out her next victim. Her eyes landed on me, flicking up and down, assessing.

There was no escaping a force like Lanie; she demanded attention and it seemed like everyone in the room was under her spell. I glanced around the room for refuge and found it when Harper Lane swept in - a breath of fresh air in cowboy boots. We struck up an easy conversation, our laughter blending with the movement of a production team and equipment.

"I'm Harper," she introduced herself, her hand reaching out to shake mine. "And I come bearing gifts." From her bag, she pulled out homemade oatmeal cookies. "My mom's secret recipe."

"I'm Willow," I replied, taking a cookie and savoring its deliciousness. "And clearly your new best friend."

"Clearly," Harper grinned, biting into her own cookie. " You sound like a true southern girl. I'm from Texas myself. Southern sisters gotta stick together."

"Especially against hurricanes like that one," I nodded then gestured towards Lanie, who was now loudly recounting some exaggerated tale to a bored sound tech.

We found a free seat and settled in with our treats.

"Ah, Lanie Tisdale." Harper chuckled. "She definitely made an impression. But we have country music in our blood and cookies in our pockets. I think we are gonna be just fine."

"Agreed." I took another bite, feeling comforted by the sweetness and reminded of family dinners back home.

"Besides," Harper added, mischief dancing in her eyes, "we didn't come here to win a popularity contest. We came to sing."

"Exactly." My gaze drifted towards a shiny piano in the corner, already imagining the notes I could create on its keys.

I leaned back on the leather couch that felt more like a cloud than a sofa, Harper's giggle ringing out over the din of conversations. It had been a whirlwind since my arrival, but finally, all twelve of us contestants were here, our anxious energies weaving together to create a feeling of excitement and hope.

My gaze settled on the guy who had welcomed every person into the place like it was his personal home. I took in his form, getting distracted by the dark blue jeans that looked tailor made for him. Heat crept up my neck and into my cheeks.

Someone really should turn the air down in here.

"Willow, girl, your face is turning about three shades of red," Harper teased, her sharp eyes not missing a beat. "You look like you've just seen a cowboy straight out of a romance novel."

I realized she'd caught me staring in the direction of where Austin stood, chatting with a couple of the other guys.

"Harper, those jeans are so tight if he had a quarter in his pocket, we could tell if it was heads or tails," I said, unable to keep the grin from my lips. My cheeks burned hotter, but I didn't mind. Being here felt like a dream, and if admiring a fine view was part of that dream, who was I to complain?

"Girl, you're bad," Harper chuckled, slapping my arm playfully. "But you ain't wrong," she said, giving her own attention to his tight Wrangler jeans, which clung to him like they were painted on.

Our chuckles were interrupted by one of the show's producers clapping her hands for attention, a clipboard in hand.

As soon as she made her announcement about dinner and the next day's schedule, the group began to disband. I found myself walking side by side with Cassidy Raye Stanton, whose quiet demeanor was a stark contrast to Lanie's boisterous presence. Cassidy offered me a gentle smile that reached her glowing blue eyes.

"Isn't this place something else?" I murmured to her, gesturing at the grandeur of the colonial-style farmhouse.

"It's like something out of a movie," she replied softly, her voice carrying the slightest hint of awe.

"Hey, Cassidy, you ever think about what it'd be like to actually live in a place like this?" Harper piped up, joining our small circle. Her drawl was rich and comforting, a reminder of home.

"Can't say I have," Cassidy admitted with a shy laugh. "It's a bit much for me."

"Me too," I agreed. "Give me just enough room to breathe and a clear view of the stars at night."

As we settled into our seats at the dining room table, the conversation flowed easily, punctuated by Harper's quick wit and Cassidy's thoughtful contributions. Laughter came often, and the tension of the upcoming competition seemed forgotten, if only for the moment.

"Here's to making music and memories," Harper raised her glass of water, and we all echoed the sentiment.

After dinner, we lazily wandered outside. The patio, bathed in the soft glow of hanging fairy lights, felt homey as we settled into our seats. I found myself next to Cassidy again, her quiet demeanor a stark contrast to Harper, who was regaling us with tales that had us all in stitches.

"Did you really ride a bull named Cupcake?" Cassidy asked, her voice basically a murmur against the laughter.

"Sweetheart, in Texas, if it moves, we ride it," Harper said with a wink. "And yes, Cupcake was a darling until he decided to toss me into next week."

Across the patio, I caught Austin's eye; he looked quickly away, but not before a smile played at the corners of his mouth. It was unnerving and exhilarating, like catching the first few notes of a favorite song on the radio.

The evening air was warm but not as humid as it could have been thanks to the huge fans above us. I did my best to coax Cassidy into sharing more about herself, asking about her hometown and her favorite songs. She was hesitant at first, but as the night wore on, she began to open up, sharing anecdotes with a gentle smile.

"Music's always been my refuge," Cassidy admitted, her eyes reflecting the twinkling lights above us. "It's where I can say what I'm really feeling without actually saying it."

"Isn't that the truth," I mused, thinking of the countless times I'd made it my own escape.

As the sky darkened to a deep navy, Austin excused himself and slipped inside the house. Moments later, he reemerged, guitar in hand, the instrument clearly an extension of him as natural as breathing.

"I think it's time for some music," he announced, and though the words were meant for everyone, I felt the invitation was somehow just for me.

He strummed the opening chords to "Dixieland Delight" by Alabama, and with barely a glance in my direction, I knew what he wanted. Our voices melded together, harmonizing effortlessly as the rest of the world faded away. It was as if we'd been singing together for years, not minutes.

Song after song poured out of us, the group joining in when they could, until the stars were fully out and the night whispered for quiet. One by one, the others bid goodnight, leaving only the echo of music and the promise of new adventures ahead.

The night felt quieter as I made my way back toward the house, the soft hum of crickets serenading the end of a perfect Tennessee evening. As I passed under the string lights that draped like twinkling stars from the patio, I caught sight of Austin's silhouette framed by the doorway. The light inside cast a golden glow on his dark hair, giving it a softness that beckoned fingers to touch.

"Hey, Austin, wait up!" My voice floated through the quiet as I called out, slowing my steps to match the unhurried pace of the night. I watched him pause and turn, a casual smile gracing his features as if he'd been hoping I might say something.

"Oh, hey," he replied, his tone grounding me in the moment. The color of his eyes seemed to pull at me, the dark brown rings around his amber colored irises like the grooves on a vinyl record, playing a song just for me.

"Wouldn't miss a chance to thank you for the music," I said. There was an easiness between us I hadn't expected but quite enjoyed.

"Thanks," he chuckled, leaning against the doorframe with an effortlessness that made my heart skip a beat. "You're not so bad yourself. Where'd you learn to harmonize like that?"

"Shower. Car. Anywhere I can belt out a tune without someone telling me to pipe down." Our laughter mingled in the air, almost in harmony as though we were still mid-song.

"Good places, all solid acoustics," he nodded, his eyes lighting up with amusement.

"We might have to make this a regular thing if we don't wear out our welcome first." His voice held a playful note, but there was a challenge there too, one I couldn't resist.

"Or get voted off," I added, flashing him a playful wink. The competition loomed over us, but in that moment, it felt distant, like a storm cloud on the horizon of a clear blue sky.

"Then let's make sure we leave 'em with something memorable," he said, his gaze holding mine—a promise of more than just songs to be shared.

"Deal." I extended my hand. He shook it, his grip firm and warm, but the electricity shooting up my arm and into my chest was far from gentle.

"Goodnight, Austin Blake."

"Goodnight, Willow Gracin."

And with those words, I turned, leaving behind the man with the guitar and the smile that could outshine any star.

Chapter 8

Austin

It was already scorching hot by the time we finished breakfast and made our way to the pool. The girls—Cassidy, Harper, and Willow—stretched out on loungers, soaking up the rays. Levi, Nash, and I, however, had different plans.

"Cannonball contest?" Levi asked, a mischievous glint in his eye.

"You know it," I replied, setting my towel on a nearby chair.

"Count me in," Nash added, a competitive smirk on his face.

The girls glanced over as we began our competition, giggling at our antics. Levi went first, leaping into the air and tucking his knees to his chest before hitting the water with a massive splash.

I stepped onto the diving ledge, rolling my shoulders, stealing a quick glance toward the lounge chairs. Willow sat up slightly, her sunglasses slipping down her nose as she watched, amused. A slow smile tugged at her lips.

Don't mess this up, Blake.

I launched into the air, trying to nail a forward flip before hitting the water. Instead, I landed slightly off-balance, sending a wave straight toward Willow and Harper.

"Austin Blake!" Willow shrieked, laughing as she wiped water from her face.

"Sorry!" I shot back, pushing my wet hair out of my eyes, flashing her a grin. "But you gotta admit, that was pretty epic."

She shook her head, still grinning. "A for effort. C for execution."

Levi clapped a hand on my shoulder. "She's got you there, buddy."

We moved on to dive contests, each of us trying to execute more daring and ridiculous stunts. Levi performed a perfect swan dive, while I attempted a flip that ended in a not-so-graceful belly flop. Nash, ever the showman, executed a handstand dive that left everyone cheering for him.

Next came the muscle-flexing segment of our impromptu show. We struck exaggerated poses, pretending to be bodybuilders. I couldn't help but notice Willow's eyes lingering on me, and I tried to keep my focus on the fun, even though my heart was racing.

"Give it up, Austin," Levi teased, nudging me with a knowing grin. "Everyone can see who you're trying to impress."

"Shut up," I muttered, but my cheeks betrayed me.

"Oh, I think we all know exactly what he's doing," Harper said, adjusting her sunglasses. "And if I didn't know better, I'd say we were at a county fair watching prize bulls strut around."

Cassidy smirked, but her voice was quieter. "Hey, at least it's entertaining."

Willow laughed, reaching for her drink. "You guys are ridiculous." But the way her eyes flickered toward me—like she wasn't quite noticing, but she was—had my stomach flipping.

Cassidy checked her phone, her brow furrowing. "Guys, it's almost noon. We should hit the showers and grab lunch. Our morning is basically gone."

Reluctantly, we pulled ourselves out of the pool and headed inside.

Nash—usually so relaxed—stood tense beside Cassidy, his hands shoved into pockets of his swim trunks. Cassidy glanced up at him, something unreadable in her expression. Her mouth opened like she was going to say something—

But she didn't.

Instead, she turned and walked off, leaving Nash standing there, jaw tight.

"Hey," I muttered, nudging him. "Everything good?"

"Yeah," he said too quickly. "Fine."

It didn't feel fine.

After quick showers and a change of clothes, we gathered in the kitchen for sandwiches and chips. The atmosphere was lighter and filled with chatter about our upcoming day.

After lunch, we boarded a bus to the studio, buzzing with anticipation. We were soon briefed on our tasks: different groups would be shooting various commercials. My group included Cassidy, Nash, and Willow.

Once on set, the director explained we'd be showcasing Nashville's Botanical Garden. Willow and I were to act as a couple in a romantic engagement scene. I gave her a high five, grinning at the challenge.

"So, how do we make this believable?" I asked as we walked toward the filming location.

Willow shrugged, her eyes sparkling with excitement. "Just be natural. And don't worry about physical boundaries with me. I'm comfortable."

Her confidence was contagious. I felt a surge of determination as we reached a scenic spot in the garden. The area was a riot of color and fragrance, the air heavy with the scent of blooming jasmine. Willow and I walked hand in hand along a winding path, her fingers warm intertwined with mine.

As we reached the arched bridge overlooking the koi pond, the director gave the signal. I dropped to one knee, my heart pounding even though this wasn't real.

"Willow Gracin," I began, pulling the ring from my pocket. Or at least, I tried to. The box was stuck. My face burned as I struggled, and Willow's barely-contained laughter only made it worse.

The ring box shot out of my hand like a rogue champagne cork, flying straight into the koi pond.

Silence.

I froze, horrified, until Willow doubled over, laughing so hard she could barely stand. Her joy was infectious, and I couldn't help but join her as the director's exasperated "Cut!" faded into the background.

"We both know how much I love making a splash" I deadpanned as the crew scrambled to fish the ring out of the pond and reset the scene.

Despite the chaos, we managed to get several good takes. Each time I got the ring out without a hitch, and each time, Willow's smile seemed brighter.

After the final take, I stood and pulled Willow into a hug, spinning her around. She giggled, her breath warm against my neck. It felt so natural that I almost wished this wasn't just an act, that there was a real reason for this embrace.

The crew, including Nash and Cassidy, cheered and clapped, the sound echoing through the garden. As we disentangled, Willow's eyes met mine, and I couldn't help but hope that maybe, just maybe, she felt the same spark I did.

The ride back to the house was a mix of excitement and exhaustion. We piled into the SUV, with Nash and me taking the third row while Willow and Cassidy occupied the seats in front of us. The air conditioning blasted full force, a welcome relief from the day's heat.

As we settled in, Willow turned in her seat to face me, her eyes sparkling. "That was wild, wasn't it?" she said, her voice bubbling with laughter.

"Yeah," I replied, grinning. "Definitely not how I envisioned my first proposal."

Cassidy chuckled, shaking her head. "That was hilarious. The director didn't know whether to laugh or cry."

Willow's laughter was infectious, and soon we were all recounting the day's events, each memory funnier than the last.

I noticed Nash smiling but staying quiet, so I nudged him playfully. "Hey, Nash, what did you think of our performance? Got any tips for a future Oscar winner?"

He smiled and started to respond, but Cassidy's expression subtly shifted, her smile fading just a bit. Nash seemed to catch it and shrugged. "You guys were great," he said simply, leaning back into his seat.

Feeling a bit of tension, I tried to keep the conversation going. "Cassidy, what about you? Any advice?"

She laughed, though it felt a bit forced. "Looser pants?"

Willow threw her head back and laughed loudly, the tension breaking slightly.

"Lesson learned," I said, shaking my head with a grin. "So, how are we feeling about tomorrow night's results?"

Willow and I talked through the previous day's performances, but it felt wrong trying to imagine anyone actually leaving after only being here a week and performing once. It barely felt like enough time to get our feet wet much less show the judges everything we've got.

As we pulled up to the house, I felt a mix of relief and anticipation for the rest of the day. Stepping out of the SUV, I stretched, feeling the day's events settling into a comfortable memory. Willow and Cassidy headed inside, still chatting, while Nash and I followed at a slower pace.

"Hey, man," I said quietly to Nash as we walked. "What's going on?"

He shook his head and attempted a smile. "Just tired. It's been a long day."

I clapped him on the back. "Well get some rest because it all starts over again tomorrow."

Nash nodded, and we both headed inside.

After a quick stop in the kitchen for some water, I headed for the living room where I'd last seen Willow talking to Cassidy, who was now walking toward the dining room.

"Hey," I said, handing her one of the bottles of water I'd grabbed. "Everything okay with Cassidy?"

Willow shrugged, a puzzled expression crossing her face. "It was weird. We were fine, just talking, and then Nash walked by and she got all quiet and left."

I frowned. "That's odd. I thought we were all getting along great."

"Yeah, I thought so too," Willow said with a sigh. "But then, out of nowhere, she just wasn't feeling it."

"Maybe she's just tired," I suggested, trying to sound hopeful. "It's been a long day for all of us."

"Yeah, maybe," Willow said, though she didn't seem entirely convinced.

The elimination show had been brutal. Wyatt Turner was the one everyone expected to sail through. After just one performance, the judges had praised him as the frontrunner, the sure thing. But when the results were read aloud, his name was the one on the list marked for elimination.

A stunned silence fell. Wyatt's face tightened, disbelief flickering in his eyes. Around the room, murmurs bubbled up—shock, confusion, disappointment. No one wanted to say it aloud, but the mood had shifted. The hopeful buzz from earlier was replaced by a heavy weight pressing down on everyone's shoulders.

I looked over at Willow, her smile gone quiet, eyes fixed somewhere distant.

Wanting to cut through the heaviness, when I knew the cameras were off, I leaned in with a grin, "So, how about another singalong after dinner? Up for it?"

Willow blinked, and then her smile returned, softer but real. "Absolutely. Meet me at the piano after we eat?"

"Deal," I said, trying to believe it myself. "Can't wait."

Dinner started off with strained conversations and forced laughter. But as everyone settled in, the tension began to ease, replaced slowly by the warmth of shared stories and quiet relief.

By the time plates were cleared, Willow was already at the piano, her fingers brushing the keys lightly.

I joined her, taking a seat beside her on the bench. "Ready?" I asked.

"Always," she said with a smile, launching into the opening chords of a familiar tune.

Willow's fingers danced over the piano keys, coaxing out a melody that filled the room. The way she closed her eyes when she hit a high note, the slight curve of her lips as she caught my gaze—it was like we were speaking a language only the two of us understood. Her voice joined mine, weaving effortlessly through the notes, and for a moment, it felt like the rest of the world had disappeared.

I should've been thinking about the competition, about how this was just a jam session, nothing more.

But when she turned to me, her eyes shining in the dim light, I felt it. A connection like nothing I'd ever felt before.

For a little while, it was just us and the music, and even when others walked in and joined us, nothing else really mattered.

Chapter 9

Willow

The moment my fingers brushed the keys, a slow exhale left my lips. The grand piano beneath my hands was similar to the one I had growing up in my parents' house where I spent hours chasing melodies that felt like they'd been waiting for me to find them.

My hands moved instinctively, shaping a tune from nowhere, something raw and searching. The notes curled into the space around me echoing softly in the oversized room.

Despite its size, it managed to feel homey. Soft lighting and cozy seating arrangements invited relaxation. It was a room that balanced luxury with comfort.

The day's events had been a roller coaster—both fun and stressful But now, with the familiar keys beneath my fingers, I was feeling far more settled. A tune floated through my mind, and I began playing, letting my fingers work out the next notes and the next. I wasn't sure where it was going or what it went with, but I stopped before getting too far into it and played it again to solidify it in my head.

Just as I repeated the melody, a subtle shift in the air made me pause. A presence—solid, warm—standing nearby. Watching.

"What's that you're playing?"

I startled slightly, my fingers slipping off the keys as Austin's voice broke through the stillness. He stood in the doorway, backlit by the soft hallway light, his expression thoughtful.

I looked up, smiling. "I'm not sure yet. Just something that came to me."

He walked over and took a seat next to me on the bench, close enough that our shoulders brushed. He hummed the melody I had just played, his voice resonating softly.

"It feels lonely," Austin murmured, his voice carrying something softer, almost hesitant.

My fingers stilled on the keys. "What makes you say that?"

He exhaled through his nose, dragging his gaze over the piano. "It sounds like something looking for a home," he said finally. "Like it doesn't know where it belongs yet."

The words sat between us, heavy in their truth.

I hadn't realized it until he said it, but he was right.

"I like it," he said.

"Thanks," I said, feeling a blush creep up my cheeks. "What do you want to sing?"

He thought for a moment, then his eyes lit up. "*Whiskey Lullaby* by Brad Paisley and Alison Krauss?"

"Perfect choice," I said, my fingers already finding the opening chords.

The first words left Austin's lips, soft and careful. By the time we reached the chorus, I felt like we'd been singing together our whole lives. His tone—warm, steady—wrapped around mine, filling in spaces I hadn't realized were empty.

We fell into the song effortlessly, our voices blending together in harmony. The lyrics told a haunting story, and as we sang, it felt like we were the only two people in the world. I glanced at Austin, catching his eye, and for a moment, everything else faded away.

His voice was rich and unhurried, like he'd lived the lyrics and knew how to give each word its weight. Singing beside him made me feel both invincible and completely vulnerable. I wasn't sure if that was terrifying or exhilarating—or maybe both.

I was so wrapped up in the music and the moment that I didn't notice a couple of the other contestants entering the room.

As the last note settled into the hush, neither of us moved. The room—everything around us—felt smaller, quieter.

Austin's gaze flicked to mine, something unreadable in his expression. For a second, I thought he might say something.

Before he could, applause shattered the moment.

I blinked, the spell breaking. Turning, I saw Harper and Cassidy grinning, others clapping from the doorway. Heat rose to my cheeks, though whether from embarrassment or something else, I wasn't sure.

"That was incredible," one of them said. "You guys sounded amazing together."

"Thanks," I replied, glancing at Austin. He smiled back, and I felt a warm flutter in my chest.

"You takin' requests?" Harper asked, as she shimmied down into one of the cushy chairs.

I looked at Austin who shrugged, smiling.

"If I know it, I'll play it," I told her.

We spent the next hour hopping from one song to the next. Some were new, some were old, some weren't even country until we got our voices on them. Whoever requested the song took the lead and the rest of us joined in when we felt the timing was right.

If this was all I'd been here for, I would have been content to spend the next eleven weeks just like this. Instead, as the last chords of *The Climb* lingered, the mood in the room shifted. Between the exhaustion seeping in from the last forty-eight hours and knowing what lay ahead the next day, the consensus seemed to be it was time to call it a day.

We offered quiet goodnights as the rest of our competitors headed to their rooms.

Austin and I were the last to leave. He lingered by the piano, his eyes catching mine in the dim light. "Thanks for hanging out tonight," he said softly.

"Of course," I replied, feeling a warmth spread through me. "I had a great time."

He hesitated for a moment, then smiled. "Maybe we could do it again sometime?"

"I'd like that," I said, unable to keep the smile from my face. Something unspoken pulsed between us, a connection that felt both new and familiar.

"Goodnight, Willow Gracin," he said, his voice gentle.

"Goodnight, Austin Blake," I replied, watching him walk away, feeling a mix of anticipation and contentment.

Once he was gone, I exhaled slowly, pressing my fingers to my lips as if to hold in the emotion still buzzing inside me.

I turned back to the piano, my hands finding the keys instinctively. The melody from earlier came without thought, but now—now it sounded different.

Warmer.

Fuller.

Like maybe it wasn't so lonely anymore.

Satisfied, I finally called it a night. I headed to my room, where my roommate, Stella, was already climbing into bed. Stella hung out more with Savannah and Lanie, but we were friendly enough.

"Goodnight, Willow," Stella said, her voice muffled by her pillow.

"Night, Stella," I replied, pulling my notebook out of the nightstand. I jotted down notes about my newly forming song, capturing the melody and the emotions it evoked.

As I put the notebook away and settled into bed, I felt a deep sense of satisfaction. The music, the connection with Austin, and the promise of more to come all swirled in my mind as I drifted into a deep, peaceful sleep.

Chapter 10

Willow

The past couple of weeks flew by packed with rehearsals, performances, and the emotional weight of saying goodbye to Wyatt then Savannah. Their departures had left a noticeable void in the house.

Savannah hadn't been part of our core group, but seeing her go was still tough—another reminder that this competition wouldn't just challenge our talent but our hearts. Wyatt, though, was a shock. He'd been rumored to be the one to beat, and he was gone first. It was hard not to let that rattle me.

There could only be one winner, and while we all knew that going in, it didn't make the eliminations any easier. Every goodbye chipped away at the camaraderie we'd built, leaving behind cracks we all tried to ignore.

Today, though, was a rare free day, a chance to breathe and reconnect. Some contestants opted to explore Nashville, but I, along with Austin, Levi, Nash, Cassidy, and Harper, stayed back. We spent the morning by the pool, soaking up the sun until distant rumbles of thunder drove us inside.

The kitchen smelled like home—vanilla, cinnamon, and the rich, buttery warmth of cookies baking in the oven. Laughter echoed off the cabinets as Harper and Cassidy worked in tandem, Cassidy rolling out dough while Harper shaped it into perfect circles.

"If these turn out terrible, we're blaming Cassidy," Harper teased, flicking flour in Cassidy's direction.

Cassidy gasped, swiping flour back at Harper, who shrieked and ducked behind the kitchen's island.

Austin, Nash, and Levi leaned against the island, watching like spectators at a wrestling match. "This might be better than the competition," Levi joked, popping a stray piece of cookie dough into his mouth.

"Y'all better be grateful," Harper said, pointing a flour-coated finger at him. "This is part of a family tradition. Every year at Christmas, we make these for the whole neighborhood."

Cassidy smiled as she sprinkled flour on the counter. "I love that."

"Oh, sure, it's sweet now, but one year my brother swapped the vanilla for hot sauce," Harper said with a groan, rolling her eyes. "We didn't know until after we'd baked and handed them out. Got some interesting feedback that year."

We all laughed, the image of spicy Christmas cookies too funny to resist.

As the cookies baked, the conversation drifted to holiday traditions. Even though Christmas was still months away, Cassidy and Harper started singing *I'll Be Home for Christmas*, their voices warm and clear. It didn't take long for Austin and me to join in.

The harmonies slipped into place like puzzle pieces. Austin's voice—deep and steady seemed to seek out and wind around mine. He didn't just sing the notes; he felt them, pulling meaning out of every lyric.

I glanced at him mid-verse, and for a second, he was already smiling at me as the melody rose and fell in perfect sync.

After the last note was out, Harper interjected with a teasing grin, "Okay, hold up a minute. You two sound like you've been singing together forever."

A flicker of something unreadable crossed Austin's face, but he covered it with an easy chuckle. "Guess we just found our backup plan."

My heart did something stupid, something fluttery. "I'll keep that in mind," I said lightly, even as my pulse hammered.

The cookies came out of the oven golden and perfect, filling the kitchen with a sugary haze. We all dug in, the sweetness lifting the mood. For a while, it felt like we were just a group of friends hanging out, not rivals vying for the same dream.

By evening, the house had quieted. I found myself alone in the music room, strumming my guitar and humming the melody that had been stuck in my head for weeks. The tune felt clearer now, but the lyrics were stubborn, slipping through my fingers like water.

The room, with its shelves of old books and the warm glow of a single lamp, felt like a refuge. I scribbled words in my notebook, crossing them out almost as soon as they hit the page.

"Hey, I didn't expect to find you here," Austin's voice broke through the quiet.

I looked up, startled but not unhappy to see him. "Hey. Just working on some lyrics."

He held his guitar, hesitating in the doorway. "I can go if you want to be alone."

I shook my head, smiling. "No, stay. I could use the company."

He walked over and sat beside me, his presence easy and familiar. "What are you working on?"

"Do you remember that tune I was messing with a couple of days ago? I think I've got it nailed down, but the words aren't quite there yet."

"Can I take a look?" he asked, nodding toward my notebook.

I hesitated, fingers tightening around the edges of my notebook. Sharing lyrics was different from singing. Singing was performance;

this was personal. These words weren't polished yet—just raw thoughts, scrawled in half-legible ink.

"You don't have to," Austin said gently, catching my hesitation. His voice was steady, patient. "But if you want to, I'd love to see."

I swallowed hard, then handed him the notebook.

"Okay," I said softly, handing him the notebook.

He scanned the pages, his brow furrowing in concentration. After a moment, he glanced at me. "Mind if I try something?"

I nodded, curious and a little nervous. He flipped the pencil in his hand and began scribbling in the margins, his lips moving silently as he worked.

When he handed the notebook back, I read the new lines slowly. My eyes widened. His words fit perfectly, weaving into the melody like they'd always belonged there.

"These are perfect," I said, my voice barely above a whisper.

Austin smiled, his eyes warm. "I'm glad you think so."

I set the notebook down and started playing the tune again, this time singing the new lyrics. The song felt whole, like a puzzle finally completed.

As I played, I couldn't help but glance at Austin. There was something about the way he watched me, like he wasn't just hearing the music—he was feeling it.

When the song ended, I set my guitar down and turned to him. "Thank you. I don't think I could've done this without you."

"Anytime," he said, his voice soft but steady.

We sat in companionable silence for a while, the music lingering in the air around us. The quiet felt comforting, like the pause after a good song, when the last note is still hanging in the air. But as exhaustion crept in, Austin yawned and scrubbed a hand down his face.

"Alright, I think that's my cue to call it a night," he said, stretching.

I smiled, stifling a yawn of my own. "Yeah, you're probably right."

He stood, hesitating for a moment as his gaze lingered on me.

"You know, these people are supposed to be our competition, but sometimes it just feels like we've all known each other forever."

His words hit home, the truth of them settling somewhere deep in my chest. "I know what you mean. It's hard not to get attached."

"Yeah," he said quietly, almost to himself. Then his eyes met mine, steady and warm. "But for what it's worth, I don't think getting attached to you is a bad thing."

The words hung between us, heavier than they should have been.

Austin shifted, rubbing the back of his neck like he hadn't meant to say them out loud. But he didn't take them back.

My fingers curled against my notebook, holding onto something solid. Something real.

"Thank you," I murmured, my own voice quieter now. "I don't mind getting attached to you, either."

His lips quirked into the smallest smile. Not cocky, not teasing. Just genuine.

"Goodnight, Willow Gracin," he said, and it sounded different this time. Like he was meditating on my name.

"Goodnight, Austin Blake," I replied, and watched as he left, the warmth of his presence staying with me.

For a moment, I remained where I was, staring at the closed door. His words replayed in my mind, the weight of them mingling with my own thoughts. These people were supposed to be my rivals, but the lines between competition and connection blurred more every day.

Letting out a breath, I turned back to the piano and played the melody once more, adding a few soft notes to the end as if to answer the unspoken questions Austin's words had left behind.

I closed my notebook and headed to bed, the sound of the music still echoing in my heart. Getting attached wasn't just a risk—it was inevitable. And maybe that wasn't such a bad thing.

Chapter 11

Austin

I hadn't stopped thinking about her since that night. When she'd asked if I wanted to help her work through more lyrics, I didn't even hesitate. Now, here we were—four days later, heads bent over the same notebook, shoulders brushing, lost in our own world.

I should have been thinking about the competition, about my performance today, about proving myself. But instead, my focus kept drifting back to her—the way her lips pursed when she was deep in thought, the quiet hum she made when testing a lyric under her breath, the warmth of her knee pressed against mine.

Being around Willow felt natural, familiar. Like I'd known her forever. Like I'd been waiting for her without even realizing it.

When she was around, I couldn't take my eyes off her. When her hair fell in waves across her shoulder as she leaned over the notebook in her lap, scribbling lyrics with such focus that her tongue poked out the corner of her mouth, it was adorable.

When she glanced up and met my gaze, those bright green eyes piercing right through me, I could hardly remember words existed.

Every time she was around, my heart did this thing—like it forgets how to beat for a split second before racing to catch up.

"What do you think about this line?" She asked, tapping her pen against the page.

My brain stalled. Not because of the lyrics—because of her. The way she looked at me made me feel like my opinion actually mattered, and I was too busy memorizing the way her lips moved to actually process words.

"Uh—" I blinked. "Read it again?"

She arched an amused brow but obliged, her voice lilting with a teasing edge.

> Your pickup truck broke down just outside of town,
> So we caught fireflies and watched the sun go
> > down.

I forced myself to focus, nodding like I had totally heard it the first time. Trying to hold back a grin, I said, "Don't you think it's a little cliché? A broken down truck in a country song?"

Willow gasped in mock offense, clutching her chest. "Cliché? More like classic."

"It has a broken down truck, fireflies, and a sunset,' Gracin."

She narrowed her eyes before smirking. "There's a reason the classics work. Is it cheesy? Maybe a little. But it works."

We stared at each other for several seconds before I played off giving in. Because she was right. It did work.

"Fine. If you insist, then I think the next line could be..." I paused for dramatic effect. "And your sweet smile made me forget that we were stuck."

Willow laughed, shaking her head. "Now that is cheesy."

The bus hit a pothole, jolting us, and I noticed we were nearing the studio. Outside, the Nashville skyline blurred by, but I couldn't bring myself to care. Right now, the only thing I cared about was sitting beside me, her head bent over that notebook.

Levi smacked me on the back of the head playfully. "Come on, slow pokes, get a move on," he teased, grinning widely.

I laughed, not realizing the bus had pulled to a stop. I closed the notebook and handed it to Willow. "Alright, alright. We're coming."

Willow tucked the book into her bag. "Shall we?"

I stood and offered her my hand. She took it, her warm fingers pressed against my palm. I let go only once she was on her feet.

We were the last ones off the bus, still caught up in our little bubble. As we stepped onto the pavement, I turned to Willow, feeling a surge of emotion. "No matter what happens, you've already been the best part of this entire experience, hands down."

Her eyes softened, and she reached out to squeeze my hand. "You too, Austin."

We were quickly herded into the studio, pulled in different directions for interviews, wardrobe, and warm-ups. The chaos of the studio was familiar by now, but today it felt different. More charged somehow, knowing that Willow was just a room away. I wondered if she was thinking about the same things I was.

As I was in makeup and wardrobe, I couldn't help but think about the song we had been working on. It felt like the perfect combination of both our styles, a true collaboration that could only have come from our unique connection. I wondered how it would feel to perform it together on stage, to share that piece of us with the world. For now, however, I had to get my head in the game. This was a solo performance day, and if I wanted to stick around, I had to bring my best.

The stage lights blazed overhead, hot against my skin. The crowd was a sea of shadows beyond the bright glare, but I could feel them— their anticipation, their energy. My heart hammered against my ribs, but the moment my fingers hit the first chord, everything else disappeared.

I sang like I had something to prove.

Every note carried the weight of late-night rehearsals; every lyric held the hunger of someone who refused to be forgotten. The audience clapped along, their energy surging toward the stage, and I rode it like a wave, giving them everything I had.

The last note rang out, and for a split second, I stood there, chest heaving, drinking in the sound of the cheers. *This.* This was why I was here.

Then the judges spoke.

Nicole smiled, giving me a flicker of hope. "Austin, I love your energy and your ability to claim the stage. You really know how to work a crowd."

Charles ran a hand through his hair, his expression unreadable. "Austin, I think you have some pretty stiff competition around you. You're good, but you'll need to step it up to stand out."

The adrenaline in my veins cooled.

Then Randy delivered the final blow. "Austin, I like you a lot. But do I think you have what it takes to go all the way? I don't know. I hope you do."

My heart sank a little, but I tried to maintain my composure.

I forced a smile, but inside, I felt deflated. The audience's cheers were a small comfort, but the judges' words stung. I walked off the stage, the high of my performance quickly replaced by a mix of embarrassment and disappointment.

She was already waiting for me when I stepped backstage, her green eyes scanning my face, seeing straight through the forced smile.

"That was kind of rough, huh?" she murmured.

I tried to play it off. "It was okay. The audience seemed to like it."

But Willow wasn't buying it. She stepped closer, close enough that I could feel the warmth of her body, close enough that the noise of the studio faded into the background.

"Austin," she said softly, reaching up to touch my arm, grounding me. "Forget what the judges said. You were incredible."

My throat tightened. I should've been able to brush this off, but the sincerity in her eyes got to me in a way I wasn't ready for.

And when she pulled me into a hug—not just a quick squeeze, but a full, lingering embrace that said, 'I see you. I believe in you.'—I felt something inside me settle.

We stood there for a moment as I let her calm seep into me before

I took a deep breath and straightened up. "Alright, back to work," I nodded in the direction of the green room.

Willow grinned, her eyes sparkling with determination. "Back to work."

Chapter 12

Willow

The day after the results show, the house felt wrong.

It wasn't just quiet—it was the kind of silence that pressed down, thick and suffocating, filling every corner of the house like a heavy fog. The laughter that used to drift from the kitchen? Gone. The sound of Austin strumming his guitar in the common room? Replaced by an empty hush that made my skin crawl.

He was everywhere and nowhere at the same time.

Harper and Levi wore their shock openly, their laughter subdued, their movements slower as though weighed down by disbelief. For me, though, it wasn't just shock. It was like a piece of my heart had been ripped away and I hadn't been given a say in the matter.

I tried to keep busy.

I cleaned. Reorganized the desk. Opened drawers only to close them again. Flipped through a book without reading a single word. Sat on my bed, then stood back up because I couldn't sit still.

Every time I thought I'd finally distracted myself, something would remind me of him. A guitar pick left on the nightstand. The faint scent of his cologne still lingering in the hallway. A memory flashing through my mind so vividly I'd swear he was still here.

And then I saw the notebook.

The sight of it stilled me. Slowly, I picked it up and ran my fingers over its worn cover, a lump forming in my throat.

As I flipped through the pages, our scribbles and half-written lyrics stared back at me, each one carrying his voice, his presence. My chest tightened with every word and chord we'd jotted down together. When I turned to the back cover, my breath caught.

There, in Austin's familiar scrawl, was a note I hadn't seen before:

Willow,

I don't know how long either of us will be here. I just know that every second I've spent with you has been the best second of my life.

Since the reality is one of us would leave before the other, I wanted to leave this behind. Not as a goodbye, but as a reminder. Just because I'm not in that house anymore doesn't mean I'm gone.

You'll always have me.

And now you have my number. I hope you'll use it often ;-)

Love, Austin.

Underneath his name, he had written his phone number.

My hands trembled as I traced the hurried strokes and careful curves of his handwriting. It was so him—passionate, thoughtful, and a little bit impulsive. Tears blurred the words as I reread the note, each time letting it hit me harder.

The tears came in earnest then, hot and heavy. I clutched the notebook to my chest, holding onto it like a lifeline. Austin wasn't here, but this note, this little piece of him, reminded me that our connection hadn't been severed just because we were in different places.

I sank down onto the edge of my bed, the notebook still in my lap, and let the emotions crash over me. I'd only known him for a few weeks. Maybe it was too soon to feel this deeply. Maybe I was rushing, reading too much into every word, every glance. But, for me, the bond we'd built already felt bigger than time, more than just music.

It wasn't just about the songs. It was about the way he'd pulled things out of me I didn't know was there—the confidence, the laughter, the hope. And despite the doubt swirling in my mind, I couldn't deny how much I'd needed that.

I pulled myself together and grabbed my phone. After adding his number to my contacts, my fingers hovered over the screen as I tried to decide what to say. I didn't want to come across as too emotional, even though I felt like my heart was wide open and raw.

Finally, I settled on something more neutral.

> Me: Hey Austin, just found your note.
> Thank you.

I hit send and stared at the screen, my heart pounding. The response came quicker than I expected.

> Austin: I'm glad you found it. How are you
> holding up?

His message caught me off guard—he was the one who'd just been eliminated, yet he was the one checking on me. It made me feel both warm all over and a little selfish. I hesitated, debating how honest to be. In the end, I went with the truth.

> Me: It's too quiet without you here. The
> house feels different.

> Austin: It's strange being back home, too.
> Almost like I never left. But not the same.

A moment later, another message came through—a photo this time. Austin stood in a sunlit field, his grin as warm as the Tennessee summer. Beside him was a man who could only be his brother, Connor, holding a tool that looked like it belonged in a history museum. The contrast between Austin's easy smile and Connor's stoic expression made me laugh through my tears.

> Me: You look like you're in your element.

> Austin: It's nice to be back with family, but it's different. Nashville really got under my skin, you know?

> Me: I get it. This place isn't the same without you.

There was a pause, then his next message made my breath catch.

> Austin: I miss you more than I thought I would.

Swallowing hard, I felt my chest tighten.

> Me: I miss you too.

The typing bubble appeared, then disappeared, and for a moment I thought he might not respond. But then it came.

> Austin: Can I call you later?

> Me: I'd like that.

I set my phone down, the ache in my chest easing slightly. Knowing he missed me too, that he still wanted to stay connected, made his absence a little more bearable.

Opening the notebook again I traced the lyrics we'd written together, remembering the way his voice had harmonized with mine, how he'd grinned at me when we nailed a tricky line. Music had always been my refuge, but now it was more than that. It was a bridge between us, a way to hold onto him even when miles separated us.

Flipping to a blank page, I picked up a pen and started writing again. Maybe the next song would be for us.

Chapter 13

Willow

The house was quieter now, and not just because Austin was gone. Nash had come down with the flu, and his once-lively presence had dimmed.

Cassidy, usually steady, seemed off balance too. I'd catch her staring out the window or fidgeting with her phone, her usual sparkle dulled.

One night after dinner, I found her in the music room, pecking at keys on the piano absentmindedly. Her fingers pressed a few hesitant notes, but there was no real melody. I slid onto the bench beside her, letting the silence settle until she was ready to talk.

"It's weird, you know?" she said, voice so quiet it almost got lost in the stillness of the room.

I waited, sensing there was more.

She hesitated, then let out a soft, humorless laugh. "I mean, I don't even know why I feel this way. Nash and I—he's become my friend. Easy to talk to. But now, every time I see him, it feels different."

I tilted my head. "Different how?"

She groaned, rubbing her hands over her face. "Like there's more to it, but I don't know what to do with that."

"Do you think you like him as more than friends?" I asked, keeping my tone light, not wanting to push her.

She frowned, biting her lip. "Maybe? I mean, yeah, probably. But it's not like I planned for this to happen. It snuck up on me. And now he's probably leaving, and I feel stupid for even thinking about it."

Her words hit me hard. I hadn't thought much about Nash before, but I knew exactly how it felt to have someone unexpectedly become important, only to face the reality of losing them too soon.

I placed my hand on hers, grounding her. "Cassidy, it's not stupid. You can't help how you feel. And you don't have to figure it all out right now."

Her lips curved into a small, grateful smile. "Thanks, Willow. I guess I just don't know what to do with all of this. It's like I'm in this weird limbo where nothing makes sense."

I smiled softly, but inside I felt the weight of my own internal limbo, the one Austin's absence had carved out in me. I realized how much his being gone had shifted everything. But just like Cassidy, I wasn't ready to admit how much that change shook me.

"Well, if there's one thing I've learned since being here, it's that nothing about this place makes sense," I said with a soft laugh. "But you're not alone. I'm here, and so is Harper."

Her smile grew a little brighter. "I know. And I'm glad for that."

We ended up staying up late that night, sharing stories and raiding the pantry a few times. Cassidy's laugh returned, and for the first time in days, it felt like she was truly present again. It was one of those rare moments where the competition felt less like a battlefield and more like a family.

The next week, Stella Mae was eliminated, and it felt surreal. She hadn't been one of my closer friends in the house, but her energy had been contagious, and the mansion felt different without her. Lanie, who had been glued to Stella Mae and Savannah, now seemed detached. She wasn't sulking exactly, but the shift was obvious.

Still, when Lanie got on stage, it was like a switch flipped. Her performance was flawless—polished, powerful, and magnetic. Watching her made me anxious. How could I compete with that?

Any time we were at the house, I found myself spiraling into self-doubt. My performances were good, but were they good enough? I spent late nights in the music room trying to answer that question with my guitar, pouring those feelings into a song I hoped would hold up under the weight of this competition.

One of those nights, as I sat alone strumming, my phone buzzed on the table next to me. I glanced at the screen and froze.

Austin: Tell me you're ready for tomorrow?

The knot of doubt in my chest loosened just a little at the sight of his name. I picked up my phone, my fingers hovering over the keyboard as I tried to find the right words.

Me: I don't know about that. I feel like I'm falling pretty short right now.

I hit send and immediately regretted being so honest. But before I could overthink it, his response came through.

Austin: Falling short? No way. You're incredible.

My chest tightened, but this time it wasn't from doubt. It was something warmer.

Me: You think so?

Austin: I know so. And I'm not just saying that because I'm your biggest fan.

I smiled, a small laugh escaping me.

Me: You're clearly biased.

Austin: 100%. But I'm also right.

I stared at his message, a warmth spreading through me that I hadn't felt in days.

Me: Thanks. I needed that.

Austin: Anytime. You've got this.

I set my phone down, the conversation replaying in my mind as I picked up my guitar again. My fingers found the strings, and the melody I'd been struggling with started to flow more naturally.

A few days later, one of the producers pulled me aside for an interview. It was standard, something we all had to do weekly. But this time, the questions were more personal.

The producer sat across from me in a cozy but brightly lit studio space. The camera lens felt larger than usual, its focus heavier, like it could see straight through me.

"Willow, it's been a few weeks since Austin left and rumor has it the two of you were quite close," she began, her tone light but probing. "How has his absence impacted you?"

The camera's red light blinked, recording every micro-expression on my face. I swallowed, suddenly too aware of the way my hands gripped the hem of my shirt.

"Um, it's been tough," I admitted. "Austin? He was kind of my person in the house. We just clicked, you know?"

She nodded, encouraging me to continue. "What do you miss most about him?"

"Everything," I said without thinking, then laughed nervously. "I mean, he made everything feel easier. He has this way of making you feel like you're the only person in the room."

The producer's knowing smile made my cheeks flush. "Sounds like you two had a special connection."

I hesitated, suddenly realizing how much I'd said. "We're just friends," I said quickly.

She raised an eyebrow but didn't push. Still, as soon as the interview ended, those words echoed in my mind. *We're just friends.*

Had it looked like something more to everyone else? Did I want it to be more? Did he?

That night, as I lay awake, I realized it wasn't just Austin I missed. Every week, it felt like another thread was pulled from our little family—our makeshift band of competitors thrown together by chance and music.

Maybe that's why Cassidy's struggle with Nash hit me so deeply. We were all here to compete, but it never really felt like that. Instead, it was like we were creating something together through our shared love for music—messy, imperfect, and raw—but definitely real.

Music was home. It lived in those fleeting moments—like the connections we'd made here. Beautiful, fragile, and impossible to hold forever.

The next morning, I sat at the piano, the soft hum of the house settling around me like a quiet breath. My fingers moved almost without thinking, tracing a melody Austin and I had started together —half-remembered, half-made-up.

The space beside me felt empty and the song itself was missing part of its voice.

Maybe that's what this whole experience was—like a song that never quite sounds the same once the people who wrote it have moved on.

But music isn't just what we play in the moment. It's the echoes we leave behind—the memories, the feelings, the parts of us that keep moving forward long after the last note fades.

I exhaled slowly, letting the final chord hang in the air like a promise.

I couldn't stop any of us from leaving. That was the name of the game. Everyone would leave until there was only one winner declared.

But I could hope the music and memories we made together never truly ended.

Chapter 14

Austin

Being back home was supposed to make things easier. The familiar rhythm of the ranch, the scent of sun-warmed hay, the weight of good, honest work—it usually grounded me. But now, every quiet moment felt like an open door for thoughts I didn't want to have.

So I kept moving.

By noon, I'd already shoveled, hauled, or hammered enough to make my shoulders ache, but no amount of work could hammer her out of my head. Nashville still felt like it was just a breath away. The stage lights, the music, the way Willow's laughter made everything feel a little lighter—it all stuck to me, impossible to shake.

"You're gonna kill that fence if you keep pounding it like that," Connor's voice cut through the midday heat, dry as the dirt beneath our boots.

I stopped mid-swing, gritting my teeth. "It was loose."

Connor leaned against the truck, arms crossed, watching me like he was seeing through all my excuses. "That fence wasn't going anywhere."

I exhaled hard, resetting the nail, refusing to meet his eyes.

"You're distracted," he said.

I kept my grip on the hammer. "Just thinking."

"Uh-huh." A beat of silence. Then— "Willow."

My hand slipped, the hammer glancing off the wood. I cursed under my breath and turned to glare at him. "What makes you say that?"

He lifted an eyebrow, unimpressed. "Because you check your phone every five minutes. Talk about her every time someone mentions the show or anything remotely related to it. You're not subtle"

I opened my mouth to argue, but he wasn't wrong.

Instead, I muttered, "She's a friend."

Connor didn't even blink. "OK."

No teasing. No smug 'I told you so.' Just two syllables, spoken like a fact. And it was. It was a fact I'd have to face sooner or later.

Then he turned, climbed into the truck, and drove off—leaving me standing there with the truth I wasn't ready to say out loud.

That evening, the house smelled like popcorn as Mom settled onto the couch with her knitting. The TV was already on, the recap from last week's competition playing. Connor sat on the other end of the couch, scrolling on his phone like he wasn't paying attention, though I knew better.

The second her name flashed across the television screen, my whole body went still.

Willow stepped onto the stage, and for a moment, I forgot where I was.

She never just performed. She owned that stage.

Her voice wrapped around the melody, steady and strong, the kind of sound that could knock the air right out of your lungs. And the way she moved? She was born for it.

I barely noticed that I'd sat forward, elbows on my knees, heart hammering.

Connor's voice pulled me back. "She's good."

I didn't look away from the screen. "Yeah."

He nodded once. "Really good."

The final note rang out, and without thinking, I was on my feet, whooping like I was in the audience.

"She crushed it," I said, grinning.

"Seems like it," Mom murmured, her knitting paused in her lap. Then she looked at me, her eyes soft and knowing. "You're proud of her."

I swallowed past the lump in my throat. "Yeah. I am."

Her gaze lingered, like she was waiting for something. When I didn't say anything, she just smiled. "She means something to you, doesn't she?"

Taking my seat on the couch, I hesitated, heart pounding.

"Yeah," I admitted, my voice quieter. "She does."

Connor, still scrolling on his phone, didn't even glance up. "You should tell her."

I frowned but pulled my phone out, anyway. I wanted to tell her. There were actually a lot of things I wanted to tell her but that she meant something to me? I didn't think I was ready for that. I opted for safe.

> Me: You were amazing.

Her reply came later that night, which hadn't surprised me. It always took time to wrap up and get back to the house.

> Willow: Thanks 🖤 I wish you'd been on
> stage, too

My chest tightened. The words hit like a sucker punch—warm, aching, bittersweet.

Because I'd wished that, too. More than I could put into words.

I typed a dozen different replies. Deleted every single one.

Finally, I set the phone down, exhaling hard as I leaned back against the couch.

The room blurred around me, her words still circling my head like a song I couldn't get out of my system.

My only thought, *I wish I'd been on stage, too. With you.*

Later that night, as the house settled into quiet, I stared up at the ceiling, my heartbeat steady but restless.

Connor's words replayed in my mind, *You should tell her.*

Mom's knowing look.

Willow's message.

I closed my eyes, exhaling through my nose.

I turned, reaching for my phone again, just to read her message one more time.

Going into the competition had come with the possibility of losing and I'd dreaded it up to the moment my name was called for elimination. There was only so much I could have done to prepare myself for it and since it had happened, there was only one other thing I was afraid of losing.

And I had no idea how to prepare myself for that.

Chapter 15

Willow

The competition had been a pressure cooker since the first performance, but lately, it felt like we were all standing on a fault line, waiting for the ground to crack beneath us. The pressure wasn't just about hitting the right notes anymore—it was in every glance exchanged backstage, every whispered conversation that stopped the second someone walked in the room. The fear of elimination wasn't just a shadow—it was a presence, thick in the air, pressing down on all of us.

And the worst part? No one talked about it.

Instead, we rehearsed harder, smiled bigger, and tried to pretend we weren't all wondering the same thing: Whose dream was ending next? Then begging the universe it wouldn't be us.

I tried to channel that tension into my music, but even the music room didn't feel as much like a sanctuary as it used to. I missed the way Austin would poke his head in, guitar slung over his shoulder, that easy, lopsided grin on his face like he had no doubt everything would work out in the end.

Now, the whole room felt different. Colder. Emptier.

I spent more time with Harper and Cassidy, our late-night chats and inside jokes keeping me sane. They knew I was struggling. But even with them, there were moments I'd catch myself turning toward the door, expecting him to walk in, only to remember he wasn't coming.

"You okay?" Harper asked one afternoon, dropping onto the couch beside me, her arm casually draped over the backrest.

I let out a slow breath. "Yeah. Just tired. It's hard to shut my brain off."

Cassidy joined us, a glass of sweet tea in hand. "Tell me about it. I keep dreaming I'm forgetting my lyrics on stage. Then the judges just stare at me like I'm a kid who wandered into the wrong room."

Harper snorted. "Better than my dream. In mine, I walk on stage, open my mouth, and just croak. Like a freaking frog."

Despite myself, I laughed. A real, unguarded laugh. They were trying so hard to keep me grounded, to keep me from slipping too far into my own head.

"Thanks, y'all," I said, my voice softer.

Harper nudged me with her shoulder. "Anytime, Willow. We've got you."

Rehearsal didn't do much to ease the tension. The stage was a sea of organized chaos, crew members bustling around and contestants trying to perfect their performances. I was running through my song when I felt a presence nearby.

Turning, I discovered Lanie leaned against the railing, arms crossed, her usual sharp-edged confidence replaced with something quieter.

"You've got a lot of heart when you sing," she said, not quite meeting my eyes. "It shows."

I blinked. Of all people, I hadn't expected Lanie to say that.

"Thanks," I said cautiously.

She hesitated, her gaze flicking away. Like she wanted to say more but wasn't used to peeling back her own layers. Finally, she straightened. "Just don't screw it up."

And just like that, she was gone.

But the words stuck.

She wasn't pleasant, necessarily, but maybe Lanie Tisdale wasn't as frosty as she wanted everyone to think.

The performance show felt like a blur of lights and nerves. Standing under the hot stage lights, I poured everything I had into the song—every ounce of doubt, hope, and longing. My soul was on display for the judges, the audience, the nation to see and judge.

When the last note echoed through the room, there was a moment of silence before the audience erupted into applause. The judges smiled, offering praise that felt genuine. For the first time in weeks, I thought maybe I was doing enough.

But then came the results the next evening.

Standing under the harsh studio lights, my heart pounded as the host announced the names of the contestants who were safe. One by one, their names were called.

And then it was down to me and Sawyer Brooks.

I felt Cassidy's hand brush mine, a silent gesture of support as I stood frozen. Time seemed to stretch, the weight of the moment pressing down on me.

"And the contestant leaving us tonight is..."

The words stretched out, impossibly slow.

My name.

The air sucked out of my lungs. The stage lights blurred, the crowd's reaction muffled like I was underwater. My ears rang, my pulse hammering in my throat.

Someone squeezed my hand—Cassidy. A small, silent anchor in a moment that felt like free-fall.

I swallowed hard, trying to hold myself together, but the lump in my throat was too big, the sting behind my eyes too sharp.

I was out.

Just like that.

The goodbye was a blur of tears, of voices overlapping, of arms wrapping around me too tight, like they were trying to hold me here, as if that could change anything.

Harper was first. She clung to me, her grip fierce. "You're incredible, Willow. Don't let anyone make you forget that."

"I won't," I whispered, even though it felt like a lie in that moment.

Cassidy's voice cracked as she said, "I don't know what we're gonna do without you."

"I don't know what I'm gonna do without y'all."

Even Lanie surprised me with a quick embrace. No sarcasm, no sharp edges—just a quiet, "They made the wrong call."

I almost lost it then.

That night, back at the house, the air was heavy with finality as I packed my things. Harper and Cassidy lingered in my room, reminiscing and making me laugh through the tears. But as the hours ticked by, the reality of leaving began to settle in.

By the time morning came, the car waiting outside felt like an endpoint I wasn't ready for.

I hugged the girls one last time, holding on a little longer than I probably should have. Harper was the last. "Promise me you'll keep going," she said, her voice thick with emotion.

"I promise," I whispered.

As the car pulled away, I stared out the window, watching the mansion shrink in the distance. The city lights blurred past, each one a reminder of the stage I wouldn't stand on again.

But in my lap was my notebook, and I clutched it tightly.

I was out.

But my music, my journey—it wasn't over. Not by a long shot.

Chapter 16

Austin

Watching her walk off that stage was like watching the final light of a candle flicker out.

She stood there under those bright lights, the same lights that had once made her shine, but tonight they felt brutal, like they were swallowing her whole. She smiled, that beautiful smile that had always come so easily. But I knew better.

Her eyes told the truth.

And the truth was, she was heartbroken.

I gripped the arms of my chair so tight my knuckles turned white. Every instinct screamed at me to get up, to run to her, to say something—anything—but all I could do was watch as she hugged Cassidy, then Harper, then even Lanie.

And then she was gone.

And I hated how final it felt.

As the credits started to roll, my family watched me with knowing expressions.

"She's going to need to hear from you," Mom said softly, her knitting needles still in her lap.

I was fumbling to retrieve my phone from my pocket when Connor added in his usual blunt way, "Call her."

"I'm trying," I muttered, pressing the call button.

The phone rang once, twice, three times. My heart pounded with each passing second. But then it went to voicemail.

Her voice came through the line, soft and warm: "Hey, this is Willow. Leave me a message, and I'll get back to you."

I swallowed, staring at the floor as the beep sounded. What was I supposed to say?

"Hey, Willow. It's me. I just," I exhaled, rubbing a hand over my face. "I just wanted to say how proud I am of you. You were incredible tonight. You always are. Call me when you can, okay?"

I hung up, but the ache in my chest didn't fade.

"You okay, son?" Dad asked from his recliner, his voice gruff but kind.

"Yeah," I lied, pushing off the couch. "Just need some air."

The cool night breeze hit me as I stepped onto the porch, but it didn't help. I couldn't shake the image of her walking off that stage, holding it together even though I knew how much it had to hurt.

She was so much stronger than I was.

I was out in the barn when my phone buzzed in my pocket.

Her name lit up the screen.

For a second, I just stared at it, my heart lodged in my throat. Then, fumbling slightly, I swiped to answer.

"Willow?"

"Hey," she said, her voice soft—too soft. I could hear the hum of an engine in the background, picturing her in the backseat of a car, her face pressed against the cool glass, watching the city disappear behind her.

"I tried calling you last night," I said, leaning against the barn wall.

"I know," she admitted. "I couldn't talk then. I wasn't ready."

"It's okay," I said quickly, because I understood that feeling all too well. "I get it."

Silence stretched between us, but it wasn't uncomfortable. It was just heavy.

"You saw it, huh?" she asked eventually, her voice half-laugh, half-sigh.

"Of course I did," I said, smiling even though she couldn't see it. "I wouldn't miss it. You were amazing. Truly."

"Thanks," she said, and I could hear the emotion in her voice. "It wasn't enough, though."

"Hey," I said firmly, standing straighter. "Don't do that. You gave it everything you had, and anyone watching could see that. It's not about them, okay? It's about what you've done, what you've created. And you've done something incredible."

She didn't respond right away, but I could hear her sniffle. "You're really good at this whole pep talk thing, you know?"

I chuckled. "Well, I had a good coach."

That made her laugh, a real one this time, and the sound was like a balm to my chest.

"I'm going to miss it," she admitted after a moment. "The house, the music, the people. Even the stress, in some weird way."

"I know," I said softly. "Believe me, I know."

She hesitated. "Yeah, you probably do."

"I've been exactly where you are," I said, my voice steady but warm. "Standing under those lights, hearing my name, knowing it's over. It's like everything shifts under your feet, and for a second, you don't know who you could possibly be without it."

She exhaled shakily. "Yes. That's exactly it."

"I remember walking off that stage," I continued, my chest tightening at the memory. "And the only thing I could think was, 'What now?' But then I realized, it wasn't really an ending. It was just the start of something else."

Her voice softened. "You really think so?"

"I don't think so. I know so," I said firmly. "This isn't the end for you. It's just the beginning. And you're going to do amazing things—I can feel it."

She was quiet again, and I could tell she was thinking, the hum of the car engine filling the silence.

"Do you remember that night in the music room?" she asked suddenly.

I smiled. "Yeah. Which time?"

She breathed a laugh, small but real. It was the first time she'd really laughed since picking up the phone, and I felt something loosen in my chest.

"I keep thinking about that song," she admitted. "The last one we worked on together. It's like—it's stuck in my head, and I can't stop hearing it."

"Good," I said, my voice warm. "That means it's worth holding onto."

She hesitated for half a second, then, so softly I almost didn't catch it—

"I miss you, Austin."

I closed my eyes. The words hit me like a punch to the chest, but in the best way.

"I miss you, too."

Another pause. Then, lighter, teasing even, she said, "Thanks for picking up."

I chuckled, shaking my head. "Willow, I'd pick up at three in the morning if you called."

"Oh, don't say that. I might test you on it."

"Go ahead," I challenged. "See what happens."

She laughed again. I'd missed that sound more than I realized.

"Okay," she said. "I'll hold you to that."

We said our goodbyes, and as the call ended, I stared at the phone in my hand. The ache of missing her was still there, but so was something else—a sense of connection that distance couldn't touch.

I slipped the phone back into my pocket and walked out of the barn. She might be leaving Nashville, but she wasn't leaving my thoughts. Not now, likely not ever.

90

Chapter 17

Willow

The moment my feet hit the Savannah pavement, I felt it— home. The air was thick with the ever-present humidity, mingled with the earthy sweet scent of pine and damp moss. Even through the glass doors of the airport, I could feel the warmth pressing against my skin. It was a stark contrast to the cool, sterile air of the competition house, but it was familiar. It was real.

And then, I saw them.

Gemma was the first to reach me, launching herself at me so hard that I stumbled back a step. "Oh my God, you're finally home!" she shrieked, gripping my arms like she needed to make sure I was solid and not some hologram.

I laughed, my throat tightening as I squeezed her back. "I missed you too, G."

Before I could catch my breath, Caleb's strong arms wrapped around me, nearly lifting me off my feet. "You did great, sis," he murmured, his voice thick with something I couldn't quite name. "We're so proud of you."

Over his shoulder, I caught sight of my parents. Mom's eyes were glassy, her hands pressed together in front of her like she was holding back the urge to pull me in. Dad, ever the stoic one, simply nodded—but there was a pride in his gaze that hadn't always been there when it came to my music.

Caleb finally let me go, ushering me toward the car. "Come on. You've got a homecoming waiting for you."

When we pulled into the driveway, I was met with the unmistakable sight of streamers tangled in the porch railing and a giant, homemade banner stretched across the front door that read: WELCOME HOME, WILLOW! The letters were slightly crooked, meaning she'd outsourced it, but I could tell Gemma had been the mastermind behind it.

I laughed, pressing a hand to my chest. "Y'all really did all this?"

"You deserve it," Dad said, stepping beside me. He placed a hand on my shoulder, firm and steady, the way he always did when he was trying to say more than words could. "You've made us all proud."

The night air was warm. Savannah didn't get the crisp fall evenings some places did, but there was a shift in the air tonight—just the slightest hint that summer was starting to loosen its grip. Crickets hummed a lazy melody, and the occasional rustle of Spanish moss swaying in the trees filled the quiet.

The evening wound down and I promised Gemma I'd meet her at home. Caleb and I leaned against my car I'd left parked in our parents' driveway, the metal still warm from the day's lingering heat.

He kicked a rock with the toe of his boot, smirking. "So, you ready for this?"

I raised an eyebrow. "For what?"

"For me to tell you that Dad, Mr. Practicality, turned into your number-one hype man while you were gone."

I snorted. "Now that I don't believe."

Caleb grinned. "Oh, you should've seen him. He passed out campaign buttons with your picture on them to everyone at work."

I froze mid-step. "No, he didn't."

"Oh, he did," Caleb said, his grin widening. "Had 'em on his desk, kept extras in his briefcase. Hosted watch parties, too."

My stomach flipped. "You're kidding."

"Wish I was. You should've heard him. 'That's my girl, right there!'" Caleb mimicked Dad's deep, measured drawl, puffing out his chest dramatically. "I swear, some of his coworkers started calling him 'Willow's PR Manager.'"

A laugh burst out of me, but my throat felt tight. I tried to picture it—Dad, who had always been so cautious about my choices, passing out buttons, bragging, hosting watch parties.

My heart twisted in the best possible way.

I swallowed. "Well, that's something."

Caleb's teasing faded into something softer. "It's more than something, Willow. He's proud of you. We all are."

The lump in my throat made it hard to answer, so I just nodded, looking out at the darkened horizon.

Caleb let the silence linger for a beat before nudging me with his elbow. "So, what I'm saying is, you've officially converted Dad into a country music fan."

I chuckled, shaking my head. "Let's not get ahead of ourselves."

Caleb smirked. "Maybe. But I did catch him humming one of the songs you sang the other day."

I laughed, shaking my head. Maybe miracles do happen.

Over the next few weeks, I settled back into life in Savannah. It was strange, at first, to wake up and not have cameras following my every move or rehearsals looming over my head.

To keep myself busy while waiting for the *Real American Country* Tour to kick off in February, I picked up a job at the local music store. It wasn't glamorous, but I loved it—the smell of aged wood and sheet music, the way customers would run their hands over guitar strings like they were greeting an old friend. Sometimes, when business was slow, I'd sit behind the counter and play, the warm acoustics of the shop wrapping around me like a hug.

At night, the house was quiet. Too quiet. No hum of contestants whispering in the next room, no guitars strumming from down the hall. Just the soft ticking of the clock on my nightstand and the occasional chirp of crickets outside my window.

I reached for my phone before I could stop myself, my thumb hovering over Austin's name in my messages.

It had been like this since he left. A text here, a late-night call there—enough to remind me he was still there, but not enough to shake the feeling that something was missing. That he was missing.

This is ridiculous, I scolded myself, locking my phone and tossing it onto the bed.

Gemma poked her head into my room a second later, raising an eyebrow. "Okay, you're staring at that thing like you're waiting for it to sprout legs and do a dance. Spill."

I groaned, flopping backward onto my pillows. "It's nothing."

Gemma snorted. "Uh-huh. Right. And I didn't just hear you sigh like a lovesick teenager."

I threw a pillow at her. She dodged, grinning. "You need to figure out whatever this is," she said, pointing at my phone. "Because I love you, but you're unbearable like this."

I exhaled, staring at the ceiling. Maybe she was right.

During one of our usual late-night conversations, I decided to ask a question that had been on my mind. "So, have you ever been to Georgia?"

A pause. "Can't say I have. Always wanted to, though."

"Really?" I asked, feeling a flutter of excitement.

"Well," he said, and I could hear the smile in his voice. "I do now."

A smile pulled at my lips, and before I could second-guess myself, I said it. "You should come down after Thanksgiving. Stay a few days. Then we can head to Nashville together."

There was a brief pause before he responded. "That sounds amazing. I'd love to."

Chapter 18

Willow

I checked the arrivals board for the third time, my fingers tapping restlessly against my phone case. The airport was bustling with post-holiday travelers, but the only face I was searching for was his.

Then I saw him.

Austin, ball cap pulled low, duffel slung over his shoulder, scanning the crowd with those familiar amber eyes. The second he spotted me, his whole face lit up.

And suddenly, I was moving.

I didn't think. Didn't hesitate. Just ran straight into his arms.

His laughter rumbled against my cheek as he dropped his bag and caught me, lifting me just slightly off the ground. "Hey there, Gracin."

"Hey yourself," I whispered, clinging to him for just a second longer than necessary.

Because it was Austin. And he was here.

And I wasn't ready to let go.

"Welcome to Savannah!" I said, grinning up at him.

"Thanks," he said, laughing as he wasn't quick to withdraw his arms either. "It's good to see you."

The drive back to my family's house was filled with easy conversation, his laugh filling the car as we talked about everything and nothing.

When we arrived, the house was alive with activity. My parents were unpacking boxes of Christmas decorations, Caleb was untangling a mess of lights, and Gemma was in the kitchen, shouting instructions at no one in particular.

"This place looks exciting," Austin said, taking it all in.

"It's our family tradition," I explained, beaming. "Caleb and I always decorate the tree, and everyone pitches in with the rest."

Caleb walked over, giving Austin a friendly nod. "I'm Caleb. Good to meet you, man. You sure you're ready for this?"

"Absolutely," Austin replied with a grin.

I made the introductions. "Austin, this is my mom, Eileen, and my dad, Frank. And you've already met Caleb."

Mom's eyes lit up as she shook Austin's hand. "It's so nice to meet you, Austin. Willow has told us so much about you."

"Nice to meet you too, Mrs. Gracin," Austin said warmly.

"Oh, call me Eileen," she insisted, clearly charmed.

Gemma appeared from the kitchen, wiping her hands on a dish towel. She gave me a quick, approving nod before turning her attention to Austin. "And this is my best friend and roommate, Gemma," I said.

Gemma's eyes twinkled with mischief as she looked Austin up and down. "Nice to meet you, Austin."

My dad stepped forward, shaking Austin's hand firmly. "Glad to finally meet you, Austin. I was sorry to see you leave the show, but I was glad it wasn't Willow that early on."

"Dad!" I chided, my cheeks burning.

Everyone laughed, and Austin took it in stride, nodding in agreement. "I totally get it, Mr. Gracin. I'm glad it wasn't her either."

I dragged Austin to the living room where the enormous

Christmas tree stood waiting to be decorated. Boxes of ornaments, tinsel, and lights were scattered around, ready for our careful hands.

Gemma joined us, her enthusiasm infectious. "This is going to be so much fun!"

My mom was already busy in the kitchen, baking our favorite Christmas cookies, while my dad was outside, untangling strings of lights to decorate the house.

Caleb and I started with the lights, carefully weaving them around the tree. Austin and Gemma handed us ornaments, sharing stories and laughter as we worked. "This one's my favorite," I said, holding up a delicate ornament shaped like an angel. "I made it when I was five."

"That is a work of art," Austin took it but, rather than looking at it, his eyes never left mine.

I blushed, quickly turning back to the tree to hide my embarrassment. The day was filled with moments like this, small gestures and words making my chest ache for more while knowing this was all it would be.

As we hung the last ornament, I stepped back to admire our work. The tree sparkled with lights and glittering decorations, a testament to our teamwork. "It's perfect," I said softly.

"It really is," Austin agreed, his gaze lingering on me longer than necessary before returning to the tree.

We moved on to other decorations, filling the house with festive cheer. Garland was draped over the mantel, stockings were hung with care, and the scent of pine and cinnamon filled the air. My mom's cookies baked in the oven, adding their delicious aroma to the mix.

By mid-afternoon, we decided to take a break. My dad came inside, wiping sweat from his forehead, and joined us in the living room. "The outside lights are done. How's the tree looking?"

"Beautiful," my mom said, walking in with a tray of cookies. "You all did a wonderful job."

We spent the rest of the afternoon relaxing and enjoying each other's company. My parents shared stories from past Christmases, and we all laughed at the funny memories. Austin fit right in, adding his own anecdotes and making everyone feel at ease.

As evening approached, my mom began preparing dinner, while my dad set the table. The atmosphere was cozy and warm, filled with the love and togetherness that defined our family.

After dinner, we spent the evening playing board games and laughing until our cheeks hurt. Austin fit in so seamlessly, it was like he'd been part of our family all along.

When everyone had slowly peeled off and headed home or to their room, Austin and I found ourselves alone in the living room, the tree casting a soft glow around us. We sat on the couch, talking quietly, our voices barely above a whisper. "Thank you for inviting me," he said, his eyes sincere. "This has been the best day."

"I'm glad you're here," I said, my heart fluttering.

We sat there for a while, talking in hushed tones about traveling back to Nashville for the show finale. Every now and then, his gaze would linger on mine, and I'd feel the ache of unspoken words hanging between us.

After yawning for the third time, I decided it was time to call it a night. I walked Austin to the guest room. "Goodnight, Austin Blake," I said.

"Goodnight, Willow Gracin," he replied, his voice soft and warm. "See you in the morning."

He stepped through the doorway but turned back to me with a smile, and for a second, it felt like this was completely normal—like he could always be here, fitting into more than just the edges of my life with ease. But I knew better. The days ahead were already numbered, and I hated how much that thought hurt.

As I walked back to my old room, the glow of the Christmas tree followed me, but so did the ache. Time always moved too fast when you wanted it to slow down.

Chapter 19

Austin

The airport was packed—holiday travelers rushing to catch flights, kids tugging on their parents' hands, flight attendants weaving through the chaos with effortless precision. I stepped off the plane, duffel slung over my shoulder, my heart hammering harder than it should've been.

Then I saw her.

She was shifting her weight from foot to foot, fidgeting with the strap of her bag like she wasn't sure what to do with her hands.

And then, like a switch flipped, her eyes locked onto mine.

Whatever hesitation had been there vanished.

She was running before I had time to brace for impact. I barely dropped my bag in time before she crashed into me, arms looping around my neck, holding tight like I might disappear if she let go.

I laughed, the sound vibrating against her hair as I pulled her in closer, breathing her in. "Hey there, Gracin."

Her voice was warm against my shoulder. "Hey, yourself. Welcome to Savannah."

I laughed, holding her close and burying my face in her hair, inhaling deeply. "Thanks. It's so good to see you."

I felt a rush of emotions—excitement, anticipation, and a nervous energy that buzzed in my veins. Having her in my arms felt like coming home, which was crazy, since home was technically 2,500 miles away.

The Gracin household was pure, beautiful chaos.

Bins of Christmas decorations were stacked in the hallway as though Thanksgiving was long-forgotten, even though it had only been twenty-four hours prior. Strings of lights were sprawled across the living room floor, half of them tangled, half of them flickering like they were trying to decide whether or not to die. The scent of sugar and spice drifted from the kitchen, where Eileen was baking cookies.

"This is a disaster," Caleb announced, surveying the mess of ornaments and half-assembled garland.

"It's a work in progress," Willow corrected, pulling a handful of tinsel from a box. She turned to me, handing over a few strands. "Think you can make yourself useful, Blake?"

I smirked, taking them from her. "I'll do my best."

"You'll have to excuse her," Gemma piped up, twirling an ornament between her fingers. "She gets real bossy around the holidays."

Willow shot her a look. "I do not."

"Sure, sweetie," Gemma said, all saccharine. "Keep telling yourself that."

I chuckled, draping tinsel over the garland draped across mantle, stealing quick glances at Willow as she flitted around the room. Her cheeks were flushed, her eyes bright, her energy infectious.

That night, we were hanging out in the living room by the light of the Christmas tree. Our conversation meandered, and we started talking about the upcoming *Real American Country* Tour. "I can't wait to travel and perform in different cities," Willow said, her eyes sparkling with excitement.

"Me too," I agreed. "I think it's going to be an incredible experience."

She let out a breathy laugh. "I just don't know how I feel about sharing a tour bus with five other women—which will probably feel more like eight or nine since one of them is Lanie Tisdale." She wrinkled her nose. "That wasn't very nice, but, man, she is high maintenance."

I chuckled. "Well, at least you don't have to share a bus with Levi. That guy talks in his sleep."

Her laughter was instant and effortless, and it unlocked something inside me that I had no business acknowledging.

Because, suddenly, I wanted to kiss her.

The urge was overwhelming—strong enough that I had to grip my knee just to keep from acting on it.

So, I forced myself into a distraction. "One time, he had a full conversation about cheeseburgers and rocket ships. It was hilarious."

She laughed even harder, covering her mouth with her hand. "Oh, I wish I could hear that! I guess I'll just have to make do with Lanie's beauty regimen at 6 AM and pack a gas mask for the amount of hairspray she uses."

We both laughed, and for a moment, everything felt perfect. The room was filled with the soft glow of Christmas lights, and the scent of pine and cinnamon lingered in the air. It was one of those moments you wanted to last forever.

The next morning, Willow and I set out to explore Savannah. The charm of the city, combined with Willow's enthusiasm, made each moment special. We visited Forsyth Park, the historic district, and quaint cafes. Each shared experience deepened our bond, making it harder for me to keep my feelings in check and my hands to myself. I loved every minute with her, but I knew the miles between us and the uncertainty ahead made things complicated.

That evening, we headed to The Driftwood—the very place where Willow had first been discovered by the producer who got her on the show. It was like stepping into a second home for her.

The bar was packed, the air thick with the scent of whiskey and old wood. As we walked in, the owner greeted Willow with a warm smile. Behind the bar, I spotted a "Vote for Willow" pin proudly pinned on the wall. Her dad had told us how he'd made it a point to stop in and hand them out on a weekly basis.

The owner noticed our entrance and drew attention to us. A round of cheers and applause went up that I knew was for Willow. She smiled through the blush filling her cheeks.

"Thanks for that, Drake," she laughed as she offered the older man a high five.

His voice was laced with amusement when he responded, "Your daddy was in here often enough offering up strongly worded suggestions about who we were supposed to vote for that it felt wrong to let your presence go unrecognized."

Willow rolled her eyes then reached for my arm, pulling me forward to stand next to her. The man studied me then asked, "You were on the show, weren't ya?"

Before I could respond, Willow answered for me, her hand still wrapped around my arm sending a steady stream of warmth through me. "This is Austin Blake. He was on the show and now I'm giving him a tour of Savannah. So be nice to him."

With a hint of mischief in his eye, Drake said, "I see. I tell you what, if the two of you will grace us with your talent, drinks will be on the house."

Willow narrowed her eyes at him then turned to me. "What do you say, Blake? Are you up for singing for free drinks?"

I pretended to think about it then shrugged, "I'll leave it up to you, Gracin."

Neither of us had instruments but that didn't matter. With a steady supply of live entertainment, a guitar was easy to come by. After about two minutes of planning, Willow relegated playing to me. I took a seat and positioned myself behind a mic as she adjusted one for herself.

The low murmur of conversation settling into an expectant hush as Willow and I made ourselves at home on the small stage.

Before we even started, I knew this was going to wreck me. Because singing with Willow was unlike anything else.

Her voice wove itself through mine like it belonged there, like we'd been singing together for years instead of weeks. It was effortless, electric—so natural it almost hurt.

Halfway through the song, she glanced at me, and for a split second, I forgot the words.

Because she was looking at me like I was the only person in the room and it made me want to never do anything else for the rest of my life.

When it was time to fly to Nashville for the show's finale, I felt a mix of excitement and bittersweet emotions. The flight was filled with quiet conversations and shared glances, both of us knowing that parting ways afterward would be difficult, even though we would see each other again in two months. But when she leaned her head on my shoulder, those worries melted away, if only for a moment.

It was a fast-paced finale filled with performances, interviews, and emotion. One of the highlights was all twelve contestants on stage singing *Life is a Highway*. It was the most fun we'd all had together since the first day of the show. The energy was electric, and for those few minutes, we were all united in our love for music and everything we'd been through.

After the finale, there was an after-party where we celebrated Christopher Jordan's win. Almost the entire night, Nash and Cassidy tried to hide that they were officially a couple, which surprised both Willow and me. I hadn't been around for that development during the show, but there had always been a weird tension between them. It was really amusing watching them sneak off to quiet corners, thinking they weren't visible. Willow and I spent most of the evening together, mingling with friends, taking pictures, and savoring the moment.

The next morning, as we had breakfast with Sawyer, Levi, and Harper, I had a moment where all I felt was immense gratitude and excitement for the future. Saying goodbye to Willow was the hardest part.

As we stood in the lobby of the hotel, our luggage in tow, I pulled a small box from my pocket and handed it to her. "I got you something," I said, feeling nervous but trying to play it cool.

She opened it, her breath hitching. Inside was a delicate necklace with a guitar pendant.

"Austin," she looked up, eyes shining. "It's beautiful."

"I thought it might be a nice reminder of everything," I said, my voice catching slightly.

She hugged me tightly. "I love it! Thank you."

There were so many things I wanted to tell her—to ask her. Like how she could feel so close and so far away at the same time. But the words wouldn't come. Not now, not yet.

So, instead of speaking, I just held on for as long as I could.

As we parted ways, my heart ached with a mix of hope and sadness. The physical separation was hard, but what could I do about it? The answer was 'not much,' which I already knew. I did, however, foresee a lot of phone calls and text messages, and that would have to be enough.

Chapter 20

Willow

My phone buzzed beside me on the porch railing, screen lighting up with a message that already had me smiling before I even opened it.

Attached was a photo that looked almost unreal—like the sky had caught fire in that split second before the dark swallowed it whole. Nearly crimson clouds, streaks of orange and gold.

I leaned back in the porch swing and snapped my own photo—the lowcountry sky cotton-candy soft, streaked with violet and peach.

His reply was instant.

Gemma appeared out of nowhere, sipping her tea like she hadn't just been watching me from the window. "You two are like a slow-burn country song, you know that, right?"

I rolled my eyes, but the heat on my cheeks gave me away. "We're just friends, Gem."

"Mmm-hmm," she said, unimpressed. "I'm calling it now—your first duet? Gonna be titled *The Line We Won't Cross*. Top Ten hit. Radio gold."

I grabbed the outdoor throw pillow and lobbed it at her head. She ducked, grinning, and walked off humming some fake country tune just to drive the point home as she walked back into the house.

Our conversations had rhythm—texts during the day, calls at night, video chats that stretched into the early hours like neither of us wanted to be the one to say goodbye.

And the music? That was where we met most fully. Where the distance between us blurred.

We weren't just writing songs. It felt like we were building something—one lyric, one chord, one late-night laugh at a time.

"Okay, what do you think of this?" I asked during one of those virtual jam sessions, tilting my laptop to get the angle right. My fingers moved across the strings, coaxing a melody that felt half-finished but promising.

Austin leaned in, elbows propped on his knees, eyes locked on me through the screen. "That bridge is solid. Maybe add a little crescendo here?" He hummed a few bars—low, rough, perfect—and I swear I felt it in my spine.

"Perfect," I said, quickly scribbling it down in the margins of my notebook.

It was always like this with us. A give and take. A dance we didn't have to choreograph.

Then he said it—"Hey, I've got an idea for the second verse." And he launched into a few lines that hit me like a punch to the chest—sharp, beautiful, and too honest.

I froze. My hand hovered over the guitar.

"I don't know," I said, eyes flicking to my notebook instead of the screen. "Maybe it's a little too raw."

He raised an eyebrow. "Raw is good. It's honest."

I swallowed. "Yeah, but—"

Sometimes it was hard to know when lyrics were stories and when they were truth. These felt personal and real. And I wasn't ready to admit how much they scared me.

Tour prep started creeping up on me like a shadow I couldn't outrun.

I packed slowly, second-guessing everything I folded. The excitement was real—Bridgestone Arena followed by a cross-country tour, a chance to keep the momentum going—but the nerves? They were just as loud.

Part of it was the music. The other part was Austin.

We'd talked every day. But being back in the same place? In the same room? On the same stage? It felt like we were heading toward something bigger and together.

The night before I left, I got a text from Harper.

> Harper: Let's hang when you get here.
> Dinner at that diner we love?

> Me: Yes, please.

I checked in with Austin next.

> Me: What time are you landing?

> Austin: Probably at the last minute. Weather delays.

> Me: That's not great. Be safe.

Disappointed, I sighed but couldn't help smiling at the thought of finally seeing him. I arrived in Nashville to a chilly but clear evening. Harper was waiting for me at the airport, and we hugged tightly, laughing and chattering as if no time had passed since the show ended.

The diner felt like a time capsule—flickering neon, chipped table-tops, the smell of grease and strong coffee in the air.

Harper slid into the booth across from me, already grinning. "So, are you and Austin still talking every day?"

"Yeah," I admitted, feeling a blush creep up my cheeks. "We've been working on songs together too."

She raised an eyebrow. "Songs, huh? Is that what the kids are calling it these days?"

I laughed, shaking my head. "It's just music, Harper. You know how much we both love it."

Harper leaned back, a playful smile on her lips. "Sure, sure."

I shifted the conversation to her world back in Texas and in true Harper fashion, she had plenty of stories that kept us both in stitches. After dinner, we walked back to the hotel, the cool night air refreshing.

The next morning, I headed to the rehearsal space, the atmosphere a blend of focus and chaos. We all knew the hard work that lay ahead, but the shared anticipation made it feel like a new and exciting adventure. Reuniting with my friends and fellow contestants felt like a family gathering, each of us slipping back into appointed roles effortlessly, as though we hadn't spent weeks competing against each other for anything.

Harper, Cassidy, and I greeted each other with hugs and laughter, the excitement palpable. We spent the morning catching up, sharing stories, and enjoying the reunion. It wasn't long before Austin arrived, just as he'd predicted, right at the last minute.

He walked in with that worn ball cap and that familiar half-smile like he knew exactly what seeing him would do to me.

And he was right.

I crossed the room without thinking. "You made it!" I said, arms already wrapping around his neck.

"Finally," he said, his arms pulling me in like he had been waiting for this moment as much as I had.

Cassidy raised an eyebrow from across the room. "Someone's happy to see Austin."

"Yeah, well," I shot back. "Someone's still blushing over Nash."

Cassidy blushed but laughed. "Okay, fair point."

It was hard to miss the way Nash and Cassidy interacted, their subtle glances and gentle touches giving away their relationship. Despite their efforts to keep it under wraps, it was clear to anyone paying attention that they were more than just friends.

The rest of the week flew by quickly in a flurry of rehearsals and instructions. Each day brought us all closer together, the excitement for the tour building with each note we sang and each step we took on stage.

When we tackled Little Big Town's *I'm With the Band*, Levi, Harper, Austin, and I gathered in a tight circle. The four-part harmony required focus and precision. As though our voices had been made to blend together, the room fell practically silent as the sounds echoed throughout as one.

As we wrapped up the rehearsal, Austin caught my eye. "You free to hang out later?"

I felt a flutter in my chest and tried to play it cool. "Yeah, sure. What did you have in mind?"

"Maybe just grab a bite to eat, catch up properly?" he suggested, his smile warm and inviting.

"Sounds perfect," I agreed, trying to keep my excitement in check.

That evening, Austin and I met up at the hotel restaurant where all of us were staying. It was quiet, tucked away and warm. Booths with soft lighting and no distractions.

Austin slid into the seat across from me, smiling in that way that always managed to sneak past my defenses and sent shivers up my spine. "This okay?"

"Perfect," I said. "I missed this."

"So, how was your trip here?" he asked, his eyes attentive and genuine.

"Good. No delays or anything," I replied, smiling. "Gah, I've missed seeing you face-to-face."

"Same here," he agreed, his smile softening. For a second, his gaze lingered on mine, and it felt like he wanted to say more, but instead, he just sipped his drink. "There's something about being in the same room that just feels right."

We talked about everything and nothing, the conversation flowing effortlessly.

It was late when we realized the place had emptied out around us with the exception of a patron or two at the bar. Checking his watch, Austin sighed.

"It's getting pretty late," he said, glancing around at the nearly empty restaurant.

I nodded, feeling a mix of reluctance and contentment. "Yeah, I guess we should call it a night."

As we gathered our things and made our way to the elevators Austin said, "I really needed this."

"Me too," I replied, looking up at him.

The ride to his floor was quiet.

The elevator doors slid open to his floor, but neither of us moved.

His gaze lingered on mine—steady, searching. I watched his throat work as he swallowed, slow and deliberate, and for one charged second, I swore he looked at my mouth. Not long, just a flicker, just enough to send chills skittering through my entire body.

His hand flexed by his side like he was holding himself back.

"I guess I'll see you tomorrow," he said, his voice rougher now, quieter than before.

"Yeah," I managed, heart thudding too loud in my chest. "See you tomorrow."

But still, he didn't move.

And neither did I.

I felt it then—the line between us so thin, so fragile, I could've reached across it without moving. It pulsed in the air, thick with everything we hadn't said and probably wouldn't.

His fingers twitched again, but then he exhaled and stepped out.

The doors closed behind him with a soft whisper, and just like that, the moment was gone.

I didn't breathe. Didn't blink. Just stared at my own reflection in the metal doors, stunned by how much space one person could leave behind.

A tiny voice whispered—*You should've said something. You should've stopped him. You should've asked him to stay.*

But I hadn't.

Because I didn't trust myself not to say too much.

Because if I let myself reach for more, I wouldn't know how to stop.

Back in my room, I curled into bed, the sheets cool and stiff against my skin. I stared at the ceiling like it had answers written on it.

It didn't.

His laughter played on a loop in my mind, soft and low, the way it got when something genuinely caught him off guard. I remembered the way his eyes softened when he looked at me, like I was something he didn't want to look away from.

It would've been easier if he were just a friend.

Easier if I didn't care this much.

But nothing about this was easy anymore.

Chapter 21

Austin

I'd almost convinced myself on the flight to Nashville—after an entire day of weather delays—that everything I'd been feeling for Willow was because of the adrenaline that came with creating music and being able to share it with someone so freely. Then I saw her.

All those excuses I'd been sorting through on the plane—every rational reason I'd tried to shove my feelings into the "temporary" box —dissolved the second my eyes found her.

She was laughing alongside Harper and Cassidy, fully involved in whatever conversation they were having. Until her gaze scanned the room and found mine. Then she ran.

Just full-on ran.

"You made it!" she exclaimed, throwing her arms around me.

"Finally," I said, barely getting the word out before she was in my arms.

I caught her, my bag dropping to the floor somewhere beside us. Her arms locked around my neck, and I held on tighter than I probably should've. Her body fit against mine like a puzzle piece I hadn't known I was missing until now.

I didn't want to let go, and for a moment, I didn't. The scent of her flooded my senses. The familiarity and comfort of it hit me like a freight train. It wasn't just the relief of finally arriving after a frustrating day of travel; it was Willow. She felt like home. My heart raced, and I knew without a doubt, that what I felt for her wasn't just friendship or the connection of two musicians. It was so much more.

And that scared me.

I pulled back, unable to hold back the smile that was hurting my face from how wide it was. "You really shouldn't be this excited to see me, Gracin."

She rolled her eyes but laughed, giving me a playful shove. "Someone has to be. Now come on, you're late, and we've got work to do."

As she led me farther inside, I followed her, feeling like my world had just shifted on its axis.

***

The first day of the tour was full of nonstop of activity. We had a jam-packed schedule of promotional events, starting with morning radio interviews. The DJs were warm and welcoming, making it easy to relax and chat about the tour. Willow shined in those moments, her charm effortless, her laugh infectious. I caught myself watching her more than I should've, completely mesmerized by the way she lit up the room.

At the pre-show publicity event later that afternoon, the excitement was palpable. Fans lined up around the block, eager to share their stories and tell us how our music had impacted them. I loved hearing those moments, loved knowing that what we created mattered to people.

But what really made my day was when Willow pulled me aside during a break. We slipped out the back of the store, finding a quiet spot on the steps where we could sit for a moment. The distant sounds of traffic and the muffled buzz of conversations from inside the store created a comfortable backdrop.

"Can you believe we're actually doing this?" she asked, leaning against the railing, her eyes scanning the horizon.

I turned to look at her, the sunlight catching strands of her hair and making them glow. "It's surreal, isn't it?" I said, smiling. "But it's everything we dreamed of."

She nodded, a soft smile tugging at her lips. "Yeah. Everything and more."

For a moment, we sat there in companionable silence. It was easy, like so many of our moments together. But beneath the calm exterior, my emotions were anything but easy. I wanted to tell her so much— about how proud I was of her, how much she inspired me, and how I couldn't imagine doing this with anyone else. But the words stuck in my throat, too heavy to say out loud.

The tour kicked off without a hitch, and the weeks that followed were a blur of performances, travel, and stolen moments. Each city brought its own magic: in Memphis, the twelve of us performed on a local morning show, the cameras capturing every note and smile. In Boston, we played to a sold-out crowd, the energy from the audience electrifying.

During a rare rest day in Chicago, Willow and I wandered down to the river, finding a quiet spot where the water sparkled under the midday sun. She pulled out her notebook, flipping to a half-finished song we'd been toying with for weeks.

"Okay," she said, sitting cross-legged on the grass. "I think I've figured out the melody for the chorus."

I sat beside her, pulling out my guitar. "Let's hear it."

She hummed the tune, her voice soft but sure, and my fingers instinctively found the chords to match. Before I knew it, we were lost in it again. Trading lines like secrets, letting a song carry the weight of everything we didn't know how to say out loud.

Every now and then, her hand would brush mine as she flipped through her notebook, and every time, it sent a jolt up my arm like I was holding on to a live wire.

This song wasn't just special—it was us. Whatever "us" was becoming.

"You know this one's gonna be special, right?" I said, glancing at her.

She met my gaze, her eyes thoughtful. "Yeah," she said softly. "I think it already is."

As the weeks went by, the lines between friendship and something more became increasingly blurred for me. Every moment with Willow—every laugh, every stolen glance, every note we sang together—felt charged with something unspoken. And I wasn't the only one picking up on it.

The meet-and-greet was buzzing with energy. Fans lined up around the block, clutching posters, CDs, and even handmade signs with our names on them. It was one of those moments where the adrenaline from performing wasn't needed—just hearing their stories was enough to remind me why I loved this life.

During a break, I caught sight of Levi and Nash leaning against a stack of instrument cases, whispering conspiratorially. The second I walked over, Levi's grin widened in a way that should've been my first warning.

"Well, look who's here," Levi said, nudging Nash with his elbow. "Mr. 'I'm Just Friends with Willow.'" He dragged out the last part like it was some kind of title.

I rolled my eyes, crossing my arms. "And here we go."

"Don't even try to deny it," Nash added, smirking. "The way she runs to you when she literally just saw you? Man, that is straight out of a movie. I swear I heard a string quartet playing in the background."

"Oh, like the first day of rehearsal? Pretty sure there were actual sparkles in the air," Levi teased. "I half-expected a slow-motion montage."

I opened my mouth to fire back, but before I could, a fan came up holding a poster with a doodle of two stick figures labeled Cashidy—Nash and Cassidy's celebrity nickname that fans had lovingly plastered all over social media. I couldn't help the grin that broke across my face.

"Oh, this is too good," I said, pointing at the poster. "Cashidy? You two are officially a brand now."

Nash groaned, scrubbing a hand over his face. "Don't even start."

"Oh, but I have to," I said, clapping Nash on the shoulder. "You've got a couple name now, dude. That's, like, one step away from matching outfits."

Levi doubled over laughing, and even Nash cracked a reluctant smile. "I hate you both," Nash muttered, though the redness creeping up his neck betrayed him.

I wasn't done yet. "Come on, Nash. You'd look great in one of Cassidy's boho-chic outfits. Maybe a crocheted floral vest to really pull the look together?"

Levi was practically crying at this point, holding his stomach. "Oh man, I can actually see it. Someone draw this. Please."

Nash groaned, rolling his eyes. "You two are jerks."

"Don't worry, man," I said, winking as I stepped back. "The fans are gonna eat up your new fashion duet on this tour. Just make sure they spell your hashtag right. Hashtag 'whipped'."

Levi wiped a tear from his eye, still laughing. "Man, I needed this. You're ruthless, Blake."

"You guys started it," I said, raising my hands in mock innocence. "I'm just here to finish it."

Then I felt a presence behind me. That familiar, electric buzz I only got when she was close.

Willow appeared, two cups of coffee in hand, her eyes narrowed with suspicion. "What's so funny?"

Like actual children, we went dead silent. Nash practically choked on his own guilt. Levi looked skyward like he'd never heard a joke in his life.

"Nothing," Nash said quickly, his voice a little too high-pitched.

Willow just blinked, handed me a cup, and arched a perfect brow. "Okay. That's definitely not suspicious at all."

I took the coffee, my hand practically wrapping around hers. She didn't pull away, not right away. And neither did I.

As she walked off, I could feel Levi and Nash trying not to burst out laughing again behind me. I shook my head, sipping the coffee she'd brought me, but I couldn't fight the smile tugging at my lips.

The teasing, the laughter, the easy way everyone fit together—it felt like the family was back together. Being on the road with this group reminded me of the best parts of the competition, of how much we'd all grown together.

But as the laughter faded and the group began to scatter—Cassidy pulling Nash away for soundcheck, Levi heading off to find food—I found myself alone, sipping the coffee Willow had brought me. My eyes wandered across the area until they landed on her. She was standing off to the side, talking to Harper, her smile lighting up the space around her.

I couldn't stop staring.

Every day on this tour, every song we sang, every moment we shared, made it harder to ignore what I felt. The songs we wrote together seemed to hold layers of meaning, like we were both saying things in the music that we couldn't say out loud.

I wanted to ask her if she felt it too.

If her heart raced when our hands touched. If the way she looked at me sometimes—eyes soft, like I was the only other person in the room—meant what I thought it meant.

But the fear of what I might lose if I crossed that line?

That's what kept my mouth shut.

Because once I said the words, I couldn't take them back. And if she didn't feel the same?

If I lost the music and her?

I didn't think I'd survive it.

So, I focused on the music. It was safer that way. Or at least, that's what I kept telling myself.

Deep down, I knew the truth. No matter how much I tried to bury it, my feelings for Willow were undeniable.

Chapter 22

Willow

Our tour manager, Kensi, had gathered us all together for an impromptu meeting where she announced that our network and sponsor, American Heartland, had struck a deal with a cell phone provider and gifted us all the latest model. Excitement filled the room as we opened our new gadgets and took photos of each other. Back on the bus a little while later, I scrolled through my phone and heard Harper and Cassidy laughing and recording an interview. Their joy was contagious and I couldn't help but smile along with them.

The next morning, I was jolted awake by Harper's excited whispers. "Willow, wake up," she whispered shouted.

"What's going on?" I mumbled, rubbing my eyes.

"Cassidy's famous," Harper announced with glee.

Cassidy laughed. "What she meant was, people really liked the interview I did with Harper. They're asking for more. Do you want to be next?"

Still groggy, I blinked at her. "Really? Like, a behind-the-scenes tour diary?" The idea intrigued me, and I felt a spark of excitement.

"Count me in. This could be fun—and good exposure," I said, my creative mind already whirring with possibilities.

As the bus rumbled along the highway, I found myself seated across from Cassidy, with Harper holding the phone steady, her face partially hidden by the oversized sweatshirt she hadn't bothered to change out of yet. The cramped space was alive with energy, the soft hum of tires on asphalt a rhythmic backdrop to the impromptu interview.

"Let's start with the basics," Cassidy said, a mischievous smile tugging at her lips. "Tell us about Willow Gracin—the journey from small-town bars to the big stage."

I shifted in my seat, leaning back slightly as I considered her question. "Well," I began, "I started playing in dive bars when I was barely old enough to get in. I'd play for tips and free sodas. Back then, I'd dream about getting a break, but it always felt like something that happened to other people, you know?"

Cassidy nodded, her expression encouraging. Harper, from behind the camera, mouthed, "Awww."

"But everything changed with the show," I continued, my voice softening. "It was scary putting myself out there like that, but it taught me that maybe I wasn't chasing a pipe dream after all."

"Definitely not a pipe dream," Harper chimed in, "You crushed it, girl."

I laughed, shaking my head. "Thanks. I guess the whole thing still feels surreal."

Cassidy leaned forward, her eyes sparkling with mischief. "Let's lighten the mood a bit. There was this commercial shoot you and Austin did—something about an engagement scene at the botanical garden?"

Immediately, my cheeks flushed, and I groaned in mock protest. "Oh, that was a disaster in the best possible way."

"Yes, the garden shoot," Cassidy said, her grin widening. "Don't hold back. The people need to know."

The memory hit me like a wave, and I couldn't help the smile that broke across my face. "Okay," I said, holding up my hands. "We were supposed to be this madly in love couple, right in the middle of this picturesque scene with flowers everywhere, getting engaged."

Harper adjusted the phone, ready to catch every word. "This is gold," she muttered.

I took a deep breath, the laughter already bubbling up. "Austin, bless him, he's cute but apparently not the most coordinated guy. So, he's down on one knee, and the director's like, 'Action!' He reaches into his pocket to get the ring, and it's stuck. Like, really stuck because," I paused, biting back a laugh, "well, we've all seen his bluejeans."

The bus echoed with giggles. Harper, hovering just out of frame, was trying—and failing—to stifle her laughter.

Cassidy smirked. "So, then what happened?"

Laughing and wiping tears from my eyes I finally managed to say, "When he finally gets it out, he's so flustered that he fumbles and—sploosh!—right into the koi pond. The ring, not Austin."

Harper and Cassidy burst into laughter, and I had to wait for the giggles to die down before continuing. "The look on his face was this mix of horror and disbelief. And me? I'm trying to stay in character, looking lovingly into his eyes while internally I'm screaming, 'Did that just really happen?' Just before I lost it."

Harper nearly dropped the phone, and Cassidy bit her lip, trying to hold herself together.

Cassidy managed to ask, her voice high-pitched with amusement, "What did you do?"

"The crew had to fish it out, and we did another take, but nothing beats the genuine shock of that first shot. Needless to say, that take didn't make the final cut, but it deserved its own highlight reel."

By this point, we were all practically in tears. "The director wasn't thrilled," I added, grinning. "But honestly? That first take was pure comedy gold."

Harper wiped at her eyes, still giggling. "I swear, I would've paid good money to see that."

"It's one of my favorite memories," I admitted, the laughter subsiding into a warm glow. "I mean, sure, it was a total disaster, but it was our disaster. And I wouldn't trade it for anything."

Cassidy reached over and lightly tapped my hand. "That's what makes it great. It's real, and people love real."

As the bus quieted down, Cassidy stopped recording, and we all shared one of those lingering moments where laughter turned into nostalgia. Harper turned the phone toward me, showing the playback, and we watched ourselves laughing, the memory immortalized.

But as the chatter shifted to other stories, I couldn't help but think about what I'd said. It really was one of my favorite memories—not just because it was funny, but because it was ours. One of those chaotic, ridiculous moments that somehow stitched two people closer without trying.

I wasn't sure what that said about us now. But I knew it meant something.

A short while later the bus was rolling up to a diner where we shuffled off the bus for breakfast. Austin and Levi were already inside saving seats for Harper and me. Nash and Cassidy walked in together after the rest of us.

As we settled in and placed our orders, the conversation naturally flowed to the interviews. I told everyone about the interview I had done with Cassidy and how Harper's had blown up overnight.

"Cassidy is really good at it, too" I said, smiling at her down the table. Her cheeks turned pink.

Levi hollered down the table to Cassidy, "Hey, I'll do an interview with you too!"

Austin chimed in, leaning forward with a grin. "For the record, I did apologize for the koi pond fiasco about a hundred times. I probably still owe those poor fish an apology. Probably thought I'd proposed then took it back. And count me in for an interview."

The table filled with chatter and laughter, the excitement palpable. We finished breakfast, and with a couple of hours of free time on our hands, we decided to hang out at the park across from the diner.

The morning air was just warm enough to kiss my skin, the sun stretching lazily across the park as if it, too, was in no rush to let the day move forward. Laughter echoed as Austin and Levi turned orange juggling into some kind of Olympic sport.

The concentration on their faces, mixed with the outcome of fruit scattering in every direction, was hilarious. I watched as Austin caught one mid-spin and bowed dramatically, a proud smile lighting up his face before Levi launched one straight at his head.

Everyone roared with laughter, the sound filling the sunny morning air.

Austin laughed, too, stumbling back a little, then locked eyes with me across the chaos. And I swear—for just a second—the whole world slowed down.

He tossed the orange back at Levi before taking a seat next to me at the picnic table. We sat with our backs against the table, our knees brushing slightly as we watched the rest of the group goof off with Frisbees and oranges. It was a moment you wished you could bottle and keep forever.

"You know," I mused, a wry smile playing on my lips, "this reminds me of the chaos of those early days on the show. Remember when the smoke machine set off the fire alarm during Sawyer's rehearsal?"

The laughter in his reply pulled a grin from me before I even opened my eyes again. "Yeah, that was hilarious."

"I never thought I'd say this, but I actually miss those days. It feels like it was so long ago but it wasn't really, you know?"

As we sat there, a gentle breeze stirred the air, and a leaf floated down, landing softly in my hair. Austin reached for it before I even noticed. His fingers brushed through a lock near my ear, careful, almost reverent.

When our eyes met, it was like all the noise around us vanished. His hand dropped slowly, the leaf resting between his fingers. But he didn't pull away.

I could see it in his face—he wanted to say something. Just as he started to speak—

"Hey, everyone! Time to get back on the buses!"

The moment snapped like a branch underfoot. He blinked, stepping back. The leaf twirled between his fingers again, but whatever he'd been about to say was buried now.

"Guess we'd better go," he said.

"Yeah," I replied, but the word barely made it past the lump in my throat.

As I walked behind him, I couldn't stop watching the way he held that leaf. Twirling it, turning it over.

I didn't know what he'd been about to say. But I knew I would've remembered it for the rest of my life.

Chapter 23

Austin

As I pulled the leaf from Willow's hair, our eyes locked, and I felt that familiar pull. I almost kissed her—again. It wasn't the first time, and I was sure it wouldn't be the last. But it should be. With several weeks left of close quarters on this tour, I couldn't afford to complicate things.

We made our way back to the buses, our almost-moment hanging between us like a song left unfinished. During the day we could ride on whichever bus we wanted to, while at night we were divided, guys and girls. For that, I was grateful because a bus full of guys for hours on end could get rowdy.

Once we were on the road, Kensi handed out the schedules for the upcoming days. Willow and I were slated to be the guest music act on a popular late-night talk show in two days.

"What are we singing?" Willow asked Kensi as she scanned the schedule.

"It's your choice," Kensi replied with a smile.

"Can it be an original?" I asked, excitement bubbling up at the thought.

"I'll run it by the producers and get back to you," Kensi said, already pulling out her phone to make the call.

A few hours later, Kensi messaged us both with a thumbs-up and *You're good to go with an original.*

Willow and I exchanged grins, the kind of grin that said we both knew exactly which song we wanted. I pulled out my notebook, and she grabbed her guitar, flipping to the song we'd written months ago, *Maybe One Day*.

As we strummed through the opening chords, I watched her lips move silently, mouthing the lyrics. The words hit differently now, like they'd grown sharper and more real with time.

"You sure about this one?" she asked softly, her fingers brushing the page.

I nodded, my gaze lingering on hers. "It's the one."

She blinked at me, her expression unreadable, before nodding back. "Okay," she said quietly. "Let's do it."

The day before the performance, we rehearsed until we could play it in our sleep, though every time we ran through it, I found something new in her voice, something raw that made my chest ache.

The afternoon of the show taping as we stood backstage waiting for our cue, my heart raced. The host's voice boomed through the studio speakers. "Austin Blake and Willow Gracin, two of America's favorites from the reality show *Real American Country*, are here tonight to sing an original they call *Maybe One Day*."

The applause thundered as we stepped onto the stage. The lights were blinding, the audience a sea of shadows. I only saw her. Willow. She glanced at me briefly before we began, and in that fleeting moment, I felt the connection between us snap into place, stronger than ever.

The opening chords echoed through the studio, and as we sang, the words seemed to take on a life of their own:

> We keep missing each other like ships in the night,
> Two hearts out of sync, never getting it right,

I'm reaching out when you're letting go,
Feels like love's a dance we'll never know.

Every line felt like a confession. Every time I sang that lyric—*I'm reaching out when you're letting go*—I wasn't sure if it was about the past or the future.

Or both.

We were giving the audience a love story.

But for me, it wasn't fiction.

And if the way Willow's voice cracked just slightly on the last verse meant anything, I wasn't sure it was fiction for her either. She looked so at ease, so beautiful under the lights, but there was a flicker in her eyes that mirrored the ache in mine. Did she feel it, too? Or was I reading too much into things?

The crowd erupted as we hit the final note, their applause filling every corner of the studio. The host joined us on stage, his grin wide and playful.

"That was incredible," he said. "So, is there something between the two of you, or are you the two hearts out of sync?" he teased, earning laughter from the audience.

I opened my mouth to answer, but Willow beat me to it. "We're just great friends," she said smoothly, her eyes sparkling with mischief.

The crowd laughed. The host grinned. And the moment moved on.

But for me? It didn't.

Those two little words pinged around in my mind completely unhinged.

Just friends.

That wasn't what the song felt like.

That wasn't what singing with her felt like.

The host laughed, clearly satisfied with her answer. "Well, whatever it is, you two make a great team."

The host grinned and sent the show to commercial, the audience still applauding. He turned to us again, his expression earnest. "I'd love to have you both on again sometime."

"Thank you," I said as Willow nodded in agreement. "We'd love to come back."

As we headed backstage, the adrenaline still coursing through my veins, I couldn't shake the weight of the song or the host's question. We're just great friends. The words felt hollow, like a chord played just slightly out of tune.

It was while I was waiting for Willow—who had ducked into the restroom to wash off her stage makeup—that the idea struck. The show must go on, and I had a very clear picture of what that could look like. It involved more stages, more songs, and Willow standing beside me for every single one. And maybe even stealing kisses before hitting the stage.

It was that last thought that sealed it for me. I wanted Willow. Not just her voice but her heart.

When she finally emerged, looking refreshed and more like herself, I hesitated. The words felt too big, too soon. But as we rode back to the buses, the city lights reflecting in her eyes, I couldn't stop myself.

"Do you remember that backup plan we talked about a few months ago?" I asked, trying to keep my tone casual.

Willow turned to me, curiosity flickering in her gaze. "The one where we joked about going on the road?"

I nodded, my grip tightening on the notebook in my lap. "Would you actually consider it? I mean, we're so good together, Willow. We've got this chemistry on stage, and off..."

She looked at me, studied me.

"Are you serious?" she asked softly.

"Dead serious," I said. "I think we could make something amazing happen if we took that leap."

My heart pounded in my ears the entire time I said it.

And still, I tried to play it cool, like this was just a fun idea.

Like it wasn't me laying everything I felt on the table without actually saying it.

But when she looked at me with those wide green eyes—excitement flickering just behind the hesitation—I knew she wanted it, too.

Her gaze shifted back to the window, her expression thoughtful. "It's tempting, Austin. Really tempting. But there's so much to consider."

"I know," I interrupted gently. "But think about it. Just think about it. We've got something special, and it could be more than just a backup plan."

She turned back to me, and this time, her smile was tinged with something deeper, something real. "I'll think about it," she said, her voice barely above a whisper. "I promise."

As we stepped out of the car and walked toward the buses, she walked beside me, close enough to brush shoulders.

I wanted to reach for her hand.

I didn't.

Not yet.

But maybe one day.

Chapter 24

Willow

The concert was electric. The energy of the crowd was like a live current surging through the venue, and every song we performed felt like a shared moment between us and the audience. But tonight, it wasn't just the crowd or the lights or the music that made it special—it was Austin. Every time our voices harmonized, every time our eyes met, it felt like we were sharing something beyond the performance.

By the time we reached the final encore, I glanced over, and he was already looking at me. That smile and the wink that may as well have been a flaming arrow to my chest? It felt like we were mid-conversation without saying a single word. Like the moment had its own pulse. This could be our life, I thought. Long nights on stage, shared laughter in dressing rooms, harmony in more ways than one.

The idea was exhilarating. And terrifying.

After the show, the usual chaos of packing up and loading out ensued, but my thoughts were miles away. Back on the bus, everyone was buzzing with leftover adrenaline. Cassidy and Harper were laughing over some inside joke in their corner, Savannah and Stella Mae were entrenched in whatever was on their phone screens.

The growing camaraderie on this tour was something I hadn't expected to love so much, and yet it was one of my favorite parts of this entire experience.

But despite the noise and the laughter around me, I couldn't seem to quiet my own thoughts. Austin's idea—the idea of us going on the road together after the tour—had taken root in my mind, and no matter how I tried to focus on anything else, it was there, growing.

Sleep was a lost cause. The bus rocked gently as it rumbled down some nameless stretch of highway, and I stayed tucked in my bunk, the quiet hum of the tires and occasional burst of muffled giggles from up front serving as my soundtrack. I cracked open my notebook, the cover bent from use, the edges frayed from late nights just like this. Each song was a timestamp. Each lyric a breadcrumb that led back to where it all started.

My pen hovered over a blank page, but I didn't write anything. Instead, I found myself staring at the song I'd played the day I met Mitch Haynes, the producer who had pulled me aside and changed my life with just one conversation.

Maybe Mitch could help again. Maybe he'd have thoughts about Austin's idea. He'd told me to reach out once things settled, but, could I reach out now? Would that be too presumptuous?

The adrenaline from the day finally began to fade, and as my eyes grew heavy, I rested my head against the wall of my bunk, the notebook still in my lap. My last thought before drifting off was a wish that morning would hurry up and arrive.

The next morning, the bus was quieter than usual. Most of the group had the morning free, and those who weren't doing publicity opted for some much-needed downtime. Austin suggested we check out a nearby café for breakfast.

"It's just a ten-minute walk," he said, showing me the map on his phone. "Come on, a little fresh air and good coffee sounds like a perfect start to the day."

He wasn't wrong. The morning air was cool, the city still stretching itself awake as we wandered through its streets. The conversation between us was easy—laughing about Levi's failed attempt to skateboard blindfolded the other day, recounting moments from last night's show, and debating whether the audience in Denver had been louder than the one in Vegas. But beneath the lighthearted chatter, there was a tension. The kind that comes when something important is hanging in the air, waiting to be addressed.

The café was a small, charming spot tucked into a quiet corner. We found a seat by the window and ordered breakfast.

Austin leaned forward slightly, resting his elbows on the table as he studied me. "How are you feeling after last night?"

I smiled, sipping my coffee. "Good. Still riding the high from all of it."

He nodded, his expression thoughtful. After a beat, he lowered his voice. "So, have you given it any more thought?"

I knew what he meant immediately. I set my mug down and glanced out the window, gathering my thoughts. "I have," I said slowly. "And honestly, Austin, the idea of going on the road together —just the two of us—is incredible. But it's also a lot. What if it doesn't work out? What if we ruin what we have?"

Then he asked, quietly, "What do we have, Willow?"

The question hung between us, heavier than anything we'd voiced before. My heart jumped, and my mind scrambled. I liked him —a lot—but saying it out loud felt like stepping off a cliff. What if I fell and he wasn't there?

I met his eyes, steady but careful. "We have something great. Chemistry, friendship, a connection that's easy and real." I paused, searching for the words. "But adding business? That's a whole different story. What if we ruin what we have?"

His hand found mine across the table, a gentle weight. "I get it," he said softly. "It's a big risk. But Willow, what if it does work out? What if it's the best decision we ever make?"

His words stretched between us, and I felt the weight of the moment. Life was full of risks, and the thought of creating something amazing with Austin—of experiencing new adventures together—was practically impossible to ignore.

"Okay," I said finally, meeting his gaze. "Let's do it."

His face lit up, a mixture of relief and excitement breaking through. "Really?"

"Really," I confirmed, smiling. "But we need to plan it out. We need to do this right."

The rest of breakfast was a blur of scribbled ideas on blank pages and dreaming aloud about what this next chapter could look like. By the time we left the café, I felt more confident about our decision. The excitement in Austin's eyes mirrored my own, and for the first time in a long time, I felt like the future was wide open.

Back on the bus later that evening, I decided to email Mitch Haynes. I attached the video of Austin and me singing *Maybe One Day* on the late-night talk show, along with a brief note explaining our idea. To my surprise, he replied almost immediately.

"Let's talk," his email read. "Call me tomorrow."

I stared at the screen, my heart pounding. This was happening. This was really happening.

Over the next month and a half, our dynamic shifted in ways neither of us could ignore. The laughter still came, the music still flowed, but there was a new weight to every glance, every brush of skin, every word left dangling in the air.

Our relationship, while still grounded in friendship, started to take on a different form. It became more cautious, more deliberate. It wasn't like we weren't still laughing together or finding joy in the music. We were. But there was an unspoken understanding between us now, one that seemed to say: I might have feelings, but we can't afford to mess this up.

Planning our future meant daydreaming aloud, scribbling ideas on scraps of paper during bus rides, and sharing late-night talks about where we saw this partnership going. But the logistics—the real decisions—would have to wait until after the tour and that meeting with Mitch. For now, all we had were dreams.

Big ones.

But it wasn't easy to stay in that safe lane, not when the feelings between us lingered, heavy and unspoken, just under the surface.

There were moments that made it impossible to ignore the spark between us. Like after last night's performance. I'd asked a simple question, and it had almost ended with me throwing every caution to the wind.

We were leaving the stage, three other members of the cast shuffled past us and production crew members hustled in every direction.

"Think that last song landed okay?" I asked, as we made our way to the green room, my voice softer than I intended.

Austin shifted his guitar to rest against his back and glanced at me, his lips curving into a half-smile. "Definitely. The crowd seemed into it. You nailed that high note, by the way."

I chuckled, tucking a strand of hair behind my ear. "Thanks. I was worried I'd flub it like I did in rehearsal which made me nervous. And you know how I get when I'm nervous."

He stopped walking and turned to face me, his lopsided grin warming my heart. "You? Nervous? Nah. You're the most fearless person I know."

The compliment caught me off guard, and I felt heat rise to my cheeks. "I don't know about that, but, thanks."

He looked at me then, really looked, and the air between us crackled. His gaze lingered on my face, tracing the curve of my cheek, the line of my jaw, before dropping to my mouth. A faint flush crept up his neck, and he cleared his throat, leaning back slightly.

"Willow," he started, then stopped, his brow furrowing.

Silence stretched between us, heavy and loaded. The inches separating us felt like miles, and yet, at the same time, they were too much. I could feel the heat of him, the faint scent of leather from his guitar strap and sweat mixing with the earthy aroma of his cologne.

"What?" I asked, my voice barely audible.

He hesitated, his fingers tightening on the guitar. "Uh... never mind. It's nothing."

But it wasn't nothing. It was everything. The way he'd leaned in just slightly, the way his voice had dropped, the way he'd looked at me like I was the only thing in the world that mattered—it all screamed that there was more he wanted to say, more he wanted to do.

I swallowed hard, my pulse racing. "If there's something on your mind, you can tell me. You know that, right?"

He nodded, but his jaw clenched like he was holding himself back. "Yeah, I know."

I wanted to press him, to push past the walls we'd built around ourselves. But I didn't. Instead, I let the moment pass, the tension easing but never fully dissipating.

Later, lying in my bunk, I replayed that exchange over and over in my mind. The way his voice had softened when he said my name, the way he'd looked at me like I was his entire world. What would've happened if I'd pushed? If I'd closed that gap?

I started noticing the space between us differently.

The inches we didn't close.

The pauses that lasted just a beat too long.

We weren't just friends anymore. We were pretending to be.

I knew that the feelings between us—whatever they were—had the power to complicate everything. So I didn't cross that line. I stayed in the safe zone, choosing our new partnership and the music over whatever might've been brewing between us.

But that didn't mean it was easy.

As much as I wanted to shove the intrusive thoughts away, I couldn't help but daydream about what it would be like if we let ourselves have more. If we weren't holding back. If we let the "what if" become reality.

And I hated how vivid the daydreams had become. They weren't vague anymore—they were specific.

I could see his hand in mine. Hear the way he'd sigh my name when we finally kissed.

The more I thought about it, the more I tried to put walls around my heart and space between us.

Austin seemed to be pulling back too. He wasn't distant, exactly. He was still kind and attentive and every bit as wonderful as he'd always been. But there was a carefulness to him more and more, a deliberate restraint in the way he moved around me.

Like he was holding back, too.

And that made it harder. Because if he did feel the same way, if this wasn't just one-sided, then what were we doing? Why weren't we saying it? Why weren't we doing something about it?

The answer was simple.

Because it wasn't just us anymore. It wasn't just two people with big feelings trying to figure out what they wanted.

But it was also bigger than that.

There was the music. The dream we were building together.

The stakes felt impossibly high, and neither of us wanted to risk ruining it.

So we didn't.

Instead, we poured everything into the music. The songs we wrote seemed to say all the things we couldn't. Every harmony, every lyric, every chord held pieces of the truth we weren't ready to say out loud.

It was both comforting and maddening to know that the music held the feelings we were too scared to face.

And as the weeks rolled by, I felt myself balancing on a knife's edge between hope and fear. Hope that one day, we'd find a way to say everything the music was already screaming for us. Fear that we never would.

But even with that fear, even with all the "what-ifs" and "almosts", I couldn't bring myself to regret any of it.

Because no matter what happened next, those songs—and what they meant—would always be ours.

And maybe someday, when the time was right, we'd find the courage to cross that line.

But until then, I'd hold on to the music and my dreams. Those at least ended with a "happily ever after".

Chapter 25

Austin

The morning after the final Nashville show, Willow and I walked into Mitch Haynes' office, and it hit me—this wasn't just a meeting. It was a turning point. The walls were covered with gold and platinum records, photographs of Mitch shaking hands with legends, and framed magazine covers that felt like glimpses of a life I'd always wanted but never let myself fully believe I could have.

Mitch greeted us with his trademark enthusiasm, his handshake firm and his smile wide. "Willow! Austin! So glad you could make it," he said, ushering us into chairs that felt too plush for my nerves. "I've been watching the video you sent me on loop. You two are amazing."

His words landed like a punch to the gut—not because they hurt, but because they were the kind of validation I'd been chasing for years. I glanced at Willow, who was perched on the edge of her seat, her notebook already open. She smiled at Mitch's praise, but I caught the tiniest flicker of nerves in her expression.

And there it was again. That pull. That ache I'd been trying so hard to ignore.

We dove into the conversation, Mitch leading us through the nuts and bolts of what a joint venture would look like. He was a pro, breaking down the business side with a precision and enthusiasm. The way he talked about branding, touring, and album strategy, it was like he could see the future we were building before we could even imagine it ourselves.

Willow, of course, was sharp as ever, asking all the right questions. She'd always had this quiet confidence, this way of commanding a room without even trying. I tried to focus on the discussion, but every now and then, my mind wandered—wondering what she was thinking, what she was feeling. Wondering if she felt the same tension I did, the same pull I couldn't seem to escape.

When the meeting wrapped up, Mitch leaned back in his chair, a satisfied smile on his face. "You two are a powerhouse," he said. "I can't wait to see where this takes you."

A powerhouse. I should've felt elated and weightless hearing that. But instead, I felt heavy and grounded—this was real in a way that scared the heck out of me. Willow looked over at me as we stepped into the hallway, her brows still raised from everything Mitch had laid out.

"You okay?" she asked.

I nodded, but the truth was, I wasn't sure. Part of me was thrilled at what we'd just set in motion. And part of me was already wondering how long I could keep pretending that this wasn't more than just music.

As we left his office, my thoughts buzzed with possibility. But underneath the excitement, there was a terrifying sense that everything was about to change.

That change hit faster than I expected.

To make sure we didn't get blindsided by any of the legalities, Willow's brother, Caleb, stepped in like a knight in shining armor. He connected us with a law school friend who agreed to become our agent, and just like that, the pieces started falling into place.

It should've felt like a dream come true. And in a way, it did. But the reality was more complicated.

Within a month, I'd packed up my life and moved to Nashville. It wasn't a snap decision—I'd thought it through, weighed my options, and had countless conversations with my family.

"You know we'll support you no matter what," my mom had said over the phone, her voice warm but tinged with sadness.

I'd gone home to pack my things, my family hovering, offering their support.

My mom handed me a stack of shirts from a drawer. "We're proud of you, Austin. But you're going to be so far away."

"I know, Mom. This is—this is where the next step is. This is the only way I can make it work."

"You've always been a dreamer," my dad had chimed in, his voice steady and reassuring. "But don't forget—dreams are easier to chase when you've got a good foundation. Just remember to keep your feet on the ground, son."

Connor, on the other hand, had just nodded when I told him, then asked, "Have you told her?"

"It's not just about her," I'd shot back, though the words felt hollow even as I said them. "This is about the music. About the opportunity."

"OK," Connor had said, leaning back in my desk chair.

"I'll be your best man," he said, dead serious, though to most it would sound more deadpan.

"We're not getting married," I snapped. Not because the idea didn't appeal to me. If I was being honest, I'd thought about what a future would look like with Willow. But those kinds of thoughts were not productive. In fact, they could jeopardize everything we were working toward.

"Yet," he stated matter-of-factly.

A few days later, I'd loaded the last box into the truck, and driven away from the only home I'd ever known. Their support meant everything, but it didn't make leaving any easier. And their words stayed with me long after I'd said goodbye.

In the end, though, there was no other choice. This was where I needed to be. Where Willow was.

She'd offered, casually, that we could find a place together to save money. Logistically, it made sense. Creatively, too. But emotionally? It would've wrecked me. Waking up and seeing her in the kitchen in her pajamas, humming while she made coffee? I'd be done for. So I thanked her, told her I already had a lead, and found a place five blocks away. The distance between our apartments was my safety net.

Every day with Willow was already a test of my resolve. Being near her, writing with her, laughing with her—it was like balancing on a tightrope. One wrong move, one slip, and everything we'd built and were building could come crashing down.

A week after officially signing the contract, we were in the studio, surrounded by the buzz of creativity. Producers, sound engineers, and session musicians buzzed around us, their energy infectious.

But even in the middle of all the chaos, it was Willow who grounded me. Watching her work was like watching magic. She had this way of pouring her soul into every note, every lyric, every take. And I couldn't stop myself from watching her, from feeling this overwhelming sense of awe.

The first time I heard her sing the bridge of our new song in studio playback, I actually forgot to breathe. She was in the sound booth, eyes closed, voice raw and stripped bare. I knew the song. I'd written half of it. But in her voice, it sounded like something else entirely. Like a confession.

My hands stayed buried in the pockets of my hoodie, clenched into fists. Because if I didn't hold on to something, I was going to say it. I was going to tell her I was in love with her.

The more time we spent together, the harder it became to keep my feelings at bay.

There were moments—so many moments—when I wanted to tell her. When I wanted to let all the emotions I'd been bottling up come spilling out. Like the night we stayed in the studio until 2 a.m., laughing over a lyric that wouldn't cooperate. Or the morning she showed up with coffee and that soft, sleepy smile that made my chest ache.

But every time, I stopped myself.

Because as much as I wanted more with her, I wouldn't risk it.

One night, after a particularly grueling day of publicity and rehearsals, I found myself sitting alone in my apartment.

The silence hit harder than usual that night. After the adrenaline of rehearsals and the high of the studio, my apartment felt sterile. Empty. No music. No Willow's laugh echoing off the walls. Just me, a takeout box I wasn't eating, and a guitar.

I pulled out my guitar, strumming absentmindedly as my mind obsessed over Willow. To the way her laugh lit up a room. To the way she'd scribble furiously in her notebook, her brow furrowed in concentration. To the way she'd looked at me after the late-night talk show all those months ago.

My fingers moved instinctively over the strings, and before I even knew what I was doing, the words came.

> *Every mile it takes, every note I play,*
> *Brings me closer, but you're still so far away.*
> *I see you in the crowd, but you won't meet my eyes,*
> *We're standing in the spotlight, under separate skies.*

The words hung in the air, raw and unpolished. They felt too honest, too vulnerable. I set the guitar down, running a hand through my hair.

What was I doing? Why was I even letting myself feel this way when I knew we couldn't afford to mess things up?

Despite everything swirling around us—the interviews, the photoshoots, the deadlines—it felt like we were simply holding our breath so as not to risk this house of cards we were stacking.

And maybe that was the hardest part. Knowing that the only

thing standing between us and the possibility of something more was the fear of what might happen if it didn't work out.

Every time she looked at me from across a mic, I wondered what would happen if I said it. Just once. If I whispered "I love you" in the space between harmonies, would she say it back? Or would I lose her?

And that's the part that gutted me. Because I could lose the music. I could lose the dream. But I didn't think I could survive losing her.

So, I kept kept singing and kept the rest to myself.

Chapter 26

Willow

Saying goodbye to my family and to Gemma this time had been harder than I'd expected. Probably because this time, I didn't have a return date in mind.

Gemma had always been my rock, my grounding force. She was my sounding board for everything—wardrobe choices, whether spending two hundred dollars on an ergonomic pillow was a good investment [side note: it is], even my doubts about moving to Nashville. And now, I was leaving her behind.

Our last night in the apartment felt surreal. I'd apologized at least five times as we packed the last of my things into boxes.

"Willow, it's not a hardship to take the apartment on by myself," she insisted, her tone light but firm, though I could see the sadness she was trying to hide. "I might look for another roommate, but honestly, I think I'll enjoy living alone for a bit. Who knows, I might even take up knitting."

I laughed, despite the lump in my throat. "Just promise you won't turn into a crazy cat lady, okay?"

Gemma rolled her eyes but reached over and flicked the tip of my braid like she'd done since freshman year. "Only if you promise not to become a tortured songwriter who wears sunglasses indoors and talks about 'vibes' all the time."

I smiled, but it felt wobbly. "No promises."

She sat with me on the floor after the boxes were taped shut, her knees pulled up to her chest.

"You love him, don't you?"

I didn't answer right away. Just stared at the spot on the rug where we'd spilled wine one night and it formed a stain that looked suspiciously like a well-defined human backside. We'd cried laughing, and was intensified when the stain refused to come up. I smiled at the memory before answering.

"Yeah," I said with a sigh. "But that's not the point. The point is the music."

Gemma didn't say anything for a while after that. She just bumped her shoulder into mine and let the silence settle like an old friend. Her lips twitched into a knowing smile.

"You know it's obvious he has feelings for you too, right?"

A pang hit my chest, but I forced a smile. "Sometimes it feels that way, but we've worked so hard to get here. I really do enjoy having Austin as a friend and writing partner. I don't want to lose that."

Gemma didn't push further, but the conversation stayed with me long after I hugged her goodbye and boarded the plane to Nashville.

Caleb, of course, had been thrilled when I asked if he'd represent Austin and me. He had this way of exuding confidence that made me feel like we were untouchable with him in our corner.

"Don't worry," he'd said when I asked about the legal logistics. "I'll handle it. In fact, I'll introduce you to Emma. She's a friend from law school who manages talent now. She's a shark, but the good kind. You're going to love her."

He wasn't wrong.

From the moment I met Emma, I was smitten. She was like the perfect blend of tough and kind, like biting into a croissant that was all crisp layers on the outside but soft and buttery on the inside. She had a warmth about her, but you could tell she didn't suffer fools. I found myself wondering how I could get Caleb to marry her so I could officially have her as a sister.

I'd made the mistake of saying that last part out loud. Caleb warned me to tread lightly. "Emma owes me a favor, but if you tell her that, she'll probably charge you double."

There was definitely a story there, but with everything moving at breakneck speed, I didn't have the mental space to dig deeper.

My dad, who had been the most skeptical about my decision to pursue music, had become my biggest supporter.

When he met Austin for the first time, he gave him a once-over that felt like a silent cross-examination. But within ten minutes, they were laughing about fishing stories, and my dad slapped him on the back like they'd been friends for years.

"If Austin gives you any problems, just let me know," Dad had said with a wink. "I know how to convince a jury of a person's innocence."

I rolled my eyes, laughing. "Thanks, Dad. I'll keep that in mind."

My mom, though, had been softer about the whole thing. She hugged me tightly the night before I left and said, "I'll help you decorate your new apartment." Her eyes shimmered with unshed tears, but her voice was steady. "Just tell me when you're ready for me to come visit."

"Give me a couple of weeks to get adjusted," I said, hugging her back. "Then we'll make a plan."

And now, in the quiet of my new Nashville apartment, I found myself alone with my thoughts and memories.

Outside, Nashville thrummed with life—neon lights blinking, laughter floating up from the sidewalk cafés below. Inside, it was quiet enough to hear my own heartbeat. I sat on the edge of the bed, the apartment still half-furnished, with only takeout containers and unopened boxes for company. The silence didn't feel empty, exactly. It felt like a question I hadn't figured out how to answer yet.

My guitar rested against the wall, a familiar presence. I picked it up, the weight of it grounding me.

I let my fingers fall into old patterns first, muscle memory leading the way. But it wasn't long before the melody changed. Slowed. Shifted. Took on that ache I'd been keeping hidden between rib bones and "we're just friends" reassurances. I didn't cry. But I felt it—this quiet ache blooming behind my ribs, stretching all the way to the back of my throat.

The words didn't come right away. They never did. But I let the music guide me, let my thoughts of Austin thread through the notes.

I thought of the way he lit up when he played, the way he always seemed to know exactly how to complement my lyrics with his harmonies. I thought of the way he looked at me often, like he was trying to tell me something without saying a word.

The words that emerged were laced with longing and hope, a reflection of the emotions swirling inside me.

> Every note, every line,
> Pulls me closer, but you're still not mine.
> We're dancing on the edge, afraid to fall,
> But maybe one day, we'll have it all.

I let the final chord linger, the sound filling the empty room.
Whatever happened, I knew I was ready to face it.
I didn't want to fall.
But I already had.

Chapter 27

Willow

It had been a year since Nashville became home—and on paper, everything sparkled. Platinum album, late-night appearances, magazine covers, sold-out shows. But paper doesn't tell the truth. The truth was pacing my living room in worn boots and a stormy stare, and the storm had my name on it.

Austin was pacing my living room, boots thudding against the hardwood floor with each agitated step, fuming about a date I hadn't even wanted to go on.

"I can't believe you agreed to this," Austin snapped, spinning on his heel like he couldn't decide whether to stay or bolt.

I crossed my arms, the tension building between us like a pulled string ready to snap. "It's a date, Austin. A fake one. For press. You know this."

"A date with *Jace freaking Buchanan*," he spat. "That guy takes more selfies than there are song credits on his last album. And that's a lot. Do you know how this'll look?"

"To who?" I snapped. "To fans? To the media? Or to you?"

His mouth opened, then clamped shut, like he was refusing to acknowledge the truth behind the question.

"Austin," I said, trying to keep my voice calm even as frustration simmered just beneath the surface. "It's just a publicity thing. Emma thought it would be good exposure leading up to the tour. It doesn't mean anything."

"Doesn't mean anything?" he repeated, his voice sharp with disbelief. "Willow, do you know this guy's reputation? The guy is a walking cliché with a cowboy hat, curious hands, and a wandering eye."

I sighed, crossing my arms over my chest. "This isn't about Jace. This is about promoting the band, the music. You know, the thing we've spent the last year building together? I thought that's what you wanted."

"Not if it means selling you out to some over-hyped player for the sake of a few headlines!" he shot back, his voice rising. "I won't stand for that, Willow."

My temper flared at his words. "Well, it's a good thing it's not your call then," I snapped, taking a step closer to him. "I'm a grown woman, Austin. You don't get to decide who I 'sell myself out' to."

He flinched, his jaw tightening as though I'd slapped him. For a moment, I thought he might yell, but instead, he let out a bitter laugh and dragged a hand through his hair. "You know what? Fine. Do whatever you want. But don't expect me to sit back and smile while you let Emma and Mitch turn you into some kind of tabloid storyline."

"That's rich," I scoffed, "coming from the guy who just gave the world a hard look at his abs and denim on the cover of Rolling Stone," I shot back, my voice dripping with sarcasm.

His eyes darkened, his hands curling into fists again. "That was different."

"Oh, was it?" I demanded, stepping even closer. My heart was pounding, and I knew I was dangerously close to saying something I couldn't take back. "You didn't seem too worried about selling yourself out when you were grinning on that magazine cover, Austin. But the second the spotlight's on me, it's suddenly a problem?"

The tension in the room was unbearable, the air crackling with the kind of heat that made it hard to breathe. For a second, we just stood there, glaring at each other, our chests heaving, our faces flushed with anger.

But beneath the anger, I could feel something else. Something deeper. Something that scared me as much as it thrilled me.

Austin's gaze softened, just slightly, and I saw a flicker of vulnerability in his eyes. "It's not just the date, Willow," he said quietly, his voice rough around the edges. "It's everything. The way our lives have been turned upside down, the constant scrutiny, the pressure to be perfect all the time. I feel like we're losing ourselves in all of this."

My heart ached at the raw honesty in his voice, but before I could respond, he took a step closer, his eyes locking on mine. "And the way things are changing between us..." he trailed off, shaking his head like he couldn't bring himself to finish the sentence.

"Austin," I said softly, reaching for him, but he pulled back before I could touch him.

"I can't do this right now," he muttered, turning away and running a hand through his hair. "I just... I need some air."

He strode toward the door, and before I could stop him, he was gone, the sound of the door slamming behind him echoing through the room.

The second the door slammed, the echo vibrated through the hollowness he'd left behind. I stared at the spot where he'd just been standing. My living room still smelled like his cologne and I hated how much I missed him when he left.

My hands were shaking. Not from fear. From the ache of almost saying everything I've been too afraid to name for almost two years.

I sank down onto the couch, my body trembling from the intensity of the fight. The silence felt deafening, and for the first time in a long time, I felt completely untethered.

Austin and I had always been able to lean on each other, to talk through anything. But lately, it felt like we were speaking different languages. Like we were both holding so much back that we didn't even know how to be honest with each other anymore.

I ran a hand through my hair, my mind spinning. I should be furious with him—for storming out, for trying to control me, for making this so much harder than it needed to be. But all I could feel was the ache of missing him, even though he'd barely been gone five minutes.

I stood up and began pacing, the same way Austin had just moments ago. I couldn't just sit here and let this fester. I needed to find him, to talk to him, to make things right.

Grabbing my keys, I headed out the door and drove in the direction I knew he'd go—to the studio. My hands were shaking on the steering wheel, but I forced myself to focus. Austin was probably holed up in the recording booth, pouring his frustration into his music the way he always did.

When I arrived, his truck was parked outside, and relief washed over me. I took a deep breath and headed inside, my footsteps echoing in the empty hallway.

The studio was quiet, but not peaceful. It felt off. Like a guitar string tuned just a little too tight. Austin sat in the recording booth, shoulders hunched, strumming something I couldn't quite hear.

He didn't look up at first. Just kept playing. A melody I didn't recognize. Something rough. Something jagged.

When he finally met my eyes, I almost wished he hadn't. Because his walls were up. And I was tired of fighting stone.

"What?" he asked, his voice wary.

"I needed to see you," I said, my voice trembling slightly. "I didn't like the way we left things."

He set his guitar aside and stood up, crossing his arms over his chest. "I'm not sure there's anything left to say."

"Please, Austin," I said, taking a step closer. "Just hear me out."

He sighed, his shoulders slumping. "Fine. Say what you need to say."

I hesitated, searching for the right words. "I know you're upset about this publicity date thing, and I get it. But it doesn't mean anything. It's just for the cameras. You and me? We're a team, Austin. Everything else? It's just noise."

He stared at me for a long moment, his jaw tight. "It's not just the date, Willow," he said quietly. "It's the way this whole thing feels so out of control. And the way... the way I feel about you. It's messing with my head."

His words hung in the air, raw and unfiltered, and I felt my heart stop.

"Austin..." I whispered, my voice barely audible.

He shook his head, a bitter laugh escaping his lips. "Forget it. I shouldn't have said that."

But I reached for him, my hand resting on his arm. "No. Don't do that. Don't shut me out."

He looked at me, his eyes filled with a vulnerability I'd never seen before. And for the first time, I realized just how much this was costing him—how much he was holding back, how much he was trying to protect us both.

"I'm not going anywhere, Austin," I said firmly. "We're still us," I said, tears threatening. "And if we keep forgetting that, we'll lose everything anyway."

His shoulders sagged, and he let out a shaky breath. "I hope you're right."

I smiled softly, taking his hand in mine. "I know I am."

He pulled me into a hug. I was fully enveloped, held tightly against his chest where I could feel his heart pounding. And as we stood there, holding on to each other, I knew we'd be OK. We still had a long road ahead of us, but in that moment, I knew we'd find our way.

Chapter 28

Austin

The tabloid pictures sat on my kitchen table like a slap to the face. Willow and Jace Buchanan in a cozy restaurant booth, leaning in close. Jace holding the door of a black SUV open for her, his hand resting far too low on her back as he whispered something that made her laugh.

That laugh was supposed to be mine.

Not mine-mine. Not in a way I had any claim to.

But still.

I knew it intimately. I knew the shape of it. The way it pitched upward right before she lost control, the way it would burst out of her when she didn't mean for it to.

And knowing he got to hear it?

It felt like someone had swapped out my oxygen for a vacuum.

I glared at Jace's smug grin. "This idiot has his paws all over her! And she's just letting him!"

My fist clenched, crumpling the flimsy paper. Rationally, I knew it was a publicity stunt. Willow had told me as much. But rationality didn't stand a chance against the red-hot jealousy coursing through me.

I chucked the tabloid into the trash with a growl, but it didn't make me feel better. Nothing would—not until Jace Buchanan's smug face was out of my head and out of Willow's orbit.

My phone buzzed on the counter, and for a moment, I thought it might be Willow. But no—Connor.

Connor: Saw the pictures. You OK?

I stared at the screen, my thumb hovering over the keyboard. He wasn't one to pay much attention to celebrity gossip, but he had some kind of fascination and even a radar when it came to me and apparently Willow.

Was I OK? No. But I wasn't about to tell him that.

I typed back a quick response.

Me: Yeah, all good.

His reply came almost instantly.

Connor: Liar

I scoffed, tossing my phone down. He wasn't wrong, but I wasn't going to tell him that. Instead, I grabbed a beer from the fridge, hoping the ice-cold liquid could cool the fire raging inside me.

It didn't.

I paced my living room, the beer barely touched, my mind spinning with thoughts of Willow. The late-night songwriting sessions where her laugh melted my exhaustion. The way her green eyes sparkled when inspiration struck. The way she looked at me sometimes—like maybe, she might be feeling everything I was but wouldn't say it.

I picked up my phone, scrolling through an article Emma had sent earlier. There it was again—a photo of Willow and me beaming at each other from the album launch party.

"Austin Blake looks at Willow Gracin like she hung the moon and stars," the caption read. "If only we all had a 'best friend' like that!"

I barked out a bitter laugh, tossing the phone onto the couch. If only they knew.

A sudden knock at the door made me freeze.

"Austin?" Willow's muffled voice came through the wood. "I know you're home. We need to talk."

My stomach dropped. For a second, I thought about pretending I wasn't there. But who was I kidding? Willow knew me too well for that.

I almost didn't open it. I stood with my hand on the knob, forehead pressed against the cool wood, hoping she'd walk away.

But she didn't.

Of course she didn't.

I took a steadying breath and opened the door.

Willow stood there, her arms crossed and a storm brewing in her eyes. "What the heck, Austin? You can't just ignore my calls and texts for three days!"

I leaned against the doorframe, forcing a casualness I didn't feel. "Didn't feel like talking."

Her eyes narrowed. "This is about the dates with Jace, isn't it? I told you—it's just business. It doesn't mean anything."

"Doesn't seem like 'just business' for good ol' Jace," I shot back, unable to keep the bitterness out of my voice. "Looked pretty cozy in those paparazzi pics."

She groaned, throwing up her hands. "Oh, please. It's called acting, Austin. And for the record, Jace is a nice guy but way too high maintenance for me. I like my guys a little less polished."

Her attempt at humor only fueled my frustration. "Right. Because everything about this is just so harmless."

Her face softened, the fire in her eyes dimming slightly. She took a step closer, her voice quieter. "Austin, why are you so upset about this? Just tell me."

I looked away, my throat tightening. Because I was in love with her. Because seeing her with another man—even as a publicity stunt —felt like a knife to the gut.

But I couldn't say that.

"I don't know what you want me to say, Willow," I finally said, my voice rough. "I'm trying to be supportive, but it's not easy watching you with him."

She stared at me, her expression unreadable. Then, in the softest voice, she said, "Then tell me to stop."

My head snapped up, my heart hammering.

She took another step closer, her eyes searching mine. "If this is too much for you, if it's hurting you..."

It was everything I wanted to hear. And I couldn't let myself have it.

She stepped forward again, and I caught the faintest tremble in her fingers.

"Tell me to stop," she whispered. "Just say the words."

And her eyes—wide, glassy, pleading—nearly undid me.

I wanted to. Every cell in my body screamed for me to take the out she was giving me.

But I couldn't take the leap. Not tonight. Not when the stakes were everything.

Not when I was still too scared she'd only catch me halfway.

I forced a shaky smile, stuffing my hands into my pockets. "I can't do that, Wills."

Her face fell, the light in her eyes dimming. She nodded slowly, tears pooling on her lashes. "Okay."

She turned to leave, and panic surged through me. "Willow, wait—"

My voice was barely more than a rasp.

She stilled, but didn't turn around.

I stared at her back, at the way her shoulders rose and fell like she was bracing for something.

My mouth opened. The words formed—

"Don't go."

"Please stay."

"I love you."

—but none of them made it out.

"Goodnight, Austin," she said softly.

And then she was gone.

The door clicked shut behind her, but it felt like she'd slammed it—loud and final.

I sat on the edge of the couch, hands tangled in my hair, heart trying to crawl out of my chest.

One more step. One more breath. That's all it would've taken.

And I'd let her walk away instead.

Because as much as I wanted her, I couldn't risk losing her.

So instead, I sat there in the silence, wondering how long I could keep this up before I finally broke.

Chapter 29

Willow

I drove home in a daze, my mind replaying the conversation with Austin on an endless, torturous loop. His words echoed in my head, taunting me. "I can't do that, Wills."

Why? Why couldn't he? And why did it feel like those words carried the weight of everything he wasn't saying?

By the time I pulled into my driveway, my chest felt like it was wrapped in metal strings, squeezing tighter with every breath. I stumbled out of the car and barely made it inside before the dam broke. Leaning back against the closed door, I sank to the floor, sobs wracking my body.

I hated this. Hated the way he made me feel so desperate, so vulnerable, so exposed. But most of all, I hated the growing distance between us. How had we gone from being the unshakable duo, the friends who could make anything happen together, to this tangled mess of emotions and unspoken words?

With shaking hands, I peeled off my jacket and kicked off my boots, leaving them in a haphazard pile by the door. The silence of my apartment was deafening, the weight of it pressing down on me. I needed something—anything—to drown out the noise in my head.

I padded into the kitchen, yanking open the freezer like it owed me answers. My eyes landed on the pint of cookie dough ice cream tucked in the back. It had been meant for a special occasion, but desperate times called for desperate measures. I grabbed the carton and a spoon, forgoing any semblance of civility. Bowl? Who needed a bowl when your heart was breaking?

The first bite was heaven, the creamy sweetness momentarily soothing the raw edges of my emotions. But by the third spoonful, anger began to simmer beneath the surface.

How dare Austin make me feel this way? How dare he act like he had any claim over who I could or couldn't be seen with?

I stabbed the spoon into the ice cream with unnecessary force, imagining it was Austin's stupid, handsome face. "Screw you, Austin Blake," I muttered around a mouthful of cookie dough. "I don't need you."

The words hung in the air, heavy with bitterness. But even as I said them, I knew they weren't true. I did need him. Needed him in a way that terrified me. And that realization only made me angrier.

The pint was empty before I knew it, and the sugar rush did nothing to quell the storm inside me. Tossing the carton into the trash with a satisfying thunk, I wiped my mouth with the back of my hand and grabbed my phone. There was only one person who could talk me off this ledge.

Gemma answered on the second ring, her voice as warm and familiar as ever. "Hey, babe. What's up?"

"Do you know what's worse than having an almost-empty container of cookie dough ice cream in the freezer?" I asked, my voice tight with frustration.

Gemma chuckled. "Oh, this sounds promising. Hit me."

"Eating the whole thing and still being angry." I flopped onto the couch, staring up at the ceiling like it might hold the answers to all my problems.

"Let me guess," Gemma said, her tone laced with knowing. "This wouldn't have anything to do with a certain set of photos making their way across every tabloid and magazine on the shelf, would it?"

I groaned, covering my face with my free hand. "You saw them."

"Oh, I saw them. You and Jace Buchanan, looking all cozy in that restaurant? His hand taking a little vacay south of the equator? Yeah, everyone's seen them." She paused. "How's Austin handling it?"

"Not well," I admitted, my voice cracking with a mix of anger and sadness. "He showed up here, all pissed off and demanding answers. Like he has any right to be upset about who I'm seen with. And then for three days, he ignored every single one of my calls and texts. And when I confronted him about his silence, he clammed up like all of a sudden, he was out of words."

"Well, can you blame him?" Gemma said gently. "Willow, the man's in love with you but is scared to death."

I sat up straight, my heart lurching in my chest. "No, he's not. We're just friends."

"Right. And I'm secretly an astrophysicist," Gemma deadpanned. "Willow, come on. Anyone with eyes can see it. The question is, when are you going to stop hiding that you feel the same way?"

"It's complicated," I protested weakly, even though the words rang hollow.

"It's only as complicated as you make it," Gemma said, her tone softening. "Look, I get it. You're scared. But what's the alternative? Letting things fester until one of you snaps completely? Or worse— until one of you moves on for real and it's too late?"

Her words hit me like a punch to the gut because they were the exact fears I'd been trying to ignore.

"What if it ruins everything?" I whispered. "Our friendship, our careers, everything we've worked so hard for?"

"And what if it doesn't?" Gemma countered. "What if it's the best thing that's ever happened to both of you? You'll never know unless you take the chance."

I closed my eyes, tears slipping down my cheeks. "I don't know if I can."

"You can," Gemma said firmly. "You're one of the bravest people I know, Willow. You've already risked so much to chase your dreams. Don't you think Austin's worth the same risk?"

I let her words sink in, the weight of them settling in my chest. She was right. Deep down, I knew she was right. But knowing it and acting on it were two very different things.

"Thanks, Gem," I said finally, my voice shaky but sincere. "I don't know what I'd do without you."

"You'd probably still be talking to an empty pint of ice cream," she teased, earning a watery laugh from me. "But seriously, Willow. Whatever you decide, I'm here for you."

We chatted for a little while longer, her voice a balm to my frayed nerves. By the time we hung up, I felt a little steadier, a little braver. But the question still lingered, gnawing at the edges of my resolve.

Could I really risk everything for a chance at something more with Austin?

I curled into the corner of the couch, the ice cream carton long gone, my stomach aching from more than just sugar.

And for no good reason, a memory rose up, sharp and sudden.

It was two months ago.

We'd just finished a show in Baton Rouge, and I couldn't sleep. The adrenaline had been too high, the comedown too steep. I found him in the hotel hallway, barefoot, holding two paper cups of chamomile tea like it was no big deal.

"You looked wired," he'd said. "Figured you might need this."

We sat on the floor of the hallway for over an hour. Talking. Laughing. Sharing earphones and listening to a rough demo on his phone. His shoulder had been warm against mine, his voice low and soft, and I'd felt safe. Seen.

Like the whole world could fall away and I wouldn't notice, as long as he was there.

I'd almost kissed him that night.

Almost.

And now?

That closeness felt a thousand miles away.

Our relationship was a constant back and forth of emotions—like a rope that starts out strong but, after being pulled back and forth too many times, begins to fray and threaten to snap.

The weight of it all settled heavy on my chest, exhaustion pulling at my eyelids. My thoughts blurred, spinning between what was and what might have been.

Before I knew it, sleep crept in.

In my dream, I found myself in a tug-of-war against a giant carton of ice cream. It was ridiculous—half-melted, dripping, and stubbornly refusing to let go.

I pulled with everything I had, but the ice cream pulled back, cold and unyielding, threatening to drag me into a sticky mess.

Somewhere between the struggle and the laughter, I realized the ice cream wasn't just a silly opponent—it was everything I wanted and feared: comfort, temptation, sweetness—and the risk of losing control.

I woke to the soft glow of dawn, the dream lingering like a secret message. Maybe the fight wasn't about winning or losing, but about knowing when to hold back and when to let go.

I was done holding back. I just had to decide when to let go.

Chapter 30

Austin

The soundcheck felt heavier than it should've, like the air in the venue was thick with everything unsaid between Willow and me. We'd just pulled into a new city, a new venue, and yet it all felt the same—another stage, another round of pretending everything was fine.

I walked into the cavernous auditorium, my guitar slung over my shoulder. Roadies worked like clockwork around us, adjusting lights, testing mics, and hauling gear, their voices echoing off the walls.

Willow was already on stage, perched on a stool, strumming her guitar with that quiet intensity she always had. Her hair spilled over her shoulder in waves, and she was humming something under her breath—a melody I didn't recognize.

She glanced up as I approached, her eyes meeting mine across the empty space. For a moment, everything else faded away, and it was just us, like it always was when the world outside got too loud.

"Hey," I said, my voice rougher than I'd intended.

"Hey," she replied softly, her fingers still idly moving across the strings.

I took my place at the mic stand, adjusting it to my height. "You ready for this?"

Willow's lips quirked in a small, knowing smile. "Ready as I'll ever be. You?"

I nodded, even though the knot in my stomach told a different story. "Let's get to it."

The band joined us on stage, and soon the soundcheck was in full swing. The first notes of the set echoed through the empty venue, and I closed my eyes, letting the music drown out everything else.

But it didn't work. Not entirely.

Every time Willow's voice joined mine, every time our harmonies locked into place, I felt it—the pull. That magnetic force that had simmered between us for years, always just out of reach.

The soundcheck wasn't perfect. There were notes to adjust, levels to tweak. But the music wasn't the problem. It was the silence between songs, the weight of everything we weren't saying, that threatened to undo me.

During a break, I wandered over to her, pretending I was just stretching my legs. But really, I was pulled toward her like always— against better judgment, against every rule we'd tried to write for ourselves.

The words slipped out before I could stop them. "So, is Jace going to miss you while we're on the road?"

Willow tensed, her fingers stilling on her guitar. "Wouldn't you?"

Her tone was light, too light. The kind of teasing that hides the real emotion underneath like a secret folded inside a joke. But the edge in her voice cut right through me.

I didn't know how to respond. Instead, I shoved my hands in my pockets and shrugged. "Yeah, I would."

Her gaze lingered on me for a second longer before she turned back to the band. "Let's take it from the top," she called, her voice clipped and even, already miles ahead of me. The message was clear. Line drawn. Conversation over.

For the rest of soundcheck, I couldn't stop watching her. The way she swayed to the music, the way her eyes closed as she hit certain notes—it was maddening. She was maddening.

By the time we wrapped up rehearsal, I was wound tighter than a coiled spring. I walked Willow to her car, the cool night air doing little to clear the fog in my head. She stood with her back to me, still and silent, her shoulders rising and falling in slow, deliberate breaths like she was trying to keep herself together. I knew the feeling. I was doing the same thing. Just quieter.

Finally, she turned, her gaze pinning me in place. "I know why you're upset," she said quietly.

The raw honesty in her tone sent my pulse racing.

"It's the same reason I'd be furious if the roles were reversed," she continued, her voice low and steady, but with just enough shake to make my chest ache. She wasn't accusing me. She was confessing. "And I'm sorry, Austin. I'm sorry I agreed to it."

Her words hung between us, heavy with meaning, and before I could respond, she climbed into her car and drove away. I stood there, staring after her, my mind reeling.

The next day passed in a blur—press, sound checks, rehearsals— everything but the one conversation I couldn't stop replaying. I thought about texting her. I thought about showing up at her door. I didn't do either. Instead, I showed up to the next venue with a full stomach of nerves and no idea what would come out on stage.

The energy in the room was electric. The kind of buzz that only came from a sold-out crowd waiting for the show to begin.

Backstage, the air was thick with anticipation. The band was gathered, tuning instruments and warming up, while the crew made last-minute adjustments to the stage setup.

I was pacing near the curtain, my hands restless at my sides. Willow was standing a few feet away, chatting with one of the sound techs. She looked calm, collected, like she wasn't carrying the weight of a million emotions just under the surface.

I wasn't sure how she did it. How she kept it all together when I felt like I was on the verge of unraveling.

"You good?" Sean's voice cut through my thoughts.

I turned to see him standing beside me, his bass slung over his shoulder.

"Yeah," I lied, forcing a smile.

Sean smirked, clearly not buying it, but he didn't press. "Well, pull it together. It's showtime."

The house lights dimmed, and the roar of the crowd cracked the tension like lightning across a dry sky. My chest surged with adrenaline, but it wasn't the kind that came from nerves. It was the kind that came from seeing her—guitar in hand, expression unreadable, and still somehow the most familiar thing in the world.

Willow stepped up beside me, her hand brushing mine as she adjusted her guitar strap. The brief contact sent a spark through me, and I had to clench my jaw to keep from reacting.

"You ready for this?" she asked, echoing my words from the day before.

I nodded, my throat too tight to speak.

The stage lights came up, and the crowd's cheers hit us like a wave as we stepped into the spotlight.

The opening chords of the first song rang out, and just like that, we were in our element. Willow's voice wrapped around mine, the harmonies falling into place effortlessly. But tonight, there was something different.

Every note felt heavier, like we were dragging our feelings behind every lyric, daring each other to say something we weren't allowed to say. It wasn't just a show anymore—it was a conversation, coded in melody, strung together with harmonies that held a thousand what-ifs.

During one of the ballads, I glanced over at Willow. Her eyes were closed, her face tilted toward the mic, and for a second, I forgot where I was. Forgot about the crowd, the lights, the band.

All I could see was her.

When the song ended, the applause was deafening, but I barely heard it. Willow looked at me then, her green eyes locking onto mine, and I swear the whole world tilted.

The final song of the night was one of our favorites—an acoustic duet that always left the crowd in awe. Willow and I stepped to the edge of the stage, the rest of the band fading into the background.

As we sang, our voices melted together and I wondered if the audience could feel it too—the tension, the longing, the unspoken words that hung in the air between us.

When the last note faded, the crowd erupted into cheers, but all I could focus on was Willow.

She smiled at me—slow, soft, the kind that tugged at something deep in my chest and left it aching. It reached her eyes, like it always did, but tonight it felt like a question. One I still didn't have the courage to answer.

We took our bows and waved to the crowd, the lights dimming around us. The audience roared, but it felt distant. Muted.

Backstage, Willow brushed past me, her shoulder brushing mine, her fingers grazing the back of my hand. An accident, maybe. Or maybe not.

She didn't look back.

And once again, I let her go.

Chapter 31

Willow

The last two months had been a blur of movement—rehearsals, fittings, sound tests, media junkets. My calendar looked like a losing game of Tetris, and sleep had become optional. But even in the chaos, Austin was my constant.

Things between us had improved. We weren't back to "normal" whatever that was. We hadn't really had time alone that wasn't spoken for. But we were comfortable again.

He always found a way to make me laugh at the worst moments, or to catch my hand in his when the crowd got too close. One glance from him could level me.

And lately it felt like he knew that.

Tonight, though, everything felt different. Bigger. So much was on the line.

We were performing at the Country Music Awards—our first time on a stage in front of our peers and coworkers. Industry veterans. Critics. Every person who could make or break the next chapter of our careers.

Our latest single had topped the charts, the buzz around us was electric, we'd been nominated for Vocal Duo of the Year, and we were set to close the show with a performance of the single. It was the kind of opportunity that could launch our careers into the stratosphere—or expose every crack.

The night was already surreal. Austin and I had walked the red carpet together, the camera flashes blinding as interviewers asked us about the tour, the album, and the rumors that constantly swirled around us.

Emma had prepped us with the usual "We're just friends" response, because that's all we had ever claimed to be. But that truth had never felt harder to tell with Austin standing so close, his arm casually draped around my waist like it belonged there.

I smoothed the skirt of my dress—shimmering gold and so tight it felt like a second skin—as I glanced at Austin. He was next to me, looking dashing in a sleek black suit that made him look every bit the country star he was becoming. His hair was tousled just right, and his tie was slightly loose, giving him that effortlessly cool vibe that made half of Nashville swoon.

"You nervous?" he asked, leaning closer so only I could hear.

I swallowed hard, trying to ignore the way his voice sent shivers down my spine. "A little. You?"

He flashed me that lopsided grin I'd come to know too well. "Nah. I've got us, Wills."

It was a simple statement, but it carried so much weight. I nodded, offering a small smile in return, even as my heart raced for reasons that had nothing to do with the performance.

We took our seats toward the front of the auditorium, surrounded by some of the biggest names in country music. Every few minutes, I'd catch Austin fidgeting—adjusting his tie, running a hand through his hair. I knew he was nervous, even if he wouldn't admit it. We were both hyperaware of what was at stake tonight.

And then came the announcement that stopped my heart.

"Here are the nominees for Vocal Duo of the Year," the presenter said, the names flashing on the massive screen behind them. My breath caught as our picture appeared alongside the others. It wasn't a surprise—we knew we were nominated—but hearing it out loud, seeing it up there, made it feel real in a way it hadn't before.

"And the CMA Award for Vocal Duo of the Year goes to..." The presenter paused, opening the envelope with practiced drama. "Grace & Gravel, Austin Blake and Willow Gracin!"

The room erupted into applause, and for a moment, I just sat there, stunned. Austin was on his feet before I could process it, pulling me up with him. His grin was so wide it was almost boyish, and his hand wrapped around mine as we made our way to the stage.

The lights were blinding, the applause deafening, but all I could focus on was the warmth of Austin's hand in mine. When we reached the podium, he gave my hand a quick squeeze before letting go to accept the award.

Austin leaned into the mic first, his voice steady despite the emotion in his eyes. "Wow. Um, first off, thank you to the CMAs and everyone who voted for us. This—this is a dream come true." He glanced at me, his smile softening. "And I couldn't have asked for a better partner to share it with."

My chest tightened as I stepped up to the mic. "Thank you so much to our families, our fans, our team, and everyone who believed in us. And to Austin—thank you for always being my anchor, even when the waves get rough."

His gaze locked with mine, and for a second, the world seemed to fade away. The applause brought us back to reality, and we walked offstage to a flurry of congratulations from everyone backstage.

But there was no time to dwell on the win. The show wasn't over, and we still had one last thing to do—perform.

After a rapid transformation in the dressing room, I took a deep breath as I stepped into the green room, my heart hammering against my ribcage. My nerves were shot, making my palms sweat and my stomach churn. I smoothed my hands down the leather dress the stylist had picked for me—a sleek, black number that clung to my curves in ways I wasn't used to. My hair was curled and teased into loose, dramatic waves, and my makeup was darker and more intense than I'd ever worn. I felt like an imposter in my own skin, like a doll someone had dressed up for show.

Austin was already there, pacing back and forth like a caged animal. He stopped mid-stride when I walked in, his eyes going wide as they swept over me. For a second, I thought he might actually forget how to breathe.

"Wow," he breathed, his voice barely above a whisper. "You look incredible."

His voice was so low I almost missed it. But his eyes didn't blink. Didn't look away.

And I knew he was seeing me—not just the dress, or the glam, or the illusion—but me. The girl behind the curtain. And somehow, that look undid me more than anything else ever could.

I felt heat rise to my cheeks. "Thanks. It's... a lot, isn't it? I barely recognize myself."

His boots thudded softly against the floor as he crossed the room to me, his hands finding my shoulders. His gaze was steady, piercing, as though he was trying to ground me with just his presence.

"That's OK," he said softly, his voice carrying a conviction that made my heart stumble. "No matter what you're wearing or how much makeup they pile on. I'll always recognize you."

His hands slid down my arms until his fingers intertwined with mine, his touch grounding me in a way nothing else could. "You ready for this?" he asked, his voice quieter now, intimate.

I nodded. But before I could respond, he pulled me closer, resting his forehead against mine. For a long moment, we just stood there, breathing each other in. The storm of nerves swirling inside me started to calm, replaced by something warmer, steadier.

Austin heaved a deep breath.

The confession slipped out before I could second-guess it. Before I could edit it down to something safer. "I love you."

I hadn't planned to say it tonight.

But there it was, raw and exposed, like an open wound.

His head shot up, his eyes wide with shock. "What?"

The knot in my chest tightened, panic blooming under my ribs. But there was no taking it back now. I swallowed hard and forced myself to meet his gaze. "I love you, Austin Blake. I'm in love with you."

For a moment, he didn't move, didn't speak. My heart sank as the silence stretched between us, the air thick with tension. Oh stars. I'd misread everything, hadn't I? I'd just ruined us.

"Austin, please say something," I whispered, my voice cracking. "If you don't feel the same way, it's okay. We can just forget I ever said any—"

"I love you, too."

The words stopped me cold. I stared at him, hardly daring to believe it. "You do?"

A slow smile spread across his face, transforming his expression into something so radiant it made my knees weak. "Of course I do. Willow, I've been in love with you from the moment we sang together on that porch with ten of our closest friends."

I didn't know whether to laugh or cry, so I did a little of both.

"Then why do you look so upset right now?" I asked with a shaky laugh, swiping at my tears.

His hands came up to cup my face, his thumbs brushing away the wet streaks. "Because you beat me to it," he murmured. "I wanted to be the one to say it first. And now your makeup is all done, and I can't even kiss you properly."

I didn't think. I didn't hesitate. I just moved—into him, into the kiss, into the moment I'd been dreaming about for what felt like forever.

And when he kissed me back, the world cracked wide open then disappeared as years of longing poured into that kiss. His lips were soft and warm, moving against mine with a mixture of tenderness and hunger that made my head spin.

He tasted like cinnamon gum—his pre-show ritual—and I knew I'd never forget the flavor as long as I lived.

A sharp knock at the door startled us apart. "Five minutes to places!" a voice called.

We stared at each other, breathing heavily, our foreheads still touching. "We should..." Austin started, his voice husky.

"Yeah," I agreed, stepping back reluctantly. I caught a glimpse of myself in the mirror and groaned. My lipstick was smudged, my carefully applied makeup slightly worse for wear. "Oh crap. Jo's going to kill me."

Austin grinned, looking entirely too pleased with himself. "Hurry back to me," he said, stealing one last quick kiss. "We've got a show to do."

I dashed off to find Jo, who gave me a knowing look as she quickly fixed the damage. By the time I returned to the wings, the house lights were dimming, and the roar of the crowd was building like a wave.

Austin was waiting for me, his guitar slung over his shoulder. He reached for my hand, giving it a quick squeeze. "Let's show them what we're made of, Gracin."

I smiled, my heart soaring. "Let's do it, Blake."

As we stepped into the spotlight, the crowd's cheers washed over us like a tidal wave. The first chords of our song rang out, and just like that, the rest of the world fell away. It was just us, our voices intertwining, our hearts finally in sync.

And for the first time in years, I felt weightless. Whole.

This was where I was meant to be. By Austin's side, in every way that mattered.

Chapter 32

Austin

Hotel rooms, backstages, adrenaline highs, and too much mediocre coffee fueled our last three months. But none of it felt exhausting. Not when Willow was there.

Every day with her had felt like stealing something rare and impossible—and we were holding on to a secret the world didn't deserve to know yet.

And I hadn't realized how much I'd needed her until I finally had her.

I'd been worried at first, wondering how giving in to our feelings would change the dynamic we'd spent years building. I'd spent weeks worrying we'd burn out the thing that had made us magic—that spark people couldn't stop talking about. I'd thought maybe finally having her would kill the slow burn that made our music crackle.

But I was wrong.

It didn't fizzle.

It roared.

If anything, the passion we shared added a whole new dimension to our music. Every glance, every harmony, every performance felt charged in a way I couldn't have imagined before. It was like we'd unlocked something that had been waiting for us all along.

And people noticed. Emma, our agent, had called it "undeniable chemistry." Mitch, our producer, said our music had a depth now that couldn't be faked. Every comment section, every fan edit, every YouTube video of our live sets—they saw what we'd been too afraid to name. They saw the way Willow's eyes would lock on mine at the bridge of a song. The way my voice would drop lower when I sang about heartbreak and she'd fill the silence like she was answering a question I didn't know how to ask.

And still, we said nothing.

Through it all, Willow and I never talked about us publicly. We'd show up to interviews the same way we always had—her in her jeans and boots, me with my easygoing smile and charm turned up to eleven. If anyone asked about our relationship, we stuck to the same script Emma had prepped us with: "We're just great friends who happen to make great music together."

It wasn't a lie. Not entirely. We were great friends.

But behind closed doors?

She was my everything.

We'd stolen moments on the tour bus when everyone else was asleep, tangled up in each other as the miles blurred past the windows. We'd shared quiet breakfasts in the corners of hotel dining rooms, talking about the future like it was some fragile, precious thing we were too afraid to jinx. And then there were the performances—standing under the lights, singing songs that carried pieces of our souls, our voices wrapping around each other like a promise.

We hadn't defined anything, not really. There hadn't been a "what are we?" conversation or a plan for what came next. It felt easier that way. Safer. Like we could keep holding onto this if we never tried to wrap it in labels or expectations.

But I could feel something shifting.

That invisible thread between us pulling tighter, asking for more.

I sat on the edge of the bed, letting the strings hum beneath my fingers while Willow zipped up her suitcase across the room. Her ponytail was slipping loose, curls falling around her face. She was humming under her breath—some melody she hadn't shared with me yet but probably would soon. She always did.

The tour was officially over. Three months on the road, and now we were finally heading back to Nashville. Back to real life, whatever that looked like for us.

I cleared my throat, trying to act like what I was about to say was casual. Like I hadn't been rehearsing it for a week straight in the mirror of every hotel bathroom we'd stayed in.

"So," I said, breaking the comfortable silence. "I was thinking. It's close to Christmas. Do you want to come home with me for a few days?"

Willow froze, one hand halfway to her suitcase. She turned slowly, her eyes wide. "Home with you? Like, to meet your family?"

I nodded, suddenly feeling like a nervous teenager asking someone to prom. "Yeah. My mom's been asking about you for weeks. She saw one of those interviews we did last month, and now she thinks you're the most amazing person in the world. I'm starting to think she likes you more than she likes me. As a matter of fact, she said—and I quote—'That girl is the only reason my son finally looks like he knows how to iron a shirt.'"

Willow snorted. "You mean, because I actually ironed your shirt."

"Details," I said, grinning. "She doesn't need to know that."

Willow laughed, but there was hesitation, maybe? Or nerves?

"Are you sure?" she asked, her voice softer now. "I mean, I'd love to meet your family, but is it a good idea? What if they don't like me?"

"Impossible," I said immediately, setting my guitar aside and crossing the room to her. I took her hands in mine, tilting my head to catch her gaze. "Willow, you're the most incredible person I've ever met. They're going to love you. I promise."

Her lips quirked into a small, uncertain smile. "You're pretty convincing, you know that?"

Her voice was teasing, but I didn't miss the slight tremble under it. She was still scared.

And I'd be lying if I said I wasn't too.

But I also knew—there wasn't anyone else I wanted to bring home. No one else I'd rather explain to my mom as "someone who matters."

Because she did.

She mattered more than anything.

"It's one of my many talents," I said with a grin. "Seriously, though. It's Christmas. Come with me."

She nodded, her fingers tightening around mine. "Okay. I'd love to."

As she turned back to zip up her suitcase, humming again under her breath, I realized something I hadn't let myself think before now.

This wasn't just a fling, or a secret, or even just a tour romance.

This was home.

And not the one we were flying back to.

The one I was already holding in my arms.

Chapter 33

Austin

I don't think I'd ever been more nervous in my life than I was as the plane started descending into Bitterroot. Not nerves like stage fright. This was different. This was hope and panic and anticipation all tangled up like Christmas lights in a box—impossible to separate, and sparking at the wrong moments.

My leg bounced restlessly against the floor, and I kept running my hand through my hair, glancing at Willow every two seconds like she might vanish if I didn't keep an eye on her.

I've played in front of packed arenas, performed on live TV, even stood on stage at the freakin' CMAs—but bringing Willow home for Christmas? Introducing her to my family? That felt like the biggest moment of all.

I glanced over at her. She was staring out the window, her green eyes wide as she took in the snow-dusted mountains rising in the distance. Her cheeks were flushed from the cold air filtering into the plane. She looked out the window like she was staring into another world. Maybe she was. Bitterroot in December had that effect. Clean snow, dark trees, a quiet kind of beauty that didn't need to announce itself.

"It's beautiful," she whispered, turning to me. "I can't believe you grew up here."

"Wait 'til you see the ranch," I said, a smile tugging at my lips. "Pictures don't do it justice."

She smiled back, but I could see the nerves hiding just beneath it. She kept adjusting the sleeves of her sweater, fidgeting with the hem, like she was already bracing herself for the pressure of meeting my family.

Truth was, I was just as nervous as she was. I wanted this to go perfectly. My family's opinion mattered to me, and I needed them to see Willow the way I saw her—to see how she'd completely changed my life.

The drive from the airport felt like it took forever. By the time I turned the truck into the long, tree-lined driveway that led to the ranch, my palms were sweating against the steering wheel. That old ache of coming home crept into my chest—familiar in the way nostalgia always was. But this time it came with a thread of fear, because now I wasn't just bringing home myself. I was bringing home the person who'd changed everything.

The house came into view, glowing with warm yellow lights, the porch wrapped in twinkling Christmas lights. A wreath hung on the front door, and smoke curled from the chimney into the crisp winter air.

Willow let out a soft laugh, her breath fogging in the cold as we stepped out of the truck. "Austin, this is incredible. It's like something out of a movie."

I couldn't stop smiling. Seeing the ranch through her eyes made it feel new again, like I was a kid. "The inside is even better," I said, grabbing our bags and slinging my guitar case over my shoulder.

Before we could even knock, the door flew open, and there was

Mom, her arms wide open and her smile brighter than the Christmas lights.

"There's my boy!" she said, pulling me into a hug so tight it knocked the breath out of me.

When she turned to Willow, her expression softened into something so warm and welcoming I felt some of the tension in my chest ease. "And you must be Willow," she said, wrapping Willow in a hug like they were already old friends. "Oh, sweetheart, it's so wonderful to meet you. You're even more beautiful in person."

Willow's face turned pink, but she smiled. "Thank you, Mrs. Blake. It's so nice to meet you too."

"Oh, please, call me Connie. And come in before you freeze! I made hot cocoa."

The warmth of the house hit us the second we walked in. The smell of pine and cinnamon filled the air, and the Christmas tree glowed in the corner of the living room, its branches heavy with mismatched ornaments collected over the years.

"Get in here, kid!" My grandfather, Shep, called from his usual spot by the fire, a steaming mug of cocoa in his hand. His grin was wide and mischievous, the kind of grin that usually meant an embarrassing story was inevitable.

"And who's this lovely young lady?" he asked as Willow stepped into the room. He stood, his joints creaking as he came over to shake her hand. "I hope you're ready for some stories about this one," he said, jerking his thumb at me. "I've got plenty."

Willow laughed, her eyes sparkling. "I can't wait."

Dad was next, striding in with his steady, no-nonsense energy. "Willow," he said, shaking her hand firmly. "Welcome to the Blake ranch. We were starting to think this boy wasn't ever going to bring you home."

"Dad," I groaned, rolling my eyes.

"What? It's true," he said with a shrug, his grin making it clear he was only half-joking. "Rumor has it, you're special."

Connor was quieter, as he always was, but he gave Willow a polite nod and a quick handshake. His three-legged dog, Charlie, lingered by Willow's feet, sniffing her boots before letting out a quiet "woof" of approval.

"Charlie likes her," he said bluntly, his voice low so only I could hear.

"Yeah? Me, too," I said, grinning despite the nerves still buzzing under my skin.

"Does that mean I pass the test?" Willow asked, crouching down to scratch behind Charlie's ears.

Before heading toward the kitchen, Connor said, "Yep."

Dinner was everything I'd been hoping it would be. The table was piled high with roasted turkey, mashed potatoes, green beans, and rolls fresh from the oven. Mom had gone all out, and the food was just as warm and comforting as the atmosphere around the table.

Every time Willow laughed, I watched my mom beam, Shep lean in a little closer, Connor nod in that way that meant he approved without saying anything. She wasn't just being accepted—she was being folded in.

Shep was in rare form, telling one story after another—most of them involving me doing something ridiculous as a kid. "And then he tried to serenade the poor girl with a ukulele that was missing half its strings," Shep said, his laughter booming across the room. "Didn't even get her name right!"

Willow was laughing so hard she was swiping tears from her face, and even Connor cracked a smile. Charlie rested his head on Willow's knee, clearly enamored with her, which just solidified what I already knew—she belonged here.

After dinner, Mom pulled Willow into the kitchen to help with the dishes, the two of them laughing and chatting like old friends. I leaned against the doorframe, watching them, my heart so full it felt like it might burst.

"She's the real deal," Shep said quietly, coming to stand beside me. "Don't let this one slip away, kid."

I didn't need him to tell me that. I already knew.

Later that night, after everyone else had gone to bed, Willow and I found ourselves alone in the living room. The fire was down to embers, the kind of quiet lingered that only existed in moments like this wrapping around us like a blanket.

Willow's hair was a little messy, her cheeks glowing from laughter and pink from the warmth of the fire. I couldn't stop staring. Curled up on the couch, a blanket draped over her legs, and a mug of cocoa cradled in her hands, she looked like she belonged here. Like she'd always been part of this place.

I sat beside her, my guitar resting against the arm of the couch, and for a long time, we didn't say anything. We didn't need to.

"This place is amazing," she said eventually, her voice soft. "Your family is amazing."

"They love you," I said. "I knew they would."

She looked at me then, her green eyes shining with something I couldn't quite name. "Thank you for bringing me here," she said. "It's perfect."

I wanted to tell her everything in that moment. How much she meant to me, how I wanted this—us—to last forever. But instead, I just reached for her hand, lacing my fingers through hers.

"Let's head to bed, Wills," I murmured, my voice thick with emotion. "Tomorrow's the big day."

We snuggled under the quilt, Willow's head resting on my shoulder. There were no words to describe how I felt other than I felt completely, utterly at peace.

She looked up at me, her green eyes searching mine.

"Sweet dreams, Austin Blake," she said softly

"Only of you, Willow Gracin," I whispered, pressing a kiss to her forehead.

It was technically Christmas Eve, but for us, it was Christmas. I woke up to the smell of coffee and cinnamon. For a split second, I didn't remember where I was—months of waking up in different hotel rooms will do that to you. But then I saw the familiar quilt draped over the bed, the snow-dusted ranch outside the window, and I remembered. Home.

Willow was curled up next to me, her breathing soft and steady. Her hair was fanned out across the pillow, and her face had that peaceful look she always got when she was dreaming. She looked like everything I'd ever wanted and didn't think I'd ever deserve. Still sleepy, still mine, still here.

For a moment, I just watched her, my heart full to bursting. I hadn't been kidding when I told her last night that today was going to be a big day. Christmas at the Blake ranch was like nothing else—gifts piled high, Mom's famous cinnamon rolls, and the warmth that came from being surrounded by family.

Her eyes fluttered open, and when they landed on me, she smiled —soft and sleepy. "Morning," she murmured, her voice still thick with sleep.

"Morning," I said, brushing a strand of hair out of her face. "Merry Christmas."

Her smile widened. "Merry Christmas."

By the time we made it downstairs, the house was alive with the sounds of Christmas morning—Mom humming along to a holiday playlist in the kitchen, Shep cracking jokes with my dad in the living room, and Charlie's nails clicking against the hardwood floors as he followed Connor around like a shadow.

Willow stopped at the bottom of the stairs, taking it all in. The fire crackled in the hearth, the tree twinkled with lights, and outside, the snow-covered landscape stretched as far as the eye could see.

"This is magical," she whispered, her voice filled with awe.

"You've never had a white Christmas, have you?" I asked, wrapping an arm around her shoulders.

She shook her head, her eyes wide as she looked out the window. "No. Growing up in Georgia, it was usually just cold, raining, or eighty degrees. This is something else."

I smiled, watching her take it all in. "Well, welcome to Montana."

The living room was alive with the warm hum of conversation. Gifts were stacked high under the tree, wrapped in brightly colored paper and tied with ribbons. Charlie padded around the room, his tail wagging as he sniffed at the gifts and nudged Connor for attention.

"Alright, let's get this show on the road," Shep announced, settling into his recliner with a contented sigh.

Connor took up the task of handing out presents, his three-legged shadow trotting faithfully behind him. He moved with his usual military efficiency, calling out names and passing gifts with no-nonsense precision.

When Willow's turn came, I couldn't help but watch her face, anticipation bubbling in my chest. My family had gone all out for her even with just a week's notice, and I hoped she could feel how much they already adored her.

First, Mom handed Willow a small rectangular package wrapped in gold paper with a perfectly tied ribbon. "This is from me," she said, her eyes sparkling with excitement.

Willow unwrapped the paper carefully, revealing a hand-stitched quilt. It was soft and beautifully made, with a pattern of mountains, pine trees, and wildflowers stitched into every square.

"It's a family tradition," Mom explained, her smile warm. "Every member of the family has one. I hope it keeps you warm wherever you are—and reminds you that you're always welcome here."

Willow's breath hitched as she ran her fingers over the intricate stitching. "Connie, this is beautiful. Thank you so much. I'll treasure it forever."

Mom reached out to give her a quick hug. "I'm so glad you're here."

Next, Shep leaned forward, holding out a small box wrapped in plain brown paper. "This one's from me," he said gruffly, though his expression was softer than I'd ever seen.

Willow unwrapped the package to reveal an antique jewelry box, the wood polished to a warm sheen. Her fingers traced the intricate carvings along the lid, and when she opened it, the velvet-lined interior gleamed like it had been made yesterday.

"It belonged to my late wife—Austin's grandmother," Shep explained, his voice tinged with nostalgia. "She always said it should go to someone special."

Willow's eyes filled with tears as she looked up at him. "Shep, I can't, I don't know what to say. This is incredible. Thank you."

He waved her off, though his own eyes were suspiciously shiny. "Just take good care of it, darlin'. That's all I ask."

Connor stepped up next, holding out a neatly wrapped package with the Blake Ranch logo stamped on the corner. "This is yours," he said, his tone as matter-of-fact as ever.

Willow tore off the paper to reveal a beanie, a pair of gloves, and a hoodie—all embroidered with "Blake Ranch."

"Since you probably don't know how to dress warm enough for Montana winters," Connor said simply, a ghost of a smile tugging at the corners of his mouth.

I laughed as Willow held up the hoodie, turning it over in her hands and resting it against herself. "You look good in Blake," I teased, unable to resist.

She rolled her eyes but couldn't hide the faint blush on her cheeks. "Thanks, Connor. This is great. I'll definitely stay warm now."

Willow hadn't come empty-handed, of course. She handed Mom a beautifully wrapped package, her smile shy but warm.

"This is for you, Connie," she said.

Mom unwrapped the gift to reveal a handwritten recipe book, filled with some of Willow's favorite Southern dishes. The pages were dotted with little notes in the margins, tips and tricks that made each recipe uniquely hers.

"I thought you might like to try a little taste of Georgia," Willow said.

Mom's hand flew to her mouth, her eyes brimming with tears. "Willow, this is wonderful and so thoughtful. Thank you so much."

Reaching down beside her chair, Willow picked up a carefully wrapped package. She walked over to Shep, who was sitting by the fire with a blanket draped over his lap and Charlie curled at his feet.

"This is for you, Shep," she said, her voice a little shy but filled with affection. "Austin told me you're an Elvis fan, and, well, I couldn't resist."

Shep's bushy eyebrows lifted as he took the package, his weathered hands unwrapping it carefully. When he pulled back the paper, his face broke into the kind of grin that lit up the entire room.

It was a vintage vinyl record of Elvis Presley's *Blue Hawaii*, the cover pristine, the colors still vibrant despite its age.

"Well now," Shep said, his voice thick with emotion as he turned the record over in his hands, "this—well, this is somethin' else."

"I found it in this tiny record shop in Nashville," Willow explained.

Shep chuckled, shaking his head as he gazed at the record like it was a priceless artifact. "The King himself. You couldn't have picked a better gift, darlin'. Thank you. Truly."

Willow smiled, relief washing over her face. "I'm so glad you like it."

Charlie barked softly at Shep's feet, as if in agreement, and Shep leaned down to give the dog a scratch behind the ears. "I'm gonna play this first thing after breakfast," he declared. "Might even show you all how to do a proper jitterbug."

The room erupted in laughter, and Willow beamed, her gift clearly a hit.

Willow reached for the next package and crossed the room toward Connor, who was now sitting in his usual spot on the couch. She smiled as she handed him the neatly wrapped box, glancing down at Charlie, who had followed her and whose tail wagged in anticipation.

"This one's for you, Connor," she said simply. "And Charlie, too."

Connor took the box without hesitation, peeling back the paper with the same quiet efficiency he did everything. Inside was a leather tool roll, carefully stitched and embossed with his initials and a smaller package that contained a bag of homemade dog treats tied with twine.

Connor ran his fingers over the tool roll, his expression unreadable at first. "Thank you," he said, his voice low but sincere.

"You're welcome," Willow replied, her smile warm.

Connor gave a small nod of approval, then tore the bag open and handed Charlie a treat. The dog barked once in satisfaction before happily chomping down, and Connor's lips twitched in one of his rare, fleeting smiles.

"Mr. Blake," she said, holding out a huge box toward my dad, "this is for you."

He accepted the gift with a raised eyebrow, his weathered hands carefully untying the ribbon. He removed the lid to reveal not one, but two Stetson hats—one in classic black, the other in a rich, sandy brown.

His gaze lingered on the hats for a moment, and then he looked up, his eyes narrowing slightly in thought.

"You notice a man's hat before anything else," Willow said, filling the silence. "Austin told me you've had your current one for a while. I thought maybe you could use a new one—or two."

Dad reached into the box, lifting out the brown Stetson. The weight of it in his hands seemed to ground him, and he ran his thumb over the brim with the care of someone who appreciated crafts-manship.

"Willow," he said finally, his voice gruff, "this is a fine gift. Thank you."

The warmth in his tone was understated but genuine, and it sent a wave of relief washing over her.

"I wasn't sure if you'd prefer black or brown, so I figured I'd cover my bases," Willow said lightly, hoping the small joke would ease her nerves.

My dad chuckled softly, his eyes crinkling at the corners. "Good call," he said, setting the brown hat aside and lifting the black one. He placed it on his head, adjusting the brim slightly. "What do you think?"

"I think you wear it well," Willow replied with an easy smile.

He tipped the hat to her in a gesture of gratitude.

My smile was wide and full of pride, and my heart felt like it might burst.

The living room buzzed with conversation as everyone admired their gifts. Charlie happily crunched on another one of his new treats, Shep was inspecting the Elvis record like it was made of gold, and Mom was already flipping through the recipe book Willow had given her.

I leaned in close, my lips brushing against Willow's ear. "You did good, Wills," I murmured.

Willow turned to me, her smile soft. "Your family's amazing, Austin. I just wanted them to know how much they mean to me—because they mean so much to you."

My chest tightened, my hand found hers. "They already adore you," I said, my voice thick with emotion. "And so do I."

Chapter 34

Willow

As I lay in bed that night, my mind drifted to the whirlwind of the last three months. It seemed like only yesterday that Austin and I had taken off on this incredible journey together, yet so much had changed in such a short time.

I thought back to the moment our relationship moved to the next level. It was both thrilling and terrifying, crossing that line from friends to something more. I had worried that it might change everything between us, that we might lose the easy camaraderie and deep connection we had always shared.

But to my surprise, our relationship only grew stronger. Sure, there were new dimensions to it now—stolen kisses backstage, fingers intertwined as we explored new cities together, a new kind of electricity that crackled between us every time our eyes met on stage. But at its core, our bond remained the same. Austin was still my best friend, my confidant, the one person who truly understood me inside and out.

These few days at the Blake ranch had only solidified that. Meeting his family had been like stepping into a Hallmark movie, complete with twinkling Christmas lights and snow-covered mountains. His mom's immediate warmth and that beautiful quilt, Shep's stories and his grin when I gave him the record, even Connor's quiet approval—it all felt like I was being accepted into something sacred.

And Austin? Austin watching me through all of it, his pride and love shining in every glance. I'd always known he was my anchor, but seeing him at home, surrounded by the people who had shaped him, made me love him even more. There was no pretense, no stage persona. Just him. The real him.

I turned to look at him, his face peaceful in sleep, and felt a rush of love so intense it took my breath away. I had known for a long time that what we had was special, but it wasn't until this last tour—and this Christmas—that I realized just how rare and precious it truly was.

I thought about Shep's words I'd overheard: "She's the real deal. Don't let this one slip away, kid." The memory made me smile and blush all over again. It was like the Blakes had pulled me into their circle without hesitation, making me feel like I belonged there. Like I'd always belonged.

As I snuggled closer to Austin, my mind wandered to all the incredible moments we had shared over the past few months. The thrill of performing together night after night, pouring our hearts out on stage. The quiet moments in between shows, writing songs and dreaming up melodies. The laughter and inside jokes, the deep conversations about life and love and everything in between.

It was like all of my wildest dreams had come true, and then some. Not only was I living my passion, sharing my music with the world, but I was doing it all with the love of my life by my side.

I slowly blinked my eyes open, a contented smile spreading across my face. Austin's arm was draped over my waist, his steady breathing a comforting rhythm against my back. His arm tightened briefly as I shifted, like even in his sleep he wasn't quite ready to let go. I smiled into the pillow.

Me neither.

My thoughts drifted again to the Blakes. They'd embraced me as though I had always been part of the family.

That sense of belonging had been so overwhelming and beautiful. But now, as much as I didn't want to leave, my heart fluttered at the thought of going home to my family. It had been months since I'd seen them, and my chest tightened at the thought of walking through the front door and feeling that same kind of warmth.

"Morning, beautiful," Austin murmured, pressing a soft kiss to my shoulder. His voice, thick and gravelly with sleep, made my stomach do that familiar, fluttery thing it always did.

I rolled over to face him, my smile widening as I met his warm gaze. "Morning, handsome," I replied, reaching up to brush a stray lock of hair from his forehead.

"You ready to go see your family?" he asked, nuzzling into my neck.

The thought made me giddy, though I couldn't help but feel a pang of sadness at leaving the ranch. "As much as I hate the idea of leaving this bed and your sweet family, I'm dying to get home."

He grinned and kissed me again before we got up and got ready for the day ahead.

Shortly after a very early breakfast, Austin and I bid a bittersweet farewell to his family in Montana, our hearts full of cherished memories and the promise of future visits.

Connie pulled me into a long, tearful hug at the door. "You come back soon, sweetheart," she said, squeezing my hands. "And don't you dare let him work you too hard."

"I'll hold him accountable," I promised, laughing as Austin rolled his eyes behind her.

James tipped his new hat to me as he leaned on the porch railing. "Safe travels, darlin'. Don't let that boy cause you too much trouble, you hear?"

"Yes, sir. Thank you—for everything."

Shep waved as Connor gave me one of his brief nods and even a small smile. "See you next time," he said.

"And I'll bring more treats next time," I added, earning a soft bark from Charlie as we climbed into the truck.

As we rode away from the house, I reached across the console and laced my fingers through Austin's. We didn't say much.

Just held on.

By the time we landed in Georgia, my excitement was bubbling over. Caleb was waiting for us at the airport, his grin wide as he pulled me into a bear hug.

"Look at you, country music star extraordinaire," he teased, ruffling my hair like we were kids again. "And you, Austin. Keeping my sister out of trouble?"

"Trying my best," Austin shot back with a smirk, clapping Caleb on the shoulder.

The drive home was filled with Caleb's animated retelling of recent family antics, and I found myself smiling so hard my face hurt. It felt like no time had passed at all, even though I knew it had.

As we pulled into the driveway, the familiar sight of my childhood home came into view. The porch was strung with twinkling lights, and the smell of roasted turkey and fresh-baked pies hit me the second we stepped inside.

"Willow, my baby girl!" Mom exclaimed, rushing to pull me into a hug that smelled like cinnamon and vanilla. She turned to Austin next, her face lighting up. "And Austin, it's so wonderful to have you here with us again. We've missed you both terribly."

Dad's strong arms enveloped me next, his voice thick with

emotion as he whispered, "Welcome home, sweetheart. It's not the same without you here."

The rest of the afternoon passed in a blur of catching up, coffee refills, and the comforting hum of family conversation. After we ate, the house settled into a lazy, post-meal calm. Mom and Dad were in the kitchen cleaning up, the savory smell of turkey and dressing lingering in the air. Caleb was sprawled across the couch, scrolling on his phone, while Austin and I sat on the floor by the Christmas tree, flipping through an old photo album I'd dug out of the closet.

"Is that you with a mullet?" Austin asked, his eyes wide with mock horror as he pointed at a grainy photo of Caleb circa middle school.

"Don't judge me," Caleb said without looking up from his phone. "It was the nineties. We all made choices."

Austin and I cracked up, and I felt that familiar sense of peace settle over me. This was home—the teasing, the laughter, the easy rhythm of people who had known and loved each other for decades.

"So, Caleb," I said, closing the album and leaning back against the couch. "You never did explain what's up with you and Emma."

At that, Caleb finally looked up, his expression immediately shifting into one of mild panic.

"Oh, this I've got to hear," Austin said, leaning forward with an eager grin.

"There's nothing to explain," Caleb muttered, clearly wishing he could disappear into the couch cushions.

"Uh-huh," I said, raising an eyebrow. "Because the one and only time I mentioned you to her, she turned bright red and practically sprinted out of the room."

Caleb sighed, running a hand down his face. "Fine. But if I tell you, you have to swear you won't bring it up to her. Ever."

"Deal," I said quickly.

Austin held up his hand, grinning. "Scout's honor."

Caleb took a deep breath, like he was bracing himself, and then launched into the story.

"It was the middle of finals week," Caleb began, leaning back against the couch with a resigned sigh. "Emma and I were studying in the library—well, I was studying. She was mostly complaining about how stressed out she was. Which was funny because she already had straight A's and was never at any risk of losing that."

"That sounds like Emma," I said with a grin.

"She was also fending off this guy who kept coming over to our table," Caleb continued. "Big guy, loud voice, thought he was God's gift to the world."

Austin raised an eyebrow. "The type who doesn't take a hint?"

"Exactly," Caleb said. "Tom had been hovering around all week, trying to ask her out. She'd turned him down a dozen times, but he just wouldn't quit. So that day, I guess he decided to try again, and she panicked."

I tilted my head, curious now. "What do you mean, panicked?"

Caleb hesitated, his eyes darting to Austin like he was debating whether to keep going.

"Come on," Austin said, his grin widening. "Don't leave us hanging."

Caleb groaned, running a hand down his face. "Fine. She jumped over the table and into my lap and started kissing me like her life depended on it."

My jaw dropped, and Austin let out a low whistle.

"She kissed you?" I asked, my voice full of disbelief and a little too much amusement.

"Oh, it wasn't just a quick peck," Caleb said dryly. "It was a full-on kiss. Right in the middle of the library. The kind of kiss that makes everyone around you stop and stare."

Austin was grinning like an idiot now, clearly loving every second of this. "And what did you do?"

"I froze," Caleb admitted. "I didn't know what was happening. One second I'm highlighting case law, and the next second she's climbing across the table to plant one on me."

I was laughing so hard now I could barely breathe. "Oh my God. What did Tom do?"

"He stormed off, of course," Caleb said. "Mission accomplished, I guess. But then Emma pulled back and realized what she'd done—and that's when things got worse."

"Worse?" Austin asked, leaning forward eagerly.

"I had a girlfriend at the time," Caleb said, his voice flat.

My laughter immediately stopped. "Oh no."

"Yep," Caleb said, popping the p. "And guess who walked into the library right as Emma was pulling away? Maddie. My girlfriend."

Austin winced. "Oof. Bad timing."

"That's putting it mildly," Caleb said. "Maddie flipped out. Started yelling about how I'd been cheating on her with Emma the whole time, which obviously wasn't true, but try explaining that in the middle of a crowded library when your boyfriend is sitting there with lipstick all over his face."

By this point, Austin was doubled over, clutching his stomach as he wheezed with laughter.

"Oh, this is gold," he said, wiping at his eyes. "What did Emma do?"

"She apologized about a million times," Caleb said. "She kept saying, 'I didn't mean to get you in trouble. I was just trying to get rid of Tom!' Like that made it any better."

"And Maddie?" I asked, still trying to process the story.

"She dumped me on the spot," Caleb said with a shrug. "Honestly, it was probably for the best. But still, I had to deal with Maddie spreading rumors about me all over campus and Emma avoiding me for weeks because she was so embarrassed."

I covered my mouth, trying not to laugh too loudly. "So that's why Emma acted so weird whenever I mention your name?"

"Probably," Caleb said. "She still feels guilty about it, even though I've told her a hundred times that it's fine. But she's Emma, so of course she was convinced she owed me something for ruining my relationship."

Austin smirked. "We appreciate your sacrifice."

Caleb rolled his eyes. The room erupted in laughter.

As the evening stretched on, the house hummed with the easy rhythm of a holiday well spent. Empty plates from a round of leftovers covered the surfaces, and the scents of Christmas filled the air. Gemma had shown up bearing a tin of her mom's famous peanut brittle and her usual energy.

"My siblings were up at 5 a.m.," she said, dropping onto the couch beside me with an exaggerated groan. "You'd think Santa brought them the moon. It was chaos. Pure chaos. I wished I'd been able to escape before they started fighting over who got the last cinnamon roll."

I laughed, nudging her with my elbow. "Good thing we're low-drama here."

"Speak for yourself." Caleb wandered into the living room, holding two mugs of coffee and wearing his trademark smirk. "You're not exactly known for your quiet tantrums, Willow."

I rolled my eyes but took the coffee he offered me. "I'm a delight, thank you very much."

"You keep telling yourself that," he shot back, settling into the recliner with the air of a man ready to stir the pot.

From my spot on the couch, I glanced down at Austin, who was sitting on the floor in front of me, his back leaning against my legs and his head tilted back, eyes closed. The faintest smile played on his lips, the kind of smile that said he was completely at ease, totally comfortable here with my family. Every so often, he would reach back to touch my legs, like he needed the reassurance of my presence.

My heart swelled at the sight of him. He fit here so naturally, like he'd been a part of this family all along.

Gemma kept everyone laughing with stories about her younger siblings' antics that morning, while Caleb tossed in sarcastic commentary that had Mom groaning and Dad chuckling under his breath. I felt like I could breathe deeply for the first time in months—no deadlines, no pressure, no sold-out venues waiting just beyond the curtain. Just family, warmth, and home.

Austin shared stories with my dad about life on the ranch versus life on the road. I could see how much my family already adored him —Mom practically beamed every time she looked at him, and even Caleb had gone from wary older brother to cracking inside jokes with him like they'd known each other for way longer than a couple of years.

There was a small pile of gifts waiting under the tree that we had almost forgotten about just by getting caught up in spending time together. I hadn't realized how much I'd missed this—the cozy chaos of Christmas, the familiar hum of my family in the background, the way everyone seemed to speak the same unspoken language.

Austin remained on the floor in front of me, his back resting against my legs as we passed around gifts.

Caleb handed out the last of the gifts, his voice teasing as he tossed a small box to Gemma. "Don't say I never got you anything," he quipped, earning a playful glare in return.

By the time the pile under the tree had been distributed, the room was alive with the rustle of wrapping paper and bursts of laughter as gifts were opened.

From Mom and Dad, I received a beautiful cashmere scarf in a rich emerald green that matched my eyes, and Austin unwrapped a sleek leather wallet.

Caleb's gifts were, as always, carefully chosen. For me, a delicate gold necklace with a tiny pendant in the shape of a music note. I fingered the chain, my chest tightening at the thoughtfulness behind it. "Caleb," I whispered, unable to say more without my voice breaking.

For Austin, Caleb had chosen a striking silver watch with a classic black leather band. He handed it over with a simple, "Can't go wrong with timeless."

Austin took the box, lifting the lid and smiling as he slid the watch onto his wrist. "Thanks, man. This is really nice."

"Looks good," Caleb said with a small nod of approval. "Don't lose it."

"Not a chance," Austin replied, glancing at the watch, then at me with a grateful smile.

Gemma, of course, went all out. She handed me a gorgeously wrapped gift bag filled with everything I didn't know I needed: a luxury skincare set, my favorite perfume, and a pair of gold earrings that sparkled like tiny stars. "You're a big deal now, Willow," she said, winking. "Gotta keep you looking the part."

"For the record," Austin interjected, leaning back against my legs and grinning up at me, "you don't need any of that to look incredible."

Gemma waved him off. "You're biased."

"And right," he added, smirking.

Austin presented my mom with a beautiful, hand-painted ceramic pie dish, one he'd picked up during the tour from a little artisan shop. "I thought it might be perfect for all those pies Willow keeps telling me about," he said, his smile warm.

For Dad, he chose a high-end embossed leather-bound folio with a matching hand-carved wooden pen.

Both gifts were met with glowing approval. Mom already started talking about which pie she'd serve in the dish first, and Dad ran his hand over the journal's smooth cover, nodding his thanks with a wide grin.

Austin handed Caleb a slim envelope, his grin almost mischievous. "You're hard to shop for, but I think you'll like this," he said.

Inside was a voucher for a weekend adventure: a guided whitewater rafting trip on the Chattahoochee River. Caleb's eyebrows shot up, and for a second, he seemed genuinely surprised.

"Didn't take you for an adrenaline junkie," Caleb said, his voice half-teasing.

"I'm not," Austin admitted with a laugh. "But I figured you'd be up for it. And maybe you'll take a plus one if you're feeling generous," he said, glancing over at Gemma. It was lost on both Caleb and Gemma, but I covered a giggle and faked clearing my throat.

"Not bad, Blake," Caleb said, tucking the voucher into his pocket. "Not bad at all."

Gemma loved the diamond earrings I'd picked out for her and Austin laughed when he opened the framed photo of us from one of the first times we sang together on the *Real American Country* Tour.

It had been an outdoor venue and the forecast had definitely promised rain but everyone decided that it would come in later than the forecast suggested. We were halfway through *Honky Tonkin's What I Do Best* when the heavens parted and we were instantly soaked. We sang and splashed our way through the rest of the song and laughed the rest of the week every time we talked about it.

He was clearly lost in the memory until Gemma asked to see the photo. Which of course resulted in having to tell the story and was then followed by more conversation about our time with *Real American Country*. Memories from the show and the tour felt so long ago but were still fresh in our minds. Never once did I ever picture this being where it led us.

The banter flowed as easily as the mulled wine Mom had set out on the coffee table, and the room was filled with the kind of joy that made me wish time would stop, just for a little while.

As the night wore on, the energy in the room mellowed. Gemma stretched out on the couch, Caleb's chin resting on Gemma's shoulder as they scrolled through photos on her phone. She was telling him about one of the projects she was hoping to wrap up at work. Mom and Dad were in the kitchen, finishing up the last round of dishes and sneaking bites of leftover pie.

An hour later, Gemma and Caleb started gathering their things. Before they finished, Austin stood and stretched, glancing toward the kitchen and then the back door.

"Hey, Willow," he said casually, his voice calm but carrying a tone that set my heart racing. "Mind coming with me for a second?"

My brows knit together in confusion, but I stood anyway, shooting Caleb and Gemma a questioning glance. Gemma raised an eyebrow but didn't say anything, while Caleb just grinned like he knew something I didn't.

Austin reached for my hand, and the warmth of his touch steadied me as he led me toward the back porch. The cool night air hit me as we stepped outside, a welcome contrast to the cozy warmth of the house. The sky was clear, stars scattered across the inky black like diamonds.

He didn't say anything at first, just stood there holding my hand, his thumb brushing lightly over my knuckles. I tilted my head to look at him, my breath catching at the way his eyes sparkled in the dim light spilling from the house.

"What's going on?" I asked softly, my voice barely above a whisper.

He turned to face me fully, and suddenly it felt like my entire world had narrowed down to just him. "I wanted to thank you," he said, his voice quiet but steady. "For coming home with me. For bringing me here. For sharing your family, your life, this piece of you that I didn't know I was missing."

"Austin," I started, but he shook his head, silencing me with a small smile.

"Let me finish," he said, his fingers tightened slightly around mine. "This week, watching you with our families, being a part of something together that is so beautiful and warm confirmed something I've known for a long time."

My heart pounded in my chest as he slowly sank down onto one knee, the world tilting on its axis.

"Willow Gracin," he said, his voice thick with emotion, "you are my best friend, my muse, the love of my life. From the moment I met you, my world got brighter, my music got deeper, and my heart? Well, it was never mine after that."

Tears blurred my vision as he reached into his pocket and pulled out a small velvet box, opening it to reveal the most stunning ring I'd ever seen—a delicate band with a center stone that sparkled like the night sky.

"If you'll remember, I've done this before but this time I'm really saying, I don't want to imagine another day without you by my side," he said, his voice cracking just slightly. "Will you marry me?"

For a moment, I couldn't breathe. The world seemed to stand still, my heart so full I thought it might burst. Then I nodded, the tears spilling over as I managed to whisper, "You didn't drop it."

Austin chuckled. "Is that a yes?"

Laughing I squealed, "Yes! Oh my gosh, yes!"

He slid the ring onto my finger, his hands trembling just slightly, and then he was standing, pulling me into his arms and kissing me like we were the only two people on earth. The cold, the darkness, the rest of the world—all of it faded away, leaving only us.

When we finally pulled apart, breathless and grinning like fools, I leaned my forehead against his. "You're full of surprises, Austin Blake," I murmured, my heart soaring.

He chuckled, his arms tightening around me. "And I've got a lifetime of them waiting for you."

From inside the house, the door creaked open, and Gemma's voice rang out. "Is it safe to come out yet, or do we need to give you two more time?"

Laughing, I turned toward the door, where my family and Gemma stood. They'd clearly been watching from the window, their faces lit up with excitement and—was that a tear in my dad's eye?

Caleb was the first to speak, crossing his arms with a smirk. "It's about time," he said, his voice full of pride.

Mom, on the other hand, was already dabbing at her eyes with the corner of her apron. "Oh, Willow," she said, her voice thick with emotion. "This is just perfect. Austin, welcome to the family, officially."

She pulled us both into a hug.

Dad cleared his throat, stepping forward with a rare, soft smile. "I know you've already asked," he said, his gaze landing on Austin. "But you've still got my blessing, son."

Austin chuckled, reaching out to shake Dad's hand. "Thank you, sir. That means the world."

"You can drop the 'sir,'" Dad said, clapping him on the shoulder, his tone suddenly deadpan. "But if you hurt her, just remember, my golf buddies include judges, coroners, and prosecutors. And they all owe me favors."

Austin froze for half a second, then laughed nervously. "Understood."

"Good man." Dad finally grinned, but his eyes were sharp with that unmistakable protective edge only a father could pull off.

I'd never been so mortified and felt so completely loved all at once.

"Dad!" I groaned, my face burning as everyone burst into laughter.

"What?" he said, shrugging innocently. "It's important he understands the stakes."

Austin turned to me, his grin wide but his voice low enough for only me to hear. "Your dad's scary."

I laughed, leaning into him. "You'll survive. Probably."

Gemma, of course, couldn't resist chiming in. "Alright, but can we talk about the ring? Because, Willow, that thing is stunning."

She grabbed my hand, her eyes wide as she admired the diamond sparkling in the soft glow of the porch light. "Austin, you've outdone yourself."

"I had to," he said, his voice low as he looked at me. "She deserves the best."

My heart melted all over again, and I knew my cheeks were probably bright pink.

Through it all, Austin kept his hand in mine, his thumb brushing gentle circles against my skin. And every time I caught his eye, I felt it all over again—the love, the promise, the absolute certainty that this was where I was meant to be.

Chapter 35

Willow

The months that followed felt like a dream on fast-forward—studio sessions, tour stops, back-to-back interviews. Our newest single had hit number one, and somehow, in the midst of all that, Austin and I had found a rhythm. On stage. In the studio. In life.

I sat at the kitchen table in our new home that we'd rushed to find soon after Christmas. I was sipping coffee and scrolling through glowing reviews on my phone.

"Listen to this," I said excitedly as Austin walked in. "Rolling Stone says our lyrics 'strike to the core of the human experience, exploring love and heartbreak with raw honesty.' Can you believe it?"

Austin grinned and kissed the top of my head. "We make a pretty great team, huh?" He poured himself a cup and sat across from me, still smiling.

Over the following weeks, we poured our hearts out onto pages and pages, drafting melodies and lyrics that felt more intimate and soul-baring than anything we'd written before. Late nights in our home studio, harmonizing until our voices turned raspy, tweaking chord progressions until they gave us chills—it was exhausting but exhilarating.

Unbreakable was one of those songs. I still remembered the night we wrote it—just the two of us in the dimly lit studio, a storm raging outside. The lyrics had come from a place of raw honesty, capturing not just the love we shared but the quiet fears and vulnerabilities we'd whispered over the years about each other to the dark. When we finished, we'd sat in silence for a long time, just holding hands and letting the weight of the song settle over us.

When we finally emerged with a new batch of songs, it felt like we were offering up pieces of ourselves. But the risk paid off. The response was incredible, the connection with our fans deepening to a whole new level.

Riding that high, everything else just fell into place—sold-out shows, surreal moments hearing crowds sing our words back to us, seeing our faces on magazine covers. It was a blur of adrenaline and gratitude, punctuated by precious stolen moments for just us.

But not everything was easy. After news of our engagement broke, the media frenzy had been intense. At first, it was thrilling to see our names trending and to read the headlines calling us the "it couple" of country music. But the spotlight burned bright and hot.

The engagement took the spotlight we were already under and cranked it up to blinding. Headlines speculated about the wedding date, the guest list, whether we'd turn it into a live-streamed "event." At first, it was flattering. But it wasn't long before it started to feel invasive.

Austin hated it. "It's our wedding," he said one night, pacing in front of the fireplace. "Not theirs."

He was right. So we drew a line—no public planning updates. No selling our story. Just us, trying to keep something sacred.

One evening we were just getting home when Austin's phone buzzed. He answered on autopilot.

"This is Austin."

He raised an eyebrow, as a grin spread across his face as he lowered the phone and pressed a button to put the call on the speaker.

"Christopher Jordan, it's been a long time, man. How are ya?"

Christopher's deep, familiar voice came through the speaker. "Austin, it's good to hear your voice. I'm doing well, thanks. How about you and Willow?"

Austin leaned back against the couch, his smile widening as he glanced over at me. "We're doing great, Chris. Just got home from the studio. What's up?"

Christopher chuckled. "Sounds like life's treating you well. I've been keeping up with your music, and I have to say, you two are on fire. I actually wanted to talk to you about that."

Austin's interest was piqued. "Oh yeah? What's on your mind?"

"I'm actually calling because I'm interested in recording one of your songs. *Unbreakable*, to be specific. It really hit home with me, and I think it could be a huge hit."

I silently screamed and mouthed, *Yes!*, as Austin chuckled and said, "Man, we'd be honored."

When Christopher mentioned *Unbreakable*, I barely contained my excitement. That song was one of our most personal—something we'd poured our hearts into during a late-night session when neither of us could sleep. To hear someone as big as Christopher say it "hit home" was surreal. This wasn't just a professional milestone; it was validation on a deeply personal level.

Austin pointed to the phone and nodded toward the office. I nodded and headed for the kitchen to start dinner. As I chopped vegetables, I couldn't help but smile to myself. How is this my life? Everything was coming full-circle in ways I could never have imagined. Just a few years ago, I'd been playing covers in local bars, wondering if anyone would ever listen to my own songs. And now here we were—writing music that not only connected with fans but was resonating with one of the biggest names in the industry.

When Austin finally walked into the kitchen, his face lit up with excitement, I knew we were just getting started.

One quiet evening in June, Austin and I were curled up on the couch when the opening chords of *Unbreakable* floated through the speakers of the radio we'd left on in the background. We froze, staring at each other with wide eyes before rushing to turn up the volume. Hearing Christopher Jordan's voice pour his soul into our song was surreal. The DJ rattled off chart stats as my eyes filled with tears.

Austin grabbed my hand, his grip tight and full of pride. "That's our song, Wills," he whispered. "We did that."

Chapter 36

Willow

The August air was warm and golden as I stepped into the open field, my white dress sweeping the grass. Wildflowers danced in the breeze, but all I could see was Austin, waiting beneath an arch of lavender and daisies, eyes locked on mine like we were the only two people in the world.

The mountains rose up around us, ancient and majestic, bearing witness to this moment we'd been dreaming of for so long.

This wasn't the grand, over-the-top ceremony the media had been speculating about for months. After weeks of headlines screaming about designer dresses, celebrity guest lists, and sponsorship deals, we'd decided to leak fake wedding plans to throw them off our trail.

In reality, we were here. Montana mountains, close friends, and a wildflower arch. Austin had said, "Let them chase a wild goose. This one's just for us." And it was.

Now, here we were. No paparazzi, no flashing cameras. Just us, standing under the open sky, with the people we loved most in the world gathered around.

As I walked down the aisle, the faces of our loved ones blurred into a sea of smiles and happy tears. But my gaze remained locked on

Austin, my partner in every sense of the word. With each step, memories flooded through me—the first time we sang together, the first time we said "I love you," the countless nights spent poring over our songs and writing our future.

Finally, I reached him, and he took my hands in his. "You look stunning," he whispered, his voice thick with feeling.

The ceremony was a whirlwind of laughter, tears, and heartfelt vows. As we exchanged rings, a sense of overwhelming rightness settled over me. This was it. This was the beginning of our forever.

"I now pronounce you husband and wife. You may kiss the bride!"

Austin pulled me into his arms, and as our lips met, the crowd erupted into cheers. In that perfect moment, everything else fell away. The challenges we'd faced, the uncertainties of the future—none of it mattered. All that existed was our love, the beautiful life we'd built together, and the infinite possibilities stretching out before us.

As we turned to face our friends and family, hand in hand, I felt invincible. The applause and cheers surrounded us like a warm embrace, and for a moment, it felt like time had stopped. Austin squeezed my hand, his gaze fixed on mine, and in his eyes, I saw everything I could have ever wanted—love, hope, the promise of a future we were building together.

Under strings of glowing lights, Austin twirled me across the dance floor as laughter and fiddle music filled the air.

My mom wiped happy tears from her cheeks during Caleb's toast, where he somehow managed to be both heartfelt and hilariously embarrassing at the same time. And Shep? He pulled out moves I was certain hadn't been seen since the 1970s, his joy radiating through every step.

And through it all, Austin never let go of my hand.

It was the kind of day I'd always dreamed of—the kind of day you hold onto when things get hard, the memory of it glowing in your heart like a lantern.

It had been only a month since Austin and I had stood under the wildflower arch, promising forever. Just over a month since Christopher Jordan's version of *Unbreakable* had swept the charts, giving our songwriting career a new level of credibility. And now, we were diving headfirst into the *Home to You* tour, riding the wave of our own momentum.

On paper, it was everything I'd ever wanted. Our career was on fire. Fans were more engaged than ever. And I was standing side by side with the love of my life, chasing our dreams together. But sometimes, when the lights dimmed and the adrenaline faded, I'd catch myself wondering if I was just one misstep away from it all crashing down.

Two weeks into the tour, those quiet doubts were harder to ignore. The exhilaration of performing night after night, connecting with our fans, and sharing our music was undeniable. But the long days, the constant travel, and the unrelenting pace were starting to take a toll. Exhaustion had crept into my bones, and no matter how much I tried to brush it off, it lingered like a shadow, growing heavier with every passing day.

By the final leg of the tour, I could feel the exhaustion weighing on me more heavily. My throat was perpetually raw, my body ached in places I didn't even know could ache, and there were mornings when just getting out of bed felt like a monumental task. During one performance, the lights felt too bright, the crowd too loud, and my vision swam for just a second before Austin shot me a concerned look across the stage. I smiled through it, but deep down, I knew something had to give.

When New Year's Eve arrived, marking the final show of the tour, I was running on sheer determination.

"Wills," Austin said, his voice gentle as he caught my wrist while I was digging through my suitcase. "You look wiped. Are you sure you're up for tonight?"

"I'm fine," I replied automatically, forcing a smile. But the way his eyes lingered on me, full of worry, made me hesitate.

He brushed a strand of hair from my face, his thumb grazing my cheek. "You don't have to power through, you know. If you need to take a break—if you need to rest—we'll figure it out."

I swallowed the lump in my throat and nodded, grateful for him even as I tried to push down the rising tide of fatigue. "I'm okay," I said softly, though I wasn't entirely sure I believed it.

As the last notes of our encore rang out and the stage lights dimmed, Austin pulled me into a sweaty embrace, his chest heaving from the high-energy performance. His eyes sparkled with the thrill of the moment.

"Happy New Year, baby," he murmured, his breath warm against my ear.

I mustered a smile, but it didn't quite reach my eyes. The crowd's cheers faded into the background as the weariness settled over me like a lead blanket. I didn't want to dampen Austin's joy, so I tucked my unease away for the time being. But deep down, I knew something had to change.

A few weeks later, back in the comfort of our home, I finally found the courage to bring it up. We'd just finished dinner, and Austin was strumming his guitar on the couch while I folded a pile of laundry. My stomach twisted with nerves as I set down the laundry basket and sat across from him.

"Hey, babe," I began, my fingers fidgeting with the hem of my shirt. "I've been thinking a lot about the future lately."

He set the guitar down, his brow furrowing with concern as he leaned forward. "What's on your mind?"

"I," I hesitated, my heart pounding. "I'm not sure I want to keep touring," I admitted, the words rushing out before I could overthink them. "It's been amazing, but I'm feeling pulled toward focusing more on writing and recording music."

Austin's eyes searched mine, and for a moment, I worried he might take it the wrong way. "What do you mean?" he asked softly. "Are you not happy touring anymore?"

"It's not that," I sighed, trying to find the right words. "I love performing, and I love connecting with our fans. But the constant travel and back-to-back shows is taking a toll on me—mentally, physically, emotionally. I just think I need a change of pace, to pour more of myself into the creative process. I'm not saying I want to stop performing altogether, but..."

I trailed off, struggling to articulate the pull I felt toward a quieter, more deliberate way of creating. I glanced down at my lap, feeling vulnerable in a way I hadn't expected.

Austin tilted his head slightly, his eyes searching mine with that quiet intensity I'd come to love so much. "Wills," he said softly, his voice steady, "we've been through so much, and I can see how it's wearing on you. If stepping back is what you need, then that's what we'll do. I just want to make sure you're okay. Really okay."

His words made my throat tighten with emotion, and I nodded. "I think I just need time to breathe," I admitted, my voice trembling. "I'm not saying I'll never perform again—I love it too much to walk away entirely. But right now, I feel like I'm running on empty. I can't keep this pace."

Austin's hands tightened slightly around mine, grounding me. "Then we'll find a new pace," he said firmly, his gaze unwavering. "We'll do this on your terms—our terms. You don't have to prove anything to anyone, Willow. Not to me, not to the industry, not to the fans. You've already given them so much of yourself. Now it's time to take care of you. Tell me what you need."

I felt the tears spill over, and I let out a shaky laugh as I swiped at them. "How did I get so lucky?" I murmured, leaning into him.

He wrapped me in his arms, pressing a kiss to the top of my head.

"I'm the lucky one," he whispered. "I've got you, and I'm not letting anything—or anyone—wear you down."

I felt the knot in my chest loosen, replaced by a quiet sense of hope. "I love you," I whispered, leaning into his touch. "Thank you for understanding."

"I love you. Always," he said, his lips brushing against my forehead. "You're my everything, Willow. And I'll do whatever it takes to make sure you're taken care of. I've got you."

Chapter 37

Austin

The normally bustling streets seemed almost serene in the early morning light, a stark contrast to the storm of thoughts swirling in my mind. Willow's hand in mine was the only steadying force, a constant reminder that whatever came next, we were in it together. Because were a team. The best team.

We arrived at Mitch's studio, the familiar sight of the building bringing a flicker of comfort. Mitch had been with us from the very beginning, a grounding presence through every high and low. If anyone could help us navigate this new chapter, it was him.

"Morning, Austin. Morning, Willow," Mitch greeted us with his usual easy smile as we walked into his office. But the moment he caught sight of Willow, his smile faltered just slightly.

"Morning, Mitch," I said, forcing my voice to sound steady. Willow glanced at me, her own nervous energy radiating through our joined hands.

Mitch gestured toward the chairs in front of his desk. "Come on in. I was surprised to see your e-mail last week. What's on your minds?"

Willow's hand twitched slightly in mine. I could feel the pulse at her wrist—a little faster than usual. I squeezed her fingers, hoping she'd borrow some of my steadiness.

"Mitch, we need to talk about the tour and what's next for Grace & Gravel."

Mitch leaned back in his chair, concern flickering across his face. "Is everything okay?"

Willow took a deep breath, her voice steady but tinged with weariness. "Mitch, I've been feeling really exhausted lately. The constant travel and back-to-back shows... it's starting to take a toll on me. I think I need to step back from touring for a while."

Watching her say it aloud—out in the open, in front of Mitch—made my chest ache with equal parts pride and sadness. Pride, because it took guts to name your limits in an industry that demanded you ignore them. Sadness, because I hadn't known how close she'd come to burning out.

Her smile was softer now, but there were still shadows under her eyes that makeup couldn't hide. I'd noticed her picking at her food lately, eating just enough to get by. And at night, when she thought I was asleep, I'd feel the mattress shift as she lay awake, staring at the ceiling. It made me want to wrap her in bubble wrap and hide her away from anything that could hurt her—but I knew that wasn't what she needed.

Mitch leaned forward, his hands clasped on the desk, his face thoughtful. "I understand, Willow. Your health and well-being come first. But what does this mean for the band?"

I tightened my grip on her hand, feeling her tension. "We're not giving up on Grace & Gravel," I said firmly. "We just need to figure out a new path forward. Maybe we can focus on writing and recording for a while."

Mitch nodded slowly. "That makes sense. We could explore some new collaborations. How do you feel about that?"

Willow's eyes brightened slightly, the smallest glimmer of excitement breaking through her exhaustion. "I like that idea. Collaborating with other artists could be a great way to stay creative without the pressure of touring."

"I'll start reaching out," Mitch said, his tone reassuring. "There have been several artists who've expressed interest in working with you two before."

I nodded, feeling a spark of hope. "Yeah, let's see if they're interested. That sounds like a good next step."

Mitch hesitated for a moment, his gaze flicking between us. "Austin, have you thought about doing some solo gigs in the meantime? Just to keep your presence strong while Willow takes some time?"

I shook my head without hesitation. "I'm not closing the door on Grace & Gravel. Willow and I are a team, and I want to keep it that way."

Mitch nodded, his expression understanding. "Alright. I'll keep that in mind. In the meantime, maybe you two should take a break. Get away for a bit."

Willow looked at me, her eyes searching mine before she nodded. "That's actually what we were thinking. We want to take a trip to Montana, spend some time with family, and decompress."

Mitch smiled, the warmth in his expression genuine. "That sounds like a great idea. Take all the time you need. Your fans will understand, and we'll be here when you're ready to come back."

As we left Mitch's office, a sense of calm settled over me. The mountains of home beckoned, promising a much-needed respite and the chance to find our footing once more.

———

The drive to Montana was long but peaceful. We took turns behind the wheel, letting the rhythm of the road soothe us. For the first time in weeks, there was no rush, no schedule to follow.

The highway stretched on for miles, and the silence between us wasn't heavy—it was full. Like both of us had finally stopped holding our breath.

Regardless which one of us was driving, Willow's hand stayed in mine. Our conversations were light, though it was obvious our thoughts were heavy.

I'd built this dream with Willow by my side. The idea of performing without her, of recording songs she might not sing, felt wrong somehow. Like trying to play a guitar without the strings. I didn't want to let my mind wander to the "what-ifs," but they lurked anyway. What if this was the beginning of something we couldn't come back from?

I glanced over at Willow as she stared out the window, the setting sun casting a golden glow on her face. She looked peaceful, a small smile playing on her lips. The shadows under her eyes were still there, but they didn't seem quite as dark.

By the time we pulled into the ranch, the sight of the familiar mountains and open fields brought a sense of calm I hadn't felt in a long time. My mom and dad were waiting on the porch, their faces lighting up with joy as we climbed out of the car.

"It's so good to have you home," Mom said, pulling Willow into a warm hug.

"It's good to be home," I replied, my chest swelling with a sense of peace I hadn't realized I'd been missing.

The days passed in a blur of quiet moments and simple pleasures. Mornings were spent hiking through the woods, the air crisp and fresh. Afternoons were filled with fishing by the river or helping Dad with ranch chores. Evenings were spent around the fireplace, sharing stories and laughter that seemed to wash away the tension we'd been carrying.

We fell into a rhythm without even trying. Willow would make breakfast with Mom and then disappear into the hills with a notebook and no plan. She came back each time with flushed cheeks and new melodies hummed under her breath.

Some days, I followed. Some days, I let her go alone. Both felt right.

One morning, I found Willow sitting on the porch steps, a cup of coffee in her hands and a plate of biscuits she'd swiped from the kitchen. "You're up early," I said, sitting down beside her.

I hadn't seen her eat this much in weeks. She laughed louder. Slept deeper. Her color came back. Her words came back. I could see her—really see her—returning to herself.

She offered me a biscuit, her cheeks a little fuller than they'd been weeks ago, her eyes brighter. "Couldn't sleep," she admitted, her voice light. "And I just wanted to watch the sunrise."

The relief that washed over me was so intense it almost made me laugh. I didn't say anything, just reached for her hand, letting the moment settle between us.

That evening, Willow turned to me, her head resting on my shoulder. When she said, "Maybe we should think about spending more time here," it wasn't wistful. It was certain.

And when I answered, "I think that's a great idea," what I meant was: I'd follow you anywhere.

She smiled, her fingers lacing with mine. "I love you."

"I love you, too," I whispered, pulling her closer.

For the first time in months, I felt a flicker of uncertainty about the future, but I quickly brushed it away. Whatever came next, we'd face it together. Because that's what we did.

Chapter 38

Willow

It had been a few months since Austin and I had returned from Montana, and the slower pace of life had done wonders for us. The days no longer blurred together in a rush of flights, call times, or dressing rooms. We'd sold songs to some of the biggest names in country music, started planning out a new album of our own, and soaked up quiet moments just the two if us. Morning coffee on the porch. Afternoons spent curled up in sun-drenched corners of the home studio. Late-night writing sessions punctuated by candles, half-finished lyrics, and stolen kisses.

The success of *Unbreakable*—the song Christopher Jordan had carried to the top of the charts—had cracked something open for us. It gave us breathing room. It gave us freedom. For the first time in years, we weren't chasing the dream at breakneck speed—we were living it.

But despite how steady everything looked on the outside, I couldn't shake the feeling that something was off inside me.

I sat at the piano, fingers drifting absently over the keys, pulling an old melody from the past—one I hadn't played since before the tour. It felt hauntingly familiar and oddly disconnected, like hearing my own voice echo from another room. The notes rang out steady and sweet, but my thoughts were knotted and chaotic.

Austin's voice carried in from the kitchen, warm and easy. "Tea's almost ready. Want to take a break?"

I blinked down at the keys before slowly standing. "Yeah," I said quietly, padding barefoot into the kitchen.

He slid a mug toward me and sat down across the table, studying me in that quiet way of his. His hand reached across the table, fingers brushing mine. "You've been off for a couple of weeks," he said gently. "Talk to me, Wills."

I wrapped my hands around the mug, letting the steam curl into my face. "I don't know," I said, too softly. "My cycles have been weird since the last tour. I chalked it up to stress at first, but something still doesn't feel right."

Austin's brow furrowed. He didn't speak, just waited.

"I've been nauseous a lot. Sore. Bloated," I went on, my voice thin. "Sometimes there's this fluttering in my stomach. I took a pregnancy test a couple weeks ago—it was negative—but I still don't feel like myself."

His thumb traced a slow circle against the back of my hand. "Maybe it was too early," he offered. "Or maybe it was a false negative. It happens, right?"

"Maybe," I echoed, but the word sat hollow in my mouth. "It's more than that. There's this pressure. A dull ache that doesn't go away. It's like my body's trying to tell me something, and I haven't been listening."

Austin's jaw tensed, and for a second, he dropped his gaze to our hands before lifting his eyes back to mine. "Then we're going to a doctor," he said. Simple. Certain. "Tomorrow. First thing."

I nodded, the weight I'd been carrying for weeks finally easing from my chest. I was still scared—but less of the unknown now, and more of what waiting any longer might cost me. Saying it out loud didn't fix anything.

But at least I wasn't carrying it alone anymore.

The next morning, the waiting room of Dr. Meyers' office was too white, too bright. I sat curled into myself, fingers tangled in the hem of my sweater. Austin sat beside me, knee bouncing a steady rhythm, his presence grounding but taut.

When they finally called my name, we stood together.

Dr. Meyers greeted us with a warm smile that didn't quite reach her eyes. "Tell me what's been going on, Willow."

I went through it all again—symptoms, the test, the feeling that something wasn't quite right. Austin sat next to me, his hand a steady weight on my knee.

"We'll run some tests," she said after I finished. "Blood work, and I want to do an ultrasound just to rule a few things out."

The blood work was over in minutes. The ultrasound, though—that was something else.

I lay on the table in a dimly lit room, cool gel spreading across my skin as the technician moved the probe across my abdomen. The monitor glowed in blues and grays, shapes I couldn't decipher flickering and shifting across the screen.

Austin stood at my side, hand wrapped around mine, eyes locked on the monitor as if he might crack the code through sheer will. The technician's expression never changed—too neutral, too careful—and her silence only made my heart pound harder.

"I'll send these to Dr. Meyers," she said when she was done. "She'll be in shortly."

The door clicked shut behind her, and the room felt too quiet. Too still.

"You're okay," Austin whispered, sitting beside me, brushing his thumb across the back of my hand. But his voice cracked just slightly on the last word.

I turned my face toward the ceiling, blinking fast.

We waited.

And waited.

When the door finally opened again, Dr. Meyers stepped inside holding a slim folder. She closed it gently and sat down, her eyes warm, but grave.

She didn't speak right away.

I sat up. Austin's hand gripped mine tighter.

The air in the room shifted.

I couldn't explain it, but somehow—I already knew. Whatever she told us would change the trajectory of our lives forever.

Chapter 39

Austin

The door creaked open, and Dr. Meyers stepped into the room with the kind of careful composure that made my stomach clench. Willow's grip on my hand tightened instinctively—her fingers cold, trembling slightly against mine—and all I could think about was how badly I wanted to take this fear away from her. Absorb it. Replace it with something safe.

But I couldn't.

Dr. Meyers settled into her chair, folding her hands on the desk in front of her. Her expression was calm—professional—but her silence stretched just a little too long. Just enough to spike my heart into a gallop.

"Willow. Austin," she began gently, her voice smooth and even, like someone trying not to alarm a skittish animal. "I have the results of your ultrasound."

Willow's breath hitched. I felt her body stiffen beside me, her shoulders tense and braced, as if her body already knew what her mind wasn't ready to hear.

I gave her hand a small squeeze, grounding her, grounding myself. Just say it. Please, just say it.

Dr. Meyers offered the barest smile, a flicker of something soft around the eyes. "First, I want to offer my congratulations. Willow, you're pregnant. Based on the measurements, I'd estimate you're around ten weeks along."

For one glorious second, everything in me stilled.

Pregnant.

Pregnant.

We were having a baby.

The word echoed in my chest like a dropped stone in still water. Willow stared at her hands for a moment, like she wasn't sure she'd heard correctly. Then she let out a shaky laugh, her free hand drifting instinctively to her abdomen, tears already slipping from the corners of her eyes.

"A baby," she whispered, her voice breaking open. "We're having a baby."

I was on my feet before I could think, pulling her into my arms, burying my face in her hair as my own tears burned hot and fast. "I love you," I whispered, over and over, a prayer, a promise, a vow. "I love you, so much."

But beneath the joy was something else—an unease that pulsed at the edges of my happiness like a dark tide pulling at the shore.

Because Dr. Meyers' smile hadn't lasted.

Because she didn't look finished delivering news.

Because the air in the room had shifted again—tilting, tightening.

"There's something else, isn't there?" I asked, even though I already knew.

She nodded, the warmth in her eyes still there, but edged with gravity now. "Yes," she said carefully. "The ultrasound showed something concerning."

Willow's hand went slack in mine.

A cold knot twisted low in my gut.

Dr. Meyers continued, her voice steady but heavy. "There's a mass on your left ovary. It could be a cyst—those are actually common during pregnancy—but the size and shape are atypical. It's large enough, and complex enough, that we need to rule out the possibility of cancer."

The word hit like a blow to the ribs.

Cancer.

I felt it physically—the wind knocked clean from my lungs, the blood draining from my face. Willow flinched like she'd been slapped, her hand going protectively to her stomach, as if she could shield the life inside her from that single, terrifying word.

"Cancer?" she echoed, barely audible. "But I'm—I'm pregnant. What does that mean for the baby? For me?"

Dr. Meyers' voice softened even more, every word coated in compassion. "I know this is a lot to process. And I want to be clear—we don't know yet what we're dealing with. There's a strong chance it's benign. But we need to take it seriously."

Willow nodded once, her tears falling silently now. I could see her retreating inward, the way she did when she was overwhelmed, when the world got too loud.

I had to speak. I had to ask the next question, even if I didn't want the answer.

"What happens now?"

"We'll schedule an MRI to get a clearer image," Dr. Meyers said. "And depending on what we see, we may need to do a biopsy. I'm also consulting with a maternal-fetal specialist and an oncologist to make sure every step we take considers both Willow's health and the baby's."

I nodded slowly, trying to absorb it all, trying to focus on logistics so I wouldn't fall apart. Willow sat completely still, her eyes glassy, her whole body curled slightly forward—like she was protecting the little life growing inside her from the weight of the unknown.

When I reached for her again, she came into my arms without hesitation. I wrapped myself around her as best I could, keeping her anchored, even if I was unraveling myself.

"We'll get through this," I whispered against her temple. "Whatever it is, whatever comes next—we'll face it together."

She nodded, but her voice cracked when she spoke. "I'm scared, Austin," she whispered. "What if it's bad? What if I can't—"

She didn't finish the sentence, but I knew what she meant.

What if I can't survive this?

What if I have to choose?

I pulled back just enough to cup her face, to make her look at me. "You are the strongest person I've ever known," I said, my voice rough with emotion. "You've walked through fire more times than I can count—and you came out stronger every single time. We are not giving up. Not now. Not ever."

Her lower lip trembled, but she nodded, a fragile smile ghosting across her lips. "I don't know what I'd do without you."

"You'll never have to find out," I said. "I'm here. Always."

Dr. Meyers gave us another moment before speaking again, her voice kind but purposeful. "We'll take this one step at a time. My nurse will call with your MRI appointment and next steps. For now, go home. Rest. Be gentle with each other."

I stood first, helping Willow to her feet. Her hand found mine again immediately, as if it belonged there. Maybe it did.

"Thank you," I said hoarsely.

The ride home was quiet. We didn't turn on the radio. We didn't talk much. We just held hands, fingers woven tight like we were clinging to the edge of something—grief, fear, hope. I didn't know.

All I knew was this: we were going to fight.

For Willow.

For the baby.

For the life we hadn't even met yet.

And I was going to hold on with everything I had.

Chapter 40

Willow

June 15th.

I would never forget that date. It burned itself into my bones like a brand—etched deep, unshakable, inescapable. The day everything changed.

"High-grade serous ovarian carcinoma," Dr. Meyers said, her voice measured and careful, like she already knew she was dropping a bomb and didn't want to trigger the explosion too quickly.

I sat there on the paper-covered exam table, my arms crossed protectively over the paper gown that felt too thin, too revealing, too helpless. The word cancer echoed through my skull, but the rest of her sentence blurred behind it. I tried to focus on the cool air brushing across my bare legs. The hum of the overhead light. The rhythm of Austin's thumb gently stroking the back of my hand.

None of it helped. I was floating—disconnected from my body, from the moment.

"What does this mean?" I asked finally, my voice small and foreign to my own ears. "For the baby. For me."

Austin didn't speak. He just stood beside me, his body rigid, one hand gripping my shoulder like he was afraid I might vanish if he let go.

Dr. Meyers' eyes softened with something close to sorrow. "It means we have a fight ahead of us. But we're going to do everything in our power to give both of you the best possible chance."

She kept talking—about staging, scans, next steps—but the words melted into background noise. A low hum I couldn't tune into. All I could hear was cancer. And pregnant. And the impossible collision of those two realities.

I felt the tremor in Austin's body before I heard his voice. "What does that look like? The fight?" he asked. His voice was tight, like he was holding back a scream. "What are the options?"

Dr. Meyers folded her hands. "The most effective path forward is immediate treatment. Surgery and chemotherapy."

"But the baby," I whispered.

Her pause said more than the words that followed.

"The chemotherapy regimen required in your case poses a serious risk to the fetus. In most instances, we recommend terminating the pregnancy before starting treatment."

The room spun.

Terminate.

The air in my lungs vanished. I stared at her, willing her to say something else—to say *unless*, or *but*, or *wait*.

I felt Austin go stark still.

"No," I said, shaking my head as the tears spilled over. "No. I can't do that. I won't."

"Willow," Austin's voice cracked beside me, raw and unsure. "Are you sure?"

I turned to him, and his face wrecked me—because it wasn't just fear I saw there. It was grief. Love. Panic. Powerlessness.

"This is our baby," I said, my voice trembling but steady. "I can't end his or her life to save mine. I can't."

Dr. Meyers looked between us with open sympathy. "Delaying

treatment is dangerous," she said gently. "But if you choose to carry the pregnancy, we'll adjust the plan. We'll fight with you."

Austin stepped forward, kneeling in front of me, both of his hands holding mine now. His eyes were shining, and he looked like he was unraveling by the second. "I don't want to lose either of you," he said, his voice barely more than a whisper.

"You won't," I promised him, pressing my forehead to his. "You won't lose me."

I didn't know if it was a lie. But I needed to believe it. We both did.

Dr. Meyers outlined a new plan: a consultation with a high-risk OB, oncology coordination, MRIs, lab work, more specialists. The odds were thin. But there was a path. A narrow, jagged, terrifying one.

And I was going to walk it.

The following weeks blurred into a strange new rhythm. Mornings filled with doctor's appointments. Evenings too quiet, too heavy. And always—always—the weight of what we weren't saying.

Nausea came in waves, sometimes from the baby, sometimes from the fear. I could no longer tell the difference.

The doctors assembled a team. Dr. Patel, the oncologist, with kind eyes and a steady presence. Dr. Novak, the maternal-fetal medicine specialist, who pulled no punches and took no crap.

Dr. Novak was the first to give me hope.

"This won't be easy," she said, cold gel already smeared across my abdomen as she prepared for yet another ultrasound. "But if you're committed, we'll meet you there."

Then, the heartbeat filled the room.

That sound—rapid, insistent, impossibly tiny but so strong—cut through the fear like sunlight.

Dr. Novak's lips tugged into the ghost of a smile. "Strong little fighter you've got there."

And for the first time in weeks, I smiled back.

Every blood draw felt like offering up a sacrifice. Every scan involved a question I wasn't sure I wanted the answer to. I was poked and prodded so often I stopped flinching.

My body felt foreign—bloated, sore, stretched thin by cancer and pregnancy and medication.

But then I'd feel it.

A flutter. A shift. A reminder.

Our baby was still there. Still holding on.

And so was I.

Austin never left my side. Not once.

When I sobbed into the pillow in the middle of the night, thinking he was asleep, he would pull me into his chest and whisper promises.

When I couldn't keep food down for days and cried over spilled soup on the kitchen floor, he kissed my forehead and said, "You're still the strongest person I know."

He was my anchor. My lighthouse. My safe place.

But I saw the cracks.

The way he'd disappear into the garage and scream. The calls he made to his brother when he thought I wasn't listening. The haunted look in his eyes when he thought I wasn't watching.

He was breaking for me.

And I didn't know how to stop it.

But through it all, I never regretted my choice.

Every time I felt the tiny movements, I remembered why I was fighting.

Every time Austin rested his hand on my stomach and whispered, "Hey, little one," I remembered what was at stake.

Every appointment that didn't bring worse news was a tiny, fragile victory.

The odds were long. The road was brutal.

But there was a heartbeat.

And as long as my tiny warrior was fighting, so was I.

Chapter 41

Willow

I didn't know how long we sat there, wrapped around each other like lifelines—Austin's arms fixed around me, his chest rising and falling beneath my cheek like the last steady rhythm in a world that suddenly made no sense.

The living room was dim, quiet. Layers of silence that seemed to wrap around us like a shroud. My tears had soaked into his shirt, warm and endless, and he never once flinched or pulled away. He just held me. Like if he stayed strong enough, long enough, maybe he could keep this from swallowing us whole.

When my stomach growled, it startled me. I hadn't realized how long it had been since I'd eaten—since anything had tasted like anything at all. Austin let out a soft breath, tightening his arms around me for a moment before slowly easing back.

"I'm going to order dinner," he said gently. His voice was hoarse, raw, but controlled. The effort it took to sound normal? I saw right through it.

I watched him disappear down the hallway toward our bedroom, his shoulders slumped in a way that made my heart shatter all over again. He was breaking in private so I didn't have to watch. That was who he was. He gave me space to feel and made space for his own grief quietly, respectfully. I loved him more in that moment than I ever had before—and I didn't think I had room left to love him more.

I stared down at the phone in my hand. I already knew what came next. What had to come next.

We had to tell them.

The people who loved us. The ones who'd raised us, laughed with us, believed in us long before we had a stage to stand on or a spotlight to hide behind. I couldn't imagine their faces when they heard the words I was about to say. I didn't want to.

But they deserved to know. And they deserved to hear it from me.

My fingers hovered over my brother's name in my contacts. Caleb. My rock, my shield growing up, the one person who could always make me laugh when I wanted to cry. I typed and deleted the message three times before finally sending it.

> Me: Hey, Caleb. I need a favor. Can you go to Mom and Dad's house? I have some news I need to share with them, but I want you to be there too. Let me know when you're with them, and I'll call.

And then I waited.

The quiet stretched like a held breath, heavy and suffocating. I must've fallen asleep because the next thing I knew, I was blinking awake beneath a soft blanket, the taste of dried salt on my lips and the ache of exhaustion deep in my bones.

Austin appeared like a ghost from the kitchen, his hands cradling a bowl that sent a warm, familiar scent curling through the air. Ginger and turkey soup from the deli he'd discovered not far from here—I'd quickly found it was my new favorite.

He knelt beside the couch, his expression tender, offering the bowl without a word. I took it with a grateful smile, my voice scratchy when I said, "Thank you."

"Anything for you," he murmured, settling in beside me. His

hand rubbed gentle circles along my spine as I brought the spoon to my lips, the warmth doing more to thaw the fog inside me than anything had all week.

We didn't speak. We didn't need to.

The soft clink of the spoon against the ceramic bowl was the only sound until my phone buzzed on the coffee table beside us.

Caleb: I'm here.

Just two words, but they felt like a weight dropped into my chest. Final. Real.

Austin saw the screen and took my hand, threading our fingers together. His eyes met mine, calm and steady. "Whenever you're ready."

I nodded, even though I didn't feel ready at all. I picked up the phone with trembling fingers and tapped the call button before I could change my mind.

It rang once. Twice.

Then—

"Willow?" Mom's voice filled my ear, warm and familiar and so achingly comforting it nearly undid me. "Caleb said you needed to talk to us. Is everything okay, sweetie?"

I opened my mouth but nothing came out. Just a thick knot of emotion lodged in my throat.

"I have some difficult news," I managed finally, my voice shaking with the weight of it.

The line fell silent, tension crackling across the miles.

"What is it, Willow?" Dad asked, gentle but strained. "You can tell us anything, you know that."

I closed my eyes and reached for Austin's hand again, grounding myself in his steady presence. My voice came low, but clear. "I've been diagnosed with ovarian cancer. High-grade serous carcinoma. And, I'm also pregnant."

The silence on the other end of the line felt like gravity itself—

thick, dense, unrelenting. And then, Mom's breath caught audibly. "Oh, Willow..." she whispered. "My baby girl."

Tears burned hot against my cheeks.

"I know," I said, barely breathing. "It's a lot. I'm scared, too. But we're fighting this. Austin and I—we're doing everything we can to protect the baby, and to get through this."

Dad's voice came next, quiet but filled with iron. "We'll be there as soon as we can. Whatever you need, whenever you need it. We love you. You hear me?"

I nodded, even though they couldn't see it. "I hear you. I love you, too."

In the background, I heard Caleb's voice—low, steady, soothing— probably holding Mom's hand, doing what big brothers and good sons do. I hated picturing her breaking. Hated knowing I was the reason.

After we ended the call, I sat frozen on the couch, my phone clutched in my hands like a lifeline.

Austin reached for me again, his arm wrapping around my shoulders, and I let myself fold into him. I didn't have to hold myself together with him. I didn't have to pretend.

"We're going to get through this," he whispered against my hair.

I nodded slowly. "I know," I said. "But it's going to be the hardest thing we've ever done."

Austin leaned back enough to look me in the eye, his voice low but certain. "Nothing worth fighting for ever comes easy."

I exhaled, long and slow. Then I reached down and rested my hand against my belly.

There it was again. That faint, fluttering sensation. The softest little whisper from the life growing inside me. A brush of hope in the middle of everything else.

"Hey there," I whispered, my voice shaky but full of love. "I don't know what the future holds, but I promise you this: I'm going to fight with everything I have to make sure you get to see this world. To feel the sun on your face, to hear the music your dad and I love so much, to laugh and dream and grow. You and me, we're in this together, okay?"

Austin squeezed my hand, his touch a lifeline in the chaos. "Yes, we are," he said, and despite everything, despite the fear and the uncertainty, I found myself smiling.

Because in that moment, I believed him. I believed in us, in the strength of our love, in the power of the tiny spark of life we had created together.

And that belief, that hope, would carry us through whatever lay ahead. It had to.

Chapter 42

Austin

The house was silent—eerily so—except for the hum of the refrigerator. Willow was finally asleep, her breathing slow and even, her fingers curled gently against the soft swell of her belly. Even in sleep, she rested her hand there like it was instinct. Like her body already knew to protect the life growing inside her, even if everything else was threatening to fall apart.

I didn't want to wake her. She needed the rest. Her body had been through enough this week—this month—and if sleep gave her even a moment of peace, I wasn't going to take that away from her.

But I couldn't sit still any longer.

I slipped off the couch quietly, careful not to shift the cushions too much, and grabbed my phone from the counter. The screen lit up in my hand as I walked barefoot through the house to the back deck, the floorboards cool beneath my feet. I eased the sliding door open and stepped into the thick warmth of the summer night. The huge back yard stretched out before me, dark and littered with soft shadows from the trees and moonlight.

I'd told my brother pretty soon after we'd found out about Willow's diagnosis. Asking him not to mention it to our parents was as good as sealing a vault at Fort Knox. Connor had promised to keep the news to himself and had been a cornerstone in moments when I needed to let my overflow of emotions land somewhere.

His life hadn't been easy—being different in a world built for others wasn't something he'd ever taken lightly. Processing emotions wasn't something that came naturally; it was an analytical task, whether sorting through his own feelings or reading those of someone else.

But love? That was something he understood in his own quiet way. When I needed him, Connor didn't flood me with words or demands. Instead, he'd show up, he'd answer—steady, calm, like a lighthouse cutting through a storm.

I remembered one night Willow had a really bad spell of nausea that seemed to never want to end. Though miles away, I'd called him feeling completely helpless. He didn't bombard me with questions or advice. Instead, he listened. A little while later, my phone buzzed with a detailed message from him.

He'd researched ways to help with Willow's nausea and found that ginger and broth could be soothing. Along with the info, he'd sent a link to a local place that made a ginger turkey soup—not far from our house.

That soup had quickly become one of Willow's favorites.

It had been Connor's way of saying, I'm here. I'm thinking about you, even from afar. Practical, quiet, unwavering.

Telling him had been easy. It was the next call that I wasn't sure how to make.

My thumb hovered over the screen, over one name—Mom—for longer than I'd meant it to.

Then I tapped the button and pressed the phone to my ear.

It rang twice.

"Austin?" Her voice was immediate, alert. Like she already knew. Like she'd felt something shift in the universe. A mother's intuition maybe? "Honey, is everything okay?"

I swallowed hard. My voice tried to come out steady—it didn't. "Hey, Mom. Do you have a minute? I, I need to talk to you and Dad."

There was a pause. A beat of quiet.

Then I heard her call out for my father, her voice lower now, more serious. A moment later, his voice filtered onto the line too, calm and solid like it always was.

"Austin," Dad said. "What's going on?"

I gripped the deck's railing with my free hand and stared out at the darkness, sounds of insects and frogs a thousand small distractions. But nothing could fully pull my focus away from what I was about to say.

"It's Willow," I began. "She's," the words stuck in my throat. "She's been diagnosed with ovarian cancer."

The silence that followed hollowed out the air.

For a second, I thought the call had dropped, but then I heard my mom's breath catch on the other end. "Oh my word," she whispered. "Austin, I'm so sorry. How is she? How are you?"

I clenched my jaw. My voice broke anyway. "She's scared. We both are. But she's trying to stay strong for the baby."

Another pause. This one sharper.

"The baby?" Dad echoed, his voice cutting through with a mix of confusion and something heavier.

"She's pregnant," I said, the words tumbling out in a rush. "Eleven weeks, actually. And she's made up her mind. She wants to keep the baby. Even though the doctors said it complicates everything. Even though they recommended terminating. She said no."

There was no stopping it now. The words kept pouring out, the dam cracked then it was broken.

"I'm trying to be strong. For her. For both of them. But I don't know how. I don't know how to hold her up when I feel like I'm falling apart."

My forehead pressed against the railing, the wood rough and grounding beneath my skin. I didn't realize my hand had curled into a fist until I felt my nails biting into my palm.

Dad's voice came first, quiet but sure. "Austin. You don't have to carry this alone. You've got us. You've got her family. You're not walking through this by yourself, son."

And then Mom again, gentler this time. "And Willow—Willow is stronger than even she realizes. You once told me she was the strongest person you'd ever known. That hasn't changed."

"I just..." My throat closed up. "I can't lose her. Or the baby. I can't imagine what that would even look like."

"You don't have to," Mom said, her voice tight with emotion. "You don't have to imagine the worst. You just focus on today. One breath, one moment, one step at a time. That's all any of us can do right now."

"And when it gets to be too much," Dad added, "you call us. No matter the hour. You hear me?"

"I hear you." My voice was barely there. "I promise."

There was a pause. And then Dad's voice softened. "Austin, we're proud of you. For standing by her. For holding on. You're doing what a good man does. And she knows that."

"I don't feel like much of anything right now," I admitted, my voice cracked open and raw. "Definitely not a rock."

"You're human," Mom said gently. "And humans are allowed to break sometimes. But love?" She paused. "Love holds. Love carries what we can't. You're stronger than you think."

I closed my eyes, their voices sinking into me like roots. I didn't even realize how badly I'd needed to hear them until the tightness in my chest loosened just a little.

"We'll be there soon," Dad said. "We'll figure out flights and get there as soon as we can."

"Thank you," I whispered. "I love you guys."

"We love you too, sweetheart."

The call ended. And still I stood there, phone dangling from my fingers, the world seemingly silent around. A plane passed overhead, blinking slowly against the velvet night. I watched it disappear, my thoughts still miles away in every direction at once.

When I finally stepped back inside, the air-conditioning hit my skin, and I shivered. The house felt heavy with quiet. Willow was still asleep, curled into herself on the couch like a question mark, her hand resting where it always did now—over her stomach. Holding the tiny life neither of us had seen yet, but both of us already loved beyond reason.

She looked so small in the dim light. So fragile. And I hated it. Hated the helplessness that wrapped around my ribs like wire. I didn't want to just sit next to her and hold her hand. I wanted to take it all away. Trade places if I could.

But all I could do was be here.

I sank into the armchair across from the couch, the weight of the day pressing down until I couldn't tell where my body ended and the furniture began. I tipped my head back and closed my eyes, the exhaustion slipping in like a tide, pulling me under before I could stop it.

My last thought before sleep claimed me was a prayer—silent and desperate—whispered to the dark.

Let her be okay. Let them be okay.

Because if I lost her, if I lost either of them? I didn't know if I'd know how to breathe again.

Chapter 43

Austin

Despite everything we'd done to keep things private, it didn't take long for the rumors to start.

At first, it was just whispers on fan forums. A blurry photo here, a vague comment there. But in the span of a week, the whispers turned to roars.

"Trouble in Paradise? Grace & Gravel on the Rocks!"

The headline screamed across a full-page spread, plastered beside a grainy shot of Willow and me walking out of a restaurant downtown. The angle made it look like we were avoiding each other, like we were cold, distant. What it didn't show was how she'd barely made it through the meal without throwing up, how I'd kept my hand on her back all night, rubbing slow circles to keep her steady, how I'd shielded her from every camera flash I could.

Then came the next one.

"Willow's Secret Struggle—All Alone?"

They'd used a photo of her sitting on a park bench. I was three steps away, throwing out our lunch trash. But the way they cropped it... she looked abandoned. Like I'd walked away and left her there.

It didn't matter that it wasn't true.

It didn't matter that I'd never been more by her side than I was now.

The words cut anyway.

Each headline felt like a blade, each photo a punch to the gut. I was trying so hard to keep it together—for her, for the baby, for all three of us—but I was unraveling. Slowly. Quietly. And no one knew.

It didn't matter how baseless or absurd the rumors were. They still hit like a sucker punch, leaving behind an ache that settled deep in my chest. I felt like I was drowning, suffocating under the weight of the media's scrutiny. They didn't know. They couldn't know. They didn't know what it was like to hear the word cancer and feel your entire world tilt off its axis. They didn't know the way Willow whispered to our baby at night, one hand pressed protectively against her belly, promising love and light and life when all we had was uncertainty.

But they were still writing their stories. Still twisting our pain into profit.

And I couldn't stop them.

I tried to ignore it. I really did. But it was like trying to hold back a tide with your bare hands.

"Grace & Gravel on the Rocks: Is Austin Abandoning Willow in Her Time of Need?"

My phone lit up with a notification as I stood in the kitchen. I didn't even want to look, but I did. I always did. Some sick part of me hoped maybe this time it would be better.

It wasn't.

That headline burned into my vision like acid.

Abandoning her.

I slammed my phone onto the counter so hard it made the silverware rattle. "What is wrong with people?" I muttered, pacing the kitchen like I was caged. "How can they write this garbage and sleep at night?"

No one answered. Of course not. The room was empty except for my rage.

I wanted to scream. I wanted to grab each headline, tear it to shreds, and shout at the world that it wasn't true—that none of it was true. But I knew better. Feeding the media frenzy would only make things worse. It wouldn't protect Willow. It wouldn't ease her pain. So I did what I always did—I swallowed the anger, stuffed it down into some dark, unreachable corner, and focused on keeping it together for her.

My hands clenched into fists, the muscles in my arms shaking from the effort it took not to punch the wall. I dropped my head, braced both palms against the countertop, and tried to breathe through it. *In.*

Out.

In.

Out.

It didn't help.

It wasn't just anger. It was helplessness. It was grief and exhaustion and desperation all twisted together into something sharp and heavy and unmanageable.

And suddenly, I couldn't hold it alone anymore.

Without thinking, I grabbed my phone again, and headed outside to the front porch where I thumbed through my contacts. I hit the one name I trusted to meet me in the middle of this storm.

Caleb.

He answered on the second ring. "Hey, Austin. What's up?"

His voice—steady, familiar—was all it took. I didn't even try to stop the crack in mine.

"Caleb, it's a mess," I said, and once I started, I couldn't stop. "The media's tearing us apart, and I don't know how to protect her from it."

The words spilled fast, fast like they'd been trapped behind a dam for days and I couldn't hold them back anymore.

"They're saying awful things—making it sound like I'm not even around. Like I left her. And with everything she's going through— everything we're fighting just to get through a single day—I can't let her see it. I can't let her believe for even a second that I'm not right here. That I'm not all in. But I don't know how to shield her from it. I don't know what the hell to do, Caleb."

My voice cracked on the last word.

There was a pause, the line buzzing with quiet.

Then Caleb spoke, low and firm. "We'll handle it."

Just like that. Calm. Certain.

"You don't have to fight this battle alone, Austin. We'll issue a statement, I'll get the legal team involved if I have to. We'll shut them down. You focus on Willow. On that baby. That's your job now."

I closed my eyes, the smallest breath of relief breaking loose from my lungs. "Thank you," I said, my voice hoarse. "I didn't know who else to call."

"You can always call me," he said immediately. "Always. You're family, Austin. And family doesn't let family go down swinging alone."

His words—you're family—nearly undid me.

"Thank you," I whispered again, my throat so tight I could barely get the words out.

"And Austin," Caleb added, his voice softer now, but no less serious. "You're doing better than you think. I know it feels like you're drowning, but you're not. You're exactly what Willow needs right now. Just keep showing up. That's the whole job."

I nodded, even though he couldn't see it. "I'm trying," I said.

And I was. God, I was trying so hard.

We hung up, and I stayed outside on the porch for a long time. When we bought our house, we chose a space away from the city. There were no houses or cars to be seen. But I thought about all the lives continuing on away from our private bubble—normal, everyday lives. Moms making dinner. Kids doing homework. Dads mowing the grass. People untouched by headlines. People untouched by fear.

And then there was us.

I loved Willow with every ounce of my being. I loved the way she fought with quiet grace, how she didn't complain even when she had every right to. I loved the way she whispered to our baby like he or she could already hear her. I loved the way she still smiled for me, even when the world felt like it was caving in.

But loving her didn't fix this.

Loving her didn't make it go away.

It just made me more afraid of what I stood to lose.

I eventually stepped back inside, the door clicking shut behind me. No lights were on, there was just afternoon light throughout he windows pouring in, peaceful, quiet.

I walked to our bedroom and stood in the doorway for a moment, just listening. Willow's soft breathing floated on the air. Steady. Rhythmic.

Alive.

I leaned against the wall and closed my eyes, letting that sound wrap around me. Letting it tether me to something real.

She was here. She was still fighting.

And as long as she was, so was I.

Whatever it took. However long it took.

I'd fight for her. For our baby. For this life.

Because even in the middle of the chaos—even when I felt like I was breaking apart—she was worth every battle.

And I wasn't letting go.

Chapter 44

Willow

He was there for every test, every scan, every silent moment in a sterile room where I tried not to cry. His hand was always wrapped around mine, warm and secure, his eyes scanning the doctors' faces for every shift, like he could catch danger before it reached me.

And when my hopes dimmed and the reality of it all pressed too hard on my chest, he'd lean in close, press his forehead to mine, and whisper, "We're going to beat this. You and our baby—you're both fighters. We're going to make it through this together."

I wanted to believe him. I wanted to believe it with everything I had. But sometimes—usually in the middle of the night, when the whole world went still and quiet—the fear crept in. It whispered doubts I couldn't silence. What if I wasn't strong enough? What if love didn't beat cancer?

We had stepped back from the public eye a few months ago. Our team released a brief, careful statement—enough to acknowledge that I was pregnant, that it was high-risk, but nothing more. No mention of cancer. That truth still lived behind a closed door, and I wasn't ready to open it for the world to gawk. Not yet.

Surprisingly, the statement bought us peace. The disparaging headlines quieted. The paparazzi backed off for the most part.

And in the hush that followed, we focused inward—on the invisible war raging inside my body, and the fragile little life we were trying to protect.

I became a full-time fighter. Every bit of strength I had went into following orders: eat the right foods, get enough sleep, limit stress. That last one felt laughable most days. But I tried. I really did.

Austin never faltered. Not when I sobbed in the shower. Not when I threw up three times before noon. Not even when the doctors spoke in careful phrases that sounded like they were trying not to shatter me with the truth.

He asked the questions when I couldn't think straight. He massaged my temples during migraines. He made dumb jokes about baby names just to make me laugh. And every night, he held me. He held me like he was trying to stitch the breaking pieces of me back together.

Still, I felt time slipping through my fingers like sand.

The cancer didn't wait. It didn't pause just because I was pregnant. It kept growing. Kept invading. I felt like I was fighting two wars—one for myself, and one for our baby. Some days I didn't know which battle mattered more.

But then there were moments—tiny, life-giving moments—that reminded me why I was still fighting.

Like our most recent ultrasound.

The room was dim, the soft whir of the machine the only sound. The technician smiled gently as she moved the wand across my belly.

"There's your baby," she said, her voice calm and full of quiet joy. "Looking healthy and strong."

Austin's fingers tightened around mine. "Look at that," he whispered, his voice rough with awe. "Our little fighter."

I stared at the grainy image on the screen—the fluttering heartbeat, the curve of a spine so impossibly small—and tears welled up in my eyes.

That. That right there was why I hadn't given up. That heartbeat. That hope.

After the appointment, we stepped into the blinding brightness of day. I could barely keep my eyes open against it. My body felt heavy—tired in a way that sleep couldn't fix.

By the time we reached the car, the ache had settled deep into my bones.

"One day at a time," Austin said, opening the door for me like he always did. "That's all we have to focus on."

I nodded, lowering myself into the seat. But as soon as I settled in, a bolt of pain sliced through my lower abdomen.

Sharp. Sudden. Unforgiving.

I gasped, doubling forward, my hand clutching my belly. "Austin," I choked out.

He spun around instantly, panic all over his face. "What is it? What's wrong?"

"I don't know," I gasped. "But we need to go back inside. Now."

Austin didn't wait for another word. He had the car door open and me out of it before I could catch my breath. I could barely register the speed at which he moved, only the pain radiating through my body.

The receptionist took one look at me and called a nurse. I was back on a table in under five minutes, the room too bright, the silence too loud.

Dr. Novak came in quickly. More tests were done. More blood was drawn.

Then came the words.

"The cancer is progressing faster than we anticipated," she said softly. "It's putting a significant strain on your body. We need to begin treatment immediately."

I stared at her, my blood turning to ice. "What about the baby?" My hand flew to my stomach like I could shield the life inside with my fingers alone.

Dr. Novak hesitated, just for a second. "There are treatments we can try that are safer during pregnancy," she said. "But they're not as effective. It's a tightrope, Willow. There are no simple answers."

I felt Austin's hand tighten around mine like a vise. I turned to him. His face was pale, but his eyes never wavered.

"Whatever you want to do," he said. No doubt. No hesitation. Just love. Just me.

Dr. Novak leaned in again, calm and composed. "Given the rate of progression and how far along you are, I believe we should consider early delivery."

My heart stuttered.

"How early?" My voice was small. Barely audible.

"Thirty-four to thirty-seven weeks," she answered. "It gives the baby a stronger chance of thriving outside the womb—and gives us a slightly larger window to treat you more aggressively once we deliver."

The words spun around me like a cyclone.

I'd pictured a full-term baby. A pink, crying newborn placed on my chest. Tiny fingers curling around mine. Now all I could see was an incubator, monitors, wires, a fight before our child even took their first breath.

I couldn't catch my own breath.

Austin pulled me back to earth. "What do we need to do to prepare?" he asked, his voice steady when mine couldn't be.

Dr. Novak laid it all out: a birth plan, NICU prep, weekly monitoring, round-the-clock coordination between oncologists and high-risk OBs. It was terrifying. But it was a plan. And that meant hope.

I held on to that.

As we left the clinic, I could barely walk. Austin helped me into the car, buckled me in with a reverent care.

We were halfway home before I found my voice again.

I placed my hand on my belly and felt the faintest flutter—just a whisper of movement. My eyes blurred with tears.

"We're going to get through this," I whispered.

Austin reached across the console and tangled his fingers with mine.

"That's right," he said, his voice full of quiet fire. "We absolutely are."

And for the first time in what felt like forever, I let myself believe him.

Even through the ache, through the unknown, through the fear—I believed. Not because it would be easy.

But because I had something worth fighting for.

Someones worth fighting for.

And I wasn't done fighting yet.

Chapter 45

Willow

On the good days—when the nausea eased, when the fatigue loosened its grip—I let myself hope.

Austin and I would dive headfirst into the nursery, like we were any other expectant couple. He painted the walls a soft, soothing green, a color that reminded me of eucalyptus leaves. I sat on the floor beside him, folding impossibly small onesies and nesting them into drawers like they were fragile treasures.

"Do you think they'll like this color?" I asked, trailing my hand across the freshly painted wall.

Austin grinned, his eyes warm as he looked at me. "They'll love it. Because you chose it."

I leaned against him, needing his steady weight beside me, needing the illusion—just for a minute—that everything would be okay. That we'd bring our baby home to this room, to soft blankets and lullabies and late-night feedings. That we'd have time.

My family came often in those weeks. My mom filled our freezer with meals she made in bulk, fussing over me while trying not to cry when she thought I wasn't looking. Austin's parents came and helped hang curtains and placed little stuffed animals on the shelves while they were here. Their quiet care heavy with the things they didn't say.

The room was ready.

But were we?

"One day at a time," Austin whispered to me one night, his lips brushing my temple as I stood in the nursery doorway, my hand resting over the curve of my belly.

I nodded, drawing strength from the way he said it. One day at a time. One foot in front of the other. Until we held our child in our arms. Until I could turn all my focus to surviving—for me, and for them.

One night, I woke to the soft, broken sound of Austin's voice drifting down the hallway.

I slipped out of bed slowly, each movement deliberate. The apartment was dim, quiet. I followed the sound to the living room, pausing just outside the doorway.

He was sitting on the couch, his back hunched, phone pressed to his ear. "I don't know how to do this, Mom," he whispered, and the catch in his voice cracked something wide open in my chest. "I'm so scared of losing her."

I leaned against the wall, silent, my hands pressed over my heart. Tears streaming down my face.

"She's acting strong. She's always strong," he went on, his voice trembling. "But I see it. The fear in her eyes. The way her hands shake when she thinks I'm not looking. I feel completely helpless."

There was a pause, his mother's response muffled. Whatever she said, it made him exhale—a tired, shuddering breath I recognized all too well.

"I know," he said softly. "One day at a time."

He murmured something else—quiet, broken—and then the room

went silent. I slipped back into bed before he could see me, the ache in my chest heavier than it had been in weeks.

Minutes later, the mattress shifted, and he slid in beside me. He didn't speak. He didn't have to. He wrapped himself around me, his face buried in my hair, his arms tight like he was trying to hold the pieces of us together.

We didn't sleep.

We laid awake listening to each other breathe, feeling our baby's faint kicks, the silence between us a fragile kind of prayer. I stared into the darkness and asked God for the same things I always did now —for time. For strength. For a miracle.

The next morning, I set my tea aside and reached for Austin's hand across the kitchen table. My fingers trembled slightly.

"We need to talk," I said, my voice soft but steady. "About what happens if..."

He shook his head instantly, eyes brimming with tears. "Don't."

"We have to," I whispered, squeezing his hand tighter. "We have to face it."

He looked away, his jaw tight. "I can't lose you, Willow. I can't raise this baby without you."

I cupped his face in my hands, guiding his gaze back to mine. "If it comes down to a choice between me and the baby, you have to choose our child."

He flinched. "Don't ask me to do that."

"I need to. You have to promise me, Austin." My voice cracked as tears spilled over. "If there's one thing you do for me, promise you'll fight for our baby. Even if it means letting me go."

His hands clutched at mine, desperate. "I can't—"

"You can," I said, pressing my forehead to his. "Because they'll need you more than anything. And if I can't be here... you have to be enough for both of us."

His shoulders shook, and for a long moment, he couldn't speak. When he finally did, it was a whisper, soaked in grief and devotion. "I promise," he said, his voice breaking. "But I'll never stop fighting for you. Never."

"I know," I breathed, wrapping my arms around him.

And he held me like I was something precious slipping through his fingers.

We cried into each other—grieving what hadn't been lost yet, holding onto the fragile, impossible hope that maybe we wouldn't have to.

Chapter 46

Willow • Austin

Willow

The world was still cloaked in darkness as Austin and I arrived at the hospital, the faint glow of streetlights casting long shadows across the parking lot. My heart pounded inside my chest, fast and erratic, a mix of fear and anticipation pulsing through me. This was it. The day we'd both dreaded and longed for—the day we'd meet our baby, and the day I would begin the real battle for my life.

Austin's hand wrapped around mine as we walked through the automatic doors, his grip strong and steady. The sterile scent of the hospital hit me immediately, sharp and familiar, a backdrop to so many of the moments that had marked this journey.

Our families were already there, clustered in the waiting room like a constellation of worry and hope. My mom saw us first. She rushed forward, tears already brimming.

"We'll be here when you're ready for us," she whispered into my hair, her arms wrapped tightly around me. "We're not going anywhere."

One by one, they hugged me—my dad, stoic and teary-eyed. Austin's parents and brother, worn from travel but steady in their presence. Caleb, his mouth a firm line, his hand squeezing my shoulder just long enough to say everything he wouldn't say out loud. And Gemma. There was no mask, no false bravado. Her arms wrapped around me, and we both cried big ugly tears. Tears of happiness, excitement, and terror.

None of us knew what the end of the day would bring. But my family was here, that's all I needed to know.

"You've got this," Dad said, his voice low and sure. "We're behind you. All the way."

I nodded, swallowing hard past the lump in my throat. "Thank you. All of you."

Austin walked me to the elevator with his arm securely around my waist. Each floor we ascended, the weight in my chest grew heavier. But beneath it, a flicker of something else: hope.

The operating room was blindingly bright, a world of stainless steel and sharp edges. I was cold, shaking—not just from nerves, but from the IV fluids, the anticipation, the knowing. This was the plan. Deliver the baby by C-section, and while I remained under anesthesia, the oncology team would begin surgery—removing the tumors, my ovaries, my uterus. A total hysterectomy. My body would never carry another child.

But this child—I had fought for with everything I had.

The anesthesiologist gave me a gentle smile as she checked my monitors. "We're going to take excellent care of you, Willow. You'll be meeting your little one very soon."

I nodded, unable to find words. My hand searched for Austin's. He stood beside me, pale but steady, his eyes fixed on mine.

"I'm right here," he whispered, gripping my hand tightly. "I'm not going anywhere."

The mask descended. I wanted to tell him I loved him. I wanted to say thank you for everything, for staying, for believing. But the words stuck in my throat, lost in the fog creeping into my brain.

So I just squeezed his hand one last time.

"I love you," he whispered. "Always and forever."

And then the world went black.

Austin

The moment Willow's hand went slack in mine, my heart cracked clean in two.

Her hand slackened in mine, her body still. Not gone, but not here either. Not with me.

A nurse touched my arm. "Mr. Blake, we need to begin. Come with me?"

I kissed Willow's hand one more time and followed them out, dazed.

They led me to a private family room down the hall—a small space with a couch, a rocking chair, and a window that looked out onto the sunrise.

"Your daughter will be brought to you here as soon as she's cleared from the NICU," the nurse explained. "And once Willow's awake and stable in recovery, we'll update you."

I nodded, barely absorbing the words. The room felt like it belonged to someone else.

Our families arrived minutes later all buzzing with quiet energy. Their presence grounded me. We waited together, filling the silence with half-finished prayers and whispered updates. Time stretched.

It felt like hours. Maybe it was.

Then the door opened.

A nurse stepped in, her arms cradling the tiniest bundle I'd ever seen. Swaddled in pink, a puff of dark hair barely visible under a knit cap, she looked impossibly small. Impossibly perfect.

"Mr. Blake," she said softly. "Your daughter is doing beautifully. She's strong. Healthy. A fighter, just like her mom."

My chest caved in as I reached for her. *My daughter.*

The second she was in my arms, the world tilted. Everything else faded. She was warm and squirmy, her eyes shut tight, her tiny fists clenching.

"Hey there," I whispered, tears slipping free. "It's me. Your dad."

Her hand curled around my finger, and I broke wide open.

Our families surrounded us quietly. My mom reached out to touch her cheek, eyes filled with awe and grief, my father behind her with a hand on her shoulder. Elaine held the baby next, whispering prayers and promises only grandmothers knew how to say. Caleb and Gemma looked on with Willow's dad, the three of them battling their emotions in their own ways.

But even in the love circling around us, my eyes kept drifting to the door.

Willow should be here.

She should be holding her. Seeing her. Breathing her in.

We were moved to another room and it was hours before the door finally opened again—and this time, it was Dr. Meyers.

She stepped into the room still in her surgical cap, her face serious, but not grim. I stood instantly.

"She's stable," she said gently. "Everything went smoothly, and we proceeded with the hysterectomy while she was under. We removed the tumor, her ovary, and uterus. Everything we safely could."

Relief washed over me like a flood—but it was short-lived.

Dr. Meyers hesitated. "But the cancer has spread more than we hoped. We found tissue involvement near major blood vessels. We couldn't remove it all without risking her life."

The words knocked the breath clean out of my chest.

My knees buckled.

I would've hit the floor if Connor hadn't moved. His arm shot out, strong and immediate, catching me beneath the elbow and gripping tight.

"I've got you," he said under his breath, steady and low.

I blinked hard, the room tilting before it steadied again. I couldn't speak. My jaw clenched against the sob rising in my throat, the kind that didn't feel like it belonged to me—something primal and guttural, forged from the deepest kind of helplessness.

Dr. Meyers softened her tone, gentle but clear. "We'll begin chemotherapy as soon as she's recovered from surgery. It won't cure the cancer, but our goal is to slow its progression and preserve quality of life."

I nodded once, jaw tight, vision swimming.

She rested a hand on my shoulder, grounding me. "She fought hard today. She's resting in recovery now. We'll let you know when she's fully awake and ready to be moved."

"Thank you," I managed, though it didn't feel like enough. Nothing felt like enough.

Connor gave my arm one more squeeze before stepping back, and I sank into the nearest chair, my mom placed my daughter back in my arms—warm and breathing and here. One half of my world safe.

Now all I could do was wait and pray the other half came back to me.

Willow

The fog in my head was thick, heavy. Like swimming through mud.

Voices drifted in, soft and muffled.

My body ached in places I couldn't name. My abdomen throbbed with a low, constant pressure, and my mouth was dry as ash.

Then I heard it—his voice. Austin.

"She's waking up," he said, and I felt his hand find mine. His thumb brushed across my skin, and I latched onto that.

When I opened my eyes, everything was blurry. But there he was —leaning over me, his eyes red-rimmed and shining. And in his arms... a baby.

My baby.

Ours.

"She's okay?" I rasped.

"She's perfect," he said, his voice breaking. "She's everything."

He brought her to me gently, and I held her—weak, trembling, exhausted—but I held her.

And I wept.

Because she was real. Because I had made it. Because I was still here.

"I'm your mommy," I whispered into her soft hair. "I've been waiting so long to meet you."

Austin sat beside us, his arms around both of us as I cried into our daughter's hair and let myself, for the first time, believe in the fragile, beautiful hope that maybe—just maybe—we'd have more time.

***

The recovery was brutal.

The treatments came hard and fast, a calculated assault on the cells trying to destroy me. I lost weight. Lost hair. Lost pieces of myself I never thought I could let go of.

But I didn't lose him.

And I didn't lose her.

Austin held my hand through every round of chemo, never missing a single appointment. He rocked our baby girl in the crook of his arm while holding my IV in place with his other hand.

Some days I didn't feel strong. Some days I didn't feel anything at all.

But I'd look at them—and remember why I was still fighting.

For her. For him. For us.

It wasn't easy.

But love never is.

And this love? This life?

It was worth every battle scar.

Chapter 47

Willow

The first few days home were a blur—equal parts joy, pain, and quiet, aching awe. I moved through them like someone learning to live in a new body, one that was stitched and fragile, slow and unsteady, but still mine. Still fighting.

The house was rarely silent. Allora's tiny cries filled the space, mingling with the clatter of coffee cups, soft lullabies hummed under breath, the shuffle of visitors moving carefully so as not to wake the baby—or me.

My mom cradled her granddaughter like she was the most sacred thing she'd ever held. I'd never seen her face so tender. She kissed the downy top of Allora's head and whispered things I could never quite hear. I didn't need to. I felt it in the way her fingers trembled against the blanket.

"She's perfect," Mom said, her voice thick with wonder.

"She's got your nose," Dad murmured, leaning in with a softness that cracked me open. His rough palm gently cupped her head, and for a moment, he looked like a man meeting the best version of himself.

"And Austin's eyes," I added, watching my husband from across the room. He smiled, quiet and proud and tired in that way only new fathers could be.

His parents were just as smitten. His mom sat perched on the arm of the couch, her eyes never leaving Allora, her fingers brushing her tiny hands over and over like she couldn't quite believe she was real. "She looks like a poem come to life," she whispered. "Every piece of her."

And for a moment, I forgot about the healing incision across my belly and the storm still brewing inside me.

This was what we were fighting for.

But when the house quieted—when our families stepped out to let us rest—the ache returned. Not just physical, though that was ever-present. The kind of ache that pressed on your soul, that curled into your bones and whispered questions you weren't strong enough to answer.

Was I enough for her?

Could I survive this long enough to watch her grow?

Every day was a balancing act—motherhood and chemo, bottle feeds and bloodwork, warm baths and icy nausea. Austin moved through it with impossible steadiness, catching all the pieces before they hit the floor.

When I couldn't lift Allora, he was already beside me. When I couldn't stomach food, he brought me ginger tea and held my hair back without a word. He wore exhaustion like a second skin, but still, he never left me to bear any of it alone.

One night, I woke to the sound of Allora's cries and found Austin in the nursery, rocking her slowly, his face hollow with fatigue.

"Go to bed," I whispered from the doorway.

He didn't look away from her. "I just want to hold her a little longer."

Some nights I held it together. Others, I unraveled completely.

One evening, when the pain in my abdomen flared and my arms felt too weak to lift her from the bassinet, I broke. I sat on the floor and wept.

"I can't do this," I whispered, my body shaking. "I want to—I do—but I'm so tired, Austin. I don't feel like a mother. I feel like a burden."

He dropped down beside me instantly, gathering me up like I was something precious. "Don't you dare say that," he murmured fiercely. "You're doing the impossible. Every single day. And Allora? She knows. She knows you love her. You're not failing her. You're showing her what it means to fight."

I didn't believe him then. Not really. But I let myself lean into his certainty, just long enough to breathe again.

My mom started joining me at chemo. She'd pack snacks I couldn't eat and stories I'd heard a dozen times but still wanted to hear again. She held my hand through every needle prick, every IV drip, every bone-deep chill that came after.

"She smiled at Austin this morning," I told her during one session, my voice tired.

Mom lit up. "Her first smile?"

I nodded. "Like she knew him. Like she'd been waiting for him."

"She's her mother's daughter," Mom whispered. "She knows what love looks like."

The nurse adjusted the IV line, and I focused on the quiet beeping, on the image of Allora's gummy grin burned into my memory.

When we returned home that evening, I was too weak to climb the stairs. Austin carried me, as I whispered apologies he didn't want to hear.

He laid me on the couch and gently settled Allora on my chest. She curled there like she'd always belonged, like she remembered that once, not long ago, we had shared the same body.

"She missed you," he whispered.

Her warmth, her tiny weight, was enough to ground me. I stroked her hair with shaking fingers, anchoring myself to her rhythm—steady, innocent, undemanding.

"You're my reason," I whispered into her soft curls. "My reason for every pill. Every treatment. Every stitch. Every breath."

Austin sat beside us, his arm around my shoulders, his cheek resting against mine.

"We'll get through this," he said, not for the first time.

But this time, I didn't flinch. I didn't resist. I nodded.

Not because I was sure.

But because I wanted to be.

Because I had to be.

Some mornings were better than others. Some mornings I walked the length of the hallway and back and called it a win. Some mornings, I changed Allora's diaper by myself and celebrated with tears in my eyes. Some mornings, I laughed. And sometimes that was enough.

Other days, I couldn't move. But Austin would bring her to me, careful and slow, and place her right against my heart.

And I'd remember.

I'd remember what it was I was fighting for.

Not just survival.

But moments.

The way she grasped my pinkie with all her strength. The way she turned toward my voice. The way Austin kissed the crown of her head like it was the center of his universe.

They were my center now.

And I wasn't done loving them.

Not yet. Not ever.

Chapter 48

Austin

The house was too quiet.

After weeks of bustle—of casseroles in the oven, baby cries competing with whispered prayers, parents swapping shifts in the kitchen and laundry room—it was just us now.

Our parents had gone home. We'd insisted. We needed to try and find our rhythm. Learn what life looked like on our own, in this in-between place where grief and love lived side by side. But as the front door clicked shut behind that final hug and goodbye, a hollow sort of silence settled over the house.

It didn't take long for the cracks to show.

Willow was fading faster than any of us had prepared for. The treatments were taking more than they were giving. Her skin grew paler, her weight dropped, and the fatigue took up permanent residence behind her eyes.

Still, she fought. Still, she held our daughter to her chest like she could will herself stronger through sheer love alone.

"Promise me," she whispered one afternoon as sunlight filtered in through the bedroom curtains. I sat at the edge of the bed, watching her eyes struggle to stay open. "Promise me you'll be there for Allora. Show her how to chase joy. How to live a big, brave life."

My heart fractured as I took her hand, the bones so fragile now, her skin like paper. "I promise, sweetheart. I swear it. But you're going to be there too. We're going to do it together."

She smiled, but it didn't quite reach her eyes. "I'm fighting, Austin. I am. But you have to be ready, just in case." She shifted her gaze to the bassinet across the room, where Allora slept peacefully. "She needs you. More than anything."

Tears slid down my cheeks before I could stop them. I leaned in and pressed a kiss to her forehead, my voice cracking as I whispered, "We're a team, remember? You, me, and her. I'm not giving up. I'm not giving up on you."

But the truth was in her silence. In the way her hand stayed curled loosely in mine even when sleep took her minutes later.

When she had the strength, Willow would nestle Allora in the crook of her arm and write in the soft leather notebooks we kept stacked on the bedside table. She scribbled furiously, page after page—our story, her dreams, fragments of lullabies and letters to our daughter.

"What are you writing today?" I asked one afternoon, curling up beside her, resting my hand on the back of Allora's tiny head.

"Everything," she murmured, a shaky smile tugging at her lips. "I want her to know it all. The way we danced in the kitchen. How you cried when we first heard her heartbeat. That she was born into a love story."

I couldn't breathe for a second.

"You're giving her the most beautiful gift," I whispered. "A piece of you she'll always have."

She nodded, brushing her thumb over Allora's cheek. "She needs to know how much I wanted to stay."

But the good days grew fewer. Her pain was harder to manage. Some mornings, she didn't speak at all, too weak to do anything but blink when I whispered to her.

On those days, I read to her. Her own words. Her letters to Allora. I read them aloud while our daughter slept curled beside her mother, unaware that the lullabies she now heard were pieces of legacy in real time.

Some nights I'd carry Allora from her crib just to feel her heartbeat against mine, to remind myself that something good had come from all this. That Willow had created something permanent. Something I could keep loving when the world tried to take everything else away.

One night, after Willow had drifted into an uneasy sleep, I slipped down to the kitchen and leaned against the counter, the coolness grounding me. I didn't cry. Not at first. I clenched my jaw and stared out the window at the dark sky, as though it might hold the answers.

But it was too much.

The grief caught up with me and knocked the breath from my lungs. I slid to the floor, buried my face in my hands, and sobbed like I hadn't in years. Not since I was a boy.

Because this wasn't supposed to happen. She was too young. We had too many things left to do. And Allora—God, she would never remember her mother's voice. Her laugh. Her lullabies.

I stayed there for a long time, until my face was swollen and my hands were numb.

And then I got up.

Because I had to.

When hospice arrived a few days later, it felt like something inside me cracked. The medical bed replaced the couch we'd curled up on a hundred times. Monitors, syringes, medical charts—it was all so clinical. So final.

But the nurses were kind. Gentle. They spoke in soft voices and taught me how to ease her pain. How to comfort her. How to listen closely for signs of what was coming.

We didn't talk about timelines. I couldn't bear to.

That night, I helped them settle Willow into her new bed, adjusting the pillows just the way she liked them. She opened her eyes briefly and gave me a tired smile.

"I'm sorry," she whispered.

I shook my head and dropped to my knees beside her. "No. You don't ever say that again. You have nothing to be sorry for. I'm here. And I'm not going anywhere."

She reached out, her fingers brushing weakly against my face. "You've been so good to me."

"You're the love of my life, Willow. There's no other way to be."

Each day blurred into the next. The nurses came and went. Allora's cries rang out in the early mornings, and I rocked her while Willow watched from her bed, her eyes glassy and semi-present.

"You're such a natural with her," she whispered one evening, her voice so faint I had to lean in to hear her. "She's going to be okay... because she has you."

I couldn't respond. My throat closed up, and all I could do was hold her hand.

She kept singing to Allora even when her lungs trembled with effort. She whispered stories, called her "my lovey," and kissed her forehead with trembling lips. She smiled through the pain.

One night, after the nurses had left and Allora was finally asleep, Willow turned to me.

"Promise me you'll tell her," she said. "Tell her everything. Don't let her forget me."

My heart shattered all over again. "I promise," I said, kissing the back of her hand. "I'll tell her every day. How brave you were. How deeply you loved her. How you fought with everything you had."

Her eyes fluttered closed. I sat there holding her hand, counting every breath she took like a prayer.

"I love you," she whispered after a long pause, so quiet I almost missed it.

I pressed my forehead to hers. "I love you, too, Sweetheart. Always and forever."

I didn't sleep that night.

I just sat by her side.

And held her hand.

Because I knew time was running out.

And I didn't want her to face a single second of it alone.

Chapter 49

Austin

The house was quiet. Not silent—Allora stirred softly in her crib upstairs, and the low murmur of the baby monitor crackled occasionally—but the kind of quiet that comes when time slows, when the weight of the moment settles thick in your chest.

It was the last night I'd see her like this. Coherent. Present.

Willow lay in the hospital bed that now dominated our living room, the frame adjusted so she could recline just enough to see the soft golden lamplight, the photographs we'd hung in a mosaic across the opposite wall, and me—sitting beside her, holding on like the world might split in two if I let go.

Her skin was so pale it looked translucent, her breath barely stirring the space between us. But her eyes—they were still hers. Tired, yes. Dimming. But still full of love. Still looking at me like I was her favorite song.

"Austin," she whispered, her voice like tissue paper on glass. "Will you sing to me?"

I hadn't sung much these last few weeks. My voice didn't feel like it belonged to me anymore. It was too fragile. Too caught up in grief. But I would've moved mountains if she asked me to.

I swallowed hard, my throat raw. "Of course, baby."

Her hand reached for mine—slow, trembling. I threaded our fingers together and held on gently, afraid I might hurt her with anything more.

The rest of the house was quiet. All four of our parents had moved into short-term rentals nearby—close enough to help, far enough to give us space. Caleb was back in Georgia, holding down the law firm so Frank and Eileen could stay here. Connor was running the ranch back in Montana so my parents could be nearby, as well. We had help when we needed it. But in this moment, we were alone. And I was grateful for that.

I took a breath, then started to sing.

It was the song I wrote for her for our wedding day. I hadn't sung it since—not fully. But it had always been hers.

I'll love you through the seasons, through the storms and through the years,

Through the laughter and the heartache, through the joy and through the tears...

My voice cracked on that line. The tears were already threatening, but I kept going, clinging to the melody like it might hold the both of us together. She closed her eyes and smiled, the lines of pain in her face softening just a little.

When the days are dark and heavy, when the nights feel far too long,

Know I'll always be beside you—my love will keep you strong...

The air in the room felt sacred. Sacred and shattering. Every breath she took was a miracle and a countdown.

She didn't say anything—didn't need to. Her hand gripped mine faintly, enough to tell me she was still here, still listening, still with me.

Forever and always, my heart is yours to hold,

Through this life and the next... I'll love you till we're old.

But we wouldn't grow old.

We wouldn't get there.

The silence after the final note felt heavier than the song itself. It settled over us like snow—soft and devastating. I reached out and gently brushed a strand of hair from her face, my hand shaking.

"I love you, Willow," I said, my voice rough, broken.

Her lips curved into the faintest smile, her eyelids fluttering closed as she exhaled. Not gone. Not yet. But fading.

I sat there for a long time. Holding her hand. Watching the gentle rise and fall of her chest. Memorizing the shape of her face. The freckles. The hollowed-out places where sickness had stolen her glow.

The baby monitor crackled, and for a second I thought Allora might cry. But she didn't. She stayed quiet. Peaceful.

And so did Willow.

Chapter 50

Austin

Cradling Allora to my chest, I rocked her gently as we stood beside Willow's bed.

She hadn't woken up in over twenty-three hours. Just a shallow breath here and there—soft, spaced too far apart. Her hand hadn't twitched. Her lashes hadn't fluttered. She was somewhere else now, somewhere just out of reach, and I was running out of ways to keep her tethered to us.

I bounced Allora slowly, her cheek resting against the curve of my shoulder, the warmth of her grounding me even as my insides twisted into knots. The tears came like they always did—burning behind my eyes, sitting sharp in my throat.

I cleared it. Once. Twice. Again.

"Tell Mommy goodnight, Cupcake," I whispered, my voice barely audible in the quiet. "Wish her the sweetest dreams."

Allora stirred just enough for her hand to graze Willow's cheek— a clumsy, perfect little gesture. A fleeting second of contact. Then her fist balled, flailed gently in that newborn way, and I shifted her to one arm to steady her.

I reached out with my free hand, brushing Willow's face with the backs of my fingers. Her skin was soft. Too soft. The kind of softness that spoke of fading warmth, of the body preparing for its final stillness.

She was still the most beautiful woman I'd ever seen. Even now.

I traced the line of her cheekbone, the curve of her jaw. My fingers hovered over her lips, her lashes, her dimples that hadn't surfaced in days. My heart cracked again—another splinter, another fault line I didn't know if I could hold together.

God, I just wanted her to open her eyes. Just once. I missed the way they saw through me, saw into me. Her eyes had always told me what she felt before she ever said a word. They'd been my compass, my anchor, my mirror. And her smile—I ached for it. I missed those dimples so fiercely it felt like a physical wound.

When I realized Allora had gone still, fully asleep against me, I leaned down and pressed a long, lingering kiss to Willow's forehead. My lips stayed there for a while, memorizing the shape of her, the stillness, the coolness I couldn't pretend wasn't there anymore.

"I love you," I whispered, my voice raw, breaking open at the seams. "Forever and completely."

I stood slowly, adjusting Allora in my arms, and walked her back to the nursery. The monitor's glow lit the corner of the room in soft blue, casting shadows over the curve of her tiny face as I lowered her into her crib. She made a small sound, nothing more than a breathy sigh, then settled again, her fingers curling around the edge of the blanket.

I pressed two fingers to my lips, then touched them gently to her cheek.

"You are everything," I whispered.

I rubbed my chest, trying to ease the aching pressure that seemed to be caving in around my heart. It didn't help. Nothing helped. Not really. But I had Allora. This incredible, beautiful soul that Willow and I had created together—our love made flesh.

She needed me to be okay. So I would be. For her.

I went through the motions—checking the monitor, adjusting the blanket, closing the door softly behind me. The house was dim and hushed, that eerie kind of stillness that makes you feel like time itself has stopped moving.

Willow was as I left her. I kissed her forehead again, whispered how much I loved her, how proud I was of her strength, and turned to face the night.

My bed was still the fold-out chair next to her, a thin blanket and a too-flat pillow my only companions once Allora was down. I crawled onto it, curling in the way you do when sleep won't come, but grief insists.

Time had lost meaning. I lived by Allora's schedule now—feedings and diapers and the sounds she made in her sleep. Some nights, I crashed at 7:00 PM without meaning to. Others, I found myself awake at 2:00 AM, staring at Willow, willing her to open her eyes, to move, to come back to me.

Tonight was somewhere in between. My body felt like it had been awake for a week. My soul... it wouldn't settle.

I shifted once. Twice. Then stilled again.

The lamp cast a halo of light across her pale features, and I watched her chest rise and fall, so slow, so soft it nearly broke me. I reached for her hand—held it lightly, afraid of how fragile it felt—and whispered once more:

"Goodnight, my love. Sleep well."

I closed my eyes. And somewhere between that moment and the next breath, sleep pulled me under. Not peaceful. Not deep. But enough.

Just enough to survive the night.

Chapter 51

Willow

It's quiet.

The world is soft around the edges, like the hush that comes just after a storm, when the air feels heavy and sacred. I can't move. I can't speak. But my mind is still mine. My thoughts float slow and gently, drifting like feathers through water.

Austin.

My love.

You're here—I can feel you. The weight of your hand in mine. The warmth of your breath near my face. The way you whisper my name like it's holy.

I wish I could open my eyes. Just once more. I wish I could look at you, really look, and tell you everything that's pressing against my chest.

But I can't. So I'm saying it here. Inside. In this quiet space where my soul is louder than my voice.

Austin... I love you.

Oh, how I love you.

You've given me more than I ever dreamed I'd have in one life-

time. A love so fierce, so true, it remade me. You were my safe place, my joy, my home. You still are. You always will be.

Please forgive me for leaving you. I wanted so badly to stay. I wanted to raise our daughter with you, to grow old beside you, to write a hundred more songs and slow dance in the kitchen long after the music faded.

But my body... my body's tired, Austin. So tired.

I held on for as long as I could. For you. For her.

Allora.

Sweet girl. My heartbeat outside my body. My miracle.

Tell her I love her. That I always have. That I always will. Tell her that her mommy fought with everything she had. That I dreamed of her before I ever knew her name.

Tell her I was there the day she smiled for the first time. That I sang to her under my breath even when my throat burned. That I memorized every inch of her, every sound she made, every sleepy sigh.

Tell her I will always be with her.

In the wind through the trees.

In the warmth of the sun.

In the quiet between notes when music lingers.

Tell her to chase beauty and make art and laugh from the belly and never forget that she was born from love so big it defied every odd.

And you, Austin—don't close off your heart.

I know the grief will be unbearable. I know the ache will live in your bones. But let it make you deeper, not smaller. Let it be a reminder of what we had, not just what we lost. Keep singing. Keep writing. Keep loving her the way you've always loved me.

You're going to be an amazing father.

You already are.

And one day, when she asks you about me—because she will—I hope you smile. I hope you tell her stories that make her laugh. I hope she hears the love in your voice and knows she was always, always my reason.

I'm not afraid anymore.

I'm ready.

Ready to rest.

Ready to let go, knowing I was loved completely and I loved just as fiercely in return.

Austin, my love...

Thank you for this life. Thank you for every moment.

I'll be waiting on the other side of the music.

And I will never stop loving you.

Chapter 52

Austin

I jolted awake, breath caught in my throat, heart pounding against my ribs like a war drum. The room was still, dim and heavy with quiet. At first, I couldn't place what had pulled me from sleep. Then I heard it.

A sound that didn't belong.

Shrill. Sharp. Unrelenting.

The kind of sound that didn't just echo through the air but sliced straight through bone and soul.

I fumbled for my phone, my hand shaking as I lifted it. The screen illuminated the room just enough to show me the time— 3:17 A.M.

Then I saw it.

The machine.

The monitor I'd accepted as background noise, like the ticking of a clock or the hum of the fridge. Always there. Always steady.

Until it wasn't.

The screen that once pulsed with promise—those soft hills and valleys tracking every heartbeat—now glowed flat and lifeless. No movement. Just a straight, unwavering line, stretching across the screen like the edge of a cliff. And that sound... that cold, merciless tone of finality that sliced the night in half.

I was up in a flash, at her bedside before the weight of reality could crush me.

"No. No. No, no, no." My voice fractured. I dropped to my knees beside her, clinging to her fragile hand. "Willow, please. Please don't do this. Baby, wake up. Please. Open your eyes. Come back to me."

I reached for her face, my fingers tracing the outline I'd memorized a thousand times. Her skin was cool, still. Still too still.

"God, please... please don't take her. Not yet. Not now."

The sob tore from my throat before I could stop it—raw, guttural, a sound I didn't recognize as mine. I collapsed onto her, curling myself around her weightless frame, desperate to make her warm again. Her head rested against my shoulder, and I rocked her like I could bring her back. Like love could do what medicine could not.

I don't know how long I stayed there. It could have been minutes or hours. Time wasn't real anymore. It shattered right alongside my heart.

Eventually, some small sliver of rational thought broke through the fog.

I had to call someone.

People needed to know.

The very idea felt obscene. Saying the words out loud would make them real. Final. Like carving them in stone. But I couldn't keep it to myself, not when so many others loved her too.

I moved with painstaking care, laying her back against the pillow, brushing the hair from her face like I had every night. Her expression —peaceful, untouched by pain—nearly undid me again. But I forced myself to stand.

My hand shook as I reached for the phone.

The first number I called was my dad's.

He picked up on the first ring. I didn't have to say a word.

"We're on our way," he said. No questions. No hesitation. Just certainty and motion. The line went dead, but those four words wrapped around me like a lifeline.

Next was Frank.

I didn't even try to steady my voice. "Frank... I'm so sorry."

Silence.

A silence that cracked and groaned under the weight of comprehension.

Then, his reply—rough and wrecked. "We'll be there soon."

In the background, I heard it.

Eileen.

Her wail cut through the air, primal and infinite. It vibrated in my chest. Matched the pitch of the devastation clawing through my insides.

I hung up.

The house was silent again, save for the still-beeping monitor, a cruel metronome to my unraveling. Reaching over I pressed a button to stop the sound.

My feet felt cemented to the floor. My breath came in shallow, fractured bursts. I turned my head, slowly, and looked at her.

Still.

Beautiful.

Gone.

There was no script for this. No road map for what to do when the center of your universe slips quietly into the dark while you sleep.

I walked back to her side, unsure how I was still standing. I traced the back of her hand with my thumb, memorizing the shape of it. The feel of her fingers in mine. The way she always made her thumb curl around mine like it belonged there.

"I love you, Willow," I whispered. My voice felt like sandpaper. "I'll never stop. You hear me? Never."

The sob that followed was quieter, deeper—an ache that lived in my lungs.

I sat beside her again. Not ready to let go. Not yet. Maybe not ever.

And somewhere, not far off, Allora stirred in her crib—her tiny cry piercing through the silence like an echo of the life Willow had left behind.

And the life I had to keep living.

For both of them.

Chapter 53

Austin

The house didn't just feel quiet—it felt suspended. Like it was holding its breath.

Outside, the sky lightened in soft streaks of gray-blue, dawn trying to cut through the thickness of a night that had broken me. The world carried on in its detached rhythm, while everything inside these four walls had stopped.

Willow was gone.

And I was still here.

After the calls were made, I couldn't bring myself to move. I sat on the couch, slumped forward, my feet planted on the thin mattress that was still wedged between the coffee table and Willow's hospital bed. She was only a few feet away, motionless. My wife. My world.

I stared at her face, at the soft slope of her cheek, the lashes resting like whispers against skin that no longer held warmth. I was watching for something—anything—some twitch of movement, some flicker of breath that would undo everything.

But the stillness was total.

And that was the cruelest part of grief: how loudly nothingness could scream.

I pressed a palm to my chest, where the pain had settled like a stone. I tried to breathe around it, but it sat there—sharp and immovable. My tears came without effort or warning, slipping down my cheeks one after another, until my whole body was shaking with the effort of holding back the scream I didn't dare release.

Then I felt it—the cushion beside me shifting, the unmistakable weight of my mom settling down at my side. Her arms wrapped around my shoulders, and I didn't hesitate. I turned into her, clinging like I had when I was small and scared of the dark. Only now the dark wasn't in the corners of the room—it was inside me.

"Mom," I gasped, the word shredded by the sobs already tearing through me. "How am I supposed to do this? I don't know how to do this without her."

She held me tighter, her palm rubbing soothing circles over my back. "Oh, sweetheart," she murmured, her own voice thick with grief, "I know, baby. I know."

The next thing I knew, my dad was behind me, his arms coming around both of us—his strength grounding me, tethering me when all I wanted to do was come undone. We sat like that for a long time, three hearts bound by love and brokenness, mourning the loss of someone we all adored.

Then, the baby monitor crackled with the soft whimper of a waking infant.

Allora.

Even in devastation, life carried on.

My dad kissed the top of my head and stood without a word. His quiet exit felt like the gentlest gift, his footsteps retreating toward her room as the weight of silence returned.

My mom kissed my temple and pulled back just enough to look into my eyes. Hers were glassy, but steady.

"Austin," she said softly, "are Frank and Eileen on their way?"

I nodded, not trusting my voice. My throat felt raw—like I'd swallowed glass and tried to speak through it.

She cupped my cheek and brushed back a strand of hair that had fallen forward. "Good," she whispered. "Now I want you to go wash your face. Get dressed. I'll make coffee. Just do those two things. That's all you need to worry about right now."

I closed my eyes and leaned into her touch for just a second longer. "I don't want to leave her," I admitted, my voice breaking again.

"You're not," she said gently. "You're just stepping away. I'll take care of her until you're ready to come back."

Somehow, I found the strength to stand. One foot, then the other. My eyes never left Willow's still form as I turned, dragging myself to the bathroom on autopilot.

The man in the mirror barely looked like me—skin pale and drawn, stubble creeping in like shadows, eyes bloodshot and hollow. I splashed cold water on my face, the sting jolting me just enough to breathe again. When I opened the cabinet to grab a towel, I saw one of Willow's lip balms sitting beside the cotton swabs. The label worn, the cap missing. I stared at it for a long moment, then shut the door gently. The tears were back in full force.

When I returned to the living room, Mom had opened the curtains. Morning light spilled across the room, softening its edges. A vase of yellow tulips sat on the coffee table. They hadn't been there before.

Then came the knock.

I didn't move at first—just stood frozen, staring at the door. My chest felt too tight. My legs too heavy.

But I walked to it anyway.

I opened the door to find Frank and Eileen on the other side, their expressions hollowed by grief.

Eileen's face crumpled the instant she saw me, and she collapsed into my arms. Her sobs were harsh and unrelenting, the sound of a mother's worst fear realized.

"I'm so sorry," I whispered, holding her tightly, as Frank stepped forward and gently placed a hand on her back.

"We'll get through this together," he said quietly, his voice shaking. I nodded and stepped aside, letting them in.

Eileen moved toward Willow like she was being pulled by gravity. The moment she saw her daughter, she let out a broken, keening sound that hit me straight in the gut. Her knees buckled, and Frank caught her, steadying her as they made their way to the bed.

"My baby girl," Eileen whispered, her hand trembling as it brushed Willow's cheek. "Oh, my sweet girl."

Frank stood beside her in silence, his hand resting lightly on Willow's forehead, the grief in his eyes as deep and devastating as the ocean.

And then, like a miracle—like Willow herself had sent her just then—we heard a sneeze.

We all turned to see my dad standing in the doorway with Allora in his arms. Her cheeks were pink, her eyes wide and curious, blinking up at us like nothing had changed.

"May I?" Eileen asked softly.

Dad gave her a nod, placing Allora gently into her grandmother's waiting arms.

"She's got magic, this one," he said quietly. "She's light in the darkest room."

Eileen held Allora like she was made of glass and gold, whispering to her in broken phrases. "Hi, angel. Hi, beautiful girl. Oh, you look just like your mommy..."

Frank stepped beside her, wrapping his arm around her shoulder, their tears falling as they looked down at their granddaughter with a love that was aching and alive.

Mom appeared beside me again, her voice low. "The hospice nurse is on her way. I also called the funeral home. They're prepared for when we're ready. Do you want me to handle it? Or do you want to talk to Frank and Eileen first?"

The word funeral hit like a gut punch. I looked toward the cabinet in the corner—the one where we had quietly, reluctantly, kept the folder.

That folder.

I swallowed, the edges of my vision going blurry. "I'll talk to them," I said hoarsely. "Just... not yet."

She nodded, her eyes full of quiet understanding. "There's no rush, honey. Just breathe."

As I watched Eileen kiss Allora's forehead and Frank rest his hand on Willow's, I realized something: this grief wasn't just mine to carry. It was ours. And maybe, together, we could hold the weight of it.

Even when it felt impossible.

Even when it felt endless.

We would love her forward.

One moment at a time.

Chapter 54

Austin

The day of the service dawned under a sky heavy with grief—thick gray clouds hovered like they knew what was coming. The air was damp and dense, the kind of stillness that makes you wonder if the world is waiting to break down with you. It wasn't raining yet, but it would. It felt like the sky was holding back, just long enough for us to say goodbye.

I stood in front of the mirror, fumbling with my tie again. My fingers, normally steady, couldn't manage the simplest knot. Every time I got close, the fabric slipped or twisted, like it was rejecting the idea of formality—like my body couldn't comprehend putting itself together when everything inside was still so wrecked.

I caught my reflection mid-frustration and froze. The man staring back at me was pale and hollow, eyes bloodshot from too many nights staring at the ceiling and trying not to cry loud enough to wake the baby. There were lines on my face I didn't recognize. Grief was aging me in real time.

Behind me, I heard the soft rustle of Allora's breathing. She was still asleep in her crib, wrapped in a soft pink blanket. Her cheeks were round and warm, her lips twitching in the beginnings of a smile.

I moved closer and leaned over the crib. Her tiny hand curled into a loose fist near her face, and I reached in, gently brushing a knuckle along her cheek.

"Your mommy was amazing," I whispered. My voice caught. "And I'm going to make sure you know just how incredible she was. I promise, baby girl."

The church was packed by the time we arrived. People lined every pew, the air thick with the scent of lilies—comforting to some, but to me, it smelled like endings. The moment I stepped inside, I could feel the weight of collective grief settle over me, heavy and constricting.

It wasn't just a crowd—it was our people. Friends, family, strangers who'd been touched by Willow's music, and names that lit up marquees and magazine covers. But none of that mattered here. No cameras. No headlines. Just broken hearts.

Nash and Cassidy Montgomery sat toward the center, hands clasped so tightly between them I couldn't tell whose fingers were whose. Harper Lane was a few rows ahead, her eyes red-rimmed, her head resting on the shoulder of a man I didn't recognize—but her grief was unmistakable. Wyatt Turner and his wife Kensi were there too, quiet, solemn, Wyatt's arm curled protectively around Kensi's shoulders. Even Christopher Jordan had flown in, sitting silently, his presence a weight in the room. She had touched so many lives. It still didn't feel like enough.

I took my seat in the front row, Allora tucked in my arms like a living anchor. Gemma sat to my left, tucked under Caleb's arm. He was unusually silent, the sharp angles of his jaw tight as he stared straight ahead. His parents sat on the other side of him, equally shattered.

On my other side, my mother kept one hand on my knee, her thumb moving in slow, grounding strokes. My dad had Allora's diaper bag and the baby carrier tucked beside his feet. He held my mother close, their grief folded between them. Connor sat stoically next to our dad, though his eyes shimmered with unshed tears.

The service began. A hymn rose through the air like a question. I couldn't sing. I couldn't even hear the words. My mind drifted.

People stood one by one to speak. To share pieces of Willow.

Gemma was first—Willow's best friend since they were little. She stood at the pulpit with trembling hands and spoke of scraped knees, whispered secrets, and the kind of childhood laughter that echoed into forever. "Willow was the kind of person who made you believe in yourself. Who made you believe the world still had magic," she said. "And now it's dimmer without her."

Mitch Haynes spoke next, voice low and raspy, grief roughening the edges. "She didn't just make music," he said. "She bled her should dry for it. Every word, every note. She made you feel like her songs were written just for you—and somehow, they were."

And then they called my name.

I stood on legs that felt like stone, every step heavy with a weight no one else could see. I made my way to the podium, heart pounding so loud I thought it might drown out my voice. I hadn't planned what to say—how could I? Every time I tried, the words dissolved into nothingness. How do you eulogize your own heart?

"Willow..." My voice broke on her name, a fragile whisper caught in the storm inside me. I swallowed hard, forcing the words out. "Willow was my everything."

Tears pricked my eyes, but I kept going.

"She was light. Not just any light—but the kind that fills every corner of the room and reaches deep into your soul. Fierce and unbreakable, but soft and tender at the same time. She laughed with abandon, with her whole body, with a joy that made you feel alive just by standing near her. She loved fiercely and without hesitation. She made me better—simply by being herself."

I paused, the silence stretching wide, holding us all in its fragile grip.

"She gave me everything. Her love, her unwavering trust, and the most precious gift I will ever know—our beautiful miracle, Allora."

I looked down at Allora, her eyes wide and shining, so full of wonder and life, a living piece of Willow's spirit.

"Even as her body fought and failed her, her heart never faltered. She was brave beyond words. Generous in every breath she took. Radiant in the darkest moments. And now, without her, the world feels colder, quieter, a little less bright."

My voice caught, but I found strength in the memory of her.

"Willow's light wasn't just something you saw—it was something you felt, deep in your bones. It's in the music she loved, the songs she sang, and in every laugh, every touch, every moment we shared. That light lives on in Allora, in all of us lucky enough to have known her."

I took a deep breath, steadying myself against the ache.

"I miss her beyond words. But I carry her with me—in every note I play, every song I write, and in every beat of my heart. Because Willow wasn't just my everything. She was the best part of me."

The tears returned with a vengeance and I swiped at my face with the handkerchief my mom had handed me that morning. I composed myself and continued.

"And so, as we say goodbye today, I hold onto this truth: Willow's light didn't end with her. It shines on—in Allora's smile, in the music that still fills our hearts, and in the love that binds us all. Though she's gone from our sight, she will never be gone from our lives. Thank you, Willow, for everything."

I stepped down to a silence that felt holy.

Then Christopher Jordan stepped forward. He sat on the edge of the stage and began to strum the opening chords of *Unbreakable*. The song Willow and I wrote together, about surviving storms. About enduring what tries to break you.

He didn't say a word. Just let the music speak.

By the end of the song, there was not a dry eye in the room.

A few days later, I found myself standing at the edge of the ranch in Montana, the horizon stretching wide and quiet around me.

In my hands, I held the urn containing Willow's ashes. She'd wanted to be here—on the land she loved. The place we got married. The place she always said made her feel most like herself.

I walked to the gentle hilltop where we'd said our vows. The wind whipped at my jacket, biting through layers, but I didn't move.

I knelt down and dug.

The ground was half-frozen, hard beneath my shovel. But I kept going.

When the hole was ready, I lowered the urn in and whispered, "I love you, Willow. I'll love you forever."

With her, I planted a young willow tree—just a sapling for now. Its branches barely strong enough to dance in the wind.

But I knew it would grow.

I hoped it would.

Because it was a symbol—not just of her, but of everything we had built. Love. Legacy. Roots.

I stepped back, dirt under my fingernails, wind in my face, the ache in my chest a dull throb.

And for the first time in weeks, I breathed in and didn't feel like the air was trying to choke me.

Not healed.

Not yet.

But not broken beyond repair.

For her, for Allora, for all the music still left in me—I would keep going.

One day at a time.

One step at a time.

Chapter 55

Austin

In the weeks after Willow's death, grief wasn't a river—it was a riptide. And I wasn't wading through it—I was drowning in it.

No one had warned me that grief could be so chaotic. There wasn't a neat progression, no gentle glide from denial to acceptance. It was a kaleidoscope of pain. I'd go from numb and robotic—barely registering the sound of Allora's cries, mechanically changing diapers and warming bottles—to full-throated rage that sent my fist into the drywall or had me slamming the kitchen cabinet shut so hard it splintered.

Sometimes the grief showed up as silence. I'd sit in the dark after Allora had gone down, the monitor blinking quietly beside me, and just listen—for something, for anything. Hoping for her voice. Imagining her footsteps. I'd whisper to the empty room, like maybe she could hear me from wherever she was.

Other times, the grief was cruelly deceptive. I'd reach for my phone to text her. Instinct. Habit. It still happened. I'd open the message app and my thumb would hover over her name. And then it would hit—like a hammer to the chest: she's not there to text back.

I begged sometimes. At night, when sleep wouldn't come, I'd lie in bed with Allora curled beside me and whisper to the ceiling, bargaining with a God I wasn't sure was listening. Please, just give me one more day. One more moment to tell her she was everything.

One afternoon, I found myself sitting next to the willow tree. The one I'd planted in her honor. I don't even remember how I got there— I'd just sort of drifted outside, barefoot, holding a half-drunk cup of coffee that had gone cold an hour earlier.

My knees were tucked to my chest, arms wrapped around them like they could keep my insides from spilling out. I didn't even know I was crying at first. I had just been staring. Existing.

And then I felt the presence of my mom settle beside me.

She didn't speak at first. Just reached over and rested her hand on my back. Gentle, rhythmic. Familiar. The same way she used to when I got sick as a kid.

"I don't know how to do this, Mom," I whispered, my voice wrecked. "How do I keep going without her?"

Her arm tightened around my shoulders, and when she finally spoke, her voice was surprisingly steady.

"Grief is like butter."

That stopped my thoughts in their tracks. I blinked at her, half-expecting her to be joking. She wasn't.

"At first, it's solid and heavy. But as you mix it in, it melts and becomes part of everything. It changes the texture, adds richness, makes things better in a way you can't quite put into words.

"Grief is like that. It starts out glaringly obvious. But over time, it becomes part of who you are. It shapes your story, adds depth and complexity. It's always there.

"Even when it's less sharp, the sadness is still there—sometimes surprising us with how strong it feels. But in that mix of pain and sweetness, there's something real and beautiful.

Life is about holding both the hard parts and the good parts together. That's what makes it whole."

I let out a sharp breath—not quite a laugh, not quite a sob.

"That's grief," she continued. "It doesn't go away. It just... transforms. You won't always feel like you're breaking. One day, you'll realize you're different. Not healed, but changed."

"And if I don't want to change?" I asked quietly. "What if I just want to stay broken for her?"

"You won't," she said. "Not because you won't want to. But because of Allora. Because of Willow. Because love has a way of rebuilding even what grief tries to tear down."

I felt torn in half.

Part of me was anchored in Nashville, a city where every alley, every record store, every quiet Sunday morning still echoed with Willow's voice. It was where we built Grace & Gravel, wrote songs until our fingers cramped and our hearts bled. Where we fell in love in a hundred little moments, most of which no one else would ever know.

And the other part of me ached for Montana. For the wide skies. For the place that had once felt like home.

The guilt of even considering leaving Nashville made me sick. It felt like betrayal. Like moving meant moving on.

But then, one night, I held Allora against my chest after a hard day—her breathing slow and shallow against my shirt—and I remembered what Willow had asked of me.

Show her how to live, Austin.

That's when I knew what I had to do.

The next morning, I called Frank.

His voice cracked when he answered. "Austin."

"I've been thinking," I began, staring out the window, the sunrise painting the skyline in bittersweet light. "I think I need to go home. To Montana."

I braced for resistance. For hurt. For guilt.

But all I heard was warmth. And understanding.

"You have to do what's right for you and that little girl," Frank said. "You'll always be family. That doesn't change with distance."

I almost cried right there. "Thank you," I said, swallowing down the lump in my throat. "That means everything."

"We'll come visit. And you'll come back. That's how this works now. We figure it out together."

A few days later, Caleb and Gemma showed up at the house like they were on a mission.

Boxes. Sharpies. Tape guns. Takeout.

We dug in.

The living room became a battlefield of cardboard and grief. Every drawer we opened held landmines—photos, letters, jewelry, baby onesies with handwritten notes tucked into their folds.

Gemma found one of Willow's journals and held it like it was sacred.

"She wrote about Allora," she whispered. "She wanted to teach her how to sing."

I took the journal from her, my fingers tracing the inked words. Willow's handwriting was messy but unmistakable, each line infused with her heart and soul. Tears blurred my vision as I read her hopes and dreams, her fears and doubts. She had written about me too, about the love she felt for me, about how she knew I would be an incredible father.

There were lyrics and chord charts, bits and pieces of songs that she had never finished. But there were also entries, honest and raw, about her goals and feelings.

I read one entry, dated just a few months before Allora was born.

"I'm scared," Willow had written, her words shaky and uncertain. "I'm scared of what the future holds, of what will happen to me and the baby. But I know that Austin will be there, every step of the way. He's my rock, my anchor in the storm."

Caleb rested his hand on my shoulder. "She knew how much you loved her. And she knew you'd take care of Allora."

We finished packing in silence.

Two weeks later, I stood at the edge of the ranch with Allora in a carrier against my chest. The sky was pale blue and wide open, the air clean and biting.

The willow tree's branches swayed nearby. Still young. Still growing.

"I'm back," I whispered.

Allora stirred in her sleep, her tiny fingers flexing against me.

I walked the fence line with her tucked close, breathing in the scent of hay and earth and coming snow.

The grief hadn't left. But it had shifted. It was less jagged now. Less like something clawing through my ribs and more like a quiet echo. A hum under the surface of everything.

We'd made it.

It was just me and Allora now.

But we were still a family.

And we were going to keep going.

One memory at a time.

One breath at a time.

Chapter 56

Austin

The morning was just beginning to break as I stepped out onto the porch, a steaming mug of coffee in my hand. The sky was pale and quiet, the horizon still smudged with lingering night. The air was cold—crisp and pine-scented, tinged with sage and something older, earthier. Familiar. In the distance, I could hear the gentle lowing of cattle, the clank of metal from the far side of the barn. The sounds of home. The sounds of a life I was still learning how to live in again.

It had been two months since Allora and I moved back to Montana. Two months of early mornings, long days, aching muscles, and quiet nights that felt too still. Two more months of standing in Willow's absence, trying not to collapse into it.

My dad was more than happy to have me back, though neither of us said it out loud. We worked side by side, tending the land, moving cattle, rebuilding fences—building something that resembled a routine. It helped, the work. Not because it erased the pain, but because it gave the pain somewhere to go.

Still, the ache was there. Constant. Quiet, but sharp. Grief had become a kind of muscle memory—something I carried without thinking. I missed Willow with every fiber of my being. I missed the sound of her laughter, the curve of her smile, the way her hand fit into mine like it had always belonged there.

The screen door creaked open behind me, breaking into the thought like a gentle knock on my chest. My mom stepped outside with Allora nestled on her hip, her little legs kicking gently against my mom's side.

"Someone wanted to see her daddy," she said, her voice soft and warm as she handed Allora to me.

I took her carefully, pulling her into my arms. She babbled, her fingers patting my cheek before grabbing a fistful of my hoodie. I exhaled slowly, pressing a kiss to her hair, and for a brief moment, the chill in my bones gave way to warmth. To something like comfort.

"Thank you," I said, my voice rougher than I wanted it to be. "For everything."

Mom smiled and reached up to brush her hand along my face. "We're here for you, Austin. Always. You and this little angel."

I nodded, swallowing hard. "I know. It's just... I keep expecting to hear her voice. To turn around and find her standing there. And every time I remember she's gone..."

Her arms wrapped around both of us, a quiet embrace that didn't need to fix anything. "She's still here, sweetheart," she whispered, laying a hand over my heart. "In here. And in her. You carry her with you every day."

A tear slipped down my cheek. I didn't bother wiping it away.

Allora rested her head against my shoulder, her warm breath feathering against my neck, and I closed my eyes.

She was right. Willow was still with us. Not in the way I wanted —not in the way I would ever stop longing for—but she was here. In the curve of Allora's smile. In the freckles on her cheeks. In every word I whispered to our daughter about love and courage and dreams.

"Come on, baby girl," I said, kissing the top of her head. "Let's go see what the day brings."

We ended up in the barn, where Connor was elbow-deep in the guts of the combine, muttering something under his breath that sounded like both a prayer and a curse.

When he heard Allora babbling, he turned so fast it startled her into a laugh.

Connor—who had never been one for touch, who'd flinched at hugs his whole life—reached for her like he'd been born to do it. She melted into his arms, babbling a string of sounds only he seemed to understand.

Watching them was like watching magic. They had their own language, their own rhythm. Two souls who had found each other exactly when they needed to.

"You good?" he asked me, his voice gentle as he tickled Allora's neck with his beard, making her squeal.

I shoved my hands in my pockets. "Some days are harder than others. I just... I miss her."

Connor nodded. No grand platitudes. Just understanding.

"I learned something in the military," he said after a moment, not looking at me. "And from being me. Life gets messy. Uncertain. And you don't always get clarity. But there's one thing that helped when I thought I couldn't take another step."

I looked at him, curious.

He smiled slightly and tickled Allora again, drawing another belly laugh. "Do the next thing," he said simply. "Doesn't matter how small. Just keep going. Your heart will catch up."

I stood there for a second, letting his words settle into the cracks. They didn't fix anything. But they didn't need to. I just needed to hear them.

"Thanks, Connor," I said, reaching for Allora.

"Anytime."

We walked a loop around the outer pasture before heading toward the house.

"You ready to go see Nana?" I asked.

Allora clapped, chanting, "Na-na-na-na!" like it was a battle cry.

I laughed and kissed her cheek. "Alright, back to Nana, then."

She babbled the whole way there. Mostly nonsense words and sounds. But I listened like they were poetry. Her first birthday was around the corner, and all I could think was how fast everything had changed... and how much I wished Willow could see it. The expressions, the tiny hand gestures, the way she scrunched her nose when she was concentrating. Willow would've adored every bit of it.

When we walked in, Dad was mid-unwrapping a banana muffin. The second Allora saw him, she squealed, "Pop-pop!"

I was pretty sure she was aiming for the muffin, but he beamed like she'd just awarded him Grandpa of the Year.

"There's my cupcake," he said, kissing her cheek. "Sweet as can be."

She reached for the muffin. He broke off a piece and handed it to her without hesitation. The two of them had no boundaries when it came to baked goods.

"Looks like we got here at a good time," I said, grabbing one for myself.

Mom was already arranging the rest in a basket. "I was just getting ready to take these down to the fire department. Thought I might swing by the nursing home, too, if that's alright. Allora and I will be back for nap time."

I nodded, watching Allora snuggled in her grandfather's arms, chewing contentedly.

"I think that sounds perfect."

I didn't say it, but the truth settled heavily in my chest: I didn't know what I would've done without them.

The rest of the day passed in steady motion. I repaired fencing along the west boundary, checked in on some irrigation valves, and helped Dad load hay bales onto the truck. Work was its own kind of therapy —hard, repetitive, grounding.

Sweat trickled down my brow, and my muscles ached with the strain of the physical labor. But there was a certain solace in the repetition—something about the way the body kept moving even when my heart struggled to keep up.

As I paused to take a swig of water, a memory hit me, sharp and sudden—Willow and I, riding horses to this very spot, a couple years ago. Her laughter had echoed across these hills, her hair lit up like wildfire in the late summer sun. She'd leaned over in the saddle and said something ridiculous about naming a calf "Sir Mooington the Third," and I'd nearly fallen off my horse laughing.

The force of it punched the air right out of my lungs. My knees buckled slightly, and I braced myself against the fence post, heart pounding like I'd been punched. For a moment, I just stood there, hunched over, letting the pain roll through me like thunder. The grief was still as sharp as ever, like losing her all over again. It came out of nowhere—just the color of the light, the smell of the earth, the exact slant of the wind across the grass.

I wanted to cry. Or scream. Or both.

But instead, I stayed quiet. I let the memory play. I let it hurt.

Because underneath the pain, there was something else. Not quite comfort. Not peace. But... presence. The memory didn't destroy me the way it might have weeks ago. It hollowed me out, yes —but it also filled me with something fragile and flickering.

I stood there a long while, my hand resting on the worn wood of the fence. Letting the ache settle without rushing it away. Willow had been here. This patch of land—it had held her. And now it held me, broken but still breathing.

When I finally straightened, I didn't feel lighter. Not exactly. But I felt anchored. Like I could make it through the next hour. Maybe the next day.

That would have to be enough.

Later that evening, Connor and I sat on the porch, watching the last golden stretch of sun disappear behind the mountains. Allora had finally gone down for the night, and the house was quiet except for the creak of the wood and the faint chirp of crickets in the grass.

"You seem lighter," he said, his voice casual, but his eyes watching me closely.

I let out a slow breath. Thought about lying. Thought about shrugging it off.

Instead, I said, "Maybe. Not all the time. Sometimes, I feel like I can breathe without it hurting so much."

Connor nodded, his expression unreadable but warm. "That's something."

"Yeah," I said, glancing toward the hills. "It is."

I didn't feel healed. I didn't feel whole. But I wasn't drowning anymore. And that, for today, was a kind of miracle.

I took another sip of my beer, the bottle cold in my hand, and stared out across the fields. The willow tree danced in the wind, its branches swaying like they were waving hello. Or maybe goodbye.

"Mostly, I'm just hanging on by a thread," I said quietly. "Some days, I think I'd rather be with Willow—even knowing I can't. But I have to be here for Allora. She needs me. So I stay."

The words hung in the quiet between us, carried off on the wind like smoke. I wasn't even sure I meant to say them out loud—but once they were out, I didn't take them back.

Connor didn't answer right away. He just stared out at the horizon, his brows drawn slightly like he was measuring his words before handing them over.

Then he said, quietly, "Good."

I turned to him, eyebrows raised.

He glanced at me, the edge of a dry smile tugging at his mouth. "Means she mattered. Means you loved her the way she deserved."

I felt something catch in my throat.

Connor shifted, elbows on his knees, his gaze distant but focused. "I've lost people too, you know. Different circumstances, same ache. And I used to think the goal was to stop feeling it—to get past it. But I think... I think some people aren't meant to be gotten over. They're meant to be carried."

He looked at me then, eyes steady. "Missing her means you're still loving her. And that's not weakness, Austin. That's the strongest thing you've got."

I didn't have words. Just a lump in my throat and a heart that ached a little differently.

Better.

Worse.

Both.

Connor leaned back again and took a long drink of his beer, then added, "But don't let missing her keep you from living your life. She wouldn't want that. You know that, right?"

I nodded slowly. "Yeah," I murmured. "I know."

"Then carry her," he said, "but don't forget to keep walking."

And just like that, he'd put words to something I hadn't been able to. Not until now.

Chapter 57

Austin

The morning of Allora's first birthday broke over the mountains in brilliant blue. The air was fresh, the sky perfectly clear, and still, I felt heavy. Grief had a funny way of distorting days that should've been beautiful. A year ago, Willow was alive. A year ago, she held our daughter in her arms for the first time. And now she was gone.

But today wasn't about loss. Today was about Allora. About the piece of Willow I got to keep, even if everything else had been ripped away.

I scooped my daughter from her crib, her curls sticking out in all directions. She blinked sleepily, then smiled—a dimpled grin so much like her mother's it brought tears to my eyes.

"Happy birthday, Cupcake," I whispered, pulling her to my chest. "Your mama loves you so much. And so do I."

Downstairs, the smell of coffee was already drifting through the house. Voices murmured from the kitchen—familiar, comforting ones. My parents were up, of course, but Frank and Eileen's presence surprised me. They'd arrived late the night before, just in time to be here for today.

"There's the birthday girl!" Eileen's face lit up the moment she saw us, her arms outstretched. Allora immediately reached for her.

I passed her over, her little legs kicking with excitement, and nodded gratefully. "Thanks for coming. It means more than I can say."

Frank clapped a hand on my shoulder. "We wouldn't be anywhere else today, son."

There was something in his eyes—something that mirrored the way my chest had been feeling all morning. We were both fathers with daughters. His was gone. Mine was just beginning. And though nothing needed to be said, everything was understood in that moment.

The house filled with people as the morning unfolded. Laughter echoed off the walls. Warmth radiated from the kitchen, where my mom was orchestrating what could only be described as a celebration feast. It should've overwhelmed me—but somehow, it didn't. Maybe I was finally building the stamina to feel joy again without guilt.

And then I saw them—Caleb and Gemma—walking in hand in hand.

"Surprise," Gemma said with a tentative smile.

For a moment, I just stared. But then a grin stretched across my face, unforced and real. "Well, I'll be."

I pulled them into a hug, my chest swelling with something like hope. "Willow would've loved this."

Caleb gave a sheepish laugh, sliding an arm around Gemma's waist. "I think so too."

Later, as Allora sat in her high chair wearing a little gold crown and smearing frosting across her cheeks, I scanned the room. These people—our people—had shown up for her. For me. For Willow. And though her absence loomed, it didn't silence the joy. It was a quiet reminder that love doesn't vanish with grief—it weaves through it.

After the candles had been blown out (with my help), and Allora was down for her nap, Caleb, Connor, and I made our way to the back patio. I lit the gas fireplace and we settled into the silence that came with shared understanding.

"So," I said after a beat, "you and Gemma, huh?"

Caleb laughed, rubbing a hand along the back of his neck. "Yeah. Still new, but it feels...right."

"How did it happen?"

He leaned back, watching the flames. "After Willow passed, I just saw life differently. Stopped holding back. Gemma's always been there—and I think I always knew. I just didn't let myself see it."

"What changed?"

"I did."

He said it like it was the simplest thing in the world. But I knew the weight behind it.

Connor chimed in, surprising me. "It was mutual?"

Caleb nodded. "She'd been waiting on me to get my head out of the sand."

I chuckled, shaking my head. "Sounds familiar."

Then I turned to Connor. "What about you? Anyone waiting on you?"

Connor smirked, but there was a flicker of something deeper behind his eyes. "Nope. I've got enough on my plate. Besides..." he nodded toward the house, "she gets my best. No sense in splitting the good stuff up."

There was humor in his voice, but also honesty. His connection to Allora was its own kind of love. One that grounded him in ways nothing else could.

"I'm happy for you," I told Caleb, meaning it. "Willow would've been too."

His expression softened. "Thanks, man. That means a lot."

We lapsed into silence again, the kind that doesn't ask to be filled. The fire cast shifting shadows on the deck, and I let the moment stretch. No pressure. No expectations. Just life, moving forward— quietly, determinedly.

There were still shadows of the past. Still nights I woke up reaching for her. Still songs I couldn't play without breaking. Still moments when I'd catch a scent or hear a laugh and my chest would seize.

But there was laughter, too.

There was light.

There was a tiny girl with Willow's dimples and her own bright fire.

There was love that didn't stop at the edge of grief—but kept going, carried forward in every person who stayed. In every moment like this.

I wasn't healed.

But I was healing.

And maybe, for today, that was enough.

Chapter 58

Austin

Three Years Later

Three Years Later

I opened my eyes to the same faded gray ceiling I'd been staring at for what felt like a lifetime. The kind of ceiling that memorizes your pain. That knows your sleepless nights, your bargaining prayers, your quiet collapses.

The sun was rising, whether I liked it or not.

I turned toward the other side of the bed, out of habit, out of hope. Just cool sheets and silence. Still. Always. I reached for her anyway, like I sometimes did in dreams, the emptiness a quiet kind of cruelty.

With a deep breath that scraped against the walls of my chest, I pushed myself upright and planted my feet on the cold hardwood. The ache in my ribs wasn't physical. Not exactly. But it had weight. Presence. A familiar shadow that never quite left.

At the window, I pulled the curtain aside and stared out across the ranch—endless golden fields, cattle grazing, the horizon tucked behind soft mountains like a secret. It was beautiful. Always had been. But sadness can dull even the brightest landscapes, like watching a Technicolor film through a black-and-white filter.

This place had always been a center of gravity. But since Willow, I didn't know if I belonged anywhere. The world kept spinning. I just couldn't feel the pull.

Still, there were chores to do. A little girl to feed and love. And if nothing else, I had made one unbreakable vow: to keep going, even when it hurt.

I made my way downstairs, each creaking board a reminder that some things hadn't changed. That some things, no matter how much else had been lost, still stood.

In the kitchen, Allora was perched at the table, spooning cereal with the kind of focus only a four-year-old could muster. My dad sat beside her, his coffee steaming quietly, his presence steady as ever.

She looked up at me with a grin so much like her mother's it nearly stopped my heart.

"Morning, Daddy," she said, milk dotting her chin.

I wiped her face with a napkin and kissed her forehead. "Morning, sweet pea. You're up early."

"Wasn't sleepy," she replied with a shrug, already swinging her legs beneath the table like the day couldn't come fast enough.

"Ranch life will do that to ya," Dad said with a low chuckle as he stood, giving her curls a tousle.

I smiled faintly, grateful that even in a world turned inside out, there were constants. My parents. My brother. My daughter. The coffee.

I poured a cup and sat across from Allora, letting her chatter fill the quiet places in my head. She talked about the horses, about her boots being "extra fast today," about how she wanted pink pancakes for dinner. I nodded and responded and smiled in all the right places, but part of me still felt... absent. Like I was standing just outside the window, watching myself through the glass.

Then she asked, "What do you want to do today, Daddy?"

Simple question. But it landed like a stone in still water. The kind that ripples long after it sinks.

My first instinct was to list off all the work that needed doing—the never-ending to-dos of ranch life. But then I looked at her, that spark in her eyes, the way her dimples deepened with hope.

"How about we go for a ride?" I said. "Just you and me."

She gasped, eyes lighting up. "Can Daddy take me for a ride, Pops?"

Dad smiled, lifting his coffee to his lips. "If I can't manage a few hours without your daddy, I need to retire."

"All right then," I said, grinning as she shot up from her chair and bolted for the stairs. "Go get dressed. Boots and hat."

As she disappeared, Dad rested a hand on my shoulder. "She's got your eyes, Austin. But she's got Willow's spirit."

I nodded, eyes stinging. "She's everything good."

He didn't say more. He didn't need to.

We rode in quiet, the morning sun stretching long shadows across the fields. Allora sat in front of me in the saddle, reins loosely in her small hands, her pink cowgirl hat slightly askew.

"Daddy, look!" she shouted, pointing toward the ridge.

A small herd of wild horses stood grazing in the distance. Their heads lifted at the sound of her voice, ears twitching, tails flicking. A memory slammed into me like a punch to the gut—Willow sitting exactly where Allora sat now, the same awe in her expression as she watched the horses run.

I blinked hard, fighting the sting behind my eyes.

"Can we go closer?" she asked.

"Not today, sweetheart," I said softly. "Let's give them their space."

She didn't question me. Just nodded and leaned back against my chest, content to feel the sway of the horse beneath us.

And for a brief moment, with the wind in our hair and the scent of dust and grass all around us, it felt like maybe—just maybe—life could hold joy again.

Not instead of grief.

Alongside it.

———

Back at the house, she chattered about horses and pancakes while I unsaddled the horses and brushed them down. My hands moved on autopilot, but my mind was elsewhere—caught between memory and possibility.

I wasn't who I used to be. That man had been buried with Willow beneath the roots of a young willow tree. But maybe I was changing.

I wasn't sure who I wanted to be, much less how to get there, but for now I wanted to be the man choosing the next right thing. And it felt possible. On a day that started with aching emptiness, I'd found something worth holding onto.

Allora's hand in mine.

Her laughter in the wind.

Her mother's memory in the silence between hoofbeats.

And for the first time in a long time, I didn't feel like a stranger in my own skin.

Just a man.

Just a father.

Just doing the best he could—one ride, one step, one heartbeat at a time.

Chapter 59

Austin

Sunlight poured across the desk in long, warm streaks, landing on a stack of notebooks that had been haunting me for a week now. I hadn't moved them—couldn't bring myself to. Just the sight of Willow's wild scrawl on the cover was enough to knock the breath from my lungs.

It was the same desk I'd once sat at doing high school homework. And now it was a place where I came to stare down the ghosts of everything I'd lost. Never thought I'd live under my parents' roof again, but life has a way of humbling you. Thank God they'd been here—steadfast, loving, and never once making me feel like I was intruding. When Allora and I came home, they opened the door, no questions asked.

The box had been tucked in the back of my closet, practically sealed in time. When I opened it, I fully expected the world to end right there. But it didn't. Instead, I found my hands lifting out those notebooks like they were made of glass.

Night after night, I'd sit here, too afraid to open them. I'd just place two fingers on the cover and whisper goodnight like she could hear me. Maybe she could. I didn't know.

The top journal had a pressed yellow wildflower sealed to it, delicate and faded now, but still holding its shape. I remembered the moment she found it growing through a crack in a grocery store parking lot.

"It's like a little bit of grace in a sea of gravel," she'd said, holding it up like it was made of gold.

That was the day Grace & Gravel was born.

I traced the edges of the flower, inhaled deeply, and—finally—opened the journal.

Her handwriting rushed up to meet me, messy and poetic and alive. A flurry of lyrics, lines of half-finished poems, doodles, ideas for melodies, snippets of conversations I remembered us having in real life. It was like hearing her voice for the first time in years—not the memory of her speaking, but her thinking. Her dreaming.

And then I saw it. The perfect script from Willow's hand I'd recognize anywhere:

I close my eyes and see a future so bright it's blinding. Music flowing through my veins, passion igniting my soul. And there beside me, my heart, my home—Austin. Together we'll paint the world with our love and set the stage on fire with our songs.

I couldn't stop the tears. I didn't even try. I pressed the journal to my chest, like maybe it could fill the hollow space I carried inside.

"Willow," I whispered, voice rough and cracking. "I still miss you every day. But I feel you here. In her. In me. In this."

Something slipped loose from between the pages—a folded note, addressed to me in that unmistakable handwriting. My hands shook as I opened it.

My dearest Austin,

If you're reading this, it means I'm no longer by your side. But know that my love for you is eternal, and I will always be with you—in your heart, in your memories, in the music we made, and the love we shared.

You have been my rock, my anchor, my forever love. Don't stop living. For me. For Allora. And for you. I'll be waiting when your road leads you home. Until then, be bold. Be kind. Love big.

Forever yours,

Wills.

I pressed the note against my chest and closed my eyes.

"I'm trying, I promise," I whispered to the still room.

The day passed as usual—chore after chore, moment after moment. I poured my energy into my work like I always had. Horses needed feeding. Fences needed mending. The ache didn't vanish, but it blurred just enough to keep moving.

Midday, Mom showed up at the barn with Allora beside her. She held a sippy cup in one hand and her stuffed horse in the other.

"She's all yours if you need a lunch break," Mom called, handing her off with a smile.

Allora shrieked with delight and ran into my arms, wrapping her legs around my waist like a koala.

"Nana said I can feed the chickens later!" she announced proudly.

"Well," I said, kissing her cheek, "just don't let that rooster talk you into anything reckless."

She giggled and tucked her head against my shoulder.

We spent the rest of the afternoon fencing the west pasture. I worked as she played nearby with a toy shovel and an imagination I barely kept up with. When the sun began to dip behind the barn roof, I leaned on the post I'd just set and looked out at the land.

Still broken. Still healing.

But for the first time in a long while, it felt like more than just surviving.

That night, after Allora was asleep and the house was quiet, I returned to the notebooks. I took them downstairs to the office away from the bedrooms. The room smelled like cedar and ink, like old paper and memories. I turned to a fresh page—lyrics, this time.

> When the night is darkest, and the path unclear,
> Remember, my love, that I'm always near.
> In the rhythm of your heart, in the whisper of the
> wind,
> I'll be the light that guides you, 'til we meet again.

I picked up my guitar. Let my fingers fall into old, familiar patterns.

The melody came fast and clear, like it had been waiting in the air. I played softly, singing into the silence, the words rising and echoing through the stillness like a prayer.

Every chord I strummed, every line I sang, pulled her closer. Not in the haunting way it used to—but in a way that made the grief more bearable. A little less sharp.

And when the final chord faded into quiet, I sat in the stillness, letting the weight of it all settle into something I could carry.

"I hope you heard that, Wills," I said into the hush. "That one was for you."

And for the first time in what felt like forever, my breath came easy.

Chapter 60

Austin

Morning broke over the Montana horizon, painting the sky in soft bands of gold and pink. I pulled on my boots —worn to the shape of my feet—and grabbed my gloves off the counter. The scent of coffee hung in the air, mingling with the low hum of my mom's voice as she moved through the kitchen, humming something gentle and familiar.

"JP and Matt are already in the barn," my dad said as he stepped inside, sipping from his chipped mug. "You better get a move on if you want to catch up."

I nodded, slinging my jacket over my shoulder. "On it."

Outside, the crisp air met my face, biting in a way that reminded me winter wasn't far off. The land stretched wide and quiet in that sacred, early way Montana had about it—cattle dotting the hills, barn standing like it always had, watching everything.

"Morning, boys," I said as I walked up to the barn. JP looked up from his saddlework and tipped his hat, his sun-worn face creasing with a grin.

"Morning, boss," he replied. "Got a full day ahead."

Matt nodded from where he was checking the fencing tools.

I pulled on my gloves and nodded. "Let's get started."

We worked steadily, nothing rushed, everything familiar. Hooves thudded softly against packed dirt, dogs barked their commands, and we moved through the motions like a well-oiled machine. My body handled the work with practiced ease, but my mind drifted.

Willow had loved mornings like this. When we'd visited, she'd sit on the fence with her notebook in her lap, one boot dangling, eyes scanning the sky like she was waiting for a melody to come down with the sun. I could almost see her there now—sunlight caught in her hair, eyes bright with thoughts she hadn't written yet.

"Boss?" JP's voice cut through, gentle but grounding.

I blinked back to the moment. "Yeah. Just thinking."

By the time I made it back to the house, sweat clung to my shirt and my muscles hummed with the kind of ache that felt earned. I was halfway up the porch steps when my phone buzzed in my pocket.

The screen flashed a number I didn't recognize. I hovered over the green button for a second. Half the time, these calls were junk—extended warranties, scams, some distant reminder of a world I didn't want to deal with.

But something made me answer.

"Hello?" My voice was rough from shouting commands across the fields.

"Is this Austin Blake?" A crisp, professional voice on the other end.

"Yes," I said, stepping into the porch's shade.

"My name is Miranda Thompson. I'm the event coordinator for the National Ovarian Cancer Research Foundation. I hope I'm not catching you at a bad time."

The words hit like a sucker punch. My fingers gripped the phone tighter, bracing against the railing with the other hand.

"No," I managed after a beat. "You're not."

"We're organizing a benefit concert next month," she continued, her tone softening. "To raise funds and awareness for ovarian cancer research. Your name came up as someone who might be willing to perform."

My chest tightened.

"I... I don't know what to say," I admitted.

"I understand this might be difficult," Miranda said gently. "But your story—your music—it could mean something powerful to people still fighting. And we'd love for it to be an opportunity to honor your wife."

I looked out over the field, toward the young willow tree on the hill. Her tree.

She'd always believed in the music. Always believed in using her voice to lift someone else. She would want me to do this. I knew that, as sure as I knew the shape of her laugh.

After a long pause, I cleared my throat. "Count me in," I said. "Tell me what you need."

The smell of pot roast and biscuits met me before I even stepped into the dining room. My mom set a plate down in front of me, her smile soft but knowing.

"How was your day?" she asked, taking her seat across from me.

"Busy," I said, looking over at Allora. She was carefully arranging her carrots into a smiley face.

"Daddy, look!" she said proudly. "It's happy!"

I smiled, ruffling her curls. "Just like you, Cupcake."

We ate the way families do when they know each other's cadence, comfortably and companionably. Allora dropped a carrot to my dad's dog, Ranch, under the table. He gobbled it up with a crunch and a happy thump of his tail.

"Allora," I said gently, "Ranch has had enough. How about you try some yourself?"

"But Daddy," she said solemnly, "Ranch loves carrots. He told me."

I bit back a laugh. "I'm sure he did. But you need them too—if you want to grow strong like Uncle Connor."

Her eyes lit up. "He lifted a tractor! All by himself!"

Across the table, my dad chuckled and shook his head. "That jack did a lot of the work."

"Not from her view," Mom said, her smile widening.

Allora held up her fork like a champion. "I'm gonna eat all of them now! Just wait!"

Her joy was infectious, the table filled with warm laughter. The kind that wraps around you and eases the weight you didn't even realize you were still carrying.

After dinner, I told them about the call.

My mom reached across the table and laid her hand over mine. "Willow would be proud, Austin. She'd be so proud of you."

Later that evening, after Allora went on a cobbler-fueled walk with my parents to Connor's cabin, I slipped into my room. The house was still, filled only with the low creaks of floorboards and the hush of night settling in.

I sat down at the desk, Willow's photo catching the light from the lamp beside it. Her smile froze me there for a second—so alive, so full.

"You can do this," I could almost hear her say. "You know what this music can do."

I let my eyes drift to the smaller photo beside hers. Allora—hat too big, curls flying, strawberry in hand. Wild, alive, bright.

"This is for both of them," I whispered, the words settling over me like a vow.

I reached for my guitar, fingers unsure at first, but it didn't take long before the chords came. Willow's lyrics echoed in my head, the ones I'd found in her notebook just days ago.

The music filled the room, soft and full. I closed my eyes and let it take me to the early days of the band, to late nights writing songs with her, to hospital rooms and baby kicks and whispered prayers.

Grief still lived inside me, always would. But it no longer ruled the room. There was something else now. Something quieter. Lighter.

I strummed the last chord and let it ring out. Then I looked toward the window, to the sky beyond it.

"I miss you, Wills," I whispered.

And this time, the quiet that followed didn't feel like absence.

The ache was still there, a hollow space that would never fully heal. But for the first time in a long time, I felt something else—a spark of purpose.

This was about using what we had created together—our music, our love, our strength—to bring light into the darkness.

And for the first time in years, I felt like I was ready.

Chapter 61

Austin

As the plane touched down in Dallas, a swell of emotions rose in my chest—excitement, nerves, and that ever-present ache that never fully disappeared. Grief, it turns out, just adapts to your life. It really doesn't leave.

I glanced at Allora, her tiny nose pressed to the window, eyes wide as she watched the bustling airport below.

"Daddy, are we here?" she asked, bouncing in her seat, her seatbelt the only thing keeping her from launching into the aisle.

I smiled despite the ache. "That's right, baby girl. We're here to sing for Mommy. And to help other people who are sick like she was."

Her face turned serious, full of the kind of determination only a child can carry. "I'm gonna sing real loud, Daddy," she said. "So Mommy can hear me all the way up in heaven."

My throat tightened. I pulled her into my arms and kissed the top of her head, breathing her in. "She'll hear you, sweetheart," I whispered. "She's always listening."

As we navigated the airport, a wave of déjà vu washed over me. The last time I'd walked through an airport, Willow had been right beside me—her fingers intertwined with mine, her laugh teasing me for overpacking. I could still feel the shape of her hand in mine. Now, I walked alone, a widower and a father, doing my best to be whole when I still felt like half.

By the time we reached baggage claim, the familiar faces of Willow's family came into view. Frank and Eileen waited with Caleb and Gemma beside them.

Eileen moved first, arms open wide as she pulled me into a tight hug. "Austin," she breathed, her voice already thick. "It's so good to see you."

I held her close. "Missed you all so much."

Frank stepped forward, resting his large, steady hand on my shoulder. "You're doing a good thing, son. Keeping her memory alive."

I nodded, unable to speak around the lump in my throat.

Caleb and Gemma came next—Caleb with a quick, strong hug, and Gemma with one that lingered. "Marriage looks good on you two," I said softly.

Gemma smiled, slipping her arm through Caleb's. "We like to think so."

When the luggage carousel rumbled to life, I took it as a cue to gather myself. "Y'all go ahead to the rental house, get settled. I've got to swing by the venue for soundcheck, but I'll catch up soon."

Eileen hesitated. "Are you sure, honey? We don't mind waiting."

I nodded, putting on the strongest smile I had. "It'll be quick. My family is headed that way and I know Allora's dying to see the pool, aren't you?"

"I wanna see the pool!" she declared.

Caleb grinned, ruffling her hair. "A girl after my own heart."

I knelt in front of her. "You be good, okay? I'll see you soon."

She flung her arms around my neck. "Love you, Daddy."

"Love you more, Cupcake." I kissed her cheek and watched them go.

I turned toward the venue, my guitar case in hand and my heart somewhere between dread and hope.

It was time to face the music.

———

Walking into the venue felt like time folding in on itself. The hum of speakers, the scurry of crew, the way the stage lights cut across the space—it all pulled me back to those early days, when Willow and I stood side by side, green as grass and full of fire.

"Hey! Look who finally shows up!"

Nash Montgomery's voice cut through the noise, and I turned just as he and Cassidy closed the distance. Cassidy hugged me first, her perfume familiar and strangely comforting even though it had been years since I'd last seen her.

"Austin! We've missed you."

I swallowed hard. "Missed you guys too."

Nash clapped me on the back with a grin. "You look good, man."

"It's good to see y'all," I said, surprised by how much I meant it.

Next came Harper Lane and Christopher Jordan. Harper wrapped me in a quiet, understanding hug.

"You're braver than I could ever be," she said softly.

Her words settled somewhere deep.

Chris smiled and pulled me into a back-slapping hug. "Been way too long."

Behind Harper stood a very intimidating man, protective and quiet. Took me a second, but then I recognized him—he'd been at Willow's funeral. Harper's security guy, then. Her husband now, judging by the rings and the way he looked at her like she held his whole world.

Chris introduced his wife next. "Austin, meet Rachel."

Rachel extended her hand, warm and kind. "So nice to finally meet you. I've heard so much. I'm so sorry about Willow."

"Thank you," I said, my voice rough.

Seeing all of them again—so many faces from a lifetime ago—unlocked something. A sense of existing I hadn't realized I missed.

As we talked and caught up, it was like the years fell away, leaving the old connection intact beneath the dust.

Then Miranda Thompson, the event coordinator, approached. "Austin, it's so great to meet you in person," she said, offering her hand.

"Thanks for inviting me," I said. "It's an honor to be here."

She led us to the stage for soundcheck. The air was warm, the kind of soft March breeze that carries the scent of spring. Everything felt set.

Then a familiar voice filled the venue—not live, but on the screen.

"Hey, everyone!"

Levi Brooks. A video message. He looked older but still grinning like a kid. "Sorry I can't be there, but I'm sending love from overseas. You're doing something amazing. Keep making noise, y'all."

Then came the first notes of *Unbreakable*.

Cassidy. Nash. Harper. Chris. They sang it—our song. Mine and Willow's. And behind them, photos of survivors, fighters, and the ones who didn't make it. Willow's photo filled the screen—smiling, radiant, strong. Then others—her during treatment, holding Allora, her eyes full of fire even at her weakest.

When it was my turn, I stepped forward slowly, guitar in hand, heart thudding.

I hadn't done this—stood on a stage without her—for nearly a decade.

I started. My voice was shaky, the lyrics unfamiliar in the absence of her harmony. I stumbled. My throat closed.

I stopped.

Everything went still.

But then—I heard her. Not out loud. Just in my heart. Like I'd told Allora.

I could feel her—calm, steady. Whispering, You've got this.

So I began again. This time, I let her memory carry me. I stopped chasing perfection and just let the music come.

And when it did, it felt like home.

After soundcheck, I invited everyone back to the house I'd rented.

"We've got a pool for the kids and a grill for the grown-ups."

Nash and Cassidy went to grab their son Weston from their nanny, and the rest of us headed to the house.

Allora stayed close at first, clinging to me, but with a little coaxing from Connor, she was swimming and laughing with Weston like they'd been best friends forever.

The grandparents slipped into the evening as though they had just seen each other last Tuesday—Frank and Dad talking ranching, Eileen and Mom chatting about holidays and Allora.

Gemma fan-girled just a little over Harper and Cassidy, who pulled her in like they'd known her for years. Soon Rachel, who was a pretty famous author from what I heard, was in the mix too, talking books and family and everything in between.

As the sun dipped low and the sky turned lavender, people began to drift home. Frank and Eileen took a sleepy Allora to bed. Nash carried a sleeping Weston. My parents and Connor said their goodnights.

Inside, Caleb and Gemma were deep in conversation with Rachel and Harper, laughter spilling out of the living room.

That's when Chris approached me quietly.

"Can we talk?"

We stepped out to the patio. The night was still.

"It's been a long four years," Chris said.

I nodded. "Yeah. Apparently a lot can happen in four years."

He hesitated. "Rachel had a miscarriage last year."

My breath caught.

"She's pregnant again," he added. "Second trimester. We're hope-ful... but everything feels fragile."

"I'm so sorry," I said. "But congratulations. Really."

Chris nodded, his eyes full of something I recognized—grief and hope living in the same space.

"I've been listening to you and Nash talk about being dads," he said. "It helps. Makes me believe I can figure it out too."

"You will," I told him. "You've got a good heart."

Then, after a moment, he asked, "Are you making music again?"

I hesitated.

"Not really. This is... the first time I've really sung since she passed."

Chris nodded slowly. "When my new studio's up and running—would you consider coming down? Maybe just for a session. Just to see what it feels like again."

I didn't answer right away. The offer was humbling, but the idea of making music for myself again—without her—wasn't something I was ready for.

"I'll think about it," I said honestly.

Chris smiled. "That's all I ask. Maybe six months from now?"

"Yeah," I said. "Six months sounds good."

Rachel's voice called from inside, and Chris stood. We hugged, and I watched them disappear into the quiet night.

And for the first time, the silence felt like space.

Like possibility.

Chapter 62

Austin

I took a breath as I stepped onto the stage, the lights momentarily blinding, the crowd's applause washing over me in a wave of warmth and nerves. I adjusted the mic and forced myself to focus—not on the cameras, not on the crowd, but on why I was here.

"Good evening, everyone," I began. "Thank you for being here tonight, for your generosity and your hearts in the fight against ovarian cancer."

I glanced toward the portrait of Willow at the edge of the stage. That smile—always so bright. For a heartbeat, it steadied me.

"A little over five years ago, my wife Willow was diagnosed with ovarian cancer. Just weeks after we found out we were expecting our daughter. One moment, we were on top of the world. The next... everything changed."

The venue quieted, holding space with me.

"We fought—together. Through chemo, through fear, through faith. Willow never let go of her joy. And when Allora was born, she became a mother in every fierce, beautiful way a woman can. For three precious months, she poured everything she had left into our daughter."

My voice caught. I swallowed hard and kept going.

"But the cancer didn't let go. Willow got weaker, but her spirit never did. She held our daughter in her arms and spoke love into her. Into me. Even in her final breath, she gave more than she ever took."

I paused, grounding myself with the podium beneath my hands.

"Losing her shattered me. Still does. But what she left behind—her voice, her love, our daughter—is a legacy I carry every day. It's her strength that gets me through, her love that reminds me why I'm still standing."

I looked out at the faces in the crowd. Some strangers. Some friends. All of them, bonded by the same things.

"Some of you have fought this battle yourselves. Some of you have lost people you love. And I want to say this: You are not alone. Grief connects us. But so does hope."

Another pause.

"Tonight, we get to give back. To fund research. To fuel the fight. To say that this disease won't win. Every dollar raised tonight is a step toward a future where no daughter grows up without her mother."

My gaze found the caregivers in the crowd. "To the caregivers: You are the quiet heroes. The hands that hold, the shoulders that steady. Your love matters more than you'll ever know. Thank you for carrying the weight. You are not invisible."

I exhaled, emotion thick in my throat. "This night is for Willow. And for every woman who's walked this road. We remember. We fight. We love. We rise."

As I stepped back, the applause surged, crashing over me. My heart ached—but it was full. Full of her. Full of purpose.

The lights dimmed. The next performers took the stage—Christopher, Harper, Cassidy, and Nash. The first notes of *Unbreakable* rolled out, and the screen behind them came alive with memories.

Harper's voice led softly, "In the darkest of nights, when hope seems lost..."

Photos of Willow flashed—laughing, singing, holding Allora. Alive in every frame.

Nash and Cassidy joined in: "We'll stand together, hand in hand..."

More images—Willow in her scarves, her smile still luminous even as her body weakened.

Then came Christopher, powerful and raw, as photos of Willow and me filled the screen. Our wedding. Her holding our newborn daughter.

"In the face of the storm, we won't bend, we won't break..."

I broke. Quietly. So did the room.

Frank and Eileen clung to one another. My dad held my mom, Connor held Allora, tears falling freely from every eye in the room. Caleb had his head bowed. Gemma held his hand. And I stood in the shadows, taking it all in.

The final image: Willow, glowing, Allora in her arms.

"Our love... unbreakable..."

The song ended. Silence fell—thick, reverent—before the audience rose to their feet in a standing ovation that carried through the walls and into my bones.

Catherine Garrick, the foundation's CEO, stepped to the mic. I didn't catch her speech—too much emotion humming in my ears—but I felt her energy, her gratitude, her fire for the cause.

Backstage, I joined my friends, exchanging tearful hugs and wordless nods.

Cassidy pulled me in tight. "Willow would be so proud of you."

"I hope so," I said. My voice didn't want to work.

Catherine wrapped up her speech, the applause swelling again. I closed my eyes and let it wash over me like a benediction.

The crowd quieted.

It was my turn.

I walked out again. And this time, I wasn't scared.

I picked up my guitar and let the room settle.

This wasn't just a show. This was a celebration. Of her. Of life. Of the fight.

I started to play.

The chords came easily, like they were waiting for me. I let the song fill the space—grief and love and something else, something brighter.

Willow was in every note. Every breath. Every echo.

I looked out at the sea of faces—some weeping, some smiling. All listening.

"Thank you for being here," I said, voice thick but sure. "For supporting this cause. For keeping hope alive. This next one's for Willow. For Allora. For all of you."

I played again. A new song. One I hadn't written until after I found her notebooks.

And when I looked out at Allora, clapping along, her smile a mirror of her mother's, something shifted in my chest.

This—this joy, this future—was what Willow had fought for.

And for the first time in a long time... I believed in it too.

Chapter 63

Austin

Over the next six months, I poured my heart into every fundraiser, every benefit stage. Each time I shared Willow's story—her bravery, her joy, her fight—I offered a piece of my grief to the world. And each time, the weight of it grew heavier.

I was exhausted. The kind of tired that sleep can't fix.

But I kept going. For Willow. For the survivors who hugged me with tears in their eyes. For the families who whispered, "She reminded me of my sister... my daughter... my wife." For the little girls in the front row who clapped like Willow's story gave them permission to believe in something good.

And then, one night after a particularly emotional event, I sat alone in a hotel room, staring down at the crumpled tie on the floor and the blinking message light on my phone.

"I miss you so much, Willow," I whispered into the quiet. "But I'm tired."

Silence. Then something else. A feeling. A memory. Her voice.

"Then take a break. But don't give up."

I closed my eyes, imagining the calm fire in her gaze. She always believed I was stronger than I felt.

The message light blinked again. A new text from Chris Jordan.

Chris: Hey Austin. How are things? Ready to get back into the studio?

I stared at it, thumb hovering. Music had become too painful to touch for so long. But now... maybe it could be something more.

Finally, I replied.

Me: Yeah, man. I think I'm ready.

And I meant it.

Allora's laughter echoed through the house, pulling me upstairs like gravity. I paused in the doorway, watching her on the floor with a toy screwdriver, surrounded by scattered plastic wheels and parts of a pink convertible.

"Daddy! Look!" she beamed up at me, her cheeks streaked with marker like pretend grease. "Uncle Connor said I can help him fix real cars, so I'm practicing!"

"You look like a pro already," I said, crouching beside her.

"I hafta make sure the wheels don't fall off," she explained, holding one up with serious focus.

I gently tightened the toy wheel, showing her how. "There you go —nice and tight."

Her face lit up. "Do you think I'm good at fixing stuff?"

I kissed her forehead. "I know you are."

She turned back to her car, humming as she worked. So alive. So sure of herself. Watching her was like watching Willow dance through the world again—fearless, full of spark. And in that moment, I saw both of us stitched into her smile.

"Daddy," she said suddenly, standing with the screwdriver clutched in her fist. "I'm gonna fix all the cars. Even the really big ones."

"I believe it, Cupcake," I said, grinning. "Just make sure you pack your tools."

She gasped, spun around, and dug into her toy chest until she pulled out her little plastic toolbox. She dropped it into her suitcase beside her sparkly unicorn shirt. "There! Now I'm extra ready!"

"You sure are," I said, voice catching.

Then she looked up at me, eyes wide and hopeful. "Do you think Uncle Connor will let me use the big wrench?"

"Maybe," I said, kneeling to her level. "But only if you listen and be super careful."

"I promise!" she said, holding out her pinky like it was a contract.

I hooked mine around hers and held it for a beat longer than usual.

"You're gonna have the best time," I whispered. "He's lucky to have you."

She gave me a huge smile. "And you're lucky to have me too, right?"

I pulled her close. "Absolutely. I'm the luckiest."

That evening, I sat on the porch with Mom, a quiet hum of crickets in the air and stars just starting to peek through the trees. Allora was still inside, packing her "tools," chatting Connor's ear off.

"Are you sure you don't mind keeping her for a couple of weeks?" I asked.

Mom looked at me like I'd grown two heads. "Austin Blake. Of course not. You think we're gonna pass up extra time with our favorite girl?"

I smiled, but the guilt lingered. "I don't want her to feel like I'm leaving her."

"She doesn't," Mom said gently. "She knows you love her. She knows you always come back. That's what matters."

I nodded, letting her words settle. "She's been buzzing about working in the garage with Connor all week."

Mom chuckled. "Those two are two peas in a pod. I think they speak their own language."

"She gets him," I said. "And he gets her. It's... special."

She tilted her head toward me, her voice softening. "Connor's always had his own way of seeing the world. And with her, it's like he sees right into her heart. No filter. No noise. Just connection."

I swallowed past the lump in my throat. "He doesn't give himself enough credit."

"No, he doesn't," she said. "But you should know—you and Connor... I'm proud of the men you've become. Willow would be, too."

Her words hit harder than I expected. I looked down, blinked fast.

"Thanks, Mom," I murmured.

We sat in silence for a while, just breathing in the air, letting the night settle over us. Somewhere inside, I could hear Allora giggling with Connor.

Something shifted in my chest—something small, but real. Not grief, not exactly. Something beyond grief.

Maybe it was healing. Maybe it was music. Maybe it was Willow, nudging me forward.

Whatever it was... it felt like a huge step.

Chapter 64

Austin

The next morning, Allora clung to my leg like she thought I might disappear if she let go. Her little arms wrapped around my shin, her cheek pressed against my jeans, muffling her words.

"Do you have to go, Daddy?" she asked, her voice trembling.

I knelt in front of her, gently cupping her face in my hands. Her wide eyes shimmered with unshed tears, full of questions too big for someone her age to carry.

"I do, sweetie," I said softly, swallowing against the lump in my throat. "But just for a little while. And you're going to have the best time with Uncle Connor, Pops, and Nana."

She tilted her head slightly, searching my face for reassurance. "Will you call me every day?"

"Every single day," I promised, brushing a curl from her cheek. "And when I get back, I want to hear all about your adventures."

Dad waited in the truck, the engine rumbling low as he gave us time. Mom stood a few steps away, blinking hard, trying to keep it together for Allora's sake.

Connor crouched beside us and scooped her into his arms.

Without fanfare or fuss, he spun her in a slow circle, and her laughter rang out bright and clear.

"We'll have fun," he said calmly, settling her on his hip. "You're helping me fix cars."

Allora nodded, her earlier sadness replaced by focused excitement. "And a campfire?"

"Yes," he replied, tapping her nose.

"Marshmallows?" she asked hopefully.

He nodded again. "Marshmallows."

Her smile lit up her whole face. "Yay! I'm gonna be the best helper ever!"

Watching them, gratitude surged through me. My family—every single one of them—had been my anchor when the storm rolled in. I didn't know how I would've survived any of this without them.

Mom stepped in and wrapped me in a tight hug. Her arms, her scent, her steadiness—it all reminded me of who I was before grief made me forget.

"You've got this, Austin," she whispered into my ear. "We're so proud of you. And don't worry about Allora. She's in the best hands."

"I know," I said thickly, my voice rough. "Thanks, Mom."

After one last round of hugs, I climbed into the truck beside Dad. Gravel crunched under the tires as we rolled down the long driveway, the ranch fading slowly behind us.

We drove in silence for a few miles until Dad finally glanced my way. His hands were steady on the wheel, his jaw tight with unspoken words.

"I'm proud of you," he said at last. "You know that?"

It hit harder than I expected. I turned to him, caught off guard. "Thanks, Dad."

"I know it's not easy," he continued. "Leaving her. Making music again. Without Willow. But this... this is what you're meant to do. She'd want this."

I nodded slowly, though my stomach still twisted with guilt. "I just feel selfish sometimes," I admitted. "I've been gone so much lately—for the foundation, the events. And now I'm going back to music... it feels like I'm choosing it over her."

Dad gave a small grunt and reached over to clasp my shoulder. "Austin, you're not choosing music instead of her. You're choosing music because of her. She'd want Allora to see you alive again. She'd want you to remember who you were when she fell in love with you."

His words cut straight to the guilt in my chest. Not to diminish it —but to name it, and then make room for something else.

"You're not leaving her behind," he said. "You're showing her what it looks like to honor love and purpose. And she knows you'll always come back."

I stared out the window at the fields we'd worked together, the trees we'd planted, the home we'd built. "Thanks, Dad. I needed to hear that."

He nodded once. "Anytime. You've been carrying this a long time. It's okay to put a little down."

We made the rest of the drive in comfortable quiet. When the airport finally came into view, I felt the knot of emotion twist in my chest—equal parts fear and hope.

When we pulled to the curb, Dad put the truck in park and looked over at me.

"Go make some music, Austin," he said. "We'll be here when you come back."

I smiled, the weight of his belief in me settling like armor around my shoulders. "Thanks, Dad. Love you."

He pulled me into a quick hug before I grabbed my bag and stepped out. "Love you, too."

Inside the terminal, I pulled out my phone. My lock screen lit up with the photo of Allora and me—her giggling, arms wrapped around my neck.

I pressed a kiss to the screen.

"I'm doing this for you too, baby girl," I whispered. "I want you to see what it means to follow your heart."

I pocketed the phone and found my gate. As I settled into my seat, I closed my eyes and let Willow's voice echo in my memory—gentle, musical, perfect.

"I'm doing this for you too, Wills," I murmured. "You always said the music was where I came alive. I'm gonna try and find that part of me again."

As the plane lifted from the tarmac, the Montana fields fell away beneath us. The ache of leaving didn't vanish—but a flicker of something else sparked in its place.

Not certainty. Not peace.

But maybe it was the beginning of coming back to life.

Chapter 65

Austin

The moment I stepped inside the studio, the cool air hit me like a balm. Outside, Alabama humidity clung to every-thing like a second skin, but in here, the air was clean, cold —quiet in the best way. That familiar scent of polished wood, leather, and warm electronics settled in my chest like a memory you don't realize you've missed until it's right in front of you.

Chris led the way down a wide hallway, lined with framed album covers and plaques that shimmered beneath the soft track lighting. History, I thought. Not just his, but music's. The kind of walls that reminded you why you started in the first place.

"I've got everything set up in the main room," Chris said over his shoulder. "Figured we could start with some of those voice memos you sent—build from there."

I nodded, feeling that flutter of nerves twist low in my stomach. It had been years since I walked into a studio like this. Years since music wasn't just therapy or memory, but work. Purpose.

But when we stepped through the door into the main room—with its warm lighting, weathered soundboards, and high ceilings that somehow felt like possibility—I exhaled for the first time in days.

This was where I belonged.

Chris handed me a guitar, a sleek acoustic with familiar weight. The second I cradled it in my arms, muscle memory took over.

"Let's hear what's rattling around in that head of yours," he said with a crooked smile, dropping into the chair behind the mixing board.

I didn't answer. I just let my fingers fall into the chords. Closed my eyes. And let go.

The first notes filled the space—low, searching, but honest. My voice followed, shaky at first, then steadying as the lyrics formed. Lines I hadn't written down but had been living inside me, waiting for this moment to breathe.

And for the first time in a long time, I didn't feel the weight of trying. I just was.

———

The next few weeks blurred in a rush of creativity and long days that bled into longer nights. Chris and I bounced ideas back and forth like old friends trading secrets. We laughed over weird chord progressions, argued about bridge placements, rewrote the same verse four times until it felt right. We were chasing something real, and for the first time in years, I was running toward it instead of away.

The glass control room offered views of the coastline just beyond the tree line. Each evening, the sky set itself on fire with shades of orange and violet. And I watched it happen like I was witnessing something sacred.

"I think we've got something here," Chris said one night, leaning back in his chair, satisfied.

I set my guitar down and stretched, rolling out the tension in my shoulders. "Yeah," I said. "It feels real."

He clapped me on the shoulder with a grin. "We'll polish it up tomorrow. Gotta head home—Rachel's probably ready to hand off the baby."

I laughed, already hearing the exhaustion in his voice, even under the pride. "Tell her I said congratulations."

He slung his bag over one shoulder and paused in the doorway. "Get some rest. Big day tomorrow."

When the door clicked shut behind him, I stayed. Just sat there in the quiet hum of the empty studio. The space still vibrated with the last chords we'd played. My fingertips tingled.

I let the silence settle, not heavy—but grounding. It didn't feel like grief tonight. It felt like coming back to life.

Reaching for my phone, I hit the speed dial and brought it to my ear.

"Daddy!" Allora's voice burst through the line, bright as ever.

"Hey, baby girl," I said, already smiling. "How was your day?"

"It was so fun! Uncle Connor let me help him at the garage, and I got to use the little wrench! And we had ice cream after dinner!"

Her words tumbled out, too fast to catch all at once, but I drank them in like water. She sounded happy. Safe. Whole.

"I miss you so much, Allora," I said softly.

"I miss you too, Daddy," she replied, quieter now. "Did you make music today?"

"I did. And I think you're gonna love it."

She giggled. "Did you write one for me?"

"They're all for you."

We talked a few more minutes, and when I finally hung up, I pressed the phone to my chest, heart full.

<hr>

Outside, the sky was a velvet blanket scattered with stars. I stood on the studio steps, breathing in the thick coastal air, letting the quiet settle in my bones.

There was still a piece of me that ached—there probably always would be. Willow's absence was a shape I'd grown used to carrying. But tonight, it didn't feel like the heaviest part of me.

It just felt... real.

This was where I was meant to be.

Making something. Healing something. Becoming something more than what grief had left behind.

And I knew—when the time came to go home, to hug my daughter and sit around the fire with my family—I'd bring this piece of myself back with me.

Not just the music.

But the man I was still learning how to be.

Chapter 66

Austin

For three weeks, I lived and breathed music.

Every morning, I walked through the doors of Chris's studio with my guitar in one hand and a notebook in the other, my heart a little more open than the day before. We spent long hours building the album from scraps of lyrics, melodies scribbled in margins, and unfinished songs that had once been too painful to touch.

Some of them were Willow's. Those were the hardest. Her handwriting in the margins, her lyrical phrasing, her raw honesty—it felt like reaching out to hold her hand across time. Singing her unfinished words was like standing on a high wire between grief and grace. But finishing them? That felt like breathing life into something sacred.

We called the album *Holding Out for You.*

The title track was one of the last songs she and I had worked on together. I'd started it at her bedside. She'd hummed the chorus softly under her breath while holding Allora. Now, it was a bridge between what we had and what I was learning to live for.

When the final mix played through the speakers, Chris leaned back with a quiet smile. "It's done," he said, his voice warm with satisfaction. "You've got something real here, Austin. Something that's going to matter to people."

I set my guitar down slowly and let out a long, steadying breath. "Thanks, man. I couldn't have done it without you."

He clapped me on the shoulder. "You were always meant for this," he said. "I'm just glad you made your way back."

Coming home to Montana felt like stepping into a new chapter of a familiar book. The air smelled like sunlight and pine. The wide-open sky seemed to breathe for me. And then I heard her—

"Daddy!"

Allora flew down the porch steps, curls bouncing, cowgirl boots thudding against the ground. I barely had time to brace myself before she leapt into my arms.

"There's my girl!" I laughed, scooping her up and spinning her in a circle. Her giggles wrapped around me like music.

She talked a mile a minute, recounting every second of the past few weeks. "I helped Uncle Connor at the garage almost every day! And Pops took me fishing and Nana made cookies and we had a real campfire and marshmallows and—"

I laughed, heart full. "Sounds like you had an adventure."

She nodded with exaggerated seriousness. "But I still missed you. A lot." Her voice softened. "Did you finish the music?"

"I did," I said, brushing a kiss to her temple. "And I think you're gonna love it."

"Can I hear it someday?"

"Someday soon," I promised. "But maybe we'll listen to it together for the first time."

That night, we all gathered around the table—Mom's cooking on full display, Connor accepting the unwanted pieces of celery Allora offered him when he thought no one was looking, Dad pretending not to notice. Laughter wove through the meal like it had been waiting for its cue to return.

I told them everything—about the studio, the songs, the long nights and the quiet mornings, the conversations with Chris about what came next.

"Caleb's back in as my lawyer," I said, reaching for my tea. "And Emma's stepping in to manage the rollout. They're already planning a soft release and maybe some small tour dates."

I looked at Mom, then Dad. "But everything—and I mean everything—is built around Allora. She comes first. That won't change."

Mom reached across the table and laid her hand gently on mine. "We know, sweetheart. And we're proud of you. Willow would be too."

For a moment, the table fell quiet—not heavy, but reverent. I looked around at the people who had held me through the darkest seasons of my life. My eyes met Connor's across the table, and he gave a small nod.

"Thanks," I said, voice thick. "All of you... I couldn't have gotten here without you."

Later that night, I tucked Allora into bed. The moonlight spilled across her blanket, catching the glitter on the unicorn stitched across her pillowcase.

"Will you sing me the song you and Mommy wrote for me?" she asked, her eyes already fluttering closed.

My throat tightened, but I nodded. "Always."

I picked up my guitar, settled beside her, and played. The lullaby was soft, simple—just a few chords and a melody full of memory. Willow's voice lived in the lyrics. Allora's heartbeat in the rhythm.

And this time, as I sang, the ache didn't hollow me out like it used to. It lingered, sure. But it was gentle. It was familiar. It was... okay.

She drifted to sleep before the last note faded. I leaned down and kissed her forehead.

"Goodnight, Cupcake," I whispered. "I love you."

I stood in the doorway for a long moment, watching her breathe—

steady, peaceful. And I felt it: a quiet shift inside me. Willow wasn't fading. She wasn't slipping away. She was here. In Allora. In the music. In me.

Moving forward didn't mean letting her go. It meant carrying her with me into whatever came next.

Her memory wasn't a weight anymore—it was the wind at my back.

Chapter 67

Austin

The next nine months were a whirlwind.

I was back on stage—spotlights in my eyes, guitar in my hands, Willow's words in my veins. *Holding Out for You* had found its way into the world, and somehow, it had found its way into other hearts too. Fans clung to the music like I had once clung to Willow's last lullabies. Every show was electric, every lyric sung louder than I expected, like the world had been waiting for the songs we'd started together.

I didn't take on a full tour. I couldn't—not with Allora at home, not with everything that mattered most still rooted in Montana. But I said yes to the moments that felt worth saying yes to—festivals, benefit concerts, weekend fly-outs, and a few unexpected spotlights that felt more like legacy than comeback.

Sometimes Allora came with me. She loved the bustle, the music, the snacks at catering. She'd twirl in the wings while I soundchecked, her cowgirl boots stomping the beat, her curls bouncing. She was always quick to point out if I missed a lyric or forgot to wave to the crowd. My mom came too, just like Willow and I had once dreamed we would do as a family. It wasn't perfect. But it was ours.

And when we were home, it was ranch life and bedtime stories. Morning waffles and pony rides. Allora and I would lie in the grass and count stars or chase chickens through the back pasture. It was chaotic and exhausting and beautiful—and somehow, even in the noise, it was quiet in my chest in a way it hadn't been in years.

Then one brisk autumn morning, with mist still clinging to the pastures, I was fixing a fence post when my phone buzzed.

Chris Jordan.

I wiped my hands on my jeans and answered with a breathless, "Hey, man. What's up?"

His voice came through, buzzing with energy. "Austin, are you sitting down?"

I laughed, glancing around at the wide open sky. "Not exactly. Why?"

Chris let the pause stretch, dragging it out for maximum effect. "You've been nominated for three CMAs."

I stopped cold. "Wait—what?"

"Song of the Year. Album of the Year. And—drumroll—Entertainer of the Year."

I stared at the ground, blinking like I could refocus reality if I just tried hard enough. "You're serious?"

"As a heart attack," Chris said. "And I don't say this lightly—you deserve it, Austin. *Holding Out for You* is the real deal. The industry knows it. The fans feel it. And this? This is what it looks like when your story finds its people."

A knot built in my throat, all disbelief and gratitude tangled together. "I... I don't even know what to say."

"You don't need to say anything," he said. "Just let yourself be proud, man. You built something beautiful out of something hard. That's rare."

We hung up, and I slipped the phone into my back pocket, my hands still buzzing.

Across the field, Allora stood watching me, brow furrowed like she could feel the shift in the air.

"Who was that?" she asked, bounding over. "You look like you found a treasure!"

I crouched down to her level, still stunned. "That was Mr. Chris. He told me something pretty exciting."

Her eyes went round. "Like what?"

"My songs got picked for some really big music awards."

She gasped. "Like prizes?"

"Exactly like prizes."

She didn't hesitate. She threw her arms around my neck and squealed, "Good job, Daddy!"

I hugged her tight, longer than I needed to. Maybe longer than she liked—she started to squirm a little—but I didn't let go right away.

Because that hug? It was the real prize. The loudest applause. The only review that mattered.

Later that evening, we sat around the kitchen table, plates scraped clean from Mom's roast and cornbread. I told them all about the nominations, and for a moment, the house lit up with joy.

"Austin, honey," Mom said, tearing up. "Willow would be so proud. We're so proud!"

Dad raised his glass in a quiet toast, no words needed.

Connor gave a rare, quiet nod. "Cool."

Allora chimed in, "Do you think I can come get the prize with you? I want to wear my sparkly boots."

I smiled. "I'll even buy you some new sparkly boots."

That night, after Allora was asleep, I stood outside under a sky full of stars. The cold biting at my skin, but I barely felt it.

I thought of Willow.

Thought of the first time we ever harmonized, the first song we ever wrote, the first dream we dared to speak aloud. I thought of the way her hand used to rest on my knee when we rode buses late at night. The way she'd squeeze it during tough interviews or long studio days. I thought of the way she lit up when she watched me sing—like she knew I was doing what I was made to do.

And then I thought about everything I'd almost let go of when I lost her.

This album wasn't just a tribute. It wasn't a goodbye.

It was proof that love doesn't vanish. It transforms. It becomes the roots we stand on and the wind that moves us forward.

This wasn't just Willow's legacy.

It was mine, too.

And I was finally ready to live it.

Epilogue

It was Allora's first day of second grade, and she was practically buzzing with excitement. The morning had been a blur of chatter about her new teacher, Mrs. Nichols, and all the friends she hoped to make. As I helped her get ready, she kept talking about everything she'd seen at Meet the Teacher night.

"Daddy, Mrs. Nichols has this huge poster of all the planets, and she said we're going to learn about space this year! There's also a reading corner with bean bags, and she told us she loves mysteries, so we're going to read some together!" Allora's eyes lit up with excitement as she went on and on.

We stopped for breakfast on the way to school, a tradition we had for special occasions. Sitting in our favorite diner, she continued to share her excitement between bites of pancakes. I loved seeing her so animated, so unbothered as her little hands waved around as she talked.

As we pulled up to the school, a wave of nostalgia hit me. It felt like just yesterday I was holding her hand on her first day of kindergarten. Time was flying by, and she was growing up so fast.

We walked into the school, and Allora confidently led the way to her classroom. But as we reached the door, we both froze. The classroom looked different from what we remembered. The bright posters and cozy reading corner Allora had described were gone, replaced by a different setup.

I double-checked the room number, confused. "This is the right room," I muttered, frowning.

A woman stood at the doorway, greeting children as they arrived, but she wasn't Mrs. Nichols.

"Daddy, who is that?" Allora asked, holding onto my hand. Just as I was about to answer, the woman turned to us with a warm smile.

"Good morning! You must be Allora," she said, kneeling down to her level. "I'm Ms. Brayton, your new teacher."

The name hit me like a shockwave. "Brayton?" I echoed, a mix of disbelief and recognition in my voice.

Studying her, my heart skipping a beat. It was Miller Conrad, my high school sweetheart. Her last name was different, and I couldn't help but notice she wasn't wearing a ring.

Miller—now Ms. Brayton—finally looked up from Allora and locked eyes with me. Her expression shifted from warm professionalism to surprise, tinged with a touch of nervousness.

"Austin?" she asked, her voice a blend of shock and uncertainty. I nodded, trying to wrap my head around the sudden twist of fate.

"Yeah. Wow, Miller... I mean, Ms. Brayton. It's been a long time."

She stood up, smoothing her skirt and taking a deep breath. "Yes, it has. Mrs. Nichols's husband got transferred unexpectedly, so they needed a second-grade teacher on short notice. I just moved back home to help my mom with my dad's health issues, so I was available."

We stood there, momentarily caught in the flood of shared memories. It felt surreal, standing in that classroom with Allora beside me, facing someone who had once been such a significant part of my life.

"Well, Allora," Miller continued, regaining her composure,

"we're going to have a great year together. Why don't you come in and find your seat?"

Allora looked up at me for reassurance. I nodded and gave her a gentle nudge. "Go on, sweetheart. I'll see you after school." She hugged me quickly and walked into the classroom, glancing back once before joining the other kids.

As Miller and I stood there, it felt like we were meeting for the first time all over again, despite all our history. I had no idea what to say, the moment hanging in the air awkwardly.

Finally, I smiled and said, "It's good to see you, Miller. I mean, Ms. Brayton. I'm sure Allora will love having you as her teacher."

Miller returned the smile, though there was an unspoken tension in her eyes. "It's good to see you too, Austin."

With a nod, I turned to leave, feeling a strange mix of emotions. As I walked down the hallway, I couldn't shake the unexpected attraction I'd felt when I saw her. It caught me off guard, a sensation I hadn't experienced since—well, since I met Willow.

It felt almost foreign, yet unmistakable. The way Miller carried herself, the warmth in her eyes, and the sincerity in her voice—everything about her stirred something inside me. It left me with a fluttering in my chest, a feeling I thought had been buried under layers of grief and healing.

Making my way out of the school, my thoughts were a chaotic jumble. It felt strange, almost disloyal, to acknowledge these feelings. But they were there, undeniable and unsettling, and kind of exciting. Who knew I was looking forward to second grade as much as my daughter?

Afterword

Dear Friend,

As you close the final chapter of Still Holding Out for You, I want to take a moment to talk about something very real that lives beyond the pages of this story: ovarian cancer.

Willow's journey was fictional, but the disease she battled is not. Ovarian cancer is often called a "silent killer" because its symptoms can be subtle, vague, or mistaken for other conditions. For too many women, it's not diagnosed until it has progressed to an advanced stage — when treatment becomes more difficult, and outcomes less certain.

There is no reliable early detection test for ovarian cancer. That's why raising awareness, funding research, and amplifying education is so critically important.

If Willow's story moved you — if her strength, her fight, or her love for her family left a mark — I hope you'll consider learning more about this disease and the incredible work being done by organizations like the National Ovarian Cancer Coalition (NOCC) or the Ovarian Cancer Research Alliance (OCRA).

These foundations are working tirelessly to fund life-saving research, support patients and families, and increase awareness so that one day, fewer women will have to face this diagnosis.

Whether you choose to donate, share information, advocate for better screening, or simply carry a bit more awareness into your life — it all matters.

To those who have faced ovarian cancer, or loved someone who has:

This book is a tribute to your strength, your resilience, and the quiet courage it takes to keep showing up — for your family, for your health, and for yourself — even in the hardest moments. You are seen. You are not alone.

And to every reader who's walked this story—thank you for holding space for love, for grief, for bravery, and for hope.

With all my heart,

Jennifer

Acknowledgments

Another book, another opportunity to say thank you.

First and foremost, I must thank my Savior, Jesus Christ, for the mind He gave me and the hope I have in Him daily. Without Him, I am nothing.

Rob, you are everything I never knew I needed. Even if you never read another word of anything I ever wrote, I'd still know that you believed in me and supported this crazy dream of being an author.

Ashley, we've done it again. I hope you never forget how to read. I need you. I can't believe Stanley didn't make an appearance this go around. We must be getting the hang of this thing. P.S., I'm sorry I made you cry... a lot.

To my beta readers and ARC team, thank you is not a strong enough sentiment. I'd name and each one of you individually but it costs more to add that many pages for printing! Just know that I hold each of you in my heart and have immense gratitude for the undertaking of helping me prep and share my work.

To you, the reader—you are the lifeblood of this project. I write for you. I edit for you. I cry over these characters and wrestle with their decisions, because I know you're out there waiting to turn the page. Thank you for trusting me with your time, your emotions, and a piece of your heart. I don't take that lightly.

Until next time.

With love and gratitude,

Jennifer

About the Author

Jennifer Carr is a romance author, lifelong daydreamer, and psychology nerd turned author.

A degree in Psychology, a Master's in Marriage & Family Counseling, multiple certifications in life/wellness coaching and brain health, and years teaching AP Psychology gave her a deep understanding of people—but it was writing that finally gave her a way to share their stories.

What started as a curiosity ("I wonder how that dream was going to end?") quickly turned into something bigger. One book became several. Passion became purpose. And a new career was born.

Married to her childhood best friend and raising a creative daughter on their quiet Alabama farm, Jennifer writes emotional, character-driven fiction with heart, healing, no spice, and just the perfect amount of swoon.

When she's not writing, you'll find her reading romance novels, listening to music, baking something delicious, or sipping strong coffee with her cat nearby.

Learn more or get signed books: jcarrwrites.com

Independent authors NEED reviews in order for their work to be discovered. If you have the time, please consider leaving your honest review on any platform for others to find.

Also by Jennifer Carr